Resurrection

The Donaghey Brothers, 2

WENDY MILLION

CHAMPAGNE BOOK GROUP

Resurrection

This is a work of fiction. The characters, incidents and dialogues in this book are of the author's imagination and are not to be construed as real. Any resemblance to actual events or persons, living or dead, is completely coincidental.

Published by Champagne Book Group
2373 NE Evergreen Avenue, Albany OR 97321 U.S.A.

~ ~ ~

First Edition 2020

pISBN: 979-8-572471-01-4

Copyright © 2020 Wendy Million All rights reserved.

Cover Art by Melody Pond

Champagne Book Group supports copyright which encourages creativity and diverse voices, creates a rich culture, and promotes free speech. Thank you by complying by not scanning, uploading, and distributing this book via any means without the permission of the publisher. Your purchase of an authorized edition supports the author's rights and hard work and allows Champagne Book Group to continue to bring readers fiction at its finest.

www.champagnebooks.com

Version_1

To my girls—I am forever grateful to be your mother.

Prologue
Carys

17 Years Ago

Finn's icy gaze is piercing, even from across the crowded Irish bar. Our gazes lock, and he smirks. It's enough to make me want to toss everyone out of the way, let him lift me onto the scarred wooden surface, and fuck me right here with an audience. *Sexual napalm.* Being around him is like an explosion in my loins. At twenty-eight, I had no idea a smirk from a man could cause my body to catch fire, until I started sleeping with Finn. I'll be lucky to escape this affair with only third-degree burns.

"Carys." Lorcan bumps my shoulder and drinks from his pint of beer. "Did you hear me?"

I toy with my straw, dropping my gaze from Finn's to respond to his younger brother, Lorcan. "Don't have a clue what you said. Sorry."

"I asked how your first day in Ireland was going."

"Took a couple meetings for my dad." I shrug. My father is trying to solidify connections here for his arms company, and I volunteered to take the lead on the negotiations. "Business comes before everything else." My focus strays to Finn again. The pleasure I mixed with my business earlier makes my legs tremble. I bite on my straw.

"Something going on between you two? Finn's hardly noticed anyone else tonight."

I raise an eyebrow and say, "Not really," before drawing the straw into my mouth.

Lorcan chuckles, and the deep, full-bodied sound is one I'd expect to hear from someone much older than eighteen. He's always been excellent at reading people, even back when I used to babysit him and his brother while our parents did business.

"Whatever you think you know." I give him a sly smile. "You don't know."

His chuckle turns into a full-on laugh, and his sandy colored hair falls into his hazel eyes. "I think you two have been fucking for years."

With a grin, I take a long sip of my liquor and then look at Lorcan under my lashes. I wrinkle my nose. "We were a bit obvious?"

If that's the case, I'm glad we've limited our interactions around my parents or his father. None of them would understand. Most of the time, I don't even comprehend our connection.

"Only if you know my *dearthair mor* like I do."

Not long ago, there would have been a hint of humor in his comment. A shift occurred between Lorcan and Finn when Lorcan's mother died. For some reason, their relationship never shifted back. I want to ask, but I'm not sure I need to. Finn can be a total jackass, and I suspect whatever has happened between the two of them, he started the trouble.

Lorcan takes my empty glass. "Another?" Peanut shells crack under his feet when he slides closer to the old, wooden bar.

When I glance up, Finn's eyes are still on me even as he chats with a university buddy. Sometimes I think I mean something to him, like now, when he's staring at me so intently I could melt in a puddle on the floor. As soon as he breaks eye contact and focuses elsewhere, the surety passes. We're not much more than friends with benefits. If I'm being honest, that uncertainty is a piece of the allure. No matter how hard I try, I can't figure him out, and it's been three years of this on and off pattern I thought we were keeping a secret.

Lorcan gives me another drink. Absentmindedly I smooth a few blonde strands that have popped out of my intricate braid. Later tonight Finn will pull the braid apart with gentle fingers. A shiver races along my spine at the memory of his hands, soothing and persistent in my hair. That's also an aspect of the attraction. The tenderness he shows me, coupled with his rough edges, is addictive. I'm valued and disposable.

"You trying to get Carys fucking drunk?" Finn's voice startles me out of my thoughts.

How did I miss him weaving toward me? He ruffles his platinum blond hair, which often signals annoyance or frustration.

"You like me drunk." I draw the straw between my lips, the fruity liquid lingering in my throat. "Don't you?"

One side of his mouth quirks up, and his gaze roams over me. "I like you all kinds of ways."

Warmth floods me, from him, from the fog of alcohol. I want to loop my arms around his neck and press myself to him as tight as I can. There's never enough with him. In my head I'm begging for more.

But I don't move. We're not into public displays of affection. My choice. Not his.

Lorcan stiffens beside Finn, and I half-turn, prepared to make a joke in case he's annoyed with our flirting. But Lorcan is focused on the entrance to the bar. Truthfully this place is more of a pub, with dim lighting and old wood everywhere. The stench of polish, peanuts, and spilled beer hangs in the large open area. There's nothing special about this Irish pub, but it's within walking distance to Lorcan's first-year student accommodation, and near to Finn's university flat. The reminder of his apartment and what we'll be doing in just a few hours is enough to kick my pulse up a notch. I can't wait to get him alone.

"McCaffery's people," Lorcan mutters.

"Bunch of jackasses." Finn grimaces. "Always looking for a fucking fight."

I rest my free hand on his bicep, and I cock my head toward the door. "Wanna get out of here?"

"Nah, they're not chasing me away." He squeezes around me to order another beer. "They want a fight? They can take their best shot."

While he waits for his drink, a tall, curvy redhead slips past me and brushes his shoulder. Lorcan has wandered elsewhere, probably thinking he's doing us a favor. I stand behind Finn and nurse my alcohol, and I restrain myself from latching onto the redhead's hair and giving it a yank. That wouldn't be fair. He can do what he likes. We aren't together. Not really. Moments like these make me queasy. I can't imagine being with anyone other than him, and yet I can't picture us going beyond a casual affair. He's not the guy a girl marries. He's the one she fucks in the back alley. And while the sex might be amazing—might even be the best she's ever had—there's never any promise of a future.

The redhead pushes her chest onto the wooden ledge and leans her face toward him. Are they going to kiss with me standing here? She gives him a flirty glance and says something too low for me to hear. He shuffles away from her and checks over his shoulder, his gaze unreadable.

Half-turning, he tosses money on the counter and tilts his beer at me while addressing the woman beside him. "You see her?"

She gives him pouty lips and then an uneasy smile, but she turns to follow the slant of his glass.

"She's the only woman in this bar I'm interested in. No, I'm not buying you a drink and you can keep your wandering hands off my dick."

She flings her hair over her shoulder and storms away.

I hadn't noticed the wandering hand, focused on her heaving breasts, her lips too close. The maneuver should have occurred to me because it's one I've used.

Before I can say anything, an Irish-accented voice calls out, "Finn Donaghey."

Finn's expression morphs from amusement to annoyance. "I'm not in the mood for your shit tonight, Patty."

He draws me closer so we're side by side. His almost six-foot solid frame of muscle makes me feel tiny at just over five feet.

Lorcan, who had been chatting with his own friends, reappears at Finn's side. There might be weird tension between the brothers, but they still stick together against anyone who threatens them or their family.

"Come on, Finnie. Agree ta one fight," Patty says.

Finn rolls his shoulders and chugs his beer before setting his glass down. "I don't do that shit anymore. I told you that."

"Afraid of yer old man? He doesn't need to be told."

Tension thickens the air. Patty is surrounded by three burly men. Lorcan glances behind him, and other guys appear. The rest of the crowd is taking notice. Finn never backs down from a challenge, but his time in Boston fighting at The Cage angered his father more than usual. I never understood why.

"My father doesn't call the shots." Finn grits out the words, his fists clenching.

That dig is a thorn in his side, but there is another insult guaranteed to set him off. I'm torn between staying close and seeking shelter. When he lets fly, sometimes people get hurt in the crossfire.

"Come fight for us." Patty removes his wallet from his front pocket and extracts a few bills. "I'll give you a fair cut."

"I don't need your money. We've been over this. The Donagheys aren't fucking broke." Finn steps toward him.

Lorcan and the men with him follow.

"And I'd have to be very poor or very stupid to get mixed up in your Mickey Mouse, bush league bullshit ring," Finn says.

My heart knocks against my chest.

"I got your fighting name picked out, Finnie. Banners made. Endorsements set up." Patty's dark eyes are alight with amusement tinged with a touch of meanness.

I cringe and slide my drink beside Finn's empty glass. What's coming won't be pretty. They must know about the name. The one thing Finn won't tolerate is the stupid nickname. Well, that and anyone but him screwing over Lorcan.

"Don't fucking go there." His tone is almost feral, a clear warning.

"Who doesn't love the friendly ghost?" Patty smirks at the men behind him. "Casp—"

Finn slams his fist into Patty's face, and the bar comes alive with shouts as the two men exchange blows while Lorcan and the guys behind him weigh into the fray. I stay by the bar at first, watching them pummel each other. When Finn gets Patty on the ground, a bud of unease sprouts in my stomach. Finn pounds on him, and blood flies everywhere. Patty's face is swelling. Is anyone going to stop him? If Finn kills him in the presence of these witnesses and I did nothing to stop him, I'll never forgive myself. I'd never let him go to jail.

After circling the other fights and dodging fists, I yank on Finn's shoulder to get his attention. He shrugs me off, but when I call his name over the chaos of yelling and furniture scraping, his shoulders relax. Without looking at me, he climbs off Patty. Then one of Patty's men charges forward out of the fray, and Finn's back is turned, defenseless. He doesn't see him coming. I step in front, shielding him. At the last moment, the glint of the knife registers. A burning, aching pain rips through my chest and I stumble, knocking into Finn, whose steady hands cradle me from behind.

"Carys, what the—" His ice-blue eyes meet mine in confusion, and then he looks down, understanding registering. "Oh, fuck." His gaze darts around the room. "Lorcan! Lorcan! I need you to call 999." Lowering me to the ground, he says, "Keep focused on me. Help's coming."

The burning has ceased, but numbness and disorientation seep in.

Lorcan appears overhead. "They're on their way." He homes in on my chest. "Holy fuck."

Finn glares at his brother, and then he smooths the stray strands of my hair. My eyelids are so heavy as I stare up. I crave sleep, to give into the heaviness. My hand strays to whatever is protruding out of my body. If I could take it out, the sting would go away.

Before I can grasp the knife, Finn wraps his hand around mine.

"Don't touch it. Leave it be. It's—Jesus—just don't." He half-turns toward Lorcan. "Which motherfucker did this?"

Lorcan shakes his head. The bar has quieted down, eerily quiet. "They're gone. Ran off."

"Doesn't matter. They all had a part in it." Finn squeezes my hand. "Every one of them."

"Finn," I wheeze out.

Speaking is a strain. My body is a raging fire and an ice bath. I shiver and sweat, shiver and sweat.

"Help's coming." He grazes my forehead with his thumb, and my eyelids flutter. "What's taking them so fucking long?"

The front door slams open, and the squeak of the stretcher's wheels draw my attention. Two paramedics loom over me, exchanging phrases in rapid-fire accented English. My heart. Something is wrong with my heart. Finn is just above their shoulder, staring at me with thinly veiled panic and far too much rage. I will him to come with me because I don't understand what's happening. The words won't leave me. My body isn't my own.

When I'm lifted onto the stretcher, I try to reach out to him, but my arm is too heavy, weighted. Lorcan stares at his brother and then follows me and the paramedics out into the cool night air. As the doors on the ambulance click closed, the last face I see isn't Finn's, it's Lorcan's.

The sirens blare as we race to the hospital. Finn didn't even follow me to the ambulance. He's not coming. Why isn't he coming? My chest aches, broken by a knife or by Finn's inattention.

After the surgery, after explaining everything to my parents, who flew in from Chicago, after talking to the police, after waiting days for him to appear, I realize something.

I'm not valued. I'm just disposable.

Chapter One
Finn

I don't know where the fuck I am, and I haven't had a clue for days. Whenever I ask the doctor, who comes around to check on my bullet wounds, he says he's not paid to answer my questions. He has a Russian accent, which could be a disaster. If the Volkovs busted my ass out of the warehouse being raided by the FBI, I'm in trouble.

Nothing about this place reminds me of a hospital. My room is a sparsely decorated bedroom in an expensive house. The décor is neutral browns and yellows. High-end. No stench of antiseptic.

Indebted to the Volkovs, who dropped me in this steaming heap of shit with Kimi the undercover FBI agent, and Lorcan, my little brother, is one of the worst things I can imagine. Hagen, the oldest son, is a braggart. I should have known he wouldn't keep his mouth shut about my father's murder when Kimi showed up in her spandex and leather jacket. Who needs a stick when the carrot looks like that?

The last thing I remember is shooting Kimi in the warehouse after figuring out she was an undercover agent. Lorcan sank a couple bullets in me in retaliation. He thinks he's in love with her. I can't believe he picked a piece of ass over his own brother.

My sheets fall out of the way, and I run my palm along my bandages. More like four of Lorcan's bullets. The doc said whoever shot me had terrible aim, but I've been to the shooting range with him. He didn't miss my vital organs by accident.

There's a quick rap of knuckles on my half-open door, and a woman strolls in dressed in light blue scrubs. I'm guessing she's some kind of nurse, but it's the first time I've seen her. She's little and blonde, and walks with a brisk purpose that's bringing part of my body back to life. If I convince her to braid her hair, she'd do in a pinch.

I angle my chin at her. "You here to look after me?"

With a sidelong glance, she examines the machines and adjusts my covers. The ring on her left hand catches the light, and I suppress a smile.

"Checking in on you." She opens the curtains.

"You want to come back later and we can get to know each other? Talk about the weather, local sightseeing tours, your favorite restaurant..."

She flashes her ring finger at me. "No, I don't suppose I want any of that."

There's a hint of an accent, but it's not Russian. What is it?

"Just an engagement ring."

With a glower, she twists the ring on her finger. "What's your point?"

"You're not married yet. There's still time for you to do better."

"I was warned about you."

I put a hand over my heart and give her my best wounded expression. "Warned about me? Now who would warn you about me?"

Her eyes light up with mischief as she backs toward the door. "You're all set here. Use the buzzer beside your bed if anything comes up."

Christ, all I need is a name or a clue where this place is located. Sun streams in from the window, but the view outside is so generic I can't tell if I'm in America or another foreign land. I should have paid more attention in science or geography class. I might be able to identify a tree or two and have a fucking idea of where I've landed. Fat lot of good my almost English degree does me now. Memorizing Shakespearean quotes was a waste of mental space.

On the bedside table is last month's MMA magazine, and I pick it up and rifle through. Wherever I am and whoever orchestrated this, they know me. From the hot blonde nurse to the MMA magazine to the sheet quality...

Hot nurse.

I grab the buzzer and hold it down. She pops her head in the door.

"Yes?"

Might as well ask. "Where am I?"

She worries her bottom lip, indecision crossing her features. "In a private home of a sort."

I frown, scanning the room. No photos. No paintings. No personalization.

"Whose home?"

She wags a finger at me. "No, no. That's all you're getting. My employer will be here soon. I've been instructed to leave you in the dark so you'll behave."

"I'm probably the best patient in this place. No trouble."

"You don't have much competition, so I suppose you're right."

She leans against the doorway, crossing her arms. "You're lucky to be alive."

"I've been told that more than once in my life." Lifting the top sheet, I readjust the covers on my lap. "I'm bored out of my skull."

"This is the first day you haven't been on heavy painkillers, so I can see why you might be restless."

I narrow my eyes. "I woulda remembered seeing you one of the other days."

She taps the side of her head. "Your brain is fried. Also you had previous injuries that weren't healed. They added to the complications of being shot half a dozen times." She hesitates. "And I only came into your room when you were knocked out cold." A smile touches her lips. "I heard you raving at the doctor about...well, everything. Wasn't too keen on getting in on that."

"Raving." I scoff, crossing my arms. "I was asking questions."

"You were demanding answers."

I stare at her, and she slides out the doorway. I open my mouth to summon her back and realize I don't know her name. "Hey—what do I call you?"

She laughs and reappears in the entry, shaking her head. "Eve."

She glances over her shoulder, and with a frown, she disappears again.

"Eve!" A second surge of annoyance rushes through me at my helplessness. Earlier I tried to get out of bed and almost fell on my face. I snatch up the buzzer and press on it again. I'm not fucking amusing myself. No TV and one magazine will not cut through my boredom. I keep my thumb on the buzzer as I twist to grab the MMA magazine with my free hand. My stitches stretch with me, and I wince. Movement registers out of the corner of my eye, and I look up.

"You're awake," she says, her voice soft, familiar.

I release the buzzer, and the magazine slides off my lap, onto the floor, hitting the carpet with a thud. At least ten different emotions war for dominance. My heart squeezes in my chest, and my cock twitches under the covers, which occupies most of my brain. Like always, the sight of her is painful.

"It was you?" I shouldn't be surprised.

Why hadn't I considered her? She's a meddler. A fixer.

She tucks a phantom piece of blonde hair into her fancy braid. Her nervous habit, and the realization she still does it, makes my heart kick. My fingers throb at the memory of being buried in her hair. There are a few things I'd love buried in her right now. Her short skirt, tight white T-shirt, and the navy blazer take me back seventeen years.

Seventeen years. Christ, I'm fucking old. She's five years older than me and looks like she's straddling thirty. How is that possible? She's forty-five.

"Surprised?" She shoves her bulky purse higher onto her shoulder, but doesn't leave the doorway.

"Yeah, considering I told you to stay the hell away."

I'm pissed off and grateful at the same time. She saved my life...again. Her caught up in my messy business is what I don't want, have never wanted.

Carys straightens, and her heels are muted by the carpeted floor as she ambles toward my bed. "I should have let you die?"

"You shoulda stayed out of it."

"Maybe I could have if you hadn't called me when you were dying in a field. Maybe if you hadn't told me you suspected the FBI was involved." Her amber eyes are thoughtful as she searches my face. "Maybe if I could stop giving a shit whether you're still somewhere out in the world, alive."

"A few months ago, when we had sex in Boston, we agreed I was...how'd you phrase it?" Not that I'd forget. "Paying my debt because you saved my life seventeen years ago." I raise my eyebrows.

The memory is scorched into my synapsis. Carys teetering off the chair in the kitchen, drunk, me catching her, swinging her up into my arms. Her lips pressed against my neck and then she murmured in my ear, *You're alive because of me. How will you pay me back?* Over and over again that night, I gave her my payment, and she screamed my name in thanks.

Her pale pink lips twist, and she crosses her arms. Her eyes narrow and then dance with mischief.

"Hmmm...is that how that night went?"

She's close enough to the bed that if my wounds were healed a touch more, I'd snatch her, yank her onto my lap. Her laughter would echo through the room like it used to years ago. Amused, aroused. But she's just out of reach, and when I shift too quickly my stitches strain at the seams.

"Happy to pay you back for this one too," I say.

Her lips rise in a rueful smile, and she eases away from the bed, more distance between us.

"You overpaid last time."

"Makes me feel like you're undervaluing my life." I stare, willing her to come closer.

She avoids eye contact and re-crosses her arms. "Who shot you?

"My *dearthair beag*." I run a frustrated hand through my hair and wince. Everything hurts. "I honestly can't fucking believe it."

"Need more painkillers?"

I give a half-smile. "I got other things in mind to dull my pain."

Something buzzes in her bag, and she slides one strap off her arm, rummaging around until she finds it. She bites her lip, and her brow creases. "I have to take this. I'll come back to check on you later." Carys heads for the door, her phone pressed to her ear before I can protest.

When she's gone, my chest strains with an ache the painkillers can't dull. The pain might be my stitches, or it just might be my traitorous heart.

Chapter Two
Carys

As soon as I'm out of Finn's room and down the hall, I hang up on the telemarketer and lean against the wall. Seeing him so haggard, so injured makes my chest constrict. Flirting with him, getting close to him, half-expecting him to toss me onto the bed to have his way with me, causes the lower half of my body pulse with desire. Never before Finn, and not once after, has the mere sight of a man made me weak with longing.

"You okay?" Eve pokes her head out of her office door.

"Sure, yeah." I straighten and tug on my jacket. "It's just—yeah, I'm fine."

"He looks rough, but he's okay. Or he'll be fine as long as he doesn't get shot or stabbed again anytime soon."

Dropping my phone into my bag, I purse my lips together. "He's been no trouble?"

Eve laughs. "I've avoided him when he's awake, until today. Some mild flirting. Thanks for loaning me the rock." She flashes her ring finger at me.

The lights catch the diamond.

"I don't need it anymore." I frown. "Finn told me once that he always checked a woman's ring finger before sleeping with her. Not that a piece of jewelry stopped him, just that he noticed."

Perhaps I should have worn the ring when I visited Kim at the Donaghey house. Of course if I'd done that, I might not have been able to save Finn. He'd be dead or in jail. I swallow. Each time my mind drifts in that direction, I want to burst into tears.

"Have you talked to Eric lately?" Eve asks.

Dragging myself away from my dark thoughts, I sigh. "More than I'd like. He's pissed about the missing content from the warehouse." He doesn't even know Kim might have accumulated dirt on us to turn over to the FBI.

"Must be hard."

"He likes to forget we broke up for a reason. Our relationship feels like a long time ago." The same can't be said for the man in the other room. Finn and I never came to an official end, and our whole affair is buried in me, like our relationship collapsed yesterday. The sting of what might have been is fresh. Breathtakingly raw. Impossible, but true.

Eve reads my mind. "Finn's intense." She leans her shoulder against the door and puts one hand on her hip. "What are you going to do about him? He can't go back, right?"

"No, he can't return to Boston."

"Will the FBI know you have him?"

"Maybe." I flutter my fingers to my hair before resting them on my purse. "They'll never be able to prove I have him. There's not much the FBI can do while we're here."

My phone buzzes, and I dig it out of my bag. This time it's a business call.

"I'll be back later."

Eve springs off the door and into the office. She's worked for the family long enough to understand how I operate. She's earned my trust several times over. Learning Kim is a traitor is a blow to my ego. I've never been fooled before.

When I understood how extensive Finn's injuries were, Eve had to be the one watching over him. No one new, no one untested, would get near him. I didn't call in favors to get him extracted, only to have someone rat us out.

Normally this building is a hospice my family sponsors, and Eve is the head nurse. We opened this place when my brother died of cancer. Since Finn has arrived, we've been turning away requests to stay in this section. Now that he's better, I need to move him into a more secure location.

I breeze out the main doors, grasping my phone. The Alps loom ahead, and I let the call go to voicemail. It's Eric, and I can't be bothered to answer his questions about why I'm back in Switzerland so soon. The company has business here, and of course my family has a house and this hospice, but it's not normal for me to be here when our warehouse in Russia is missing weapons, ammunition, and who knows what else.

The waiting car sits in the circular drive with Jay, my bodyguard and right-hand man, behind the wheel. Once I'm in the backseat, our gazes connect.

"Eric just called me, asking for you."

"What'd you tell him?" I drop my phone into my purse and wish it would get lost in there.

"I was at home with my family. Didn't have a clue where you might be."

I laugh. "I bet that went over well."

"He said the company trace on my phone told him I was a lying motherfucker and we were in Switzerland again. You don't want him to know about Finn, but he's going to wonder if you had something to do with the warehouse theft."

My back stiffens at the implication. "Why would he think I stole from my company?"

"Because he's Eric."

When we began dating, my father took a shine to him. A corporate man. Smart. Athletic. He ticked my father's boxes, and with my brother long gone, he gave my father the son he almost had. Eric can be an asshole, so he ticked the only box I seem to require in a boyfriend. When it turned out I had a cap on the jerk quotient, we broke up. He campaigned my father for control of the company when he retired. Another reason we would never have worked out. His confidence overrode his common sense. My father may love him like a son, but Eric is not family.

"I'll call Eric when we arrive at the house," I say.

"He said he's flying here to figure out what you're up to."

"Wonderful."

Jay chuckles. "You think Eric and Finn will get along?"

"Not a snowball's chance in hell."

Eric will be livid when he realizes the laws I broke and the favors I called in to lift Finn from the warehouse without a trace. Given how little notice I had to save him, I made sketchy deals and poor compromises. Eric will rake me over the coals for exposing the company. As the head of the Van de Berg Ammunitions, I should be more careful. His criticism is valid, but I don't want to hear it.

We drive in silence through the streets of Zurich, headed to the countryside and our luxury chalet which cost my father a fortune years ago. Now we use the house as a hideout, or a base, or just a retreat from the real world. As soon as the large wooden structure looms ahead, my spirits rise. The gorgeous green hills, the snowcapped mountains, and the lake have a calming effect. It's been hell the last few weeks, between keeping Finn a secret, discovering Kim is a traitor, and then the theft of the goods in our Russian warehouse. I've been spinning, and it's about time I stopped.

When the car glides to a halt outside the chalet, I hurry into the house. Lena, my housekeeper, is in the kitchen getting dinner ready. The high vaulted ceilings, huge windows, and wide-open living room, dining room, and kitchen make this area of the house one of my favorites.

"Smells delicious." I kick off my heels and collapse into a plush leather couch.

"Long day?"

"Long life at this point." I shrug off my blazer. "We'll be having a guest join us."

"Eric is on his way?"

I grimace. "Yes, but not him. Well, perhaps him. I'm going to try to convince him a hotel makes more sense."

Eric won't agree, but the discussion is worth making him understand he's not wanted.

"I need the room furthest from mine, the one with an attached bathroom, for my guest."

Lena raises her eyebrows as she stirs something in a pot on the stove. She's eleven years older than me and still as beautiful as the day I met her. Snow White comes to mind. Lena's worked for my family for so long she sometimes treats me more like her child than her employer. She started just after my brother died. My dad consoled himself with this chalet…and Lena.

"Is this guest a man?"

"He is."

"Would that person be the fugitive the FBI is searching for? A certain Finn Donaghey?"

I pucker my lips and turn away.

"He can't return to America." Lena comes around the island and perches on one of the couches across from me.

"I know." I stare at the beams running across the ceiling. "I'm getting him on his feet."

"In your house."

"Yes."

The heat of Lena's gaze is palpable, but I won't meet it. She's wondering what else I'll do to get him on his feet. But I've been down that route with Finn before, and I don't intend to go there again. My father taught me men can't be faithful. That kind of loyalty isn't in their DNA. My engagement experiment with Eric proved I can't turn a blind eye. At least not anymore.

"I'm not a twenty-eight-year-old girl addicted to bad boys and danger. I've grown up. I'm a forty-five-year-old woman who knows better."

A smile is in Lena's voice when she says, "Let's hope so." She rises and goes back to the kitchen to stir her pot. "He's a fugitive from the FBI. That's not a life for anyone. Certainly not the head of an international arms company who likes to pretend she's squeaky clean."

I sink deeper into the couch and put my feet on the coffee table. Pretending might not be an option about a lot of things.

Chapter Three
Finn

I hold the buzzer again. Eve pokes her head in the door and doesn't quite suppress her sigh.

"Come fluff my pillows."

She raises her eyebrows.

"Please."

As she walks toward the bed, I lean forward, and she bunches the pillows, making them bigger. I just wanted to see if she'd do it. I've been coming up with shitty jobs for her since Carys left. No phone. No internet. No TV. No books. I'm not sure what Carys thought I would do with my time, but annoying the nurse seems to be it. And digging for whatever she doesn't want me to find out.

"That ring." I gesture to her left hand. "What's your boyfriend's name again?"

"Uhh." She bunches her hands into the sides of the pillows with more determination. "Peter."

I smirk. She said Paul earlier.

"It's funny. Looks a lot like something Carys would wear."

"Oh? You think she'd like this?" She eyes her handiwork and steps away from the bed.

Stifling a groan, I ease onto the pillow. There's nothing about Carys I don't notice. Nothing in this room is to her taste, which is surprising. The yellow and brown tones aren't colors she'd choose.

"Peter-Paul live around here?"

"In Zur—" Her eyes grow wide, and she blinks.

Zur-Zur-Zurich? She smuggled me to fucking Switzerland. "Ah, the Alps." I wink at her. "I won't tell her you spilled the beans."

Eve's accent makes a lot more sense now.

"When do you have to return her ring?"

She stares at me, turns on her heel, and hauls ass out the door. Right now, I guess.

I sink further under the covers and wonder whether I can get the nurse into the room again. Perhaps I went a bit too far. Amuses the shit out of me that Carys gave her a fake engagement ring to wear, but didn't coach her on the backstory. After having my ass handed to me by Kimi, my very own undercover FBI agent, Eve's ineptitude is laughable.

"I'm glad you find this whole thing funny." In the doorway, Carys has her arms crossed.

Gone are the skirt and tight white shirt, and in its place are dark jeans and a flowing, girly shirt. The other outfit was better.

"You gotta admit," I say, "giving her a ring and not helping her build a backstory is careless."

She shrugs and then wanders into the room. "I wanted you deterred, not deceived."

"We're in Switzerland, huh? You woulda had to break a shit-ton of laws to get me here."

"You won't be able to go back." She stops near my bed, out of reach.

She must be able to sense what will happen if she gets too close.

"What information do the feds have?" I say.

"You're missing. That's the news story."

"Kimi will make sure they suspect you."

She squares her shoulders and stands taller. "There's nothing they can do if you're here. I paid everyone involved very well. I had to string the extraction together last minute, so I didn't use my best, most trusted people, but it'll be fine."

"Christ, Carys. I don't want you going to prison trying to save my ass."

"It's done. You were unconscious, so you didn't get a say." Her lips rise at the corners, not quite a smile.

"How'd you find out? Lorcan?"

He didn't kill me. Maybe he made sure I'd come out alive, too.

She shakes her head and bites her lip. "Sean."

"Sean."

The truth drops like a piece of lead. Pisses me off that she could buy information from a key man in my organization. But without Sean caving, I'd be in custody. Death woulda been preferable to jail.

"I need to transport you out of here tonight. Can you walk?"

"I've made it to the bathroom and back a few times." My gaze rakes over her, taking in the no-nonsense flats she's wearing, as opposed to her heels. "I had to lean heavily on Eve."

Without missing a beat or breaking eye contact, she calls out to someone named Jay. A burly, olive-skinned man appears in the doorway.

"Finn needs to lean on you on the way to the car." She tilts her head at me, a challenge.

"I need some fucking privacy to get dressed. I'll be fine."

She holds out a hand to the man beside her and he places a shopping bag across her fingers. She swings it forward and lets it go so it lands beside my bed. She's done that maneuver before.

"We'll be out of here when you're ready." She closes the door behind her.

Easing myself to the edge of the bed, I wince as I grab the bag from the floor. Designer jeans in my size and a black T-shirt. I dress so slowly that at one point, Eve knocks to ask if I need help. It's not her hands I want trailing across my body, even if it was fun to pretend for a while.

With a sigh, I tug the shirt down and straighten. My stitches stretch with every movement, serving as a constant reminder my little brother chose a woman he'd only known a few months over me. An FBI agent. I didn't think Lorcan had a clue about Kimi until we were face-to-face in our warehouse, and then it was pretty fucking clear he understood who Kimi was and what she'd been doing.

When I open my bedroom door, there's a waiting room directly outside and an office to the left. Eve leans against the office entry. Jay and Carys are sitting in the recliners, and she flips through a fashion magazine with one hand, her phone clutched in the other. She notices me as her phone buzzes.

"Ready?" She peeks at the incoming message and sighs. She drops the magazine on the table beside her, and stands.

"Eric?" Jay hoists himself out of the chair.

"He landed." She eyes me for a second, indecision written across her face.

"Who's Eric?"

The ring on Eve's finger. The way she sighed at his text. Adds up to something I don't like. Was she engaged when we had sex months ago? Is she still engaged? The vice around my chest tightens.

She glances at Jay. "A business associate."

My instinct is to demand more information. Instead I grunt and start toward the door. None of my business. She doesn't belong in this shitstorm I've created. We had a single night a few months ago and nothing more. Just because she saved my life doesn't change our reality. I gotta keep the head on my shoulders in charge, instead of the one in my pants.

"Finn." Her voice is soft, almost sad beside me.

I raise by eyebrows in silent response.

"You're moving pretty slow. Do you want help?"

I grit my teeth and shake my head. "I'm fine."

The words, *are you sure,* hang between us, but she doesn't dare vocalize them.

"Thanks, Eve." I smirk and give her a wink on the way past. "You understand how to look after a guy. Your fiancée, Peter-Paul is a lucky man."

A blush rushes to Eve's cheeks, and she turns away. Carys makes an exasperated noise, and I run a hand down my face to hide my grin. There's something very satisfying in besting her.

We file out into the cool, dark night. When we get to the car, I maneuver into the backseat with care. Carys sits in the front with Jay. Determined to avoid being close to me, I guess. Fine by me. I don't need more complications. Easier to think when she isn't within arm's reach. As soon as she is, burying myself deep inside her is all I want. Years ago, being with her ran through me like a wildfire. Took her almost dying to snuff it out.

As the vehicle accelerates through the city streets, I try to focus on what the hell I'll do now. Getting revenge on Kimi is a happy thought, and I linger there, but it's out of the question. There's no way to go after her without dragging Carys, and possibly Lorcan, down. I'm not doing that. Lorcan might have shot me, but he's still my brother, my last piece of family. Should I have looped him in when I allowed the Volkovs to murder our father? Probably. Can't go back.

From the front seat, Carys says, "Are you going to tell anyone else about Lorcan and Kim? The FBI connection? The truth is being covered over, but we could blow the whole thing wide open."

"Who would I call?"

"Byrne brothers. Volkovs. Zhangs. Any of them?"

"Fuck 'em." I grab my neck and wince at the straining skin and stitches.

I can't even remember the last time I felt good. Apparently getting stabbed and then shot is a bad combination.

"If they're too dumb to figure out the truth, fuck 'em." If they figure it out, they'll go after Lorcan. We've got our problems, but nobody else better touch him.

"You worried about the fallout for him?" Carys says.

"He didn't kill me."

"You make the gunfight sound like a fistfight in your parents' basement."

"That's the code." I turn my gaze from the window to see streetlights dancing across her half-turned face. "Same rules apply.

He's my brother. I'm not giving anyone anything that'll get him killed."

"Are *you* going after him?"

I chuckle. "You worried you saved my ass just to have me put it on the line again?"

A hint of a smile touches her face. "Wouldn't be unheard of."

"Surprise. I'm finally growing up." I smirk and spread my hands wide.

Her laughter echoes through the car, warming my chest. I press the heel of my hand into the warmth and focus on the scenery outside as the city recedes and countryside takes over. In the distance a chalet is lit up like a landing strip. That's gotta be hers. Charles Van de Berg has always been a big fan of extravagance in every aspect of his life.

"Small and quaint," I say.

"You know my father."

I used to until I almost got his daughter murdered. Standing toe-to-toe with him outside her hospital room, covered in the blood of the men who put her there, is my most vivid memory. That and her expression when she realized she was stabbed. *Christ.*

"You all right back there?"

Her voice draws me out of my dark thoughts. *Jesus.* The number of people I've killed in my life, and the thing guaranteed to undo me every time is that expression on her face, startled, scared, full of disbelief. There was *nothing* I could do.

The tightness in my chest eases at the realization she didn't die. Close, but the doctors at the hospital worked their magic. Letting her go was the best decision I ever made. Might be the only choice in my life I'm proud of. "Fine. Thinking about how the hell to get out of Switzerland and on with my life."

From my profile view, her smile fades. "Yeah," she says. "The sooner you're on your feet, the better."

As we start up the long drive, Carys and Jay talk in low voices up front. I can't quite hear what they're saying, but when another vehicle is in the driveway, she lets loose a stream of curses.

"Eric?" I try to catch a glimpse of his car.

"When we go in, can you please keep out of it, Finn? Or else stay in the car until I get rid of him."

I sit forward while the car glides to a stop. Eric and I will not get along if she's already warning me. The pretentious Alfa Romeo in the driveway doesn't help.

"I'm not staying in the car," I say. "And if he's a dick to you, I'm gonna shut him up."

Carys sighs. "Just remember you've already been stabbed and

shot in the last few weeks."

I chuckle. "Don't worry. I'm sure I could still throw a mean right hook if I had to. Somebody can repair my stitches."

From her seat, she holds up a finger. "Promise me. Promise me you won't touch Eric, no matter what."

With the door open, I ease myself out. "Has it been that long, Carys?"

Straightening in the cool, night air, almost every part of my body aches. More drugs. I hope to hell she's got good painkillers in there.

"I never make a promise I can't keep."

Chapter Four
Carys

I lead the way into the house. Each step is quicksand, tugging on my feet, sucking me deeper. Rescuing Finn was more instinct than intellect. For seventeen years I ignored anything to do with him. Then a whiff of the Donaghey brothers, thanks to Kim's scheming, and I've been hauled into their vortex of death and danger.

Not that the international arms business is sunshine and roses. I've grown up with those dangers, and my father is well-established. Everything in this world makes sense to me. Finn's brand of rage, sex, and violence has always turned me on, but I never understood why.

I stride through the house, my flats making me silent on the wood floor. Usually I make more of an entrance. Finn and Jay are far enough behind that I should be able to warn Eric before the two men come face to face.

Sitting on the couch, suit jacket open, feet propped on the table and a drink in his hand, is Eric. Like this, he makes my breath catch. He's the opposite of Finn in his build and coloring, but his aura of power draws me to him.

"You didn't have to come all this way," I tell him.

A sly smile spreads across his lips. "You're hiding something from me."

"We haven't been engaged for years. I'm also your boss. I suppose I can literally hide anything, and you can't do shit about it."

His grin fades, and he turns in the couch to inspect me. "Don't be a bitch. We're missing a massive amount of product in Russia, and you're more interested in a skiing vacation than tracking a thief? You can't tell me that's normal behavior for you."

"That's the thing about being the boss. I assigned people to gather the information for me while I'm here. I don't have to do everything myself. The word *delegation* was invented for that."

Eric raises his cranberry vodka soda and swishes it around his glass. He saunters over to me with the ease of a man who knows how this will go.

"I can delegate with the best of them. There are people who require a more *personal* touch." He grazes his fingers over my collarbone as he pushes my hair behind my shoulders.

Normally his familiarity would cause a shiver to race down my spine. But I am so achingly aware of Finn's approach, Eric's caress barely registers.

His rich brown eyes search me, trying to figure out what's different. He might be an asshole and a cheat, but he can read people. He's known me for so long in so many ways, my lack of reaction must jar him. "What are you doing here in Switzerland?"

"Me." Finn's deep timber responds from behind me.

Eric darts his gaze over my head, and confusion mars his face. "And you would be?"

I half-turn, willing Finn to use an alias, any alias. Eric's never been a threat to me outside the business arena, but I'm not sure what he'll do about me harboring a known fugitive. One who almost murdered an FBI agent and, if he could do it again, would simply have better aim.

"Finn Donaghey."

Eric's eyes widen and he glances at me before straightening to his full height. It's impressive. He's six-foot-four to Finn's six-foot stature. But Finn's fighting motto has always been, *the bigger they are, the harder they fall.* Size never intimidated him. Eric's lean, ropy, a runner. Finn's bulkier, a brawler. Most people wouldn't want to come across him in a dark alley.

Unbidden, the image of him pressing me up against a cold brick wall, pushing his hands up my skirt, the ache to be with him, to have him inside me, is more than I can bear. It was the last time we were together before I was stabbed.

Heat rises to my cheeks, and I turn from Eric, hoping he's too focused on his rival to notice my sudden arousal.

"Is he the reason the fucking FBI has been sniffing around the office in Chicago?" Eric's drink sloshes over the edges as he gestures toward Finn.

Not his first alcoholic beverage since arriving.

"Yes." I swallow, willing myself to stay in the moment and stop getting lost in the past.

Finn's not capable of feeling for me what I once believed I felt for him. He doesn't do commitment. Most men don't. Least of all Eric.

"I'm helping him get sorted," I say, "and then I'll be back to the office. I have people figuring out what happened at the warehouse."

"Not just what happened, Carys. We need to comprehend why

and who was involved and whether it's likely to happen again. If we were a smaller organization, that theft would have ruined us. As it is, we don't have a clue where those arms are headed. Our proverbial fingerprints coat them."

Lashing out is tempting, but when Eric's been into the alcohol, he's too easily riled. Given that Finn has already reminded me about his quick temper, I keep my anger in check.

"I'm aware of the questions that need answered," I say. "You being here instead of in Chicago or Russia isn't helpful for any of them."

Finn moves around the two of us and crosses to the couch Eric vacated. Easing into the soft white leather, he takes us in with his flinty gaze.

"Don't mind me," Finn says. "Pretend I'm not here. Carry on." He waves his hand and then rests them over, last I checked, an impressive set of abs.

"Are you going to get arrested?" Eric focuses on me, his jaw tight. "For the guy who almost got you killed years ago?" He brushes his fingers over the spot on my chest where the faint remnants of a scar still lie underneath my shirt.

Finn raises his eyebrows. "You're fucking lucky I'm recovering from bullet wounds, or you'd be having your ass handed to you right now. That's your one asshole comment. I'd prefer to let my stitches heal. But if you poke this bear, you're going to get the claws and my teeth."

"He's not kidding." I give Eric a pointed stare.

His face contorts with disgust and disbelief. "A bear metaphor? That's the best you've got?" He tucks a stray strand of my hair behind my ear.

His constant points of contact are annoying me. He's never this affectionate anymore.

Tension vibrates off Finn. Is it the familiarity Eric is showing with me, or my ex-fiancé's disrespect of him?

"You have the shittiest taste in men," Eric says. "He probably doesn't understand metaphors."

Finn holds up two fingers. "Two credits shy of getting a business and literary studies degree. I could give you a better metaphor, but you seemed like a simple guy. I didn't want to overwhelm you with my intellect." He smirks and laces his fingers together across his middle again.

"I'm simple? How the fuck, in this day and age, do you stay two credits shy of getting a degree?"

"Well," he says, drawing out the word. "You start by murdering a bunch of people in Ireland and then you keep killing people." Finn shrugs. "Seems I was cut out for a path in life which didn't require a degree."

My heart races, and my knees are unsteady. I can't decide if I'll vomit in disgust or faint with longing. Terrible taste in men is an understatement because everything he said makes me want to haul him upstairs and reacquaint my body with his.

Eric pales at the implications of Finn's words, and then he wheels on me.

"We need to have a discussion in private. I'm extremely concerned about what you're getting yourself into here."

With a sigh, I purse my lips together. "I'll show him where he's staying, and we can chat."

"Jay can do that." Eric nods toward Jay, who is by the main entrance.

"No, he cannot. He's guarding the door from anyone who might want to burst in here. I'll show him to his room and come back."

"I'm not tired yet." Finn settles deeper into the couch.

There's no way I am pleading with him to leave the room. "Fine," I grit out. "Eric and I will go spend time in *my room, alone,* to get privacy then."

Finn holds up a hand. "I can show myself to my room. It's fine. Where is it?"

As he rises, it's clear he's still stiff and sore. Seeing him weak softens me toward him and his stubbornness.

"Up the stairs, fourth door on the left. The last one."

"Where's your room?" He angles his head toward Eric.

Eric meets his curious stare. "Not your concern, I don't think."

"I'll see you in the morning, Carys." His gaze trails over me, my skin prickling with desire.

"Right," I agree. He will not go to bed. He'll retreat to the top of the stairs and find somewhere to eavesdrop. The upper level of the house has a balcony which overlooks the living area, and voices drift up. Eric is so intent on berating me, he hasn't even considered this idea.

After Finn disappears from the room, Eric takes the next hour to try to 'talk sense into me.' I counter every argument with two responses—he's no longer my fiancé or I'm his boss.

He continues to suck back the vodka and becomes less interested in turning me off Finn and more interested in turning me onto him.

We've fallen into a post-breakup routine of sleeping together whenever we're in any city but Chicago. Part of me wonders whether he flew here just to get laid. If I wasn't so desperate to propel Finn out of my head, I wouldn't even entertain sleeping with him tonight. He's being an obnoxious dick who doesn't recognize his place in my life or the organization.

When he heads upstairs before me, I don't tell him he can't go to my room. When I get there, I'll find him naked, waiting. Any other time, his presence would be a bit thrilling. Sex was never the problem between us. Rather, the sex he was having with other people behind my back. Tonight he's a means to an end. I need a release before my sexual frustration rages out of control.

After I've put the glasses in the dishwasher, I wander up the stairs. On the landing just outside my door is Finn.

"I assumed you'd be asleep by now." I keep my voice low. Eric doesn't need to realize he was eavesdropping.

"Did you?" Finn pushes his hands into his pockets and shrugs. "You knew I'd be listening."

"Hear anything of interest?"

"Eric's a dick."

"What can I say? I have a thing for dicks."

He smirks and glances away from me. "You've had a warehouse theft?"

"Yes. But we'll get it under control. Eric is overreacting."

He isn't, but I don't need Finn trying to ride to the rescue when he has to sort out his own life.

Finn scans me with his ice-blue eyes. "He's in your room?"

"Probably." My heart hammers.

Whether Eric's in my room shouldn't matter to him.

Finn grips the back of his neck with one hand, while his other disappears deeper into his jean's pocket.

"You don't have to sleep with him to prove a point to me."

"Is that what I'm doing?"

"I still feel it, Carys. The connection between us. It's humming right now. You can't tell me you don't feel it, too."

Goosebumps rise on my arms, and I rub them. His sixth sense is accurate. When Finn and I are alone in a room together, something lives and breathes in our space. Back when this whole thing first started, the sensation freaked me out. Then I wondered if the tension in the air might be love. Now I recognize it as good old-fashioned lust. I can take care of that myself.

"If it makes tonight easier for you," I say, "I would have had sex with him even if you weren't here." Backing away from him, I place my hand on my bedroom door. "I'll see you in the morning."

He shakes his head but doesn't meet my gaze. "You're better than this, Carys."

With pursed lips, I examine him for a moment. "Maybe. But this is all I want."

Then I turn the handle and walk into my room.

Chapter Five
Finn

The sun streams in from the blinds I didn't bother closing last night. My sleep was restless and painful, and just fucking terrible. I shoulda sucked it up and asked Carys for the drugs. That's why I waited for her on the landing. Since the other doors were open on the second floor, I knew Eric was in her bedroom, waiting for her. Her settling for that guy is the equivalent of having someone piss on my cornflakes. I didn't walk away from her the first time for her to end up with a guy like him.

The sun keeps hitting my eyes, and I throw my forearm across them, wishing I could will myself back to sleep. While I'm lying here, I need to figure out how to get out of this house. Being around Carys is a bomb with a lit fuse, fizzing away, getting closer and closer to exploding. My instinct is to stay, to watch it go off, to relish in the chaos and destruction.

Not this time.

I climb out of bed and grab the other set of clothes someone put on the dresser before I got here last night. My movements are slow and careful, but I get dressed as quickly as I can and amble down the stairs to see what I can find for breakfast. As I come into the main room, I suck in a deep breath filled with greasy bacon and coffee. Doesn't get better than that. Standing at the island, meat sizzling on the grill in front of her, is Lena. Her black hair is in some kind of bun thing, and she hasn't noticed me yet. We only met once, years ago, when Charles Van de Berg introduced us at a party, and it became clear she was playing the role of Mrs. Van de Berg, in Switzerland. Carys talked about her a lot back then—how she enjoyed Lena's company, how her feelings were a betrayal of her mother.

"You're still working here? You a glutton for punishment?"

Lena jumps, let's out a squeak, and touches a hand to her chest.

"Sorry. I didn't mean to startle you."

I'm shoeless, and I've always had a tendency to approach in silence. It's instinct.

"No, no. That's okay." Her smile stretches across her face, not connecting with her dark brown eyes. "I wasn't expecting anyone to be up yet. Usually the smell has to get under her door before she'll even open her eyelids."

With my hands in my pockets, I saunter over to the island and ease onto a heavy wooden bar stool. Carys has two paces in the morning. Up before the birds, making deals, or a cave dweller who only emerged for food.

"She's not an early riser here?" I say.

Lena shakes her head, and she uses tongs to turn the bacon.

Glancing up at the balcony overlooking this room, I run my hand through my hair. *Is he still up there?* The thought turns my stomach.

"He's gone." Lena has her back to me as she grabs a plate from a cupboard behind her.

"That was quick."

"Always is. He got what he came for."

I'm sure I've grasped her meaning, but I say it anyway. "Which was?"

"Raise his leg to everything in sight and go home to screw whoever he wants in Chicago."

I snatch a piece of sizzling bacon from the pan and drop it in front of me when it burns my fingertips.

"Not a fan of Eric?"

"Are you?"

"The reason I don't like him isn't the reason you don't like him."

She raises a shaped eyebrow. "You might be surprised. Charles loves Eric, though, and I've heard he's good at his job."

"Can't be too good if they've had a major theft."

"He's not in charge of that region," Carys says, from behind me. "And you're right, Lena, my father loves him. They're very similar."

I'm not the only one who can make a stealthy approach. Twisting in my seat, with difficulty, I catch a glimpse of her standing in the entranceway in an oversized men's dress shirt. If it's not his, she wants me to think it is. Her point wears thin on my patience.

"That's what you're wearing today?" I ask.

Lena cracks the eggs and drops them into the frying pan.

"With the right belt, it would do in a pinch." Carys wanders over to the couches and takes a seat. The furthest spot from me she can choose.

"Lots of room at the island," I say.

"I'm fine over here," she replies.

I purse my lips in irritation and catch Lena smiling. "It's not fucking funny."

Lena's grin widens. "It kind of is." She flips the eggs and raises the spatula in one hand while the other perches on her cocked-out hip. "I hear you're stuck over in this area now."

Scowling, I snatch another slice of bacon. This time the piece isn't too hot, and I take a big bite.

"Fucking FBI."

"At least it's not the CIA," Carys says from the couch. "Domestic, not international."

"Not in the mood for your tiptoeing through the daisies comments," I say.

Her laughter peals through the room. "Are you ever?"

"No," I grumble and eat more bacon.

When we were together, Carys was perpetually sunny when faced with my doom and gloom. I pretended to be annoyed by it, but her optimism was a trait I used to love. At least that hasn't changed.

"You got any drugs?" I say.

"Oh." She rises and saunters into the kitchen, opening a corner cupboard.

"Sorry. I completely forgot you were injured. I should have remembered because you move like an old man with arthritis."

Lena stifles a laugh with her hand.

"I don't look that bad."

Carys passes me a bottle, and I check the label before popping the top. I was hoping for morphine, but whatever this is will have to do.

"Where are you going to live now?" Lena slides an egg onto a plate and then does the same a second time.

"We should go over the list I put together at some point today." Carys takes a slice of bacon and pulls it apart with her fingertips, inserting pieces into her mouth.

Lena piles the plates with bacon, eggs, and a potato mash thing she fried in the pan. She passes a plate to me and to Carys. Mine has twice the amount of food. Normally I'd have no trouble wolfing it down, but my time in and out of hospitals has meant I haven't been doing anything normal.

Carys stands on the other side of the wide island, eating her food in slow, meticulous bites. Watching the fork go from her plate and slide into her mouth is torture. The drugs haven't kicked in yet, and my body aches. The tightening in my pants isn't helping.

"Do you have access to any of your money?" she says.

Her lips close around her thumb to catch a smear of egg yolk. Her tongue swirls, and I swallow. Right now, I want to fuck her on the kitchen counter while Lena watches. I'm shit at resisting temptation, and Carys is the shiny, juicy apple. Even when the fruit is poisoned at first bite, she's impossible to resist.

"A bit." I sip the coffee Lena placed in front of me to wash down my pills. "Probably not enough. It'll depend on the country. I had lots of cash on hand at the house, and I took some to the warehouse with me. Figured if I came out of there alive, I'd at least have something to help me start over."

Carys frowns. "You didn't arrive in Switzerland with a bag."

"Probably still in the warehouse, with the FBI, or with whoever whisked me out. How *did* you get me out, anyway?"

"Paid off someone in the raid party."

"FBI?"

"Who else would be in the raid?" She raises her eyebrows at me as the fork slides into her mouth again.

"Impressive."

"I've got friends in all kinds of places."

I smirk. "I bet you do."

"Keep your mind out of the gutter, Finn."

My gaze roams over her leisurely. "I hate that fucking shirt."

"I'm making a statement."

"Been made. Go change."

"No." Her amber eyes connect with mine, full of challenge. "What was it you said to me? Your voice means nothing in this house anymore."

My lips twist in annoyance as I focus on my plate. "I shouldn't have fucking said that, okay. I was surprised to see you at my house, meeting with my brother, talking about shit you knew nothing about."

"Fine. But you don't appreciate why I'm wearing this shirt." She flicks the collar with her fingers.

"Whose is it?"

"Eric's."

"Then I understand exactly why you're wearing it."

"The shirt is comfortable."

"Bullshit. You're telling me to stay the fuck away. You don't need to. I have no intention of trying to get in your pants." I trail her body again, greedy for the curves barely outlined by the oversize button up. "Or up your shirt. As soon as we've worked out the details, I'll be out of your life again."

She tucks her hair behind her ears and avoids eye contact. With her fingers, she takes apart another slice of bacon.

The dishes Lena's been washing in silence clatter into the second sink. She glances over her shoulder and bites her lip.

"Sorry."

"Want help?" I rise from my seat and bring my dish over to slide it onto the counter beside her.

When I turn around, Carys is gone.

"She's not as tough as she seems." Her voice is quiet beside me.

"I know," I say. "That's why I need to stay the hell out of her life. I blow lives up; I don't keep them safe."

"You're starting over." She plucks a dish towel from the rack beside me. "Maybe you can restart that attitude, too."

I give her a long look, searching her open, serious face.

"You're one of those people."

A smile touches her lips. "Those people?"

"Like Carys."

I take my dish and place it into the dishwasher. Sliding my coffee off the island, I walk away.

"You want to see the good in people, even when it's not there."

Chapter Six
Carys

I'm in my office, behind my desk, a pantsuit on, hair tied back in a messy bun. All business in here. Professional. What he said earlier doesn't matter because I don't want to sleep with him either. I didn't wander down the stairs in Eric's shirt, fantasizing about what it would be like to have Finn rip the buttons off me and fuck me on the counter in my kitchen. Nope. Didn't cross my mind. Not even once.

God. I slept with Eric to unwind me, make these residual emotions easier. Instead I spent the night with him, lost in thoughts of Finn. Eric's lips, close to my ear murmuring about how wet I was, how good I felt, made me want to scream, and not in a good way. Eventually I had to tell him to shut up before he ruined the mood. And by mood, I mean the fantasies in my head his voice kept destroying. I wanted to shut my eyes and dream of Ireland.

Turns out I'm a forty-five-year-old woman still addicted to the danger that's about to walk into my office any minute. I asked Lena to bring him to me so we could go over places to live. No extradition treaties. Isolationist, or not overly friendly with the USA, would be best. It's a small list.

Knuckles rap on the outside of the door before Finn opens it with his fingertips. I rise behind the desk as he saunters in. As he eases into the chair across from me, I sink into mine.

"What have you got?" he says.

Picking up the sheet in front of me, I double-check it before sliding it toward him. He looks good since he took those drugs earlier. Better coloring. More relaxed. Probably the opposite of what he sees in me right now.

"This is it?" He waves the list at me, frowning. "Cuba, Switzerland, Russia, and Iran?"

"There's Iceland, too." I frown. Did I forget to add it?

"Saw that. Any place with the word 'ice' in the name is an automatic no." He eases deeper into the chair. "I guess I'm staying here."

I clear my throat and point at the paper. "As you can see, I also outlined Switzerland as the most expensive option."

"You're telling me I'm too poor to live here?" Finn's flinty gaze bores into me.

"Maybe?" I shrug and shift in my seat. "I don't know what your finances are like. You were vague earlier."

"I can fucking afford to live in Switzerland if I want."

"Without having to work? I don't know if you saw—"

"Yes. I can read. Cuba and Russia are the cheapest options. Russia is the best at bucking extradition requests and for a higher quality of life. Your five hundred graphs and charts are clear."

"Oh, good." I sit up straighter, cross my legs, and rock back into my chair. "*Privyet* to Russia, then?"

"Not a chance. Russians are snakes in the grass. I'm not going there."

"The Volkovs aren't even real Russians. That'd be like calling you and Lorcan Irish."

"We are Irish."

I laugh and run my hand along my brow. "Staying in Switzerland isn't a good idea for you."

"The country is big enough for you to visit this place and for me to live in another city." Finn slides the paper across the desk. "From what I've seen, I'll enjoy settling here."

"You've seen the inside of my house and the Swiss landscape in the dark. Unless you somehow saw through your eyelids when you were unconscious."

"You told me to pick. I picked."

The phone on my desk rings, and I jump.

Finn smirks. "You're still wound tight. Eric must not have done his job last night."

My cheeks flame as I lift the phone and hold the receiver to my ear. "Carys Van de Berg."

"A package got delivered for you at the front of the chalet. What do you want me to do with it?" Jay's voice lumbers along the internal line.

"Can you tell who it's from?"

"No address other than yours. Kinda a medium-sized box."

I glance at Finn who is scanning my face with an intensity I'm not sure I like.

"Don't open it. I'll come look." With the receiver back on the cradle, I rise from behind my desk. "I need to take care of something. Consider Russia or Cuba. Seriously. Switzerland is expensive as a long-term solution."

He's frozen in his seat. "Why are you worried about a package delivered to the front of the house?"

"Not worried," I say. "Just cautious. I called in favors to get you lifted. People can be overeager to cash those."

His eyes narrow, and he heaves himself out of the chair with a grunt. "I'm coming to see this package."

"It's not something you need to worry about."

As I come around the desk, he slides across the chairs quicker than his injuries should allow. His bulky, broad body partially blocks my hasty exit.

"You thought that was a suggestion." He clicks his tongue, his ice-cold gaze connecting with mine. "You saved my life, or maybe just my sanity this time. Either way—anyone who comes after you, gets me."

"Mess with the bull and you'll get the horns?" I smile.

My heart races out of control at the heat radiating off his body. His familiar spicy scent drifts toward me. Eric did not do his job last night. Not even close.

"You're the bull? I'm the horns?" He smirks.

Oh, God. Horns. Long, hard horns.

He closes the space between us. My pulse threatens to explode out of my neck.

"A wolf doesn't always need to pretend to be a sheep," he says as his fingers touch the spot on my throat where my pulse flutters, his favorite place to caress, the pads gentle against my skin. Then, he balls his hand into a fist and jams it his pocket. "Sometimes being a wolf is enough."

"You can sense fear?" I reply.

We make eye contact, the connection searing in its intensity.

"Among other things." The words drop between us, a threat, a promise. Me. Him. Against the wall, on the floor, in a bed, everywhere, anywhere. Desire hums, a current, poised to electrocute us both.

I swallow and take a wide berth around him; careful we don't touch. As I do, I glance down, and Finn's hand is flexing in his pocket. A single step toward him, and we'd both cave, give in, fuse. My body is waging war on my head.

When I get to the door, I turn back at him. He's only half facing me, focused on the wall, his jaw tight with tension.

"Are you coming?" I say.

He raises his eyebrows, a mixture of amusement and annoyance clear on his features.

"Now you want me to come? Could you be any more fucking confusing?"

"When did I say I wanted you to come?" At his expression of disbelief, I give him a sly smile. "I was simply saying I'll *allow* you to come."

Finn chuckles as he ambles toward me. "Allow me?" He rakes his gaze over me, amusement winning out. "Doesn't work that way."

"If you follow me," I say, going out the door. "I think it does."

His chuckle warms my chest and spirals to other areas. A grin splits my face as I lead the way to the front door. We don't take long to reach the entrance, and Finn stays behind me the whole time, which is both thrilling and unsettling.

"Where is it?" I ask Jay as soon as I catch sight of him in the entryway.

"Left it outside."

"Good." I open the huge wooden door to find a small, wide package off to the right.

I don't need to check to know Finn is behind me, just beyond my shoulder.

"Why didn't you let Jay open it?" His voice is gruff.

"He's got a family." I squat to pick it up and head toward the driveway, away from the house.

"He's your bodyguard. This is his job. What the fuck do you think is in there?" Finn's footsteps are heavy on the driveway.

"I don't know. But he's got kids, a wife."

"And you've got a whole company full of people depending on you." His hand comes around the side of my body and snatches the package away.

"Finn—don't—" But I'm too late. He's ripped the packaging off and yanked back the cardboard.

Inside is the same thing I've been getting for a couple weeks now. An old-fashioned alarm clock lets off a shrill ring as soon as the parcel opens. Scrawled across the face are the words *time is ticking*.

He takes the clock out of the box and cradles it in his hand, tossing it into the air. "This some kind of warning?"

When I don't answer, he hurls the clock at the garage door. It bounces off the metal and shatters on the concrete driveway.

"Who is this and what'd you promise them?"

I take a deep breath, willing my heart to return to normal. The box always holds an alarm clock, but each time I wonder if it'll be a bomb. "The FBI mole."

Finn squints at me and shakes his head. "An alarm clock?

What's the ticking for? What's he want?"

"Money. A lot of money." I shrug. "I paid him already, or I believe I did. The transaction was through a third party. He could be trying to get more, or the cash got held up on the way to him."

"Either way, an FBI dickhead doesn't threaten you. Fucking amateur. You don't send a piece of shit alarm clock. You find the thing that matters most, and you dangle it over a ledge." His quick angry strides toward the house are the smoothest I've seen him so far. Rage looks good on him.

"Finn," I call, following him. "You can't get involved. You need to keep a low profile."

He turns on me. "Do you know where this guy is?"

"He's in Russia, but—"

"Perfect. We can put this dog down."

"Finn."

"Why'd you want to open it instead of Jay?"

"I told you why."

"Which means every time one of these arrives, you think it could be a bomb."

I purse my lips and don't answer him. My hand flutters to my hair.

His hard gaze softens. "We go to Russia. We put the agent in his place. I'll help you figure out the warehouse theft. When we're done there, I'll stay behind, get out of your way, let you live your life free of me and my bullshit."

At his words, a flood of mixed emotions rushes over me, and I'm not sure which to address first. Sadness. Anger. Uncertainty. "I don't want to kill anyone. That's not how I work."

He breaks eye contact with me and one side of his mouth quirks up. "You won't have to kill anyone." Shifting away from me, he heads into the house. Just before he opens the heavy door, he calls back, "I'll do it for you. People don't fuck with you and live. Not while I'm around."

Chapter Seven
Finn

There's not much to pack as I shove the few things Carys bought me into a bag. I will need to figure out how to get more money while I'm in Russia. There's a knock on my bedroom door, but it can't be Carys. She had to go out to secure my new identity quicker than expected.

"What is it?" I rest a hand on the side of the bed to ease the strain on my stitches. Who knew getting stabbed and then shot would have such a steep recovery?

Lena's head pops around the doorframe. "You all right?"

I grimace and straighten. "Just old."

She laughs. "You're not that old."

"Last time I was wounded this badly, I was in my twenties. Didn't take this long to get better."

"Maybe your memory is faulty." She grins.

One side of my mouth quirks up in response. "Could be. Either way, it means I'm old. What can I do for you?"

"Carys asked me to deliver the rest of the clothes she bought you."

I take the bag from her and shove it in the small suitcase I've been packing.

"Not even going to look?"

"Doesn't seem like it. Anything else?" Truth is, it's unsettling that Carys knows the things I'm likely to wear, after so many years. Comforting, too. I'm not sure what bothers me more. I'm too volatile, too dangerous for her. She's a liability for me. Anyone who comes after me will realize Carys is who you dangle over that ledge. Lorcan knew it. Wouldn't take much for someone else to discover my weakness.

Lena crosses her arms and indecision floats across her face.

"Generally I like people who say what they're fucking thinking," I say.

Another brief laugh escapes her. "I'm worried about Carys."

"I'm gonna help her figure this shit out, and then I'm out of her life." With a sense of finality, I zip up the suitcase. "I won't hurt her."

"Surprisingly, it's not *you* I'm worried about."

I frown. "Eric?"

She shakes her head. "Charles, her father, has done a lot of dirty deals in Russia. A few of them behind her back since he *retired*. These packages...Carys isn't sure they're from the FBI guy. She hasn't been able to trace them."

"So, what?" I say. "You think they're tied to him or some sort of bad deal?"

"I don't know. But she hasn't talked to him about the threats, even though I told her she should. She's forbidden me from telling him."

"Fuck it. Tell him anyway."

Lena chuckles and shifts her feet, not meeting my gaze. "It's taken me a long time to be this close. I—what I've been doing with Charles... She means a lot to me, and she wouldn't forgive me for interfering."

My chest swells at her words and I brace my hands on my hips, trying to determine what she wants from me. "You want *me* to tell Charles?"

"If he found out she was the one who saved you, he'd start a nuclear war. Seriously. Last time the two of you were together, she almost died."

I grit my teeth and focus on the wall over her shoulder. "I'm aware of what he thinks of me." He was very clear in the hospital's hallway when Carys was clinging to life. Carys and I didn't make sense. Carys and I were too different. Carys and I would end with her dead and me in prison, or we'd both be dead. If I hadn't been forced on a plane the next day by my father, I would have overruled Charles. Never would have listened to him. But once I'd had time and distance, I realized they were right to drag me away. She made me better, and I made her worse.

"I wanted you to understand that what's going on over there might not be what she thinks," Lena says.

With a sigh, I ruffle my hair and grab the back of my neck. "How pissed will Carys be about her father's dealings?"

"Livid. She caught him one other time and told him if he wanted to work for her, he was welcome to. Otherwise he needed to...how did she phrase that? Stay the fuck out of her way." Lena winks at me. "She's got a backbone when she wants."

I smile and glance at Lena. "You don't say." I grab the bag off the bed and stifle a groan. I want to fast-forward time so I'm not so sore. When I head toward the door, she stays put. "Something else?"

She worries her bottom lip. "I heard what you did to the men who almost killed Carys."

I stare at her and say nothing for a moment, the suitcase clutched in my hand. "She tell you?"

"Charles."

A bit of a surprise. Of course, he knew what I did. I showed up at the hospital covered in blood, and it wasn't from his daughter. "He called me a hothead and a fool."

Lena's smile is weak. "Probably true, right? He's got his own temper issues. He knew you would have done anything to protect Carys if you could. It's just—the lifestyle you lead—you couldn't keep her safe. Her happiness is his priority, but he also wants her alive."

"Ah, the irony." I roll my shoulders and continue toward the door. "The threat she's facing right now might not even have anything to do with me."

"You'll help her whether or not the problem is because of you?"

I grab the edge of the door and stand, poised to exit, to meet Carys back at the front of the house. I half-turn to Lena, not quite meeting her gaze. "What I did in Ireland, killing those men. I'd do it every day for the rest of my life if it meant keeping Carys safe. There's nothing I wouldn't do." I yank the door wider. "Including leaving her alone once this threat is done."

"What if that isn't what she wants?"

"It is. It will be. And even if it isn't, we all know I'm not the happily ever after guy." I walk out the door.

Chapter Eight
Carys

There have been several times in my life when I've been grateful for a private jet. But flying a known fugitive from Switzerland to Russia, even on a fake set of documents, makes me appreciate the luxury more than normal.

When we got on the plane, I picked my usual seat, expecting Finn to settle into one near me, close enough to at least talk. Instead he sat as far away as possible, asked for earbuds, and has been drinking Irish car bombs and listening to something—maybe music, maybe a string of angry profanity—who knows?

Every time my focus strays to him and his relaxed pose, I want to scream. It's irrational, but I hate him for ignoring me so completely that switching off and forgetting I exist when we're locked on the same plane is easy. Since the moment he opened his damn door to me and Kim, my Finn obsession has been reborn.

Kim. Fucking Kim.

A few seats away, Jay catches my eye. "You all right?"

"Fine." I draw circles on the side of my head. "Thinking, thinking, thinking."

He chuckles. "About where we're going?"

"Should be. But no. About where we've been. Never good." I shift in my seat, straightening my spine and grab the *Vogue* magazine from the cushion beside me.

"Him," he says tipping his chin toward Finn. "Or Kim."

A smile threatens at how well he knows my thoughts. "Both, actually."

"Ouch."

I flip through the articles, seeing nothing, skimming over the latest trends. I can't focus.

"Just go tell him he's pissing you off. He seems like the type of guy who appreciates a straightforward approach."

I laugh. "You're right there. Finn only likes games if he's the person playing...and winning." After a glance at Jay, I shuffle through a few more pages of my magazine. "I will not talk to him. What happened between us is old news. Old, dangerous, get-me-killed news."

"Any room the two of you are in positively crackles." Jay leans forward in his seat. "Even right now, you're not talking. But you see the slant of his shoulders." He uses his finger to draw an invisible line on Finn. "He's so fucking aware of you it's unreal."

I shake my head. "The slant of his shoulders?" My voice drips with disbelief.

"You pay me to notice this shit."

I close the magazine. "I do. Doesn't mean I don't consider it bullshit."

"Stand up."

"What?"

"Stand up. I bet he goes tense."

My lips twitch. I'm amused despite myself. "Just stand," I clarify.

"Stand up. Wiggle, like you're pulling your shirt or readjusting your clothes. He might not look, but I guarantee he'll notice."

With narrowed eyes, I start to rise.

"No, no," Jay says. "Don't look at me. Watch him."

"Sure. Sure. I'll watch the slant of his shoulders." Tossing the magazine on the seat between me and Jay, I keep my focus tuned to Finn. Sure enough, as I tug my shirt, he straightens in his chair. His head angles in my direction, not enough to see me but almost as though he's listening or waiting for something to appear in his peripheral vision. A predator. A shiver zips through me. Why is that movement, that instinct in him, such a turn on? God, I have issues.

After falling back into my chair, I glance over at Jay who is chuckling. He makes a shooting motion with his finger and then blows on it. Then he pretends to rotate his gun before holstering it. A laugh escapes me, louder than normal. Finn twists in his chair and our gazes connect. My smile slips, and he turns around again.

Fuck it.

With a quick push on the armrests, I'm out of my seat, and I wander to him, my hands in the pockets of my loose black dress pants. When I sit, I keep an empty seat between us. He doesn't acknowledge me, and I yank out the closest earbud. His jaw tightens, and when he faces me, there's a hint of anger.

"Can I do something for you?" He removes the other earbud and keeps them bunched in his hand.

Now that I'm over here, next to him, I'm not sure what I want. The only thing I don't want is him ignoring me. "Should we come up with a strategy for when we arrive?"

"You organize shit. I'm the mindless muscle."

I cock my head and tuck a stray strand of hair behind my ear. "No offense, but you're not exactly in prime mindless muscle fitness."

"Doesn't take much to shoot a gun." He swirls the last of his Irish car bomb. "You sure these threats are coming from the FBI guy you paid?"

My fingers flex on the armrests. "Not exactly sure."

"Give me a percentage."

"Um...fifty?"

"I'm going to murder someone over a fifty percent chance. I suppose I've killed for less. I'm surprised you like those odds though."

"I told you I don't want anyone killed."

"Yeah, well, I'm not a guy who makes those sorts of promises." His icy gaze rakes over me. "The desire to murder an FBI agent is still thrumming through my veins. Wouldn't take much to set off my instinct."

"Finn."

He sits forward and leans across the seat between us. "This is who I am, Carys. I am the guy who does those things."

Anger rises in me like a tide, and I gather myself, meeting him in the middle of the free seat. "I understand exactly who you are. But if you're out there representing me and my business, you fall in fucking line. I put my life, my company at risk by rescuing you. Do you have any idea what Kim gathered on me in the time she worked for me? 'Cause I don't. But I sure as hell know she's got lots on you."

Finn opens his mouth to speak and on instinct I cover his mouth. Electrical currents shoot through my arm. I ignore the sensation, and Finn's gaze locks on mine.

"You want to help me," I say. "You help me. You don't douse the situation in gasoline and light a match."

Behind my palm, his lips quirk. Carefully, I remove my hand.

"I wouldn't *drop* the match."

"Yeah, you would."

"It might accidentally slip out of my fingers."

"You shot Kim."

He scowls. "She fucking deserved it."

"Your plan, such as it was, seemed to be simply not to die."

"Not true." He settles back in his chair and avoids eye contact. "I didn't believe, when it came down to it, Lorcan would pick her over me."

"That's a mindset, not a plan."

He waves a dismissive hand. "You want to put a collar on me? Fine. Done. I won't kill anyone without your permission."

"Not just a collar. There's a leash, too."

With a smirk, he turns to examine at me. "You into role play now, Carys? You always liked to experiment."

Heat floods my cheeks, and my anger dissipates. Using the armrests, I vault myself into a standing position and ignore his innuendo. "When we get there, we'll go to the warehouse first. I have an employee I'll need to meet with to see what's been determined."

He stares at me for a moment and then sticks an earbud back in. "I'm starving."

"We'll grab dinner after the warehouse and meeting. I'll even let you pick."

"Anything I want?" His gaze roams over me in a hot, leisurely way, suggesting far more than I intend to consider.

His fingers twist and turn the other earbud, distracting me.

I long to press my cool hands against my face. Why is it so scorching on this plane? "Within reason."

"Shame." He looks away. "I can think of lots of unreasonable things." With the other earbud in his ear, he settles deeper into his seat.

I make a beeline for my chair, my heart pounding. Jay grins when I flop beside him.

"Not so bad?" he says.

"You know when you're out somewhere and there's a fruit tray and a brownie tray? Why do we always want the brownie?"

Jay gives me a look of disbelief. "Because brownies are fucking delicious."

"Yeah, but they're bad for you."

"When you bite into one and the chocolate goodness hits your tongue, do you care? You don't. No one does. Sometimes the bigger sin is not digging in."

"What if you're allergic to brownies, and they could kill you?"

His smile fades. "He ever lay a hand on you?"

I frown. "Never. No. I—he's a lot of things, but he's not *that*."

"And this whole affair was when?"

"Seventeen years ago."

"You're not even the same people. Maybe you eat the brownie and you find out you don't have a sweet tooth anymore."

I give him a long look. He doesn't need to realize I've sampled the brownie recently and the sweet tooth might just eat me. "Your wife is lucky."

He gives me a rueful smile. "Next time we get in a fight, I'm putting you on speakerphone. You'll have to yell it really loud though, maybe several times. Sofia's got a temper."

I laugh. "That's a deal."

Over the speaker, the pilot tells us to prepare for landing. "As soon as we're on the ground, I need you to find out where we can meet Valeriya," I say.

"You got it," Jay replies. "Car should be waiting on the tarmac when we touch down."

"Customs? Passport control?"

"Valeriya took care of it."

"Perfect."

One less worry. People criticize countries where money can buy things, powerful things, such as entry into the country without passing through customs. The truth is—people don't care about right and wrong. They just wish they had enough money so they didn't have to care either.

Volgograd isn't a major city, which is also helpful.

"You worried about what we're gonna find?" Jays says.

I seek the back of Finn's head, almost on instinct. "Not anymore."

Chapter Nine
Finn

The warehouse is huge. It's also empty. Carys's heels tap dance on the concrete floor as she searches the few offices off to the right. Jay stands beside me, fiddling with his phone.

"I don't understand what I'm looking at here." I put my hands on my hips, and the coat Carys gave me in the car stretches across my shoulders. When she handed it to me, annoyance and gratitude fought for dominance. Just like every single thing she's done for me since I woke.

"An empty warehouse." Jay tucks his phone into his pocket.

"Gee, thanks. I got that part. But how full was it? Quarter? Half?"

"Try loaded to the gills."

I rock on my heels. "Fuck off."

"I'm not kidding, man. Eric wasn't wrong to be raging over this loss. It's huge. A smaller company would have folded for sure. I'm surprised Charles isn't here reaming her out for incompetence."

Of course her father *could* be the reason the warehouse is empty. Would he do that to his daughter? I can't decide. Their relationship has always been tense. She and I were drawn together by our complicated family structures. She both loved and hated her father. At the time, I understood her conflicted feelings. For me, the hate won out.

"Jesus Christ." I leave him standing near the main entrance, and I head toward the clicking of her shoes. In the last office, Carys is in the center of the room, her arms crossed, disbelief on her face.

"The robbery is worse than they told me. There's nothing left. Not a single weapon. We were completely cleaned out."

I run my hand through my hair and sigh. "Eric is a dick. But if this was my organization, heads would be literally rolling. This took serious resources and massive planning. It stinks of an inside job."

"The theft happened at the same time you were in trouble." She leans against the wide desk in the middle of the room. "I delegated. I would have normally handled this myself." She squeezes the messy bun at the nape of her neck. "I should have done more. The inventory has been gone for weeks now. Tracing it will be tough. And Eric's correct—our fingerprints are on everything. Depending on who has our products, it could appear we're making deals we aren't doing." Her smile is fleeting. "We do questionable things for profit, and if I got caught on those—well, fair enough—I made my choice. But if we get prosecuted over this…"

"Valeriya. She's in charge here?" I say.

"Yeah." Carys pushes off the desk. "Next stop is to her. I just—I can't believe this."

"You can't tell me no one's ever stole from you before."

"I mean, of course, but never like this. Never this big. And none of us have a clue who did it. Not my father, not Eric, and I sure as hell don't have any ideas."

"Valeriya's fingers are in the pie."

Carys laughs. "You haven't even met her."

"Don't need to."

"Well, unlike you, I'm reserving judgment until I speak to her. That's what a good employer does."

"My employees never complained."

She leaves the office. "When the result of a complaint is a bullet between the eyes, not too many people want to stir the pot."

"Exactly. Make 'em sorry they even thought about fucking you over," I grumble.

"Right—again with the murdering."

"Sound as if that's a problem for you, and I know it's not." Her heels clack on the floor ahead of me, but I've got my head down. "You understand better than most how I was raised."

When she stops, I have to throw my weight in reverse to avoid ramming into her. When I glance up, her amber eyes are soft with understanding. Stupid. Why'd I bring up the past? We used to confess so many things to each other under the cover of darkness. I've worked hard to coat my underbelly with a steely resolve. Sometimes I think she might be the only person who ever realized it existed.

"What happened with Lorcan—it gives you a fresh start, Finn. You don't have to be the man you were. Your father is dead. You can't return to your organization."

I keep my hands in the pockets of my jeans to prevent myself from reaching for her. So easy to loop my arm around her waist, tug her to me, lose myself. "People don't change. We are who we are."

She makes a frustrated noise and glares at the wall behind me.

Her hand strays to her hair. She crosses her arms and then focuses on me, searching for something. "A long time ago, you told me—"

"Too many years ago."

"But if people don't change..."

"There was a moment, I'll give you that. Two roads diverged in a wood." I smirk. "I chose the bloodier one."

"You don't have to be flippant about this. I'm being serious."

"Me too. I'm a lost fucking cause. You can't reform me, remake me, change me. There are two things I do really well. You've already experienced one of them." I lean in so my lips are close to grazing her ear. "And the other one is killing." Then I brush past her and make my way to Jay at the front of the building. After a minute, her heels sound behind me.

~ * ~

Valeriya is a skinny-ass blonde Russian with eyes a similar shade of piercing blue to mine. She's also a fucking liar.

"You've had three weeks." Carys crosses her legs on the oversize recliner. "Three weeks and you've discovered nothing?"

We're in Valeriya's apartment in an upscale neighborhood, and the place is much nicer than it should be on her salary. Her necklace and earrings catch the light when she turns her head. They're too real for her pay grade.

"No, I'm sorry. Nothing." She shrugs as though Van De Berg Ammunitions didn't lose a shit-ton of money.

I run a hand down my face and glare. One good threat and this woman would spread her knowledge like butter on bread. There's not a doubt she knows something. Whoever took the weapons and ammo must have more clout than Carys and is therefore worth Valeriya's loyalty. The realization pisses me off.

"Can I?" I growl.

"No," she says, tight-lipped. "You may not."

"Who is he? And what can he do?" Valeriya re-crosses her long legs and examines her chipped nails.

"Kill you," Carys deadpans.

Valeriya's startled gaze flies to mine. A sly smile crosses her face. "You would not do that in this country. My father—"

"I don't give a shit who your father is. Someone stole a warehouse full of material. You think I wouldn't put a bullet in your head? I've killed for less. Google Finn Donaghey and thank your fucking stars she's got me on a collar...and leash."

Carys sucks in a deep breath. "Don't Google him." On her feet, she stares at Valeriya. "I'm coming here tomorrow. You need to reconsider where your loyalty lies. I want something concrete—a direction—a name."

Valeriya rises to her full height. Without her heels, Carys would be dwarfed by her. "I tell you. I know nothing. Tomorrow will not change that."

"There are other ways to make someone's life difficult other than murder." Carys runs her hand along the back of the leather recliner she just vacated. "Money is a powerful motivator. If you want to keep your money, and I don't just mean what *I've* paid you, reconsider your attitude."

"You can't touch my bank accounts."

Carys narrows her eyes and opens the purse she has clutched in her hand. She removes a slip of paper and passes it to her. "Those account numbers? They're yours, sweetie. I've got lots of friends in lots of places. You want to be broke? Fine by me."

Valeriya stares at the page for a moment, her mouth a tight line. "I know nothing."

"That necklace." Carys points her index finger at Valeriya's neck and then her earlobes. "And those earrings say otherwise. Maybe you don't understand enough, but you do know something. Get me enough by tomorrow."

"What time?" Her voice has lost the insolent confidence of earlier.

"First thing in the morning." Carys walks to the front vestibule and opens the door to Jay who has been standing watch. "I'm recovering weapons or I'm recovering cash. Your choice."

Christ. She is so fucking hot right now I have to keep my hands deep in my pockets to stop myself from grabbing her around the waist as we exit the apartment. I've never seen her do business before. Her playful sense of humor, her softness, the way she sees me in ways no one else does, lure me in. But this—her cool control—almost puts me on my knees.

"How'd it go?" Jay asks as I close the door behind me.

"Snakes in the grass," I mutter.

She laughs. "Valeriya will come around. No one wants to be poor in Russia."

He leads us out of the building. She trails him, and I bring up the rear. When we get to the bank of elevators, she turns to me. "Still hungry?"

"Do bears shit in the woods?"

"That's a yes, then." The elevator pings. "I have a place," she says.

"You want me along?" Jay asks as we step into the metal box.

"You'd better." She's focused on the closing doors. "If Valeriya calls her father to tell him I threatened her, there might be trouble."

"Who is he?" I say.

Her eyes twinkle in amusement, a smile playing at the edges of her lips. "Russian mafia. Your favorite."

"Think *they* could have taken your product?" I suggest.

"Doubtful. They use my business in Russia to clean their money. But it's good to be sure." As the elevator doors open, she exits.

"If Valeriya doesn't tell Daddy you threatened her…" I slot the pieces together.

"Exactly." Carys glances over her shoulder. "She doesn't want him to realize what she's been doing behind both our backs."

"Impressive."

She mocks a tiny curtsey. "Why thank you, kind sir." Her southern accent peeks out, reminding me of the other times she's let me hear it. My chest aches at the memories.

Jay holds the door of the car as we both climb into the rear seats. With the middle space between us, we head to dinner. I stare at the scenery outside as we glide through the streets, determined to keep these old feelings for Carys from rising too far.

Chapter Ten
Carys

I'm on my third glass of vodka in the quaint restaurant down the street from the hotel my family frequents in Volgograd. The place is a bit of a dive bar, grungy even, but I love the Russian food. Their kebabs are exceptional. If the man across the table from me wasn't so distracting, I'd be in heaven.

We've barely said two words to each other since we were seated and ordered. I'm praying for our meals to come faster even as I gulp more vodka. Drinking this much is a mistake, but I can't stop myself. *Liquid courage.*

"What are you thinking about?" As soon as the question leaves my mouth, I curse the alcohol. The stupidest, most girly ask in the world.

The vinyl on the chair squeaks when Finn leans back and crosses his arms. "Trying to puzzle out your employee."

"Valeriya?"

He raises his eyebrows.

Another stupid question. More vodka makes its way past my lips.

"Who has more clout than you?" He picks up his drink. His pain must be substantial because he took painkillers and opted for water instead of alcohol. Weirdly responsible.

"In Russia?" I reply. "Pretty much everyone. I'm a small fish here."

The ice in Finn's water clinks together as he rotates his glass. "Do you suspect your father? Could he be the reason for the theft?"

"My father?" I rear back, my glass dangling from my fingers. Wasn't my first idea when I found out. In fact, he would be one of the last people I'd accuse.

"Charles never liked to play by the rules." Finn stays focused on the swirling water.

"He's retired."

He glances up at me. "He never sticks his nose in? Never once had remorse over giving up control?"

My glass clatters, almost tumbling from my fingers when I lean across the table. Jay rises from his seat near the door, but I wave him down without diverting my attention from the man in front of me. "My father is a lot of things, but he wouldn't force me into this position."

"He used to enjoy testing you—giving you impossible tasks, seeing how you'd get out."

"And your father used to set a gun in your hand and tell you real men kill people who get in their way."

Finn grabs my drink from me. He teeters on the legs of his chair and puts my liquid courage on the table behind him. The cheap white tablecloth shifts as he pushes the glass along the top. We're the only people in here. The waitress, who is coming out of the kitchen with our food, gives me a puzzled look but continues to our table, the food held high on a platter over her head.

"Give me my drink," I say.

"You're drunk, and you're bringing up shit that will piss me off. You're done drinking."

The waitress sets Finn's food in front of him and then passes me mine.

"Another drink?" She indicates the almost empty glass behind Finn.

"Yes."

"No." Finn's voice drowns out mine, and he's far more intimidating than me.

She scurries away. She'd better bring my drink.

We eat in silence for a moment before I throw back my chair, storm around him, grab the glass, and chug the last bit.

When I pass him, he snakes his arm out to my waist and tugs me into his lap. Our eyes connect and my breath catches in my throat. The slightest movement forward will reunite our lips, put me out of my misery. He's hard beneath me, straining to be released. "You need to stop drinking."

"Why?" My gaze flicks up to meet his and then I focus on his lips, willing him to close the distance.

"We agreed months ago we weren't doing this." His voice is gruff, and he's so still beneath me I wonder if, like me, he's afraid to move.

"Did we?" The words are whispered between us. My fingertips brush his brow.

"You're right. *You* said we weren't doing this again."

"Maybe I misspoke."

"You're drunk."

"I am."

Finn shakes his head. "You want no strings sex? I'm game." He slides his hand into my hair, loosening my bun. "But I'm not fucking you while you're drunk." Finn brings my forehead to his. "I don't want to be a regret in the morning when you're sober. Not again."

"What I said to you that morning—"

"Doesn't matter if you meant it. You said it. Not again. We do this, you make the choice stone-cold sober and you understand it's just physical."

I climb off his lap and stand, straightening my clothes. His words shouldn't burn. But they do. A hot iron pressed against my heart. I sink into my chair on the other side of the table and pick up my kebab, pulling it apart with my fork and fingers. The silence between us is all-consuming.

"You don't want me, Carys."

With an annoyed sound, I drop my fork, letting it clatter onto my plate. "I'm old enough to decide what I want."

"Okay," he says while he chews. "What do you want?"

An excellent question. One I haven't let myself consider too closely. On a very immediate level, I want to get laid, by him, and the sooner the better. Beyond that? I can't say for sure. A long time ago, I wanted so much more, first from Finn, then from Eric, but I couldn't secure the connection. I would be so close, and happiness would slip away. So, I stopped hoping, stopped wanting.

"Come on. If you're old enough to know what you want, spit it out." Finn sets his fork on his plate and leans closer. "You want me to clear this table? Fuck you on it while Jay watches?"

Yes.

"You want me to take you back to our hotel and show you the ways your body can come for me? Is that what you want?"

Yes. The idea makes my legs tremble with desire. "Don't be an asshole."

"I'm just asking. 'Cause for someone who is old enough to decide what she wants, you've been confusing the hell out of me."

"What I said in Boston—"

"Nah, I want to talk to sober Carys. That's the person I'm interested in right now. Drunk Carys is horny as fuck and hunting for a way to get off."

"Screw you, Finn."

His mouth quirks up, and he gives me a told-you-so smirk.

"God, you're so infuriating. Why couldn't you have sex with

me without being an asshole about it?"

"Tomorrow morning I'm all yours." He throws out his hands. "Tonight—you're gonna sleep it off alone. You realize what'll happen tomorrow? You'll go back to skirting around me." He makes a walking motion with his fingers. "Pretend like this conversation didn't happen."

"Maybe I won't." But my resolve slips. I want him, but I don't want the complications from having him.

"You will. It's safer that way."

When the waitress appears behind Finn, I say, "Can we get the check, please? I think we're done here."

Chapter Eleven
Finn

The next morning, Carys wears dark glasses and won't meet my gaze. Is she pissed at me for what I said last night, or does she regret coming on to me? Probably both.

We file into the car. Jay eyes the two of us in the rearview mirror but understands Carys well enough not to speak. We're headed to the location where the FBI agent is holed up, waiting for his forged documents to start over. Jay runs a tight ship for Carys, and his ability to get shit done is impressive.

"How far away is this place?" I ask as the city fades into the distance.

"About half an hour," Jay replies.

"Perfect." I peek at Carys's stony face and settle deeper into the seat. I slide my hands along my thighs, and I consider the least assholeish thing to say. "Sleep okay?"

"Shut up, Finn."

Guess that wasn't it. "Jetlag can be a bitch."

Carys tips her glasses down her nose and looks at me over the top of them. My mind flashes to every sexy teacher fantasy I've ever had. As though she senses the tightening in my pants, she takes her sunglasses off with a sigh.

"I'm sorry about coming on to you. I shouldn't have done that."

Without her glasses on, it's obvious she didn't sleep well, and she's very hungover. "How do you want to handle FBI guy?"

The awkward post-coital conversation is a reason I didn't sleep with her last night. If we're going to have the discussion anyway, I might as well have fucked her for my trouble. At least I would have enjoyed that.

"You don't want to talk about it?" she says.

"I said what needed to be said. Today we're focused on getting your shit back and eliminating whatever or whoever is threatening you."

With her fingers, she twists and turns her black shades. "I'll take the lead in the conversation."

"Approaching on our right," Jay says as the car glides to a stop outside a short, squat, white-sided house that has seen better days.

"I'd say he didn't get your money," I say.

"Not everyone is frivolous." She slides her glasses back onto her face.

"Guy was cash-strapped enough to grab me out of a warehouse overrun with agents. The money was for something imperative to him. Guaranteed."

Carys mutters an agreement as Jay opens her door. I slide out behind her, happy with my view of her ass. The bright pink skirt she has on stretches and clings to the right places. I slide my gaze up her, over the loose black shirt fluttering in the wind to her hair in a tight bun at her nape. The combination of buttoned-up and wild has always appealed to me. I enjoy watching her come undone.

We pause at the door, Jay tense, alert.

Carys checks on me over her shoulder. "You gonna be cool?"

"Like a deep lake at the start of spring." I wink.

She sighs and raps her knuckles on the steel. I take my position on the other side of Carys so Jay and I are flanking her. Anyone answers who is bad news, she's getting shoved behind me. Her lovely ass is better off hitting the cracked concrete than anything more violent.

"Who is it?" A deep male voice calls from inside the house.

"Carys Van de Berg and her associates." She drags her purse higher onto her shoulder.

The door inches open, and a pair of brown eyes peer out. Once he's scanned us and the landscape behind, he creates enough space for Jay to slip in. I shoulder past Carys so she brings up the rear. People who sell their loyalty set me on edge.

"Why are you in such a shithole?" I say.

The question is more instinct than curiosity. Carys paid him a ton of money, and the furniture in the living room could have come from Goodwill. There are takeout wrappers scattered across everywhere. The guy's been existing on cheap burgers.

"Finn." Carys shoots me a warning glare.

My jaw hardens. Easy to forget I don't run the show. We will have to talk about this collar and leash business. It's a choke collar instead of something kinky and fun.

I raise my eyebrows. "You don't want to understand why the guy who accepted so much of your money is living in the pit of despair?" I pick up a wrapper from a chair. "You can't even afford a garbage can?"

FBI guy crosses his arms. "I rent. And what the fuck is it to you how I live?" He scans me. "Jesus. I can't believe you lived, and you're already walking around."

I smirk. "Knock me down, and I come back twice as hard."

He shakes his head. "So much God-damned blood all over me. I had to go get tested to make sure I didn't catch anything off you—guys like you, you just never know."

I growl and step toward him.

Carys throws out an arm to pin me in place. "You don't speak to him like that." She presses her arm into my chest when I push against it. "Finn's question is valid. I paid you a fortune. Why are you living here?"

"Told ya. I rent. Also, you've only paid me half my money. I've been trying to figure out how the hell to sort that out."

Out of the corner of my eye, her mouth tightens, and her arm drops from my chest.

"I paid you the full amount. Half the morning of the raid, half when Finn made it to Switzerland alive."

"First half came, second half never appeared."

With a frown, she examines Jay. "Explain this to me."

Jay is focused on his phone. "Working on an answer now, boss. Doesn't add up to me." He sizes up the FBI guy. "You screwing with us Ricardo?"

"You want bank statements?" He grabs his phone from the greasy table.

I'm not the cleanest person in the world, but I've had a maid service for long enough this level of filth is repulsive. "What are you doing with the money?" I cross my arms.

"Not your business." He concentrates on his phone, swiping through screens. "I need the second half of the transfer next week or I'm fucked." He stares at Carys, ignoring me. "I get fucked? I find ways to fuck other people."

I take a step forward. "You the person sending her the alarm clocks?"

Ricardo's face morphs into disbelief tinged with annoyance. "I just said two minutes ago I was trying to figure out a plan to contact her. You think if I had an address, I'd be sending her an alarm clock?" He nods at Carys. "What kind of warning is that? Vague. Stupid. You want someone's attention, you find what matters to them." He passes his phone to Jay and then glares at me. "For example, I want to get to Carys, I'd wager I target you. She risked a hell of a lot to save you." Calculation is clear in his gaze. "And your posture tells me the feeling is mutual. Aww. Ain't that sweet. Mutually assured destruction."

I straighten, annoyed that my protectiveness is so obvious, so different from the way Jay treats her.

"Get me my money or I'll figure out a way to make sure both of you pay with your own form of hell."

"You don't threaten me," I growl.

He chuckles. "I just did. What are you going to do, Finn Donaghey? You're nothing without your patsy guards."

"I wouldn't be so sure." Carys takes the phone from Jay and scans the information. She removes a handgun out of her purse. Without a word, she passes it to me.

The weight of it in my palm is relaxing, and the tension in the room dissipates. Is this a green light? I take a deep breath as I check it over.

"Before we came," Carys says, "he said he still had this intense urge to murder someone from the FBI. I told him I wasn't keen. Usually I prefer to handle things much more civilly. Make no mistake, Ricardo—you threaten me, you threaten Finn or Jay or anyone else associated with me, and I'll set him loose. He's been murdering people since he was fourteen. He knows all the ways to do it, and some of them you won't see coming. The only thing holding him back is me."

I focus on the gun as she talks. Her description of me as a barely restrained animal is painful and thrilling. As a kid, I didn't have a choice. Lorcan was the soft one, and so I became harder and harder to protect him, to protect myself. Shoot first. Apologize later. Still my wildness is a big part of her attraction.

When we got together, watching me fighting in The Cage made her realize I wasn't a boy anymore. I was a man. She'd never deny it. Those qualities which are hard for her to resist are also why I can't be with her. At some point I'll make a mistake like last time, and she'll pay the price. A consequence I cannot bear.

Jay nudges my shoulder while Carys and Ricardo negotiate new terms for their agreement. "Don't shoot him."

My lips quirk up, and I tuck the gun into the back of my jeans. "He'd probably already be dead if Carys wasn't here. You don't negotiate with disloyal people."

"I hear ya on that. But disloyalty in others is sometimes the only way we can get shit done."

I put my hands on my hips and only half-listen to Carys discussing the details of the money transfer. "Why didn't you see it?" I ask Jay.

"See what?"

"Kim—Kimi."

"Ah." Jay rubs his face. "That's a difficult question. We run a different organization here. You get me? The illegal stuff isn't so brutal most of the time. Kim blended—she was easy to like, quick to gain our respect. Backstory held up when we ran our checks. Smart. Funny. Tough as nails in a tight spot. And Carys loved her in a very genuine way as only Carys can. I think she saw herself in Kim." One eyebrow cocks up and then he tips his chin. "Why didn't *you* see it?"

There had been noticeable shades of Carys in Kim—made sense they'd gravitate together. No nonsense, tough when needed, with this vulnerability underneath most people didn't catch. I saw it a few times in Kim, much more often in Carys. Carys loved her—trusted her. I wanted to believe Carys hadn't been fooled.

I run a hand through my hair and then return it to my hips. "I did, and then I didn't. And then I did again. Lorcan—he—I don't fucking know. But I needed to be sure if I was going to pull the trigger. To keep my brother on my side, her death had to be justified to him." I give a humorless chuckle. "Little did I know, he understood what she was and didn't fucking care."

"You thought you could make Kim's death justifiable to him?"

With a shrug, I puff out a breath. "I misread that one."

He chuckles.

"All right." Carys turns on her heel to me and Jay. "Let's go. I need to trace this money now. Jesus Christ. I rescue you and my whole business goes to shit."

"Uh, thanks for that, by the way. Not sure I've said those words."

Carys waves me off as she strides to the front entrance. With the door ajar, she glances over her shoulder. Her mouth is open, ready to say something. Instinct kicks in when a sharp *ting* hits the gutter and waterspout. Time slows, narrows, focuses. Blood rushes to my brain, roaring, drowning out everything but Carys. *Save her.*

Grabbing her arm, I haul her to the ground, shielding her with my body as Jay yells, "Shots fired. Get down! Get down!"

Chapter Twelve
Carys

Finn's chest is pressed to my face. He's grappling for the gun at his waistband as his other arm helps shield me. It has to be the adrenaline. His injuries are still healing, and I've watched him walk enough the last few days to know he's stiff and sore. His movements are sure, fluid, painless.

He glances at me, tucking his chin to meet my eyes. "Were you hit?"

I swallow. My shoulder stings. Is the pain from a bullet or how he dragged me to the ground? "I'm fine."

Finn breaks eye contact to scan the rest of the area. "Jay!"

"Here."

"Ricardo?" Silence greets his second rollcall. He has me pinned so close to the floor I can't see what else is happening.

"He's down." Jay shuffles to the door.

"Dead?" Finn says.

"Not sure."

"Shit." Finn's free hand holds the gun, but our position means his back is to the entrance. "Any more shots?"

"Haven't heard anything for a minute."

"Target?"

"Take your fucking pick. Could be you, Carys, or Ricardo. You're all hot depending on who's shooting."

The pain in my shoulder isn't lessening. Finn is half-turned toward the wall. He's not touching the part that's burning, so the sensation is not from any pressure he's putting on it.

"Can I get up?" I take a deep breath, willing the sting to leave.

"No," Jay's and Finn's voices ring out in unison.

"I'm going to get Carys secured away from the door," Finn says. "Cover me."

"Ready," Jay says.

With astonishing swiftness, Finn rolls off me, scoops me up and carries me to the back of the tiny house. There are no pings or curses from Jay, so I'm hoping there are no more bullets. Finn sets me on the floor by the white kitchen cabinets and crouches to meet my eyes.

"You do not move until I call clear or Jay does, okay? You stay here."

I don't have a chance to respond before he's gone. My shoulder aches, and I rub it in circular motions. The skin rotates under my fingers, making the burning worse. With a frown, I remove my hand and stare at my fingers. Wet. Bright red. *Shit.*

Scanning the kitchen, I grab the dishcloth hanging on the stove. When I hold the cloth against my injury, a sharp breath escapes me. Should I call for Finn? If television can be believed, a bullet to the shoulder is probably the most minor gunshot. Jay or Finn shouldn't be distracted if there is danger at the door.

Worry eats at me. The silence in the other room is almost too much. In any other situation, I'd never sit here waiting for someone to help me. I can shoot a gun. But I gave the only weapon I carry to Finn. It would be stupid to charge into the other room unarmed. I could take a knife, but the joke about bringing a knife to a gunfight is only funny when you're not the one stupid enough to do it.

My brain circles for ideas, but the niggling thought I've been trying to keep at bay sneaks in. I could have died. If Finn hadn't hauled me down, I might have died. Closing my eyes, I let my shoulders rest against the chipped cupboards.

"All clear!" Jay's voice rings out.

I haul myself to my feet and take the towel away from my shoulder. It's covered in blood but given the time I've been sitting there, there's not a ridiculous amount.

With a deep breath, I drop the cloth into the sink. There's a mirror above it and the neckline of my shirt is wide. My finger finds the hole and slips in. Definitely shot.

"You okay?" Finn's voice is quiet in the kitchen.

I snatch my hand away and whirl toward him. "Fine." My smile is tight.

He tips his head at my shirt. "What were you doing?"

"Oh, it's—well—just—"

He sets the gun on the counter and closes the distance between us. He touches my shoulder, and I gasp. His fingers find the hole. His gaze connects with mine, anger and worry warring in his pale depths. "You were fucking shot?"

"Um." I press my lips together. "I think so?"

"Jesus Christ, Carys. When were you going to tell me?"

"I'm sure it's not an actual bullet wound, a graze, a scratch probably, a burn." I tug my sleeve over the mark.

Finn pushes my shirt away from my arm, and his fingers land on the three buttons at the top that'll make the material very loose.

I cover his hand, stilling his progress. "Don't."

"I need to see." His free hand circles around my neck, his thumb grazing my cheek. "You might need a doctor."

I move his hand aside and undo the buttons myself. There is something deeply intimate in letting him undress me, especially when he's like this—tame, concerned, almost loving. After a storm of violence, he's often gentle, and his tenderness makes my chest ache with longing.

My sleeve slips down, and he turns me. With the cloth from the sink, he washes the wound. "A graze."

"Lucky," I whisper. His proximity, the tangy scent of him, this kindness will undo the immunity I've fought for today.

His thumb grazes the top of my arm, just beside the mark, and then he bends his head to kiss my shoulder. A shiver runs through me. Electrifying.

"Finn," I murmur, and my body is liquid, pliable. He could do anything to me, and I'd let him.

His arms slide around my waist, and he buries his face in the crook of my neck. "God, how do you always smell so fucking amazing? Someday when I die, I hope the way you smell is the last thing I remember."

I relish the simplicity of this moment. I breathe him in, letting my awareness of him flood my senses. Our desire won't be fulfilled, not here in this house with danger outside the door. He'd never risk my safety. Being able to acknowledge the yearning between us makes me less unstable, more solid.

"Jay? Ricardo?" I ask when he eases away.

"Jay is fine. Ricardo is dead."

"Dead? How?"

"We got lucky. Ricardo was a direct hit through a window."

"Oh." I smooth my hair at the top of my head. "Right. This is…I mean, I know we deal with weapons, but they aren't often used on us." I lean against the counter while Finn opens kitchen cabinets. "What are you looking for?"

"First aid kit. I can patch that up, no problem." He nods toward my shoulder.

"There'll be a kit in the car's trunk." The graze is still trickling blood, but the pain isn't the same as before. "What's Jay doing?"

"Calling the Russian police and figuring out how we can pay them off to keep us out of this." He winks at me. "Money can solve almost anything if you get the right people."

"Except you hate disloyal people."

He chuckles. "Only when it doesn't go my way." He reaches for me and then he thinks better of it, sliding his hand into his front pocket. "Let's get you to the car. We can wait there for Jay to finish, and I'll patch you up."

"Thank you," I whisper. "If you hadn't—"

His jaw tightens, and he won't meet my gaze. "But I did. The lesson here is that you are *never* to be the first person in or out of anywhere, not a car, not a house, not a boat, nowhere." He stares at me. "You got me?"

"I don't want you or Jay hurt or killed either."

With a shake of his head, Finn purses his lips. "Jay's paid to do this. It's his job. He doesn't want it; he can go work somewhere else. And me? I'm disposable. I got nothing going on right now except for helping you. What's another bullet wound?"

"You're not disposable to me."

He doesn't miss a beat, gliding over my comment as though my husky voice filled with need sounded matter-of-fact instead of desperate. "For the purposes of entering and exiting places, we'll pretend I am. Also, I could use my own fucking gun."

I keep an arm crossed over my middle as though it can shield me. "Okay."

He leads the way out of the house. We pass Jay on the phone in the living room. He has my gun in his hand as we walk to the vehicle, ready to aim and fire at any moment.

"Maybe they were after Ricardo?" I say.

"Maybe." But Finn doesn't sound convinced.

I get into the backseat, and he grabs the first aid kit from the trunk. He opens the door and settles beside me. For a moment, he sits with the red bag wedged between his hands. His gaze trails over me, assessing. As he unzips it, he says, "Take off your shirt."

"You can put a bandage over it if I slip my shirt off my shoulder."

His fingers skim my shoulder, and he shakes his head. "'Fraid not. I'll do a shitty job." When he shifts in the seat to bandage my shoulder, a wince escapes him.

"What about you?" My brow furrows, remembering his injuries and the way he moved in the house. "You could have torn stitches."

"Oh, I'm sure something is torn."

"Let me see."

He smirks. "I'll show you mine if you show me yours."

"Not the best line I've heard."

He eyes me with amusement. "Well, you're sober now. I suppose I should have known I'd have to up my game."

I find the hem of my shirt and hesitate. Should I take it off? "And you think *I'm* confusing."

He eases away from me, giving me space. When he ruffles the hair at the back of his head, he winces. "I won't touch anything but your wound. I swear."

His promise is both what I'm hoping for and what I'm afraid of. His hands on my body are enough to send other parts of me into overdrive. Steeling myself, I remove my shirt in one swift motion. True to his word, he homes in on the gouge in my shoulder. He works in silence for a few moments, cleaning the wound and then finding the right dressing for it. As his fingers dance across my skin, my body heats, minimizing the sting from my injury.

"Might scar," he says.

"I have people who can fix it if it does."

He indicates the scar on my chest as he packs up. "Why didn't you fix that?"

The knife that pierced my heart.

I brush my fingers against it. "Feels like an old friend now."

He squints and then frowns. "What the fuck kinda friend is that?"

"One who reminds you of the places you don't want to go again." An asshole thing to say when he's been so kind. Instinct drives me to draw him to me, but also to repel him as far away as possible. I open my mouth to apologize when his jaw tightens. I may not know what I want, but I know what I need. The responsible choice. Distance. The closer we inch together, the closer sober Carys is to saying *fuck me, please*. There's still enough of me that cares about the consequences.

He forces the zipper on the kit. The metallic sound of the teeth clicking together is loud in the tense silence.

"You should let me look at you." I try to take the bag and our fingers brush.

The driver's door pops open, and I yank my shirt back over my head in a fluid, frantic motion. Finn chuckles beside me.

Jay's gaze connects with mine in the rearview mirror, and he raises his eyebrows. His eyes flick between me and Finn but he says nothing about the blush raging across my cheeks. "You hurt?"

"A graze." Finn settles deeper into the seat near the door, far from me. "A brush with danger."

Satisfied, Jay shifts the vehicle into drive. *A brush with danger.* If only that was it. But his flames lick at me from across the car, enticing me, biding their time until they can burst into an inferno, consuming me whole.

Chapter Thirteen
Finn

Cary insisted on going to a Russian doctor she has on-call to get me patched up before venturing to Valeriya's again. I let him check me over while Carys and Jay are out in the waiting room.

"All clear?" I ease my shirt back over my head.

"Minor issues," the doctor says. "Be more careful. You're not healed yet."

I grunt as I slide off his examination table. "You service the Van de Berg employees?"

The doctor scribbles a prescription for pain on his notepad, rips it off, and holds it out. "Yes. Why?"

"Valeriya? I hear her father is some kinda mafia kingpin." I don't take my eyes off him, trying to assess his level of knowledge.

The doctor's face is granite. "I cannot discuss her with you."

"She's a client?"

"Enough that I cannot discuss."

I fold the prescription and tuck it into my back pocket. For a moment I stare at him, wondering if I can get him to say more. My instincts tell me she's making dirty deals. She's been working an angle or more than one behind the scenes. Whoever she's working with, Valeriya thinks they have more clout than Carys. *Who?*

The last time I was blindsided by something I should have known is still fresh in my mind. I'm not keen to start a pattern. Poke, prod, dive to the bottom of any person who might have information. The doc isn't budging, but at least Valeriya has been here. Routine appointments? Or more than that?

The doctor opens the examination room and ushers me out with his hand.

Carys and Jay rise from their plush seats when I amble toward them, my hands shoved into my pockets.

Her worried gaze meets mine. "Everything okay?"

"Fine." I shrug. "More drugs."

We get into the car, and Jay navigates the streets to Valeriya's place with ease.

"What if she doesn't talk?" I focus on the scenery while we cruise into a more upscale section of the city. Blackmail—maybe the doc has something we can blackmail her with. Access will be key.

"She will," Carys says.

I run my knuckles across my cheek. "I don't like it. Half the money to Ricardo goes missing. You've got an empty warehouse that should be full. Your showrunner here is a mafia princess with a chip on her shoulder. The situation is a fucking mess."

"Thanks for the summary." Carys removes her lip gloss from her purse and presses it against her lips. As she screws the gloss down and caps it, she looks at me. "Valeriya has been with me a few years. I've never had an issue with her."

"This doesn't seem like an issue to you? Seems like a big fucking problem to me."

"She'll be back in line today. I'm telling you, nobody in Russia wants to be poor."

"Someone is backing whatever she's doing. You'll need to be tougher on her."

She sits straighter in her seat. "You don't have a clue how I run my business."

"You're right. But I understand when someone is getting fucked over. Unless you locked her accounts, she'll have moved her money. Will you be able to find it again? Who knows?"

She crosses her arms. "I don't need a Plan B. She'll fall in line."

My lips quirk up in a half-smile. "Care to wager?"

"Wager?"

"If I'm right." I don't give myself time to consider the wisdom of this bet, spurred on by the desire to prove to her I'm more than a physical asset. "You and me, dinner tonight—no alcohol."

She narrows her eyes. "And if I'm right?"

"Whatever you want."

Her cheek caves as though she's biting the inside of it. "I don't know what I want."

"Yeah, that's clear." I lean across the seat with my hand outstretched. "I don't mind living on the edge. You win? You can decide your prize after. There's nothing you could ask for that I wouldn't give you."

Her eyes always remind me of whiskey, and they're filled with uncertainty even as she grasps my hand. "Seems too good to pass up."

I wink at her. "That's 'cause you aren't going to win, anyway."

"On your right," Jay calls out, as we glide up to Valeriya's building.

The concierge comes out with a valet to park our vehicle.

We climb out and take the elevator up to her fancy apartment. As the doors to her floor open, a tingle of unease skitters up my spine. On instinct I draw the gun Jay slipped me earlier from its spot on my lower back. Carys has her gun in her purse. At my movement, and perhaps sensing the same thing I do, Jay removes his gun before we step out of the elevator. Down the hall on our right, two burly guards stand outside Valeriya's door.

"Those are her father's men," Carys says, from behind us.

We slow our approach when the guards see us and draw their own weapons. Carys or Jay need to take the lead, or I'll shoot first and worry about the consequences after.

"We're here to see Valeriya," Carys says.

"With guns?" The taller of the two men raises his eyebrows. "Why guns?"

"Jay and Finn didn't recognize you." She slips past me and leads the way.

Jay holsters his gun, and I dam up a flood of annoyance because she's out front again. Reluctantly, I slip my gun into the waistband of my jeans.

"What's going on?" Another voice emerges from inside the apartment.

"Demid." Carys rushes toward him. "We were here to see Valeriya."

A tall, broad man with blond hair and light blue eyes similar to his daughter appears in the doorway just as we arrive. "She's not here. I have not heard from her in a few days, so I came to check on her. She's not answering her phone." He leaves the entrance to let us in.

Carys goes in first, and the tide of my annoyance rises.

"I don't know. The door was locked, but her keys are here." With his fingertips, he lifts them off the side table. "Her phone is gone but her purse is in her room."

She frowns and glances at me. I've been so busy cataloging the security mistakes she's made, I haven't been listening.

"She's missing?" She scans the room.

"Yes." Demid gestures to the immaculate apartment.

"Where's her phone? Did you find it?" I search the main room, checking the logical places it might have been left. Without waiting for an answer, I go through the main bedroom, too.

"I did not see it," Demid calls.

"Has she been acting oddly lately?" Carys says, from the other

73

room.

"No more than normal. Why? What do you know?"

The defensive pitch of his voice isn't a good sign, and I come out of the bedroom to stand at the entrance of the living room.

"Nothing. Just trying to help." She seeks me out over Demid's head. Is she thinking about how we threatened Valeriya yesterday?

"One of my men is getting the security footage for the last twenty-four hours," Demid says.

"She seemed fine yesterday when we saw her." I lean against the doorframe. "Visiting a boyfriend? A friend out of town?" That's not what I think, though. She took her money and got the hell out of town, maybe out of Russia. But where did she go? Who did she go to?

"You were here yesterday?" His voice is sharp, and he glares at Carys.

"We've been having problems at our warehouse," she says.

Demid's gaze rakes over her and then shifts to me. "I recognize him." He points to Jay. "You. You look familiar but not from here."

I nod. "I'm not from here." Unlike the situation with his daughter, my killer reputation won't be a useful piece of information now. The last thing I want to do is drop Carys any deeper into this shit.

He grunts and then examines Carys again. "She's valuable to you, no?"

She takes a beat. "She is."

"You'll find her?"

"We will," I chime in from across the room. We make eye contact, and the unspoken communication is so loaded I wonder if Demid can sense the weight. Does she want me to help her? Now, she doesn't have a choice.

"No stone will be left unturned. You have my word." I cross the room and offer Demid my hand. He takes it in a firm shake, straightening his shoulders.

"You have kids?" he says. "You understand?"

I release my grip. Carys tenses beside me. When we were together, she wanted it all. The kids. The husband. The home her parents hadn't provided for her. I'd never been sure what I wanted, what I could give someone, and so I'd said nothing in return. Life hadn't worked out as she'd expected. Sometimes I want to ask her what happened, but the timing is always off, and her answer probably won't satisfy me.

"No kids." I rock onto my heels. "But I understand what it means to love a person beyond reason. To do anything to keep someone safe."

From the corner of my eye, she turns her head away, her fingers pushing a strand of her hair back in place.

"I'll give you a week to find her. If you don't," he eyes Carys who is focused on her feet, "I will send out my more aggressive people."

If we haven't managed to track her or narrow her potential locations in the next forty-eight hours, the search is a lost cause. Anyone who has ever hunted someone knows the first forty-eight hours are gold. Everything after is a crap shoot.

"That's fair." I lead him to the door.

Carys has been oddly silent, and Jay took up the search of the apartment I abandoned. He's banging around the bathroom even as I get Demid to the exit.

"We'll check here more for clues," I say. "Trash, diary entries, whatever we can find. She has her phone. Keep trying to call her. She might pick up."

When I shake Demid's hand in the doorway again, his man approaches from the hallway. When the guard gets to us, Carys hovers by my shoulder.

"Security footage?" I say.

It'll be one less thing we'll have to mine.

The man checks for his boss's consent before speaking. "She left alone, phone in hand, about three hours after you came here yesterday."

"Bags?" she asks.

"Nothing. Just the phone."

"Can you send the video to Carys?" Hopefully their technology is good enough we don't have to go looking again ourselves. Sometimes there are clues to a location or direction nobody sees at first.

The guard takes the outstretched phone from Carys to copy her email address.

Demid is lost in thought for a moment. Then he half-turns back to Carys. "Was she in trouble with you?"

"We don't know," she says, her voice steady. "We came to see whether she could help us track our missing product from the warehouse. She was…evasive."

He grunts. "You don't fucking touch her when you find her. If she did something wrong, I'll deal with her. She's screwing with my business, too."

"I appreciate how these things work." Her voice is firm. "I didn't think you realized what was going on."

Promises are dangerous, so I'm not making any. His daughter

75

is on the run. Who knows what'll happen when we track her?

Demid gives me a last appraisal, as though he's assessing my trustworthiness. I don't blink. The only person I owe any loyalty to is Carys, and if someone is threatening her, that trumps everything else.

He wanders along the hall with his men, his back hunched. A brief surge of longing for my father zips through me. The man I'm mourning isn't my father though, it's some idealized version of him I let live in me for a while. He was never the man I needed, and I wasn't the son he wanted. I take a deep breath and roll my shoulders, trying to keep the past buried.

After securing the door, I turn on my heel, a smirk on my face. "What was it I said earlier? Something about Valeriya fucking you over, wasn't it?" I grin. "A bit of a pump and dump, but definitely feels like she fucked you."

Carys lets out a frustrated huff. "You don't want to eat dinner with me when I'm sober. I'll bore you to death. I'm a lot more fun when I'm drunk."

I brush past her, and I chuckle. "Guess we'll find out."

Chapter Fourteen
Carys

We've made Valeriya's apartment base camp while we sort through her papers, search for clues. Jay is phoning airlines, checking security footage, calling taxi companies. Finn's on a conference call with an IT company. They're supposed to be hacking into her phone records or her email—preferably both.

Seems like Finn's right about Valeriya fucking me over. But since we don't understand *why* she vacated her apartment, he can't declare a complete victory yet. Or at least, that's what I told him. Really the two of us sitting down for a sober conversation over dinner, discussing things beyond this work, terrifies me. There's only the tiniest thread of my willpower intact.

As I sort through the papers in a desk drawer, I come across a pile that stops me short. The surrogacy documents she signed. Back when I was with Eric, Valeriya responded to an advertisement I ran for a surrogate to carry a baby for me. In the end, the timing hadn't been right, and I changed my mind. But I liked her enough to offer her a junior job in my Russian office. She worked her way up to the second in command to Ekaterina. A lot of time and determination went into her getting this position. Why would she do this to me?

I'm about to rip up the contract when Finn appears in the doorway.

"Find anything?" he says.

I twist my mouth as I drop the pile of documents into the drawer. "Nothing useful." Turning to him, I close it with my hip. "We need to follow the cash."

"You got someone who can trace where her money went?"

"Maybe. I need to call Ekaterina."

"And she is?"

"The lead person of this division. She's in Moscow working on getting us more contracts, but she might be aware of something. We believed Valeriya was on top of the warehouse theft."

Finn shakes his head, his shoulder on the doorframe. "The only thing Valeriya has been on top of is her own agenda."

"Any luck with the IT company?"

"Gotta give them a few hours, and you'll need to wire the payment to them."

Finding her might cost more than backing down. I can't waste time and resources on a dead end. "At some point, it'll be more expensive to find her than to let her go."

"I'm sure she's counting on your level-headed approach."

I laugh. "And your approach would be?"

A hint of a smile touches Finn's lips. "You're aware."

"Pursue her to the ends of the earth and burn her on a stake?"

He holds up his hands. "My revenge isn't always rational."

"Not always, huh?"

His expression is pensive. "Maybe never." He cocks his head. "In my business, you needed a rep to keep people in line. Everyone in Boston understood you didn't mess with the Donaghey family. First, because my old man was such a terror, and then because I was even worse." There isn't a hint of remorse in his words.

"You're proud of that." I cross my arms and stare at him.

Not an accusation, more of an observation. I've never considered how Finn feels about the reputation he's built. Perhaps part of me hoped he regretted at least some aspect. Yeah, he's impulsive, reckless even, but he makes himself sound as though he doesn't even have a conscience.

"Come on, Carys. You don't think I should be? After my father died, the organization didn't collapse. We got stronger, bigger."

On the tip of my tongue are the words, *you also got raided by the FBI*, but I'm the one who led them there. "When your father died." I punctuate each word with a pause. "Finn, you played a role."

"I didn't kill him." He springs off the doorframe and shoves his hands into his jean pockets. "I just didn't stop the Volkovs."

"Semantics."

He shrugs. "Sure, but it's also true. Are you that upset about one less bad man in the world?"

I cross the room so we're standing close enough I can read his face. "I find it difficult to believe his death doesn't bother you even a bit. Did you and your father have a complicated relationship? Yeah. Did he have your mother killed? Yeah, he did. But he was still your father."

"And the world is a better place without him."

His expression is hard, impenetrable. I'm heading into areas Finn doesn't enjoy discussing. Even when we were younger, his father, the business, the things he did, they weren't topics we delved into beyond a surface level. He didn't dwell on the choices he made for his father, for the business when he was with me. To me, that meant he didn't like making them, didn't enjoy doing them.

"Look, Carys. I'm an asshole. I've never pretended otherwise. Whether or not you admit it, that gets your engine revving." He closes the distance between us even more. "You might not want to want me," he lowers his lips to my ear, "but you do."

His breath breezes across my neck. My heart explodes, galloping, straining for more. His assessment is true. I don't want to want him, and yet he's all I want.

"People don't change," he says.

"Some do," I whisper, and his jaw tightens.

"Too late for me. I'm an old dog."

Jay clears his throat behind Finn, and we spring apart. I hadn't realized how close we'd gotten, though my body is warm, languid with desire. Without Jay as a buffer, I would have slept with Finn on every conceivable surface at every location we'd gone to in the last twenty-four hours. The tension between us is almost more than I can bear.

"Valeriya?" I ask Jay over Finn's shoulder.

"No, but I got a lead on who intercepted your money transfer to Ricardo."

I raise my eyebrows in question.

"Charles put a stop to it."

A shot of annoyance mixed with confusion mingles in me. "My father? How?"

"He has privileges on the account you used. The bank says he would have received an automatic alert about the money in transit, and he would have rerouted it back."

Placing my hand on my forehead, I make small circles with my fingertips. Why would my father bother to step in? He'd have no reason to interfere unless he found out why I was using the money. My relationship with Finn was a sore spot for him, partly because it ruined a business relationship, partly because it almost ruined me.

"The money went back into the same account?" I say.

"No, into a separate account." Jay hesitates and then says, "Must not have wanted you to know Ricardo didn't get the transfer."

Motherfucker. "I'll deal with him later," I say. "Ricardo is dead, so the delayed payment isn't an issue anymore. My warehouse, Valeriya, those are priorities."

"And the threats," Finn adds. "We don't have any idea who was threatening you and why."

"Even you said those were Mickey Mouse." I close the desk drawers and step around him into the main living space. "As far as I'm concerned, that's also on the back burner for later."

"The threat in Switzerland was amateur, yeah. But if it was the same person opening fire at Ricardo's piece-of-shit house, that ups the ante." He doesn't follow me, only increases the volume of his voice.

"Any news from the airports? Taxi companies?" I ask Jay as I grab my purse off the couch and riffle through it for my phone.

Finn's sigh of annoyance echoes in the apartment. Those threats are the last thing I need to worry about. Doesn't matter what he thinks.

"No record of her taking a taxi or leaving via a traditional airline. She could be traveling under another name. Fake documents are easy enough to get here," Jay says.

"Finn, your IT guys are going to email me or text me information?"

"They'll be in touch. I've used them before. They're good. If there is something to be found, they'll find it."

"I want to go to the bank, talk to my contact in person, see if he knows where the money went. Follow the money, right?" I check with Finn and Jay for confirmation. "The money won't lie."

Chapter Fifteen
Finn

Carys goes into the office at the bank by herself. The building is shiny windows, gleaming metal, and polished floors. I'm not sure what I expected of a Russian bank, but not this modern. Jay and I are outside the door in case there's any trouble. He's glued to his phone, trying to chase up leads on Valeriya or the warehouse or any of the other fucking things going wrong. I miss having a device. Standing here with nothing to do gives me too much time to think.

Part of me is annoyed Carys didn't see Valeriya for the lying bitch she's turned out to be. Carys has always been that way—loves hard, finds the best in people, even when she shouldn't.

The office door swings open, and she hitches her purse onto her shoulder. Jay and I flank her.

"And?" I ask.

She takes a deep breath. "She didn't move the money."

"That's a good sign." Jay stops fiddling with his phone and tucks it into his pocket.

"She cleaned out her accounts. There's no way to trace her."

"At least you were right about one thing." If she's gone, we have even less time before the scent fades. We're wasting our energy here, so I head for the exit.

"And what was that?" Carys trails behind me.

"Nobody in Russia wants to be poor." At the exit, I scan outside and check my gun in my waistband. "Also means we're at a dead end to find her unless Jay can pull a rabbit out of a hat."

"Lots of hats," he says. "No rabbits yet."

The car is parked close to the curb. We're careful to keep Carys between us, searching for any signs of danger. I hate not knowing who shot at us earlier. If they were after Ricardo, we might be in the clear. Until we know for sure, I'm not taking any chances.

"I bet you really want a drink." I tease her as I open the door to the backseat. My head stays raised, my focus on sweeping the buildings and other cars.

"My life for a glass of wine." She climbs in and scoots over so I can follow behind her.

"Shame you won't get one tonight."

"She could have taken the money out through coercion."

Look at her trying to wiggle out of our deal. "Did the manager mention someone else?" I settle into my seat and give her a mild look.

Her lips twist, and she takes in the view out the window. "No."

Jay slams his door and starts the engine. We leave the curb and ease onto the busy streets.

"I get it. No one wants to admit they misread a situation. Happened to me recently. It was a killer." I offer her a sly smile, and she shakes her head. I muffle my amusement with a splayed hand before continuing, "She's fucked you over. We don't understand why, but it's safe to say it's happened."

"She must be involved in the warehouse theft." The scenery whizzes past us as we head back to the hotel. "Why else would she run?"

"Maybe," I concede.

"You're not convinced? You believe she's screwed me over, but the most logical answer doesn't make sense to you."

"You've got all this shit swirling. Your business is a toilet bowl right now. The warehouse. The threats. Valeriya missing. FBI dickhead dead. Charles interfering with the cash transfer. Could everything be connected? Possibly. Coincidences this great don't exist."

"Even still, Valeriya's piece of the puzzle has to be the warehouse."

I stare at her for a moment. "You ask the bank manager for the video footage of Valeriya taking out her money?"

"I did. Jay always likes to check."

"I will too when it comes in."

Carys smooths her brow. "None of this is your problem, Finn. I don't—you don't have to take this on."

"You think I'll leave you wading through this on your own? I don't give a rat's ass when I resettle somewhere. I have no plans. I gotta figure out which banks accounts the FBI didn't freeze or find ways to recover cash from the house in Boston so I can start over, anyway."

"I can go to Boston, get you the money if you give me the codes."

"Nah." I flex my hands. "They'll be watching the house." What I don't say is that if Lorcan told the FBI anything, they'll understand the easiest way to get to me is through Carys. Hauling her in will get my attention.

A buzzing sound emanates from her purse. She digs around for a minute before her hand emerges with her phone in triumph. When she sees the caller, she frowns.

As soon as she answers, and I realize she's talking to my IT guys, I keep a close ear on the conversation while staring out the window. Valeriya doesn't have any suspicious email activity, but she made a five-minute call to someone in Chicago after we left the other day. Carys takes a pen and a pad of paper out of her purse and starts writing the digits. She doesn't finish, though. Instead she brings the pen to her lips, and she chews on the tip as the person on the other end keeps explaining something.

"Is that the only time the number was called?" she asks.

I can't hear the reply, but her frown deepens.

"Right. Okay. Thanks. This is helpful."

When the call ends, I give her a minute to tell us the details, but she's focused out the window, not bothering to speak.

"And?" I prompt.

Her sigh is heavy. "She contacted someone in my Chicago office before she went to the bank."

"In Chicago?" Jay's grimace is visible in the rearview mirror. "We got a fucking mole?"

"The timing is suspicious," Carys admits, twirling the pen. "But she's called that number several times in the last few months. The general switchboard. Your IT gurus said they couldn't get an extension off her log."

I rub my jaw and then cross my arms. "Would it be normal for her to call there? Who would she talk to? You?"

"Possibly." She stares at the seat, the pen spinning across her fingers. I'm tempted to snatch it. The motion is fucking distracting. "There are a few people. Eric. Hailey. Eliza. Daniel."

"They each have something to do with the Russia division?"

"Sort of. They're employees she could call, and there would be a plausible reason to speak to them. Accounting. Product movement. Storage. Ordering." She peers at me. "Ekaterina might be able to account for some calls. The IT company is faxing a list of the days and times to the hotel."

"When can we meet with her?"

"She sent me an email. She's back in the area tomorrow." She drops the pen into her purse. "I have two hundred people working in the Chicago office."

I nod. She doesn't need to tell me what that means. If those calls weren't placed to the four individuals she mentioned, we'll be chasing our tail. "The front reception," I say. "Who answers when a person doesn't have the extension?"

"Lilly. Most of the time, it's Lilly."

"We start with Ekaterina. If that doesn't work, we see if Lilly remembers Valeriya calling for anyone in particular."

"You can access employees through their last name in the system without ever speaking to Lilly."

"People get lazy. Get in a hurry. Multitask. We follow the leads until there's a dead end, and then we bulldoze a new path."

She laughs. Her face, alight with amusement, makes my stomach clench.

"I like your thinking, man." Jay points to me in the mirror. "I'll drive the dozer."

"First," I say. "We go to dinner. I saw a gourmet burger on the hotel bar's menu."

"You want to eat a burger in the hotel bar?"

"I'm in the mood for a burger and a beer. What are you going to get?" I tip my lips up. "Oh, yes. You can't drink tonight. Just the burger, then?"

Carys twists a ring on her right hand and gives me a sideways glance. "You weren't serious about that bet, were you?"

"All bets are serious. Always. I don't make them unless I can win. And when I win, I collect."

Our gazes connect before mine wanders over her body, the ever-present desire humming between us once more.

"I would've been happy to have you collect if you'd won," I say.

A dull pink rises to her cheeks. "You don't even know what I would have asked for."

I chuckle. "Don't I?"

Her blush darkens, and I laugh again.

"On your right," Jay says as we sidle up to the hotel. "What's the plan, boss?"

"Dinner at the hotel, I guess." She closes her purse. "You can go to your room. We'll be fine."

"No." I shake my head. "You can eat at another table or in the lobby. We don't understand what's going on. You're not minimizing the little security you have. If anything, we should call in more people."

Her jaw tightens, and she purses her lips. "I've never been under a direct threat before."

"There was that stalker," Jay chimes in from the front before taking a valet spot.

"Years ago," Carys says. "And in Chicago, which was both better and worse. I had lots of guards."

"You had a stalker?" I frown, wondering where this person might be now.

She gives me a wry look. "He saw me in a magazine. Had a vision we were married. With kids, no less. He had a very elaborate life cooked up."

"What happened to him?"

"Got too close for comfort." Jay slides out the driver's side. When he opens the passenger door for Carys, he continues, "Ended up being committed to a psychiatric ward by his family."

She climbs out, and I round the car, my gaze zipping the perimeter for any threats. If she stays in the same hotel, it would be very easy for someone to track her. "How long ago?"

"Ten years." She glances at Jay for confirmation. "It was the catalyst for my relationship with Eric."

"Eric didn't seem like such an asshole back then," he clarifies.

She grimaces. "Oh, he was always an ass. He just hid it under fancy clothes for a while." When she gazes at me, her expression changes, but I can't read it. "Most men don't turn out to be who you think they are."

I'm not sure which of my missteps she's talking about, but the comment is aimed at me as much as Eric. Being lumped in with that arrogant prick makes me clench my fists. I deserve her wrath for things I did in the past. Knowing she's been messing with Eric off and on for the last ten years causes an ache in my chest. A relationship with him is nothing like what she talked about having—the opposite, actually.

With a final check around the area, I lead the way into the hotel. Jay slips the keys to the valet who comes out to greet us. I enter the building first, followed by Carys, and then Jay.

"You're eating at the bar?" He nods at the big open space in front of us. Stools line the bar, and a few tables spot the perimeter. Off to the right is a dimly lit restaurant. Bright bar. Dim restaurant. The wise choice is lit up, a neon sign. Lights. Less atmosphere. Business versus pleasure.

"We'll eat in there." I gesture to the restaurant. Who doesn't enjoy living on the edge? With Jay in mind, I scan the bar, I say, "You eat—"

"Table right there." He points to one straddling the main hotel entrance and the door to the restaurant.

"Table right there," I confirm.

Carys rocks on her heels, her purse clutched in front of her, tapping her knees.

"Hungry?" I take in her hot pink skirt and her fluttering black shirt again. My fingers itch to remove the tight bun at the base of her neck, flick my tongue across the spot below her ear that always makes her moan.

"Starving." She doesn't head toward the restaurant, and she doesn't make eye contact.

Is she cataloging the ways we used to find satisfaction in each other? The longer I spend with her, the more my willpower slips. The more I convince myself I could take the next few days, weeks, or months fucking her and still walk away.

I did it once. Seventeen years ago, my world began and ended with her. Leaving her a second time can't be any harder. "Let's eat." I rest my palm on the small of her back, guiding her toward the restaurant.

Her deep breath is audible before she moves forward. Through her thin shirt, my hand is seared by the contact. I fight the urge to sweep her into my arms, carry her to my room, and have an entirely different meal.

Sleeping with her would ease the aching in my pants and in my chest. Sex would make my worry for her justified, more immediate instead of a residual thing from days past. We don't know each other anymore. These emotions are a reflex, instinct, a lack of closure. My thirst for her is endless. That's all. A relationship would never work. We're not meant to be more than this naked desire.

We're shown to a secluded table, and I slide in across from Carys. I'm aware of our reality. I'm the guy she fucks in an alley when she thinks nobody is watching. The guy she gets drunk enough to screw and regret. I'm not her final destination. I'm her pitstop.

The waiter flips open the menus and passes one to us both. Over the top, I watch Carys tuck a tendril of her hair behind her ear. She peeks up and our gazes connect, the moment pulses with recognition.

Everything I've thought is true, and the energy between us is unmistakable. Tonight I'll be the one who slips inside her in a Russian hotel room, who brings her to climax over and over, knowing I might be who she wants, but I'll never be who she needs.

Chapter Sixteen
Carys

Finn orders a burger and a beer. I get a salad and mineral water. I'm tempted to feign a trip to the bathroom to have my drink changed to vodka and soda. He'd never suspect unless he got close enough to smell my breath. A personalized breathalyzer is entirely possible. Since the lobby, he's been looking at me like he could devour me instead of the burger.

"Well," I place my phone on the table, "you wanted me sober. What were you hoping to discuss?"

Finn smirks. "I didn't need you sober for the conversation portion of the evening." He turns his hand as though he's flipping an imaginary object over. "Only for what comes next."

His eyes are ice chips as they sweep over me. Ice isn't what's running through my veins. Heat. So much heat I want to fan myself. Instead I squeeze my thighs together and pray for the server to have understood mineral water meant vodka.

Clearing my throat, I'm grateful when the waiter puts our drinks in front of us. "I should have asked before. Thoughtless of me, really. Is there anyone in Boston you need me to contact to let them know you're okay?"

"You mean besides my backstabbing fucker of a brother? No." He raises his beer and takes a long pull. "Not a fan of attachments."

"Right. Yeah. I guess that's always been the case."

He leans back in his chair and crosses his arms. "Not always." He skims the restaurant before focusing his intense gaze on me again. "What about you? Seventeen years ago you were marriage, kids, white picket fence."

I was so naïve. That's what I want to say. How often does anyone's life turn out how they expect? First, my heart couldn't quite master marriage, and then my body wouldn't let me carry a child. He doesn't need to be told those things, though. Why would he care? "Marriage. Kids. Both liabilities. Loving anyone more than you love yourself makes you weak."

He chuckles and sits forward, scanning the room in an exaggerated fashion. "Where's Carys? Who the fuck are you?"

I shake my head. "I'm serious."

"No, you're not. That's a bullshit line people like you use to cover up their oh so tender heart."

"Well, if you're so smart, you tell me why I didn't end up married with kids."

Our food arrives, and I twirl my fork in my hand before stabbing my lettuce. His perceptiveness is annoying, even if it's probably what's kept him alive all these years.

"You got shitty taste in men."

"Genius. Why didn't I think of that?" I stuff a forkful of lettuce into my mouth.

He laughs and picks up his burger. "All right then. Tell me the real reason."

I slow my angry chewing and try to give off a carefree air. "It didn't work out. I don't know."

"You used to light up whenever you talked about the future." He watches me as he takes a bite.

A sad smile plays at the corners of my lips. "I must have scared the shit out of you."

He chuckles. "Nah. You never gave me the impression *I* was your first choice to fulfill those duties."

I angle the fork into another piece of lettuce and stare at my plate for a minute, letting his words sink in. "Didn't I?" I search my memory for those moments when I might have made it clear, but he was so wild, untamed, and I worried I'd spook him. "You never wanted to settle down? Have kids?"

His cool gaze scans my face as he bites into his burger, contemplating my question. "Why would anyone want that with me? I'd get them killed." He flicks his finger to where my scar lies under my shirt. "You're the proof of that prophecy."

"I didn't die."

"Took that as a warning."

"Strings of women were what you were used to, anyway. You never had trouble attracting them."

"Your tone of voice makes that sound less complimentary than I'd like."

I give him a wry smile. "Oh, does it?" I pick up my glass of water and take a sip. "Marriage is archaic. I grew up with a deeply unhappy mother and a philandering father. Men aren't capable of being faithful."

He chews for a moment, eyes narrowed, and sets his burger on his plate. "You lumping me in with those men?"

"You're a man, aren't you?"

"With a capital M." He winks.

"Then, yeah, I am. Whatever. We screwed around for the better part of three years. I never expected you weren't doing whoever else on the side."

His eyes become slits. "You wondered if I was sleeping with other people?"

I shrug. He'd never given me a sense either way. We did what we did, and we didn't talk about what it meant, or where it was headed, or even, most of the time, what we were doing.

"I was a shitty boyfriend."

"Probably most men are shitty boyfriends between twenty and twenty-three. I wouldn't be too hard on yourself. Besides, were you my boyfriend? Fuck buddy, maybe."

"Why didn't you ever ask?"

"I wasn't going to be one of those needy girls."

He picks up a French fry and sweeps it through mayonnaise before popping it into his mouth. As he chews, he stares at me. I want to raise my hand for the waiter and ask for some alcohol. Having this conversation sober is torture.

"I came to the hospital," Finn says.

I refocus on him and frown. "What?"

"When you were stabbed. Before my father had me tossed on a plane, I came to see you."

"Oh."

"I told you that night in Boston. It was after we'd had quite a few more drinks. Figured you were too drunk to remember it."

"I always thought—"

"You said. But it's not true. I came. Christ, I'm not sure anything coulda stopped me from making sure you were alive."

My heart squeezes at his words, at the intensity on his face. "You didn't see me, though."

"No."

"Why not?" His appearance would have changed everything. To know he'd come, that I meant something to him.

His mouth quirks up, but there's bitterness in his expression. "Charles and I had a heart to heart in the hall. He wasn't wrong. Staying with me woulda been a death sentence for you."

"I should have been given the choice."

He shakes his head. "No. I'm glad I wasn't given a choice

either. Without even thinking too hard, I can come up with at least five instances where you might have died because of my foolishness."

Part of me doesn't care. A life with him, however short, would have been better than the one I've led so far. "I had seven miscarriages and then I found out he'd been cheating on me the whole time. Got one of his side pieces pregnant and paid for her abortion." The words leave my mouth almost before I can consider them. I can't look at Finn—don't want to witness whatever emotion crosses his face. Pity, probably. Maybe anger because I let Eric humiliate me.

His burger rattles his plate when he throws it. "You gotta be fucking kidding me."

I don't respond and instead continue eating my salad. He was right. I created a false narrative to tell people, strangers, friends, business acquaintances, to protect myself. "Since we're giving each other the truth, that's mine. I wanted it. I wanted that future so badly. But I just couldn't get that version of my life to stick. It wasn't supposed to be mine."

Tension radiates off Finn from across the table. He takes a long drink from his beer and avoids eye contact. His silence speaks volumes.

"Sometimes," I say. "No matter how much you want something, it just isn't meant to be. And now, well, now it's too late."

Chapter Seventeen
Finn

Rage courses through me, an old friend. Last time I felt this surge, I shot an FBI agent. I'd love to shoot someone again.

Eric.

I take another bite of my burger and chew without saying a word to her. She's eating her salad in silence, an air of grief around her causing a corresponding ache in my chest. I hate that fucking pressure bearing on me. I do pretty much everything in my power to never experience regret and longing. Since she rescued me, they're constant fucking companions. Whenever they rear their heads, I tell myself, *that's the stab wound* or *that Goddamned gunshot just reopened.*

I've never been a fixer. Lorcan is, Carys is, but me? I'm usually the guy creating the chaos. My mind churns with ways to fix this feeling in me, in her. The best I can come up with involves going upstairs and using our bodies to forget, to remember, to fucking drown in each other. There's only one other solution which would satisfy me. Catch a plane to Chicago and take care of Eric. FBI watchlist be damned.

When I look over, she tucks the stray strand of blonde hair that's popped out of her bun behind her ear again. In a sense, I get why she clung to him. She's never been good at giving up on people. I didn't think she could find a guy worse than me. I should have known better. She's an overachiever.

I place my plate to the side. Even with a healthy dollop of mayonnaise, the French fries taste like cardboard. "Why are you still letting him touch you, Carys? Why are you allowing him to lay a single whoring hand on you?"

She sets her fork aside. "Because nothing matters anymore. The sex is good—who cares if he's giving it out to everyone else as well? All men are Charles or Eric or—"

"Me."

When she insinuated the comparison earlier, I didn't feel like setting her straight.

She shrugs but doesn't meet my gaze.

"The least you can do is look at me when you're making shitty accusations."

Carys crosses her arms. "Am I wrong? Let's not bullshit each other."

She was so guarded when we were younger. Everything between us had to be a secret, and I went along with it because from the moment she let me slide into her, I was a goner. Hell, I was probably gone long before that. I kept tabs on her throughout my teenage years, jerked off so many times with her name on my lips I sometimes wondered if I'd call out *Carys* at the wrong time, with the wrong person.

Once we were together, she could have asked me for anything, and I would have done it. But she never did. I thought I was temporary—the frog she kissed before she found her prince.

Being around her, hearing her side, the reality my twenty-some-odd self couldn't see is staring me down, impossible to ignore. My anger subsides as I catalog her face, save the tiniest details for later. This was never just lust between us.

Maybe I should tell her the truth—that I never slept with another woman in the three years we were together. Never even considered it once I had her. Or I let her continue to think the worst of me.

"Yeah," I say. "You've got me pegged."

Honesty does nothing but give her false hope. Whether I loved her then or I love her now isn't the point. I'm not good for her; she'd never survive me. I don't save people or fix them. I ruin them. Maybe I am like Eric, like Charles but not in the manner she thinks.

Carys shakes her head and purses her lips. "Acting offended, just to admit I'm right." When the waiter approaches, she piles her cutlery on the plate and lets him take it. "I don't know why everything has to be a battle with you."

I chuckle and lean across the table toward her. "You want me to be easy?"

"Do you have any idea what easy looks like?" Carys raises an eyebrow as she pays the bill.

A surge of annoyance goes through me because she's picking up the tab again. I need to prioritize access to my money. Or find another means to pay her.

I stare at her for a moment. I should leave her comment alone. Impulse control isn't a strength. "I can recognize easy." She glances up at me and our eyes lock. "Easy is me, going back to your hotel room, sliding off those shoes, pushing up your skirt, tugging your panties to the floor. Easy is me, trailing my lips from your ankles up to your inner thighs, spreading your legs and flicking my tongue across your clit until you can't decide what you're begging for. Do you want the release, or do you want to stay in that state forever?"

Her breathing is shallow, and I'm sure if I could put my finger on her pulse, I'd find it racing with desire. Her panties will be wet, so wet when I yank them off it'll be all I can do to stop myself from sinking into her, the warmth and wetness surrounding me.

"Finn." Her voice is breathy, filled with longing.

Later her breathiness will be in my ear, echoing around me, smothered by my mouth covering hers.

I should have suggested room service.

Her phone beeps.

She presses her fingers to her forehead and breaks our eye contact as though she's remembered something important, like she's coming out of a trance. She snatches the phone off the table with one hand while the other circles her bun and squeezes. Her cheeks are flushed a pretty shade of pink.

"Jay has news." She braces herself against the table before stooping to grab her purse from the floor.

Before I rise, I adjust myself. My pants are so fucking tight they're almost painful.

Her hand shakes as she swings her bag onto her shoulder. Even still, she leads the way out of the restaurant with remarkable poise. Will her pupils have returned to size when we exit?

Jay meets us in the foyer. "Here, or…?"

"Upstairs." She gives the lobby a visual sweep. "Who knows what ears are listening."

She's flustered in the elevator and selects the wrong floor button. She mumbles something incoherent before hitting the right number. Jay slides an amused glance in my direction, and I smirk. He knows I caused her misstep.

We stop outside her room, and Jay enters first to sweep for bugs or anything else that might cause us trouble. While he's gone, she stands with her legs crossed at the ankle, her phone clutched in her hand, avoiding me.

"Did you enjoy my example?" I say. "Did it seem apt?"

"Shut up." She types a message, avoiding me. "Don't be an ass."

"You used to like my ass. In fact, I remember—"

Jay pops his head out the door. "All clear."

She expels her breath in a whoosh, her shoulders dropping. She grabs the door from him and enters the room. I follow behind her and sink into the closest chair while she leans on the king-sized bed.

"Well?" she says.

"My contact said a private jet went out late last night with an incomplete passenger list. Not uncommon from this airport, as you know. Followed the flight up at the port of entry—Belfast. Any guess who was on that plane?"

"Valeriya." She sighs.

"Bingo."

"In Ireland." Carys frowns. "She must have googled you, Finn."

"You got a hotel? Firm location?" My jaw clenches in annoyance.

"Working on it," Jay says. "I hope I'll have something by the morning."

"Prep our pilot. We're probably headed to Ireland tomorrow." She strides to the mini-bar, picking up each of the liquors and examining their label.

"All of us going?" Jay looks between us as he heads to the door to prepare.

"No." She glances at me. "Finn will stay here."

"Will I?"

She glares at me and snaps the lid off a bottle. "I didn't pay a massive amount of money and risk getting a jail sentence of my own so I could drop you into the only country completely off limits. You'll either end up dead or in prison."

Jay ducks out saying nothing more. Smart man knows when he's not needed or wanted. He's growing on me. The door clicks closed behind him, which leaves us alone. I wander over to the mini-bar, feigning nonchalance. She's not winning this argument. No fucking way.

After removing my gun from my waistband, I slide it across the counter. Then I pluck the bottle from her fingers. The vodka streams straight down my throat. When it's empty, I wipe my mouth with the back of my hand.

Our gazes connect.

"I opened that for me," she says.

"I'm a guest in your room. Shouldn't I get served first?"

"You can't come to Ireland." She swallows, and the pulse at the base of her neck jumps. Without hesitating, I brush my thumb against it. She sucks in a sharp breath.

"My contacts, everyone who knows me, they live in the south,"

I say. "Belfast is north. I'll be fine."

"The FBI—"

"Isn't the CIA. Weren't you the person who declared that a bright side?"

"You'll still be on a watchlist."

"You worried your document forger isn't any good?" The gap between us is inching closed. I drink her in. With each breath, her flowery scent invades my senses. We're on the cusp. Even if backing down is the right thing to do, I have no will to do it.

"I rescued you—"

"And now." I trace my fingers across her collarbone before sliding them into the bun at the back of her head. "It's my turn to rescue you from whatever or whoever is trying to hurt you."

She goes onto her toes and her forehead touches mine. Her chest rises and falls as though she's been running. We both know where this is headed. But I need a green light from her. I'm not having her tell me tonight, tomorrow, any day soon, this night was a mistake. She only gets to use those words against me once more, and that'll be when I'm walking out the door for good.

"The only thing I care about is keeping you safe. I'm coming with you."

"Finn," she whispers.

My heart gallops, sure of where this tension is headed. Our lips are so close the slightest movement on either of our parts will reconnect us, send us spiraling down. I slide my free hand up her side, under her shirt and around to trace her spine. When our skin connects, an electric pulse shoots through me. She arches her back and her gaze flicks up to mine.

"Oh," she says, as though she's surprised, as though this wasn't always the path with us.

"Tell me." My voice is gruff next to her ear as I tighten my hold, letting her understand how much I want her. "Tell me what you want."

Chapter Eighteen
Carys

The smart thing would be to ask him to leave my hotel room, to step back, to readjust my shirt. After he leaves, I'll satisfy my lust in another manner—that's the smart thing. The tiniest part of my brain still knows that even as the timbre of his voice sends a shiver of desire racing down my spine.

Whenever Finn is this close, my mind short circuits, and it's all I can do to remember my name. The sharp, tangy scent of him, the way he worships and devours me, the way his skin slides over mine, makes my senses go into overdrive, hyperaware, poised for release.

"Fuck me," I whisper, rising on my toes to press my lips against the sensitive spot on his neck.

"I didn't hear you." His voice is guttural, on the edge of losing the control he has left.

Glancing up at him under my lashes, I smirk. "Then I guess you should leave so I can take care of myself."

He deftly releases my bun. "I enjoy hearing you say you want me."

"You always liked it when I talked dirty."

He searches my face. "Hmm. Unbelievably sexy." Then he draws me even tighter, and his lips descend on mine. I meet his kiss. Eager. Hungry. Anything to avoid thinking about what I'm doing. My shirt goes over my head in a fluid motion, our lips barely breaking apart. When I tug his T-shirt, he helps me get it over his head. He sucks in a sharp breath but keeps kissing me, his tongue reminding me of the amazing things it can do.

As soon as his top is gone, I run my hand up his side and bump into a bandage. I break the kiss and step back, the spell broken at the reminder. His torso is littered with bandages of various shapes and sizes.

"Finn." I float my hands float across his body, taking in each of his injuries. "Doing this will hurt you."

He chuckles. "Not doing it will hurt a hell of a lot more." His arm comes around my middle and tugs me against him again. "Unless you're saying no, it's a hell yes from me."

"I'm not saying no, but…" I brush the bandage near his shoulder. He's been so good at pretending to be fine since the shootout I forgot about his injuries. There are so many. "Can you—"

"You're not really asking me that." His hand sweeps my long blonde hair away from my face, and his expression is amused. "I may not be able to do fast and hard, but I can certainly manage slow and steady."

I swallow. "Slow and steady?"

He leans down so his lips graze my earlobe. "So slow and so steady you'll be quivering, begging, so jacked up that when I finally let you come, you won't see stars, you'll see Ireland. And you'll think I managed teleportation in an orgasm."

I laugh even as my body tingles at the thought. "Shut up and fuck me already."

"Just one last thing."

I trail my hand from his shoulder down his arm. "That is?"

"Protection. I want to make sure I keep you safe."

I close my eyes and place my forehead on his chest. Admitting this and making eye contact is strange, more intimate than what we're about to do.

"I take a monthly shot." I kiss his chest, and he sucks in a breath. "And you had a full workup when you first came to the hospital. I didn't want them to miss anything, so they tested for everything. Because of what happened with Eric, what's still happening with him, I get checked regularly."

"Carys, please tell me you don't let him—" His tone is gruff, angry.

"No." I shake my head. "No. We're—I insist on being extra careful. I—there were a lot of years where we weren't. Obviously he wasn't sensible with whoever else he was seeing on the side."

Finn is so tense beneath my hands I'm not sure what he will say or do.

"Finn?" My voice is hesitant. The sun has slipped below the horizon, and although the curtains are still open, the room is only lit by a few streetlights. His face is granite in the half-light.

"When I think about how he's treated you, I want to fucking kill him."

"I let him—"

"No, fuck that. Your job isn't to follow him around and make sure he keeps his dick in his pants. That's on him. Nothing to do with you. Nothing."

"I thought you might pity me," I whisper, avoiding his gaze. "I didn't want to be her, and I'm exactly like her."

Both his hands dig into my hair, and he tilts my face toward his. "You're not your fucking mom. You didn't marry him. You didn't have kids with him. Cut him loose." His voice is rough.

"I don't want to talk about it anymore." At the window, I draw the curtains. I tried to fire Eric right after I found out about his betrayal, but my father wouldn't let me. He said Eric was too much of an asset to the company, and I needed to take one for the team. And then, as the weeks passed, it got easier to let things keep going on as they were. Even when my father retired, I didn't kick him out. He's excellent at his job. He's just not a decent person.

"Look, maybe this was a bad idea," I say.

As if Finn knows proximity is his key to winning me around again, his bare chest brushes my back as soon as I bring the curtains together. What little light was in the room is extinguished, and I'm glad for the cover of darkness.

"Do you want me to leave?" His tongue flicks out, catching my earlobe, drawing it into his mouth. His hands slide from my shoulders to my arms and then across my middle, securing me flush against him again. There's no doubt at least part of him wants to stay. But I'm not convinced this path with Finn leads to happiness for either of us. What I do know is someday, when I reflect on the days I had with this man, I'll wish I had lived in the moment. I want him. I turn in his arms, meeting his kiss, wrapping my arms around his neck and hauling him close.

Fuck the right thing. I'm doing what feels good.

As we walk toward the bed, Finn unzips my skirt, and it drops to my feet. When he undoes my bra, it slips down onto the floor. His hands cup my breasts before his head dips, taking the nipple into his mouth. His teeth graze my taunt bud, and I gasp, digging my fingers into his hair.

From the moment I sidled up to him at the bar after a cage fight, sex has been like this with him—electric. His touch is a defibrillator bringing me to life. I never knew I could be with someone and still long for them at the same time. A constant yearning for more—closer, deeper, more. Back then, if I'd thought there was even the slightest chance he returned my feelings, I would have done anything to stay that way forever.

I tug on the top button of his jeans, and his mouth traces a path up to my lips. He deepens the kiss while I work to undo his pants and push them over his ass so they fall to the floor. We step out of our discarded clothes. He locks me tight against him as he buries his face in my neck, kissing, licking, and sucking the most sensitive spots, the ones nobody else bothered to find. Electricity pulses through me.

I moan and dig my nails into his shoulder blades. He shudders and cups my ass, pulling me so close to him his hardness is clear against me. My hand slips into his boxer-briefs, trying to free him.

"No," he murmurs against my lips. "Slow."

"Please." I arch toward him and deepen the kiss. I'm slick with need.

The back of my knees hit the bed and he lifts me up, dropping me in the center of the mattress before following me, kissing and licking a path up my body. When he runs a finger along the lip of my panties, I dig my hands into the sheets and wriggle.

"Not yet." His tongue navigates the same route as his finger.

"Please." I'm pleading for a release, for these sensations to go on forever.

He skims my folds over my underwear, and I try to squirm closer. He's barely touched me, and I'm already wound so tight.

He crawls up my body, our lips reconnecting as he rocks his hips against mine. His cock brushes my clit through what's left of our clothes, and I release the sheets to grip his ass, securing him against me.

"Oh," I breathe out, closing my eyes, curving toward him.

"Look at me," he commands from above.

I open my eyes, but I'm almost dazed with need. "More," I beg. "I want more."

He pushes against me harder, and I wrap my legs around his waist. I sigh at the pleasure, and he scoops my lips up and then deepens the kiss while he rocks slow and steady. The flex and release of his hips propelling me nearer to the edge.

His hand skims my side and comes up to cup my breast, his thumb grazing my nipple, causing it to bead, and little fires shoot to my core. Easing back, he works his way along my body, his lips creating a path to the corner of my underwear. He puts two fingers on either side and maneuvers them down my legs until I hear them hit the carpet.

He licks his fingers and then slides them between my folds, his thumb circling my clit while his other fingers slip inside me. A gasp escapes me, and I fist the sheets.

"Oh, God," I cry as he keeps up a consistent pace for a few strokes before removing his hand to lift my hips and flick his tongue across the same area.

I wriggle beneath him, and he chuckles and swirls his tongue, the pressure exquisite.

"Finn." My body clenches. "Please."

"Not yet." He retreats to kiss his way up my body.

When he tries to meet my lips, I press against his shoulder, guiding him onto his back. And then it's my turn to shower affection over the parts of him not covered by bandages. When I get to his boxer-briefs, I ease them along his hips, and they drop on the floor.

My tongue circles his shaft before I take him into my mouth. His hands are in my hair, and I love the power, that I can cause a man like him to lose control. His breathing is ragged. When I peer up, he's biting his lip.

"Jesus, Carys. I forgot how talented you are at that." His breath is a hiss when I take him deeper. "We'll never make it to the main attraction if you keep going."

I crawl up him and then straddle his waist, positioning myself above him. "Fuck that." I smile. "I want to see Ireland." Then I slide onto his shaft. When I grind, he raises himself, giving me the friction I need.

"God, you feel *fucking* amazing," he mutters as I sink onto him, creating an intense rhythm.

I lean over, and he rises, one hand going into my hair, drawing me into a deep kiss. His other hand sits on my hip, locking our connection as we rub together. The sensation is so earth-shattering that if I were to die in this moment, I wouldn't care. There's nothing in the world but him and this room and this pleasure.

I whimper into his mouth when my orgasm rocks through me. He locks me to him, grips me harder as he meets my orgasm with his own.

Collapsing onto him, I sigh. Impossible to believe I could have forgotten how incredible sex is with him. But my memory didn't do him or us justice. Perhaps he was right to insist I was sober.

"Ireland?" The word is soft in my ear.

I kiss his chest. "Maybe England. Ireland's pretty far from here."

He chuckles beneath me. "Something to aspire to."

~ * ~

I've been lying awake since Finn fell asleep beside me with one arm thrown over me, his head inches from the crook of my neck. Every time I turn my head to examine his injury-riddled body, I gain courage. Letting him go to Ireland with me in the morning is the easy thing to do—easy for me, anyway. I want him with me. I enjoy having him around. He makes me feel safe, protected.

But I'll spend the whole trip worried about him. Will he end up in jail? Will the McCaffery family find out he's back and order a hit on him?

Carefully, I extract myself from under his hand. His breathing hitches, and I freeze. Then he resumes his regular pattern. My heart pounds with betrayal, but this is for the best. I can't allow him to throw his life away to chase my rogue employee.

With an eye on the clock, I dress and gather my things together. It's four in the morning, but I need to get out of here before Finn catches me.

Once I have my bag packed, I take some money out of my purse and leave it on the dresser. Not enough for him to follow me, but enough to eat and stay here for a week if he's careful.

When I get to Jay's door, I knock. A few minutes pass before he appears, bleary-eyed. He presses the heels of his hands into his eyes and squints, checking behind me. "You don't want him coming?"

"No."

"You sure? He will be fucking pissed."

I swallow and stare at the room I just left. "I'm sure. He's safer here than there."

Jay gives a curt nod and steps back for me to enter. He flies around his room and is ready in less than five minutes.

When he reopens his door, I half expect to see Finn standing there, naked and pissed off. But the hall is clear.

As we pass my hotel room, I give it one last glance. He might not forgive me for this. But if he died or ended up in jail, I'd never forgive myself.

Chapter Nineteen
Finn

Before I'm fully awake, I sense something is wrong. The room is too still, the spot beside me too cold. Her flowery scent lingers, but not in the way it does when she's present.

I sit up and rub my eyes. A hint of light peeks between the curtains. I don't remember the last time I slept so soundly. Rare for me to tune out noises in the background, even in sleep. Alert is alive.

Her stuff, strewn across the floor last night, is gone. I slept through her packing. Throwing off the covers, I check the bathroom to be sure, but I realize what's happened. She went to Ireland without me. On the dresser is a mound of bills.

Jesus. She paid me like I'm a fucking prostitute.

Snatching my jeans off the floor, I tamp down the spurt of rage threatening to escape—at myself, at her. My room key is in my back pocket. Will my passport and other forged documents still be there?

I dress in hurried movements. The money sits on the dresser. Not taking what she's left is stupid, even if having the neat stack pisses me off. Grabbing the bills off the wooden surface, I stuff them into my pocket.

I check the room to make sure I haven't forgotten anything. *Gun.* I stride over to the mini-bar and shove it into the waistband of my jeans. My brain ticks through my options, but they're limited, almost nonexistent with little money.

No vehicle to get around the city, no contacts, no fucking phone. I don't even have a god damned internet connection.

I slip out of her room and into mine. With no problems I locate my passport and the other forged documents. At least she didn't go that far to keep me away.

While I pack, I take stock. I have three phone numbers memorized. My other contacts live in a phone I no longer have or on the internet I can't access. The first is Carys, and I'm not giving her a heads-up I'm building a plan. The second is Lorcan. I can't fucking call him. Even if his number still exists, he'll likely have Kimi or the FBI screening his calls. Fucking pussy.

The third is Hagen Volkov. A call to him makes my blood boil, but I need cash. Even if he doesn't realize it, he sold me out to the FBI. He owes me.

First, a phone.

Then a plan. Or rather the plan can formulate after I have funds.

I head to the front desk and get directions to the closest place to purchase a phone. Thankfully the store is within walking distance of the hotel. I'm banking on Hagen giving me an IOU, but he's an unpredictable asshole. He may not come through for me. Without cash, I'll be twiddling my thumbs until Carys graces me with her presence.

The process for the phone is ridiculous—partially because we barely communicate between the sales guy's mangled English and my non-existent Russian. How the fuck am I supposed to live here when this is over?

When I get back to the hotel, I wait until I'm in my room to dial Hagen's number. It rings so many times I wonder if the fucker knows how to set up his voicemail. I hang up and call again. Finally someone answers.

"Who the fuck is this?" His impatient voice snaps me into focus.

"Your favorite Donaghey brother."

"Ah, you fucker. You survived? I heard Lorcan put a cap in your ass and you died."

I grit my teeth and wish I was there to put a cap in Hagen's ass. He's such a useless, arrogant fool.

"You're in Russia? Ah, the homeland. Good choice." His voice is full of mockery. "Where exactly?"

"Doesn't matter. I need money." I rub my forehead when silence descends the line.

"Sean Kovatz has taken over your empire. Call him. How are you going to pay me back if you're not in charge?"

"You think I don't have cash stashed places? I gotta secure transportation, and then I can get my hands on it." I also don't have Sean's number. The FBI is probably tracing those transactions, waiting for me to reach out.

A car lock beeps in the background, followed by a door slam.

"I can't get you money. Even if I wanted to, I can't. Whatever went down between you and Lorcan in the warehouse has cops crawling across our organizations. I can't believe you killed your brother. Never thought the two of you would come to blows like that."

"Should be a lesson to you, Hagen or a warning."

Did Lorcan die? There's a tightness in my chest at the thought. I don't let the idea stick. Carys would have told me if Kimi and Lorcan were dead. She didn't. She asked if I was going after them. It's more likely the FBI have him hidden somewhere, poised to testify if they ever find me.

"I value my life above all," I say. "Don't think I can't get to you. Someone will give me funding, and when they do, you're on my shit list."

"Hold up. Hold up." The car starts. "I can't get you money. I didn't say I wouldn't help you. The Kuznetsof family—Russian mafia in Volgograd. Tell them I sent you."

Kuznetsof. Valeriya's family. Christ. I hate when the world is too fucking small.

"Address?" I grab the pen and a pad of paper next to the phone in the room.

Hagen scrambles in his car for a minute and then rattles off an address. "Just don't—"

I hang up before he can get anything else out. The number of fucks I give about what Hagen wants or doesn't want is at less than zero. Ripping off the top sheet from the pad, I hurry down the stairs back to the front desk.

~ * ~

Demid Kuznetsof's house is on the outskirts of the city. A regular American property transplanted into Russia—two-story, two-car garage, gray brick—but the lot is huge. A brief pang of longing for my mansion in Boston, for the life I led a few short weeks ago, surges through me.

Begging at people's doors isn't my style. But the money I paid the cab to get here ate into the funds Carys left me. This negotiation needs to work.

My gun is tucked into the back of my pants as I ring the doorbell. One of the burly men from yesterday opens the door a crack, and I realize the front entrance is reinforced. He eyes me up and down.

He says something in Russian.

Here's hoping he speaks English, too. "I'm looking for Demid."

"He know you're coming?" His switch to English is effortless and almost without an accent.

"Not unless he's psychic." Or Hagen called him. Also possible. But no point in name-dropping to security.

"Wait here."

I'm not sure where else he thinks I'd fucking wait, but I don't say anything before he closes the door in my face. I should move to Russia to show Demid and these other two-bit hacks how to run a decent mafia empire. He didn't even search me.

A minute later the door swings wider, and the guy is back, but behind him is Demid. "Hagen called me." When he steps around his security, his smile fades. "I recognize you."

"Yes."

"You work with Carys."

I purse my lips. "Yes."

He runs a hand through his hair. "You're coming to me for money?" His eyes narrow.

I had a feeling this might be complicated. "We've located Valeriya."

He stills, and his gaze bores into me. "And you're here."

"I am."

"I can't help you."

"Won't help me."

He shrugs. "Same—same. Carys didn't take you wherever she went. You're a wanted man. Your reputation for brutality precedes you, Mr. Donaghey. I don't want you near my daughter."

"Because you know she's a liar and a traitor to the Van de Bergs."

"She's my daughter. Someday, if you have a child, you'll understand. She could shoot me in the back, and with my dying breath, I'd still love her."

There are two people who own me in a similar fashion, and neither of them will ever be kids. "I can pay with interest."

"Do you intend to go after Carys, and by extension, my daughter?"

I shrug and consider drawing my gun, doing this conversation with more force. How many guys does he have in the house? How bloody could a confrontation get? He hasn't even let me in the door.

"Valeriya would not have done this on her own," Demid says.

"Something we can agree on." But our reasoning is different. "Do you have information?"

"She's been acting oddly for the last ten months to a year. Not herself. Distracted. Trips out of town. Said she had a boyfriend, but never wanted me to meet him."

I squint, trying to figure out if there's any relevance to the timeline. The warehouse was cleaned out in the last few weeks. Carys indicated that the packages have only been arriving for a few weeks. Then there's the murder of the FBI agent, which might be unconnected but can't be ruled out.

"Her boss?" I say.

The name is on the tip of my tongue, but I can't quite grasp it.

"Ekaterina Petrov," Demid agrees. "She may know more, yes."

"If I promise I won't touch your daughter, will you give me Ekaterina's contact details and a hundred-thousand-dollar loan?"

"What is your promise worth, Mr. Donaghey?"

My instinct is to smirk and offer a smart-ass reply. My promise is worthless if I get to Ireland and find Valeriya has put Carys in more danger or hurt her. I say nothing.

"Hagen vouched for you," Demid says.

A smile tugs at my lips. "What's that mean to you?"

To me, his approval is worth dick-all. Hagen's a cocky, dumb fuck who rides on his father's impressive coattails. But if Demid thinks Hagen's opinion is valuable, I will not argue with him.

"To keep the peace with him, I do as you ask and hope your promise has weight." He gives me the once-over. "One hundred thousand—American?"

I nod.

"Wait here."

The door closes in my face once more, and I take a deep breath to reign in my temper. After he's been gone a while, I sit on the steps of the house and work on figuring out my Russian phone. I'm not sure what time Carys snuck out of the room, but it's mid-afternoon. There will be a limited number of flights to Belfast today. There may not be any.

When the door reopens, the guard has a duffel bag, and Demid has vanished.

"No parting words?" I rise and take the sack from his hand.

"Mr. Kuznetsof is busy at the moment."

I raise my eyebrows. "Too busy to watch this money walk out the door?"

"An employee of Ms. Van de Berg called. They located Valeriya."

"Ah, I see. Is he working on getting her back here?"

The guard hesitates and then sighs. "In a way." He frowns. "She's dead. Bullet to the head."

An execution. My heart rate jacks up about fifty notches. Valeriya is dead. Did they find her dead, or was there an incident? He said one of Carys's employees called. Not her. Jay. *For fuck's sake.* If anything has happened to her...

This morning I've alternated between annoyed, angry, and

frustrated, but right now, I'm not any of those.

Carys.

Her name is a drumbeat reverberating through me. Very few things bother me, so this tightening in my chest, borderline panic is my gut, is new and unwelcome.

I stare at Demid's guard. "I'll give you ten grand to drive me to the airport immediately."

Chapter Twenty
Carys

The morgue is in the basement. I haven't been in many, but the environment is perfect for dead bodies. Linoleum floors, white walls, bright lights. The distinct smell of disinfectant and decay latches onto my clothes, seeps into my pores. Later, when I take a shower, I'll be expelling death.

The attendant sitting across from me and Jay has a picture on the table turned facedown. Jay was in the middle of calling Irish contacts when he got a text alerting him of a body being dragged out of the Belfast Harbor. We didn't think it could be Valeriya. What were the chances?

My phone pings in my purse and I tense. Jay's sideways glance is accompanied by the tiniest smirk. If we weren't here doing this, I'd tell him to shut up. He knows I'm anxious because half of my brain expects Finn to call, to show up, to do something reckless even though he doesn't have the means.

The younger man offers a kind smile. His baby-faced good looks only reinforce my advancing years. "You're Valeriya Kuznetsof's employer?"

"I am." With my hand, I draw my purse closer to my body while the other rises to touch the side of my crown braid.

"I'll show you a photo of a person we believe to be Valeriya Kuznetsof." He continues to drone on, detailing her facial injuries, the bruising, the bloating from being in the water, and finally the gunshot wound to her temple. "Do you understand?"

Briefly, I close my eyes before opening them again. "Yes. I—this isn't the first time I've seen a dead body."

The attendant turns the photo over, and I wish I'd kept my eyes closed. It's Valeriya, but I'm grateful I'm making this identification and not her father. Demid would be devastated to see her so beat up. While she might have turned out to be a traitor, I'm not sure she deserved this send-off.

"That's her," I confirm as he slides papers across the table for me to sign. "Am I able to notify her father?"

"Check with the police. I'm only the morgue attendant."

"Right, okay." I won't be checking with the police. Demid deserves to be told as soon as possible, not when the authorities get around to it. Rising, I stare at Jay who is tuned into his phone. His wife must want to throw the damn thing across the room sometimes.

When he glances up at me, there's concern in his brown depths. A new complication must have arisen. We'd better get out of here. Frowning, I turn to the attendant and offer my hand.

"Thanks for your time."

"Just doing my job." The attendant's smile is brief, and he peruses my fitted white skirt and my dark purple top. "You in Ireland for long?"

My smile matches his. Then my thoughts drift to Finn. He'd lose his mind if he saw the hunger in this guy's eyes. "Flying visit. Taking care of business."

"Ah, shame."

"We gotta go." Jay takes my elbow. As soon as we're out the door, he shakes his head. "We can't be anywhere without a guy thinking he can get a look in."

I laugh. "It's not that bad."

Truth is, I enjoy having men want me, especially if they aren't tied to the company. Someday men won't gaze at me with the glint of interest in their eye. I'll miss their attention which is why I fight the signs of aging with everything money buys.

"I know what you were doing last night," Jay says. "Don't try to tell me he'd be okay with your little exchange."

My cheeks light on fire, but I am not discussing what happened between me and Finn with Jay. "Why were you in such a hurry to get out of there?"

"You won't like my news."

"I love when you start that way." I point at him as I loop my purse higher onto my shoulder. "And by love, I mean the opposite."

We trample up the stairs to the exit door.

"What was the frantic texting in there? I thought maybe your wife was telling you to get your ass home."

"Nah, sometimes she's happier when I'm gone."

"I doubt that." But I've never been married, so perhaps that's their truth. "Anyway—hit me with it." I make a winding motion with my hand.

"When I started making inquiries into Valeriya, a couple people went squirrely on me. Evasive. Giving me bullshit I realized wasn't accurate. I've been digging."

I frown as he opens the heavy exit door and glances outside. "Okay."

"You heard of the PLA?"

I follow him out. We're in an alley on our way to the car. I search my mind for the acronym. "Irish?"

"Yeah."

My head bobs in acknowledgement as I remember. "They contacted me...months ago...years ago? I can't recall and exact date. They're the IRA wannabes, right? Approached our European connection here to do something under the table. I didn't think the risk was worth the reward."

He scans the alley as we walk. I slide my hand into my purse in case I need to draw my gun. Confined spaces aren't ideal if we end up under attack.

"Valeriya was here to take a meeting with them." He stops beside our rental where the alley widens into the street and opens the passenger door.

I hold onto the doorframe and stare at the narrow passage, lost in thought. "Selling off things from the warehouse?"

"Could be. Don't know. Could she have been hoping for protection from you and Finn? It's strange though. Why Ireland? Why them?"

Finn's name and Ireland in the same breath takes me to the night before. I swallow as my senses are flooded with memories. He'll be furious with me. When I return to Russia, I'll make him understand why he couldn't come.

"Can you get me a meeting?" I say.

"I've been trying. They're closed up tighter than a frog's asshole."

"That watertight, huh?"

Jay grins at me as I get into the car. "So far. But frogs have to shit sometime."

When he slides in beside me, I glance out the window. There's something comforting in Ireland—like coming home, though I've never lived here, even though I almost died here.

"Let's go for a drive. I assume you've researched the areas they frequent?" I ask.

"You're going to try a bump?"

"Why not? It's low risk. I feel like a drink." God knows I need one. "We'll find a bar."

"You got it, boss." He starts the car, and we navigate toward the best area of Belfast to hunt the PLA.

~ * ~

We drive for a while before Jay receives a strong enough lead to pick a spot. Similar to other Irish bars within a two-block radius, except there's an odd flag posted on the doorway as we enter. Not a combination I've seen before—vertical lines of orange and brown with a huge yellow star laid over top. Jay enters first and leads us to a booth in the middle of the dimly lit bar. The place probably hasn't had a remodel since the 1800s. There's wood everywhere, and the floor is sticky with stale beer. Our table number is etched into the wooden surface.

"I'll get us drinks," I say.

I'm clutching my purse when the door opens again. A group of people enter, talking and laughing. I weave my way to the bartender and dig out money from my bag. I sidle up to the edge of the worn wood. When the server gets to me, I order us each a beverage and use the codename for a specific drink Jay heard will signal our interest in a non-alcoholic transaction. The group that came in is loud, and they keep drawing my attention while I wait for the drinks or for a contact—whatever comes first.

Once I get our brimming glasses, I return to Jay, hoping some action happens soon. Jay points to a few people by the bar as subtly as possible. "One of them kept checking you out."

He's paranoid. Men don't hit on me everywhere I go. "Men don't fall at my feet constantly."

He gives me a half-smile and sips his drink. "Woman this time. Brown skin. Short hair. Petite."

"Admiring my purse or my shoes or my three-hundred-euro skirt. I wouldn't worry about it."

"Used to be true—no real worries, a single stalker—then people died, other people shot at us, you harbored a wanted man." He raises his eyebrows and takes a drink of his diet coke. "Lately trouble is everywhere."

Wanted man. The words get stuck on a loop in my head as I stir my fruity cocktail. One man, and he'll be in a rage when we go to Russia. A part of me I'm trying to keep under control desperately wishes he was here. Strange to miss him, to long for something—someone—I put to rest years ago.

"Why didn't you let him come? We had the documents."

I'm startled he's read my thoughts. We've spent a lot of time together over the years. He's been my constant for security, and he's become my jack of all trades. I travel light, and he'll do anything I ask.

"A very long time ago, he murdered a few men here in Ireland. There's a kill-on-sight order out from the McCaffery family. He can't be here. And even if that wasn't true, there's the other thing."

He laughs. "Yeah, those *other* people." He takes another sip of his drink. "What's the story with the dead Irishmen?"

I focus on my glass and open my mouth to tell him what I've believed for years. Before the first word can leave my lips, I glance up at Jay. "I used to think he killed them because of his pride. They were rude to him." I grimace at the memory, still fresh despite the years. "But I'm not sure anymore."

"The time you almost died?"

With the straw between my fingers, I take a sip. "Yeah."

Jay lets out a low whistle. "You know better, right?"

What does he mean? Do I know to stay away from Finn? Do I realize he killed them because they hurt me? Do I understand having a relationship with him will never end well? I laugh and drain my drink. "This is a bust. Doesn't anyone in this place work for the PLA? Wasn't the code word supposed to spur people into action?" After sliding out of the booth, I gesture to my purse. "Watch that. I'll be a minute. Ladies room."

He tries to come with me, and I wave him off as I head to the bathroom around the corner and at the end of a narrow, poorly lit hallway. A frisson of unease shoots from the base of my neck, an arrow down my spine. I glance over my shoulder, and the woman who was watching me at the bar is behind me. When I face forward, another man is coming out of the men's room. There's not enough space for all of us, and they're closing fast. Turning on my heel, I try to sneak past the woman to safety, my heart hammering, but she won't budge. Finn had a point about my personal safety.

"Carys Van de Berg?" Her gaze is assessing. "Do you have a minute?"

I frown and touch a hand to my braid. "No, I don't. I need to get back to my companion." Whether they're PLA or another organization, having this conversation without protection makes my stomach churn.

"Jay Fernandez is fine where he is. We have people monitoring him. Not to worry."

When I glance behind me, the other man is still there. Stupid to leave the table without my purse and Jay. No gun. No muscle. "Who are you, exactly?"

"CIA," the man behind me answers.

The woman steers me toward the emergency exit past the

bathrooms.

"I can't go with you right now. I have appointments, and I need to see ID." My heels aren't the best shoes to gain purchase on the old wooden floor, but I dig them in. I'm torn between screaming and using fighting maneuvers Kim taught me one night when we'd had a drink too many. Clues to her identity everywhere, and me, so clueless.

The woman flashes a badge in front of my face while guiding me closer to the door. "We're going to speak to you in the van. We have a few questions."

"Questions?"

"About Finn Donaghey and his whereabouts."

~ * ~

A few questions in the van turns into a trip to a set of office buildings on the outskirts of the city when I seal my lips tight. Another thing Kim taught me. When you're cornered, say nothing, not a single word. A crack in the dam will lead to a flood.

From their line of questioning, I've gleaned I took Finn to either Russia, Cuba, or Switzerland. They haven't nailed a definite country. These are the people in charge of international security?

We're headed into the fourth hour of this stalemate. Does the CIA work the same as the police? "Lawyer."

The petite, brown woman across from me, who the other two guys have been calling Anu, sits straighter in her chair. "You want a lawyer."

"Yeah. *My* lawyer."

"Might take a while."

"Or you can get me FBI Kim. I'll accept one of those two people. But if you're going to ask me questions regarding Finn Donaghey, then I have nothing to say. I haven't seen him in months. We aren't exactly friends." The fucking dam is breaking. *Seal it up, Carys.*

Anu exchanges a glance over my head with the other agent who has been pacing and lounging for the last few hours. He can't decide if he's super tense or super relaxed.

"FBI Kim?" he clarifies as though confused.

I don't answer him. There's nowhere else I need to be. Valeriya is dead. Finn is stuck in Russia. Jay is…well…freaking out because he's lost me. If they want me to talk, they'll have to bring me one of those two people. My lawyer is in Chicago. Kim should be recovering from a gunshot wound somewhere in the US, likely removed from the FBI. I may be here a while longer.

An hour later, there's a knock on the door before it cracks open and a tall, slim, but muscular woman slips in. She's dressed in jeans and a black T-shirt from an Irish bar, with her leather jacket obscuring the full name. Her dark hair is in its usual ponytail, and when her brown, almost black eyes meet mine, they're both familiar and foreign. She's the kind of pretty that's jarring. Her skin causes a shot of envy to slice through me—tanned but without the sun damage and smooth, not a wrinkle in sight. Of course, she is fifteen years younger.

"That was quick." I let the words sit between us.

She was already in Ireland. Had to be. Otherwise the CIA has invented time travel.

Kim scans the room. "I asked for the recording devices to be switched off. You never know, though."

She searches everywhere, checking the corners, and then sweeps under the table, first with her eyes, then with her hands. Her movements are stilted. Is she still injured under her layers of clothing? Finally she slides into the seat on the other side of me and links her dusty brown hands together before meeting my gaze.

"You wanted to see me?" she says.

An amused smile threatens. "Wanted to see you? Only if you're rotting in hell."

"Do you have Finn?"

"Of course not. You realize how I feel."

Kim nods. "I do." She unlaces her hands, and her index finger traces a gouge in the wooden surface. "I understand what it's like to connect that way with someone. The things you'd do to protect them, the lengths you'd go to." With a brief glance up, she gives a tiny shrug. "You're worth so much more than someone like him could ever give you."

"Don't pretend to know things." I lean across the table, rage welling up in me.

"The friendship we had was real, Carys. It killed me to report on you."

"But you did it, didn't you?" I grit my teeth. "And you're not dead."

"Look, I have two things I want to say to you before they come in here and decide this conversation was a waste of time and resources. You're not going to give up Finn, whether or not you have him. I get that." She stares at me for a beat. "The PLA has a contact somewhere in your organization, and they have been purchasing guns from you. I don't think you're in on the transactions, probably didn't realize they were happening. I didn't hear so much as a whisper in the months I worked for you, and the CIA seems to believe these exchanges have been happening for almost two years."

Two years. Was that when they approached me, and I turned them down? Valeriya? Wouldn't that be nice? She's dead—problem solved. My father? Would he go behind my back again? He never had a moral objection to reckless, idiotic extremist groups if they could pay.

I give her a mild look, feigning disinterest while my brain kicks into overdrive. I sit in my chair, crossing my arms. "And the second?"

"Finn—" she hesitates before continuing, "and Lorcan were trafficking women and children while I worked for them. Women, like you and me. And kids...of every age."

I raise an eyebrow. "And this should bother me because?"

"You can pretend you're hard-hearted, that's fine. You do that. But I'm familiar with the Carys under your cold front. Women and kids are the line you said you could never stand for anyone to cross."

She's right. I'm surprised she remembers. But I guess that was her job. Gain my confidence, use it against me.

"You want me to track these women and children and help them? Is that your point?"

Kim shakes her head. "No, that's not the point. We're cleaning up those messes. My point is—you're harboring a man who does those kinds of things with no remorse. He let his father be killed with no remorse. He shot me and felt no remorse. He aided in the trafficking of hundreds of women and children and felt no remorse. There's no goodness in him, Carys. Whatever decency you think you see, that man is an illusion. Smoke and mirrors. You can't save him; there's *nothing* in him worth saving."

Although I'm reeling from her trafficking revelations, having her lay into Finn in such a callous, judgmental way makes my blood boil.

A few short weeks ago, I'd have agreed with most of her assertions. Years ago, he hurt me. But I'm not sure I read him or the situation right. Is Kim seeing things clearly? There was always this intriguing mixture of darkness and light in her. She'd hate to realize the darkness won out when she fell in love with Lorcan. No, he can't be bad, so it must be *all* Finn.

"He loves his brother," I hedge.

Kim laughs. "Does he? Enough to put him first? Lorcan loves me, and Finn shot me, intended to execute me in front of him. When has Finn *ever* put anyone but himself first?" Her expression is expectant. "I can wait while you search your memory." She taps the tabletop. "It hasn't happened. It'll *never* happen."

I stab my nail into the wood. "You're a fucking FBI agent. Did you think he wouldn't protect himself and protect Lorcan from you?" I narrow my eyes. "It should have taken another eight or so hours for them to get you here. What, have you changed over to the CIA? You going to fuck people on an international level?"

"I can't answer that."

"Cameras are off. You claim our friendship was real. You broke the rules for Lorcan."

Kim leans back in her chair, her mouth set in a firm line. Her dark eyes flicker. She's considering something, but what? "Yes."

My laugh is bitter. "That's all I get?"

"I'm here getting the lay of the land." Her stare is laced with meaning. "I still have stitches that need to finish closing and a psych eval to pass."

"You're good at pretending, so I'm sure you'll have no problem."

She sighs and places her elbows on the table again. "I shouldn't say this, but if you want proof I care, here it is. Someone in your organization is fucking you over—"

"No shit," I mumble.

"The PLA and whoever they're dealing with are making the trail seem like *you're* in on the weapons sales. That means, if the CIA takes down the PLA or goes after their suppliers, your head will be on the chopping block. Not your company, but you, personally. That's how the paperwork reads. You'll end up in federal prison."

I stare in silence for a moment and hope I don't look shocked while my insides swirl. For whatever reason, I didn't take her earlier warning to heart. Someone was dealing to the PLA. An annoyance, an avenue to be checked into, not a path to jail. Now, I'm not so sure I want the culprit to be Valeriya. Dead people don't make good witnesses.

"You're sure?" I keep my voice neutral.

"I'm being brought up to speed. I didn't—I never got very much on you when I was there. For lots of reasons. You were careful. I was reluctant. Doesn't matter. But this—what I'm seeing—like fucking Christmas. Wrapped up neat and tidy. Nice little bow on the top of your impending sentence."

I swallow and splay my hand on the table, my mind churning. "Do you have a timeline?"

"To move ahead? No. Nothing yet. But the threat is real. You need to get to the bottom of it before me or someone like me comes knocking."

I sigh and cross my arms. "What do you want from me?"

"I'd like to say nothing."

"But you can't—so what do you want? The cameras are off. People in your position don't switch them off unless they're trying to hide their actions. Approval doesn't happen unless someone else believes what you're getting is worth the risk."

"You won't give up Finn?"

"Finn? What would I know? Maybe he's dead." Those words, spoken out loud, make my stomach clench.

She laughs and settles deeper into her chair. "Sure." For a minute she eyes me. "When you figure out who is fucking you over, you give them over to us. We'll prosecute, or we'll turn them into an asset to help with our larger investigation."

"And if I don't agree?"

"It seems like you're the one doing the illegal supplies, Carys. If that's true, and you are the one dealing with the PLA, you are welcome to come on board, and we can work together to take them down."

"It's not me. You know that." I uncross my arms and stretch my hands out along my skirt. "I'll need product numbers so I can determine the originating point for the weapons. Narrow my search."

"I can get you that." Kim gives me a calculating appraisal. "You're agreeing to help us?"

"What choice do I have? I don't want to go to jail." There's still a leftover instinct in me to divulge too much to her, to trust her more than I should. Considering what else has been happening to me lately, her story rings true.

"I care about you. You don't need to go to jail for contacts you didn't make."

A smile touches my lips. "But if I did these deals..."

An answering smile hints at the corners of Kim's mouth as she stands. "Maybe not then either. It's not you—I'm confident. I'll do what I can from my end as long as you're keeping the lines of communication open on yours." She slides a card across the table.

I pick it up, fingering the edges.

"And if you've got Finn, keep him off the fucking radar. He's a loose cannon—you don't need that."

I raise my shoulders. "Don't have a clue what you're talking about." The card has a letter "K" and a phone number. Interesting strategy.

"I'll get someone to drive you to your hotel."

"Did anyone tell Jay what happened to me?"

Kim opens the door. "I doubt it. He'll be freaking out, glued to his phone, trying to pinpoint where the hell you've gone. Probably already called his wife Sofia to proclaim how much he loves her."

She's right. Exactly right. Strange to realize how well she knows me and my organization, and yet this incredible, insurmountable distance exists between us.

On the way to the hotel, my mind drifts to Finn again. All day, I've alternated between wishing I'd let him come and being grateful he's not here. I'm glad he's in Russia and hasn't spent the last however many hours chasing his tail like Jay.

Despite what Kim imagines, Finn isn't the loose cannon he was in his youth. But he's still quick to anger, quick to act. At least if he's doing any of that, he's far away from here.

Chapter Twenty-One
Finn

I'm fucking broke. Again. But I'm in Ireland, and I'm in Carys's hotel room sitting in the dark, waiting for the FBI or the CIA or whatever government organization cornered her in the PLA bar to bring her back.

At what point do I stop waiting? I don't know. I've been chasing my tail since I got here.

Demid's guard got me Jay's phone number, helped me organize a private plane to Belfast, and drove me to the airport. Turns out, he wasn't as inept as I thought. Once I was here, getting to Jay was easy.

Figuring out what happened to Carys? Hard and expensive. The temptation to put a bullet in Jay's head for losing her was overwhelming. My anger has been on a rapid boil just under the surface since I arrived. He's more suited to the role of a personal assistant than a bodyguard. Fucking useless. He's been running around Northern Ireland like a chicken with his head cut off.

After every decent option hit a dead end, I called Thomas Byrne in Dublin to have pressure applied to his Belfast contacts. Given I have almost no money or influence anymore, I didn't want to owe him. The Byrne family is a tie to my old life in Boston, to Lorcan, to my lost empire. Calling him was like shooting a flare into the night sky. *I'm still alive. Here I am.*

I run my hands over my face and let out a sigh of frustration before sinking deeper into the overstuffed chair in Carys's suite. If she arrives—*when* she arrives—we'll have a chat about what it means to take personal safety seriously. Today has been a shitshow from start to finish.

None of the Byrne contacts were certain, but the most reliable source thought Carys was nabbed by the FBI or the CIA. The CIA has been sniffing around the PLA. Google tells me they're low rent IRA wannabes—dangerous—gaining power. According to Jay, Valeriya, the Russian snake, was supposed to be meeting with them. Can't say

I'm upset she met a watery grave.

There are three reasons I figure the FBI, or the CIA, would nab Carys from a public bar. They're fishing for information on me, in which case, being in Ireland just became even more dangerous. Or Kimi gathered and submitted sufficient evidence on Carys or the Van de Berg empire to bring its legitimacy into question. Or Valeriya was poised to fuck Carys over by doing a deal with the PLA with the missing merch from the warehouse.

Jay is still running around Belfast trying to get a lead, but I had to come in. If they return her, it'll be to here. Being out there made me want to murder, beat, burn the world to the ground until I got an answer, until I had the truth, until I got her back. The realization she's in trouble is enough to send me into a free fall.

My elbows rest on the top of my thighs, and my hands clench and release as though I'm warming up for a boxing match. The next person who walks through this hotel room door better be Carys, or I may end up with another reason I can't be in Ireland.

At the sound of the clumsy clatter of a key in the lock, I jerk my head toward the door. I rise from my seat in the far corner of the suite, the darkness thicker here unless she turns on a light right away. When the door swings open, the person in the doorframe is too tall and broad to be Carys. From height alone, the figure could be Jay, but this guy has the rangy leanness I recognize. I contemplated flying to Chicago to murder him. The good news? I'm still in a murderous mood.

I draw my gun from the waistband of my jeans but keep it loose at my side. Eric probably hasn't come here for a fight, but he'll get one. He enters the room and then says over his shoulder, "She must not be here."

Another figure emerges in the light from the hallway, causing a sigh of annoyance to escape me. Charles. Her father. Well, fuck me. I can't kill him, which means I can't kill Eric either.

They haven't turned on a light yet. Instead they're standing in the dim doorway chatting at a decibel I can't quite catch. I'm not one to hide—ever. But the things that've happened to Carys since I woke up point to a level of interference from one or both men. When opportunity knocks, who am I to deny it entrance?

To the right of the chair is an armoire with enough space between it and the window for a person my size to slip between. I sneak over, hoping the two men are deep in conversation and ignore any movement. My chest strains against the heavy, old-fashioned furniture as I slide down as far as I can. My hand with the gun faces out in case I need to take care of a snitch or two.

The light flicks on, and Eric's and Charles saunter in, their footsteps muffled by the carpet. They head in the direction of the mini bar.

"All the alcohol is here, so she obviously hasn't been in the room for more than a drop off," Eric says, and the thump of his foot connecting with something, maybe her suitcase, reverberates around the room.

A glass clatters onto the wooden tabletop, and then liquid splashes into it. "Drink?" Charles asks.

"No. She gets pissed when I start without her."

"At this point, it's best to play by her rules, I suppose." There's a pause and then a glass thuds onto the table. "Who'd you say told you about the CIA?"

Eric chuckles. "I didn't."

The chair in front of me creaks, and my heart kicks in response. I'm concealed by the armoire and curtains, but I'm not naïve enough to believe I can't be discovered. They could turn me in to the Irish mob or the CIA. Could I kill them to stay alive and out of jail? Yes. Would she ever forgive me? Not a chance in hell.

"I'm concerned you're fucking up our plan with whatever side deals you've been working. Why was my daughter in a PLA bar? Why is Valeriya dead? Nothing should put Carys at risk. I didn't sign up for this."

"The answer to the first is Jay's good at his job. Perhaps too good. We may need to plant false leads to keep him off the scent. She'll know someone in the organization has been dealing with the PLA either through Jay or, I imagine, the CIA. I suppose that can't be helped now. The second question, well, that's more complicated and you don't want to know."

Liquid being poured into a glass echoes through the room again. "When are you going to make your move?" Charles asks.

"Roughly a month. The timing of these things is always vague."

There's a quick flapping noise, and I picture Eric flicking his suit jacket open like he did the last time I met him.

Charles grunts. "A month? And she's holed up with Finn Donaghey? Christ. She'll either be pregnant or dead by the time your plan comes through. I agreed to this ridiculous plan with the understanding—"

"Her pregnancies don't tend to stick." Eric's smooth, emotionless voice cuts off Charles. My fingers twitch on the gun. "The original miscarriage, wasn't it? With him? A literal knife to the heart and a figurative one as well." Eric's voice hardens. "I don't think she's stupid enough to put herself in either situation again."

My heart slows in my chest. What-the-actual-fuck did he just say? My brain is processing through mud. She was pregnant? With *my* child?

"You didn't see how broken up she was," Charles says.

"Doesn't matter." The chair creaks again as Eric rises, then he crosses the suite. "I've made mistakes—paying for that bitch's abortion being the biggest—she forgave me every other indiscretion. This time around, she'll be happy. Once I reveal everything to her, once she knows how serious I am, she won't want to say no." His laugh is ominous. "She won't be able to."

A glass hits the wooden table. Liquid pours into it.

"Then Carys and I will finally run this company together," Eric says.

I press my forehead into the armoire and brace my free hand against it as Charles and Eric do a toast to the future of the Van de Berg kingdom. The roaring in my ears almost drowns out the sound of the suite door opening and closing.

"Oh," Carys says, her voice breathy with surprise. "What are you doing here?"

The tension, coiled tight in my belly, releases in a rush. My heart strains at the music of her voice. *She's okay.*

Another frisson of anger chases the comfort away. She shouldn't be saying those words to them; she should say them to me.

Chapter Twenty-Two
Carys

When I realize the lights are on in my suite, I assume it's Jay. A part of me both hopes and dreads it might be Finn. But he's not the type of guy who waits in a well-lit room. No, he'd much prefer a dark corner, scaring the shit out of me to prove a point.

When I step into my suite and find my father and Eric toasting each other by the mini-bar, it causes my heart to sink.

"What are you doing here?" I say.

Eric turns toward me, sliding his tumbler along the polished mahogany table. "Sook called me."

I frown and cross the room, taking the last glass from the mini-bar to pour myself a drink. "My lawyer called you, but she didn't bother to show up?"

"Sook said she could make the calls to get you released without coming. They didn't have a reason to detain you. Chance and circumstance." He grimaces. "Harboring a fugitive tends to make you a target for the authorities."

It's not uncommon for him to come to my rescue. Despite everything, he can be strangely protective. I used to find it sweet. Today I'm annoyed.

"What I do and who I do it with outside of office hours isn't any of your concern." I swirl my drink around, watching as the whiskey comes close to slipping over the edge. "It has been none of your business for years."

If Sook solved my legal troubles without even coming to Ireland, it means they sent Kim in as a last-ditch effort to get something out of me before they had to release me. I'm growing weary of subterfuge and half-truths. Is it that hard for people to be honest?

"When you're using company funds to pay off an FBI agent, it becomes our business." My father arches his eyebrows.

He doesn't have a single gray hair. The inclination toward vanity is one of the few things we have in common. He appears so much younger than his actual age. Another half-truth.

"I was in a hurry and needed access to cash. With time, I would have paid the money back from my personal accounts and investments." I swallow my drink and then slide the glass onto the table next to Eric's. "Instead, I only gave him half what I owed and almost died trying to sort it out."

"Don't be so melodramatic," my father scoffs.

Shoving down the sleeve of my shirt, I reveal my upper arm and the bandage still gracing it. "The FBI agent who helped me is dead. There was a shootout at his rental in Volgograd. So, if you two geniuses thought you were helping me out by cleaning up my mess, you almost cleaned me up with it."

Eric holds up his hands. My father's face has lost color. Either they're both incredible actors or they don't understand why Ricardo's house ended up riddled with bullets.

Eric tries to caress my injured arm, but I step out of his reach.

"I don't suppose either of you knows why I've been getting packages in Switzerland with an old-fashioned alarm clock and various versions of *time is running out*, do you?"

Out of the corner of my eye, my father gives Eric an annoyed glance.

"Not a clue," Eric says in a breezy voice as he pours himself another drink. "But doesn't seem like a legitimate worry."

He used that voice whenever I asked about the women I was sure he was fucking while we were engaged. He uses the same attitude in the office with people he believes are being irrational and stupid. Just before Kim went to Boston, he tried his patronizing tone with her. She threatened to shoot him. I should have let her.

"I realize you're lying." I point at him and then wander toward the windows.

I need space from the two of them before I strangle them both. They've cooked up a scheme, and it'll be me who pays the price. "I've got other, more pressing things to worry about right now. Who the fuck is dealing with the PLA behind my back?"

Another uncomfortable silence materializes, settling between us. As I approach the corner of the room furthest from them, I glimpse a duffle bag under the armchair closest to the armoire. Familiar, but I can't place why. Then the realization hits. The bag is from my house in Switzerland; it's the one I gave to Finn.

Shit.

Shit. Shit. Shit.

My heart rate skyrockets. He could be hiding somewhere in the suite, which wouldn't be like him. Or he's out with Jay searching for me. He might return at any point. If my father or Eric see him, they'll turn him into the authorities, or they'll alert the Irish mob. They've both made it clear they don't agree with me fishing him out of the FBI's net.

"Well." I spin on my heel. "Is someone going to answer my question? 'Cause if not, both of you can get the hell out of my hotel room."

"Carys," Eric says in that tone I hate. "It seems obvious to me Valeriya was the person screwing you over. She came here to meet with the PLA, and now she's dead."

"Doesn't explain where our products have gone from the warehouse." Valeriya's involvement doesn't explain the paper trail the CIA claims they have or the two-year timeframe. Outright theft is a first, but if the PLA are using goods linked to me, then someone's been stirring the pot, maybe for years.

I spot my purse on the bed and stalk over to it, yanking it open and grabbing my phone. Did Finn put it here? Jay? Ignoring the panicked texts on my home screen, I type a message to Jay.

Finn. Where is Finn? A surge of panic hovers below the surface.

When I glance up, Eric and my father are exchanging uneasy looks. I'm missing something; there's an undercurrent between them.

A message pings. The blood rushes out of my body.

Finn's in the hotel somewhere. He has to be. He isn't with Jay.

"Look." I drop my phone into my purse, willing my heart to calm the fuck down. "I'm tired. It's been a long day. You're lying to me about something—both of you. But I'm too exhausted to care. Go to your rooms, wherever they are, and when I see you tomorrow, you need to have answers. Ones that make sense." I don't bother asking for the truth because, at this point, I'm convinced they won't give it to me.

Eric pours himself another drink and nods to my father. "I'll see you in the morning, Charles."

"Oh, no." I cross my arms. "You're not staying here. I'm done with lies, and half-truths, and so much bullshit your eyes are even browner than normal. No. Leave. Go. Get out." I point to the door.

"Carys," Eric cajoles.

"No." I grab his duffel bag off the floor by the bed. When I get to the door, I open it and toss it into the hallway. "I hope my father got a room with two double beds. Otherwise, you'll be both literally and figuratively in bed with each other. Won't that be nice?"

Finn might be somewhere in this hotel room. If he is, if he's heard them, it's a God-damned miracle my father and Eric are still alive. I can only imagine the things they said before I arrived. About him. About me. About who knows what else.

My father steps out the door, into the hallway. "Room 561," he says to Eric over his shoulder.

He stoops to pick up his bag and stares at me. "This is really what you want? I could help you relax after such a stressful day."

"Could you?" I meet his gaze. "I doubt it."

He flushes with annoyance. "Someday you'll understand."

I laugh. "Oh, I think I understand enough already. Goodnight, Eric."

With a last frustrated huff, he heads down the hall toward the elevators. I shut the door and flip the lock into place. For a moment I focus on the fake wooden surface, gathering my strength for the next round.

Turning, I'm about to call Finn's name when I see him by the window, leaning his shoulder into the armoire, the gun loose at his side.

All I want to do is go to him, wrap my arms around him, lean into his chest, and let myself be safe for the first time today.

And then I remember what Kim told me.

And then I remember how much danger he's putting himself in by being here, the danger I might be in.

"You shouldn't be here."

He doesn't respond, doesn't leave his place near the window. The panic and anger I've kept at bay surges in me. Everything is collapsing around me, and he couldn't care less.

"Did you hear me?" I stride over to the mini-bar and pour myself a second drink. "You shouldn't be here."

The silence from him is oppressive as I take the shot of whiskey.

"Doesn't matter if you're angry at me for leaving you like that," I say.

Except anger isn't what is emanating from him, reaching out toward me. The emotion is one I can't pinpoint. When I've gathered my outrage, I spin around. "You're giving me the silent treatment?"

"Just waiting for you to get drunk enough to tell me the truth."

"Fuck you."

Finn's empty hand ruffles his close-cropped hair and then clings to his neck. He slides the gun into the waistband of his pants near his spine. "It was the CIA?"

"Yes."

"Were they after me?"

"Of course."

"Did they say anything about Lorcan?"

I hesitate and stall by sliding my tumbler onto the table. In the car I wondered whether I should mention Kim to Jay or Finn. But I'm so tired of being lied to, lying to other people.

"Kim was there."

He straightens, springing off the armoire in a burst of alertness. "What? Why?"

I cross my arms and lean my hip against the table. I will not be the first to bridge the distance between us. He isn't raging against me leaving him in Russia. I'll take this version of him, even if I don't understand it.

"I asked for her," I reply. "But I think they agreed with the hope she'd get under my skin."

"Kim's like a sliver."

"Gotta dig it out, or it'll become infected." I stare at him, pondering my next move. "She told me about the trafficking."

Finn's head nod is almost imperceptible. "Course she did."

"It's true?"

"You doubted her?"

I swallow and shrug. Did I? Maybe not. But I hoped Kim was trying to needle me, get me away from him. Tears prick behind my eyes. I turn my gaze to the ceiling and take a deep, shuddering breath. "Years ago—"

"I'm not that guy anymore."

A tear falls. I wipe it away and then re-cross my arms. "Sometimes." I shake my head. What I'm about to say isn't smart, but the sentiment has been playing in my mind on repeat. "Sometimes, I wish we could go back. Have a redo."

"What would you redo?"

"I don't know." Another tear escapes and trickles down my face. "I don't know." But I do. I had too much time to think when I was trapped with the CIA. Lately it feels like the night I was stabbed was a turning point. Not everything that came after has been shit, but nothing in my life has ever felt as good as it was before.

"Did you know?" Finn's gruff voice hauls me right into the present.

"Know what?"

"The night you were stabbed, did you know you were pregnant with my baby? Had you already decided I wasn't fatherhood material?"

"Oh, my God." My knees buckle, and I reach out blindly to brace my hand on the table. "Who told you?"

Chapter Twenty-Three
Finn

Color leaves her cheeks in a rush, making her washed out, too pale. My head and my heart war over whether to go to her. Before I do anything else tonight, I need the truth.

"I drank that night. Do you honestly think I would have been drinking if I was aware I was pregnant?"

I search her face, checking for any sign she might be lying. "You found out..."

"When I woke up from surgery." Her gaze connects with mine across the divide before slipping away. "I never had the chance to tell you."

"In the hallway, when I spoke to Charles, when he warned me off..."

"He knew, yeah. My father." She secures a stray strand of hair into her braid. "He's always had these misguided ideas about what's best for me. I'm not sure he's ever understood me."

"Seems he still doesn't," I say as she brushes a few more tears from her cheeks.

I clench my hands and shove them into my pockets. My chest aches with longing, with the desire to go to her, comfort her. Touching her is a bad idea. Too much will spill out. The words are there, but they won't help either of us.

"Tweedledum and Tweedledee are conspiring against you."

Carys sighs and toys with the glass on the table beside her. "Yeah. I just don't know why."

"You understand what they're up to?" I narrow my eyes.

She gives an unsteady laugh and points at me. "Okay. I don't have that information either. They aren't being honest with me." She smooths both hands over her face. "What did you hear?"

"Some sort of PLA involvement. Eric knows something about Valeriya's death. The conclusion of their plan comes down the pipe in a month." I don't tell her he's sure he can get her back. That seed won't be planted by me.

Carys frowns and rubs her forehead. "A month?" She massages as though she can conjure unknown details from her memory. "I can't remember something the company is doing that'll be concluded in a month."

One side of my lips quirks up. "Hence the conspiracy."

She's stopped crying, thankfully. I'm not sure how much longer my willpower would have held out if those silent tears had continued. Each one shred the bit of heart still beating in my chest. Men have begged me for their lives, and I've felt nothing. But her sadness burns through me, leaves a scar.

I clench my hands.

"Neither of them would hurt me on purpose," she says.

The sound of Eric's grating laugh as he mentioned Carys's first miscarriage—our miscarriage—echoes in my ears. He cheated, lied, shown her who he is, but she doesn't want to see it. "Eric is a dick. You're wrong about him. He doesn't give a shit if you get hurt."

"He can be misguided. So can my father." She shrugs and doesn't look at me. "They're men."

Her comment sets me off. "I don't understand what that fucking means." She's constantly lumping me in with them, and I don't deserve it. I leave my corner of the room and stride closer to her. "That's the second or third time you've implied men can't be trusted."

"Sometimes men do stupid things. Then," she says, her gaze connecting with mine, "I have to figure out a way to forgive those men for those things."

Fucking hell. She's got me there.

When we're only a few feet apart, I pause. If I get close enough to touch her, to slide my hand around her waist, tug her flush against me, there won't be any more talking. These events happening to her, between us, around us, are creating fires of need, of desire, of another emotion I've never admitted to anyone. I enjoy playing with fire. Who doesn't? But she's the last person I'd want to burn.

"How did you get here?" she says.

I smirk. "You won't like it. Though I was pretty fucking pissed when I woke up and found you gone."

"I'm surprised you aren't still angry."

"There are more pressing emotions aimed at other things." Like that fucker Eric. My mind swirls around any and all solutions to make sure he never gets a second chance with Carys. It wouldn't be a true second chance, anyway. He seems to have screwed her over at every turn. What he's done makes me vibrate with suppressed anger.

"How?" she says.

129

"Demid. One hundred thousand dollars. A private plane. Thomas Byrne. A few other people I owe favors if I ever have any money or influence again."

"I can help with Thomas, pay back Demid." She turns away and her fingertips dance across the mini-bar bottles. "You shouldn't have come. The risk…"

I stare at her back. She doesn't know? Seems impossible she wouldn't realize. The inferno threatening to consume us surges, forcing the words out. "Did you really think I'd want to be anywhere fucking else? Throw me in prison. Gun me down in the streets. I'd go to hell and have that shit happen on repeat it if meant you were safe and happy. That's all I've ever wanted for you."

She goes still at the table. Her back tenses. When she turns toward me, she braces her hands on the table. Tears are trickling down her face. My gut twists in response. "Finn—I—"

"The whole time I was listening to those two dickheads spout off, I couldn't stop thinking it's my fucking fault. It's my fucking fault her life is like this."

"Finn." She steps toward me, but I step back. "It's not—"

I clear my throat and ask the second question that's plagued me since Eric laid it out. "The other miscarriages—the fact that you haven't been able to have a baby—is it because of that night?"

She shakes her head and closes the distance. Her fingers trail from my bicep down to my wrist and she links our hands together. A simple touch, but it electrifies my body, makes me even more aware of her in this room, the bed behind us.

"The first miscarriage was trauma related." She swallows. "The others? There was no reason. Every test money could buy said I should be able to get pregnant and sustain a pregnancy." Her shoulders rise in the tiniest shrug. "It just wasn't meant to be."

Another tear slips out unchecked, and I tug her toward me, locking her against my chest. Her cheek is over my heart, and I squeeze her tighter. "Do you ever—" I don't have the guts to finish my question. Asking wouldn't be fair. I can't offer her what she wants, what she needs.

"Finish it."

"Carys."

"I'm tired of lies and half-truths and bullshitting each other. Ask me."

Silence lays between us for a beat. The question is dumb. But after listening to Eric and Charles talking, after realizing she hasn't gotten the things I wanted for her, I can't stop wondering. I'm plagued by a giant what if?

Regrets are for indecisive, weak people, aren't they?

I bend my head, my lips close to her ear, as though my weakness is a secret. "Do you ever wonder what life would have been like if that night hadn't happened?"

She presses her forehead into my chest. "I never used to. I thought I understood, realized what we'd meant to each other."

The implication is that she'd meant nothing, we'd been nothing to each other. God, I was such a fool. Still am. This road with me does not lead to any happiness for her. I shouldn't ask. "And now?"

"And now, I can't stop thinking about how happy I used to be with you." She still won't meet my gaze, and her manicured fingertip traces figure eights across my chest. Her closeness muddles my thoughts, turns my focus to the way her body fits against mine, how good it is to be skin to skin, buried deep inside her.

The path we'd walk is impossible. Wrong, maybe. I have no right to hope, to ask. "For the rest of my life, I'll be a wanted man."

"I know."

"With me, you'll always be checking over your shoulder. The CIA, the FBI, other mob organizations, they'll be searching for ways to draw me out."

She raises her head and meets my gaze, her lips only inches from mine. "I understand the reasons I shouldn't be with you, Finn. You think I haven't had them on repeat since I rescued you?" Her amber eyes sear me with sincerity. "What do you want?"

"I want you to be safe and happy."

"What if I can't be both?"

I run my knuckles along her cheek. "Then I want you to be safe."

She takes a deep, shuddering breath. "And I've decided I'd rather be happy."

"The things you used to want—"

"I gave up on those a long time ago. Years ago. I'll never be a mom. I'm not telling you I'm not sad. But the other thing I wanted? It was a partner I could trust, who would be honest with me, who would love me." Her eyes waver from mine, a hint of unease in their depths. "You tell me the truth, even when it's not something I want to hear."

I stare at the wall, contemplating her words. When we were younger, she told me if I ever wanted to stop sleeping with her, all I had to do was some human trafficking. It was a hard line for her. We were in bed, and I laughed. Told her it was weird to be okay with murder and not okay with trafficking. Then I promised her I'd never do it.

Easy to lie, to tell her I forgot our conversation when Zhang's trafficking business landed in my lap in Boston. When Antonio asked what we would do with the human arm of Zhang's business, I thought of Carys, of the promise I made, of how after we had sex in Boston she told me she was so drunk and horny I could have been anyone. I kept Zhang's business because I was pissed I meant so little to her when she meant so fucking much to me.

She tries to back away, and I clutch her closer.

Her nervous laugh is muffled by my chest. "Clearly, I misread this. Forget I said anything."

"I'm thinking." I smooth her hair and kiss the top of her head. Agreeing to be with her makes me a selfish bastard. Normally, I'm quite happy with being a bright, shining example of what it means to be both selfish and a bastard. God knows I've had both thrown at me so many times I've lost count.

"You shouldn't have to think this hard." She tries to escape my grasp. "If you can't—if you don't believe you can love me—"

I chuckle, and she slaps my chest and struggles with more force, trying to break free. "It's not fucking funny, Finn."

Love her? I barely remember a time when I didn't love her. My body may have belonged to others, but my soul, what's left of it, is hers. My obsession started when I was thirteen, jacking off into a sock at the idea of her, and it'll end with me whispering her name on my death bed. I laugh again, and then I realize why she doesn't find it funny. Swallowing down my amusement, I let her get away from me.

She strides halfway across the room and stops, her back facing me, as though she's not sure what to do with herself.

Can I let her tie herself to me? Can I be that selfish?

"You think I don't love you?" I say.

"You've never said it."

I shrug and quirk my lips up, but it isn't with amusement. "I've never said it to anyone."

When she turns, her expression is pensive. "No one? Ever?"

"Maybe my mom." I grimace. Remembering her is a sharp thorn in my side. "She was murdered when I was five, so I don't recall saying it." I dig my hands into my pockets. "Donagheys never say it. Not out loud. Never occurred to me you might need to hear them."

She searches my face but doesn't come back to me. Her hands are linked, and she stares at them. One of her rings goes around and around. "Sometimes I felt it or thought I felt it. Maybe you did." A sad smile flits across her face. "You were hard to read." Her smile vanishes. "You're still hard to read."

"Are you sure about this?" I shove my hands deeper into my pockets, trying to keep the rational distance until she's decided.

Letting her go last time was almost impossible, but I did it because I was standing in the way of her getting the things she wanted. Once we fall back into each other, could I pull myself out? Walk away? I don't know. I don't want to find out.

"Yes." She closes the space between us and places her hand on the side of my face. "I want to be happy. Being with you, around you, makes me happy." She rises on her toes to mold herself to me. In my ear, she whispers, "I've loved no one else the way I love you."

The heaviness in my chest eases. I draw her tighter to me. "I love you, too." Those words, from her, from me, crack me open, lay me bare. I'll do anything to make her happy, and whether or not she wants it, to keep her safe.

Chapter Twenty-Four
Carys

Finn's hands cup my face, bringing my lips toward his. I meet his kiss, driving my fingers into his hair, pressing myself as tightly to him as I can manage with our clothes on. His tongue massages my mouth, and he skims the hem of my shirt, easing it up, circling my back. At the skin-to-skin contact, I shudder with pleasure. He grips my ass, molding me to his erection. *God, I love the way he feels.*

When his mouth leaves mine to seek the most sensitive places along my neck, I moan and clutch onto him, afraid my legs might give out. My adrenaline spikes. His declaration of love is a drug coursing through me. Impossible to believe someone like him could love me.

"Say it again," I murmur.

Finn chuckles against the curve of my shoulder. "You going to make me say it all the fucking time?"

"Consider it the price of admission." My voice is breathless, and I'm already reaching for the button on his jeans.

He sucks on my earlobe and nibbles. "I fucking love you, Carys. Just you. Always you."

His gruff voice in is like another shot of desire.

Is there anything better than hearing those words from him? I'll never tire of being important and precious.

"Promise me." I tug his shirt over his head. Our lips barely break apart, and he makes short work of my clothes as I strip him bare. "It'll only be me and you. I can't do that again."

He grabs my hand and presses it to his heart. His lips trail a line from my jaw to my collarbone as he speaks, "What's in here," he drags my hand from his heart and settles it over top of the prominent bulge in his underwear, "and what's in here are yours and yours alone."

I circle his cock and squeeze. He groans, and his lips find mine again as he disposes of my bra.

"You think you can do that?" I say.

I'm practically panting as his hand slides into my panties, his finger gliding across my folds.

"I did it last time without you asking."

His words are muddled by the sensations rushing through me. I'm drunk with need, with love, and his fingers slipping inside me only intensify those feelings.

"What?" I bring my hands up to cling to his shoulders, to hold myself steady.

"You heard me." He lifts one of my breasts to his mouth and tugs on the nipple with his teeth.

I gasp.

"Then why did you—oh, *God*, do that again."

His thumb grazes my clit a second time with the right amount of pressure to make every nerve ending spring to attention.

"Because..." He picks me up and carries me toward the bed. He tosses me on top, and I shriek as he follows me. "I was young and stupid. Then I was old and cynical."

His eyes, such a pale, pale blue, examine me with such intensity my breath stalls. "I didn't want to ruin your life a second time."

With my finger I trail a path from his temple to his lips. "You won't ruin me. You'll show me what I've been missing."

His hand skims up and down my bare leg, and he seems lost in thought for a moment. Impossible to read.

"Finn?"

Both of his hands slip under my shoulder blades and he rocks against me, his underwear the only barrier between us. I arch to meet him.

"I don't understand how a bastard like me got another chance with you." His face sinks into my neck, and I run my fingers through his hair, my breath hitching each time he slides against me. "But I'm not letting you go this time."

His lips work their way to my mouth, and he deepens the kiss as his hips rock against me again. "You're mine. Just mine."

I grip his ass, locking him tight to me. "I want to feel you. All of you."

"Don't worry." He's going down my body again. "You'll get it all." He kisses my inner thighs, making me squirm. "When I'm ready to give it to you." His tongue flicks along my center. "Anticipation is half the fun."

While his tongue and fingers bring me to the edge over and over, I dig my hands into the covers on the bed and then slide them through his hair.

"Finn," I murmur. "Please."

He rises off the bed and removes his boxers. His body is still riddled with bandages, but his movements are sure and fluid. "Turn over."

I don't need to be asked twice. I flip onto my stomach and rise onto my knees. Finn kisses my back before sliding into me. His hand comes around and rubs my clit in a circular motion. Each thrust is slow and deliberate, so slow I try to increase the rhythm, but his grip on my hips slows me every time.

I moan. My body is so rigidly strung I'm not sure what I want more. Half of me never wants the pleasure to end, and the other half is begging, straining for the release.

"Faster," I pant. "Please."

He picks up the pace for a few thrusts but doesn't increase the pressure of his hand. I take one of my own and urge his fingers to rub against me.

"I want you to come so hard you forget where you are."

His lips brush my neck as he plunges even deeper. I gasp.

"And then I'll get you to do it again."

His fingertips circle me as he glides in and out faster and harder, and I have to put my hand back on the bed, pressing my face into the mattress to muffle my scream as my orgasm rocks through me.

With a few more thrusts, he follows me over the edge and collapses onto my back.

"I think I saw Ireland," I mutter.

He chuckles, and my heart warms. "Fuck Ireland." His voice is rough in my ear. "Next time, we're aiming for the stars."

~ * ~

I stuff the last few things in my purse, and I glance over at Finn who is still lying in bed, the covers snug around him. He's drinking the coffee I made him and watching me pack. We didn't get much sleep last night. But I saw stars. An abundance of stars.

"Intergalactic travel is hard on me." He raises his cup to his lips and smirks.

I laugh. "You think we discovered new planets last night?"

"You realize the obvious joke is something involving Uranus, right?" He winks at me.

Another laugh escapes me. "You'll stay here? You're not going to appear suddenly at my breakfast meeting."

"I'm staying here. I got plans for you when you get back." He twists to put his coffee cup on the nightstand. "But when we land in Switzerland, we need to discuss security for you. Most of the countries and cities you visit, I can't go without taking a massive risk. What happened yesterday isn't fucking happening again."

"I know. Jay will be with me. I'll be more careful. The meeting will be fine." I pick up the hotel notebook and consider putting it in my bag along with the pen.

"Yeah. Jay's stellar—as a secretary. Yesterday proved he's shit at keeping you safe. That's unacceptable."

"We can talk about it later." I gather my purse and check my phone. "I don't want them coming to the room, so I need to go."

"You're eating at the hotel restaurant, right? You're not leaving the hotel."

I sigh. "Yes. If I said no, what would you do?"

"Get dressed and tail you."

"I'll make sure we stay here."

"Jay will text me if you don't."

I roll my eyes. "And why would he do that?"

"Because after yesterday, he knows better than to leave me out of the loop." Finn's gaze pins me in place. "Valeriya is dead. Charles and Eric are organizing something behind your back. We were shot at a couple days ago. The CIA is on your ass. Somehow, you're mixed in with the PLA. If you give me a couple minutes, I can probably come up with ten other reasons you need to be fucking careful."

At the edge of the bed, I run my hand along his face. "I'll be careful. I promise." He circles my neck and pulls me into a kiss. His other arm swoops around my waist, and I can guess what he's going to do. If he gets me in the bed, I'll never leave.

Stepping back, I give him another quick kiss, moving out of the way before he can deepen it. The weight of his words tries to rest on my shoulders. But when I open the door, I'm so happy and light they can't settle. "I won't leave the hotel." When I close the door, I glimpse his face. He's frowning into his coffee. Something is still bothering him, but I haven't had the guts to ask. I have him. He loves me. I'm not rocking the boat. This is what happy feels like—been too long.

Jay meets me in the hall. "Your guest doing okay?" he asks as we walk.

"Same old." I give him a sideways glance. "I hear you're tattling on me now."

"You didn't see him yesterday when he found out you'd been taken, and I knew dick all. He was a man possessed. I honestly thought he would kill me before we got the CIA lead."

"That made him feel better?" I raise my eyebrows.

"The chances of the CIA killing you weren't high. Imprisoning you, maybe." He rubs his temple. "He spent a hundred grand trying to track you yesterday."

"He told me."

"You two sharing secrets?" He opens the door to the main lobby.

"Something like that."

"When we're done talking to Charles and Eric, we'll need to regroup."

I spot them across the lobby. "Finn overheard some things in the room."

"I wondered." Jay tips his head at my dad and Eric in acknowledgement while he scans the lobby. "I got more info late last night, too."

"Anything I need to know right now?"

He doesn't have time to answer because Eric comes striding over, annoyance vibrating off him.

"There's a thirty-minute wait for a table here." He glances at his watch. "Your father and I fly out in a few hours. We don't have time for a lineup." When he looks up, his eyes narrow. "You look tired."

I shrug. "Hours of interrogation will do that." The hours of orgasms didn't help with the tiredness. Intergalactic travel is so fucking amazing I'd never complain. A wisp of a smile rises at the memory.

Eric's eyes are slits, and he opens his mouth to speak when Jay says, "Place across the street seems decent."

"Done," I say. "We'll slip over there, have a quick chat over a coffee, and come back here."

Jay raises his eyebrows as he gets his phone out of his pocket. I cover his hands as he types something.

He scowls at me. "You weren't there. My head and my shoulders enjoy being attached to each other. Nobody likes a headless Jay."

Eric's gaze shifts between the two of us, and I drop it. Stopping him isn't worth alerting Eric or my father to who's upstairs and why my body is so deliciously sore.

My father strides toward us, agitated. He and Eric are far too similar sometimes. Why did I ever believe Eric could make me happy? "Did you decide, Carys? You were the holdout for staying in the hotel."

My sweet smile strains my facial muscles. "We'll go across the street. Not nearly as busy."

"Probably shitty food," my father grumbles.

"Remind me again why you and Eric are here?" I lead the way toward the hotel exit. Jay picks up his pace to leave ahead of me. I may not have seen Finn raging yesterday, but the evidence is written across Jay like a billboard.

"You're my daughter. You were missing. Where else would I be?"

Several places spring to mind without me trying hard, and none of them is a second-rate hotel in Ireland. There are few times I can remember my father putting his wants, his needs, *after* mine.

"And you?" I glance at Eric.

He scoffs and shakes his head. "We were engaged once. Those feelings don't just turn off."

"Well, I suppose that was the problem with our engagement. You couldn't turn off those feelings for anyone."

Beside me, Jay snorts and then covers it up with his fist and a cough. When we get to the pub across the street advertising an Irish breakfast, Jay enters first and the three of us stand outside the door for a minute.

"This is the new protocol?" My father puts his hands on his hips. "He sweeps the place before you ever enter? Seems to be an overreaction to a CIA meeting."

I sigh and purse my lips. Impossible to win. "How about me almost being shot? How about Valeriya being murdered? How about the PLA doing business with my company behind my back? Any of that seem worth extra precautions?"

Eric's hand settles on my hip, and I step away from him. Jay pops his head out the door and nods to me. We file in and find a booth in the rear.

Jay orders our food from the bar and then slides in beside me. "The PLA." He stares at my father and Eric. "My intel says one of you is behind at least a few of those deals."

My father shrugs. "I never had a problem working with people who could pay. The politics is none of my concern."

My temper simmers below the surface. "The last time you interfered, I told you to say out of the business or to be all in. You've completely fucked me. The CIA has a file which makes me appear solely responsible for those deals."

"You didn't let me finish." My father holds up his hand. "I stopped dealing with them when you told me to step away. However irrational and ill-informed your wishes might have been, I respected them."

I turn to Jay. Was my father being truthful?

"The last deal happened a week ago. And the products they bought came from our warehouse theft." He picks up his phone and finds the email before handing it to me.

I sigh and scan the information. "He's right. The product

numbers match."

Eric sips his coffee and remains silent. Finn said Eric had something to do with Valeriya's death, and Valeriya was coming to meet with the PLA.

"You met Valeriya a few times, didn't you, Eric?" I cock my head at him as the waitress delivers our food.

He clears his throat and takes another sip of his drink. "Possibly." He sets cup onto the table before picking up his knife and fork. "Not everyone is memorable."

He's a fucking liar. Not that I'm surprised. The smoothness of the lies as they tumble out—that's what astounds me. Was he always like this?

My father's phone rings, and he takes it out of his pocket before silencing it. When our gazes connect, he sighs. "Your mother. She's having a late-in-life crisis. I'm giving her space to deal with it."

I shovel a mouthful of egg into my mouth to keep my rant from spilling out. My father has never been supportive of emotional outbursts. Any time I wanted his attention, I had to make damn sure I was stoic, controlled, no hint of emotion. Dealing with my brother's illness and death were a million times worse because of my father's unspoken rule.

"Why's she upset?" I ask.

"The past. Always the past. The thing she doesn't understand is you can't go back. Once a choice is made, you might as well forget you had a choice. It's that simple."

I frown and take another forkful of food, chewing while I think. "Is this something you did or something she did causing the regret?"

"Something she did—but she's upset because she says I asked her to do it—no, demanded it. Which is ridiculous. I'd never do that. Her memory is faulty."

Whenever he becomes the blustering old man, he's covering a lie. A weird tell, but that's his. He goes too far with his denial.

"All these years she never talked about it—like it didn't happen," he says. "I don't understand what's gotten into her."

"Are you going to tell me why she's upset or just talk in half-truths?"

He glances up at me as though he's realized what he's saying. "I can't tell you. Her shame, not mine."

I scratch the nape of my neck and decide I'll never get to the bottom of their issues. My mother and I aren't close—not anymore. When I broke my engagement to Eric, a switch flipped in her. Every time I went to see her, she asked about him. When would I forgive him?

When would I take him back? He was, after all, such a *nice* man.

"When are you returning to Chicago? Regular work needs to resume," Eric says as he polishes off the last of his breakfast.

An image of Finn, surrounded by plush white covers pops into my head, and I have to suppress a smile. "Technically I'm still working right now. I came to identify Valeriya, my employee. Prior to that I was in Russia trying to track our stolen goods."

"And before that you were in Switzerland harboring a fugitive." Eric's gaze is stony when it meets mine.

The urge to tell him I've been harboring Finn all over the place is almost irresistible. "My personal life is mine."

"When it interferes with business—"

"My father," I gesture toward my dad, "can give me a hard time about mixing my personal life and my job. He's my father. He used to run and own everything. I'll take that. From you? Not one more word. If you can't remember your place in my life and in this company, you'll find yourself on your ass hunting for a job."

Eric raises his hands. "All right. All right. Settle down, Carys."

My father glances at his watch. "We need to catch our plane." He rises from his seat and tosses his napkin beside his plate. "You'll take care of the bill, Carys?"

"Of course," I say. "We'll be heading back to Switzerland later today. You can call me at the house if there is anything urgent. I'll be trying to sort out a few things while I'm there."

Such as what Finn will do for a job or how I'm going to get his money. He hates being too dependent on me.

My father gives a curt nod, but Eric's face is stormy as he stands. "You won't keep him there forever."

I tilt my head at him. "He's safe there. Whether he stays there forever is up to him and me."

His gaze searches mine for a moment. "He's a murdering fugitive. There's no forever with a guy like him."

"Not your concern who I spend forever with, Eric."

His eyes narrow and then his face clears, and he smirks. His fingertips trace the side of my face, and I stare him down, cool, defiant. He kisses my cheek. My father waits impatiently at the door. He tips his head toward the outside. With one last lingering look, Eric follows my father out.

"What was that about?" Jay drains the last of his coffee.

I sit back in my chair. "I don't know. Did he always treat me like that?"

"He did."

"Huh." Silence fills the space between us for a beat. "Finn knows we're here?"

"He does."

"I'm in trouble."

Jay's lips twist in amusement. "You're probably in for a tongue lashing."

A burst of laughter is out before I can catch it. I dig money out of my purse and drop it onto the table. I give him a sly smile. "I do enjoy the way his tongue lashes."

"I heard." He grins. "My room is right next to yours, and those walls aren't as thick as you'd think. Then my wife heard the two of you through the phone, and I got an actual tongue lashing on how I don't do enough for her anymore." He chuckles. "Might have to get pro-tips from Finn. Calm my wife the fuck down."

I shake my head and hold my hand over my eyes as I laugh. My cheeks are hot, but I am also impossibly, absurdly happy.

"It looks good on you." Jay opens the door and steps into the street ahead of me.

"What does?"

"Happiness."

Chapter Twenty-Five
Finn

We've been in Switzerland for a week with no problems. Things have been so good between me and Carys, but there's this weird heaviness in my chest. I've always been content. I'd never have labeled myself as happy, but I had the business, my brother, a shit-ton of income, and enough women to keep me from longing for the one I've got now.

She travels around the office getting things organized to talk to Sean about my money. She's sure we can secure it without having to go to Boston and without the FBI catching on. I am less convinced. Broke is better than Carys being in jail. I couldn't care less about what happens to Sean or anyone else from my old organization. That life is so far away.

Even though I'm worried, I can't very well live off her wealth. For the rest of our time together, I'd be a kept man, or I'd slide into something illegal just to have control. I hate her solution, but I don't have an avenue around it. Cash equals independence.

At the darkest corner of my mind, like a fucking ticking clock, is Eric's determination to get Carys. Whatever he's attempting behind her back, he's confident his plan will draw her closer to him and not farther away. Late at night when she sleeps, I wrack my brain trying to determine what he's got, what he's doing to make her want him.

"You won't be able to stay in Switzerland long-term with your head office in Chicago," I say as she settles behind her desk.

"I know." She doesn't meet my gaze. "I've been thinking of a solution. We'll have to figure out a way to make it work. I can fly here on weekends or work from here if there's nothing urgent there. Delegate more. Have virtual meetings."

I press my fingers into my forehead. "A lot of fucking work."

A slow smile spreads across her face. "You're over there glowering. Are you happy?"

Her amber eyes are shining with so much love it's impossible to break eye contact.

"Yeah. I am." With a deep breath, I run a hand down my cheek. "Makes me paranoid something will knock me a peg or two."

She comes around the desk to sit on my knee. "Well, there's still a lot going on. But there haven't been any more packages since we returned. No more thefts. At least some product from the original warehouse went to the PLA. We haven't been shot at, and no one has died in the last week."

I laugh. "You're making my point for me. Things are going too fucking well." My loose hold around her waist isn't enough, and I tug her closer. "We still don't have a clue what your father and Eric will drop in your lap in a few weeks."

She grimaces. "Whatever it is, we'll be fine. It can't be anything too serious or Jay would have caught wind of it. He hasn't seen his family in so long. I'm feeling like the worst employer ever."

My mouth quirks up. "He's still alive. You're not the worst employer."

She slaps my shoulder, and I haul her against me so her face finds the crook of my neck. "What time is Sean calling?" I murmur in her ear.

"Any minute. He needed a secure line that couldn't be traced."

"I have a minute or two."

She laughs. "That's not going to satisfy me." When she gets off my lap, I give her ass a little swat.

"Would have satisfied me. Temporarily." She holds my gaze as she goes to her seat. Our minds are in sync. "You're thinking about it, aren't you? Pulling up your skirt, bending over the desk, me coming up behind you, my hand—"

The shrill ringing of the phone on her desk makes Carys jump. I grin.

"Hold that." She picks up the receiver, breathless.

Bank numbers and routing codes go back and forth between them, with her clicking through various websites. She asked an IT guy at her company to set up the backdoor shit she's doing with Sean right now. Makes me fucking nervous. It's unnerving to care this much for someone else and to be unsure everything will work out, that she'll be safe, unharmed by the fallout I brought to her door.

When she gets off the phone, her gaze meets mine.

"It's done. Modest amounts in dozens of bank accounts, but you've got money again. We can go to the bank later today and decide which account you want to use as your primary."

"I'm surprised Sean was fine with handing over that much equity." I search her face. "He give you any resistance?"

"The legal side of the exchange. He's not keen to go to jail for aiding you." She winks at me. "I told him a broke Finn was an angry Finn with nothing to lose."

I smirk and glance away. That's not true anymore, but I can understand how her argument would be persuasive.

She kneels between my legs, and my chest aches at the sight of her. Shouldn't giving into these emotions have stabilized me or at least not made them worse? My desperation, to keep her safe, to keep this closeness forever, has peaked. Anyone who hurts her will suffer my wrath.

I smooth a piece of her hair behind her ear. "When does Ekaterina arrive?"

"Two hours." She undoes my jeans and gazes at me under her lashes. "I wonder how we can pass the time?"

I slide my hand up her leg and under her skirt to caress her ass. She's not wearing any panties. *God, I love her.* "You want to see the stars?"

Her smile is wicked as she frees me from my jeans. "I love mapping the constellations."

Cupping her ass with both hands, I lift her onto her desk. "Well, who am I to deny you?"

Her laugh gets swallowed up when my lips descend on hers.

~ * ~

There are still rooms in the chalet I didn't realize existed. We're in the boardroom above the garage. I thought the door into here was a closet. Architecture is not my forte. Lena is showing Ekaterina through when she arrives. While we wait, I make a mental note to revisit this space. The wooden table stretches across most of the room with rolling chairs at regular intervals. Table. Chairs. Projector wall. I want every nook, crevice, surface in this house to remind her of me, of us, of how good being with me is. No matter what Eric's got planned, she won't be able to consider anyone or anything other than me. She's mine, and I have no problem playing dirty to keep her.

"Finn." Carys grabs paper off the printer. "Did you hear me?"

Her voice brings me out of my head, and I raise my eyebrows at her in silent question.

She frowns and finds an imaginary hair to stuff into the complicated braid. When it's the two of us, she wears her hair loose around her shoulders. The braids and buns and whatever else she designs seem to be part of her defense against the rest of the world. Every day I discover something I didn't notice the first time.

With a sigh, she sinks into a chair a few seats away from me.

"At the risk of being the girliest-girl, what were you thinking about? I haven't asked any of the other times because I'm not sure I want to know. But maybe I should know. Whatever it is, it's bothering you."

"It's nothing."

She lets the lie sit between us for a beat, and I can't meet her gaze. "A week ago, I said I wanted a partner I could trust, and then I said you were always honest with me, even when I didn't want to hear it. That's the guy I love. That one." She frowns. "I love this guy too." She swirls her finger at me in a circular motion. "Who is lost in his own thoughts. But I prefer the other guy. The honest one." She gives me a pointed look.

I wince. Except she isn't the person who doesn't want to hear it, it's me. My jaw tightens, and I glance toward the door. "Just something I overheard Eric say."

Carys rises and steps around the chairs between us to roll my seat back and perch on my lap. "Tell me." Her fingers stroke my furrowed brow.

"He seems to believe that whatever he and your dad have cooked up, it'll bring you and him closer together." I clear my throat. "You'll pick him."

She grins and wraps her arms around my neck. "Never in a million trillion years. There is nothing he could say or do to make me leave you and go to him."

"He seemed very confident."

Her lips quirk up in derision. "That's his thing—he's confident even when he's wrong. One of his worst qualities." Carys's gaze focuses above my head. "He *is* a win-at-all-cost sort of person, though." Her expression morphs into one of determination. "I wouldn't be with him even if he threatened to kill me."

I tighten my arms around her at the suggestion. "He'd never get a chance. He'd be dead as soon as the idea entered his head."

There's a sharp knock on the door. She tries to stand, but I increase my grip on her. She brushes her lips against mine, and her hand rests on my chest over my heart. She skims my earlobe with her teeth, and she whispers, "I'm yours. Just yours. Always."

I move my hands from her waist to frame her face. There's another knock on the door, but I pull her into a kiss anyway. When whoever knocks again, I let her go with a sigh, trailing along whatever part of her body I can connect with before she gets too far away. She glances at me over her shoulder. *So fucking sexy.* I can't wait for this meeting to be over. A tug on the thighs of my jeans shifts the tightness enough to make it bearable.

Carys opens the boardroom door, and instead of Lena, she's met with Jay and Ekaterina. I ignore the new woman and stare at her bodyguard. He has one fucking job—guard the front door. What's he doing in here?

He tips his chin at me. The urge to throttle him causes my hands to clench.

"I hired more security. Got two guys on the door." He reads my mind.

I'd ask if they are competent, but Jay's idea of apt security and mine aren't even close. I grunt and rise to offer my hand to Ekaterina. Her dark hand slips into mine. She scans me with her midnight eyes. She's little and round, but she carries an air of confidence and authority.

"Finn Donaghey?" she asks.

"The one and only." I release our handshake and sink into my seat. "You heard of me?"

"CIA is offering a tidy sum for information on your whereabouts."

"CIA can go fuck themselves. I'm not going to jail." Is she threatening me or warning me? "And I'll kill anyone who tries to get me there—reward or not."

Ekaterina laughs and goes to the other side of the table, away from me and closer to Carys. "I wasn't suggesting I'd be turning you in."

She has almost no trace of an accent. If it wasn't for her name, I might mistake her for American. Jay leaves a seat between us and slides into another closer to Carys who sits at the head of the table with her various charts and graphs printed.

"Thanks for coming here." Carys's smile is strained.

"I'm hoping you can give me insight into what the hell happened with Valeriya," Ekaterina says. "I go to Moscow for a meeting, and when I return she's flown to Ireland and gotten herself killed."

"We're trying to put those pieces together."

"She wasn't always the most reliable employee, but she didn't deserve that end."

"She wasn't reliable?" Carys frowns.

"Last four or five months, she was full of herself. Seemed to think she could do what she wanted. Followed her schedule, not mine."

"Why didn't you mention something to me?"

"Eric was around at least once a month to check on things at the warehouse and to speak to Valeriya about her attitude. I thought you arranged that. I thought you knew."

Carys leans back in her seat, her frown deepening. "Once a month?"

"Like clockwork." Ekaterina taps her nails on the table. "He said you were aware of the problems with Valeriya, and you'd asked him to step in."

"I wouldn't have undermined you like that. Not without talking to you first." Carys checks her papers and then glances at Jay. "Did you realize Eric was going to Russia so much?"

He shakes his head. "I pulled the expense reports and phone records for those five or six people we thought might be in touch with Valeriya. Eric was one of them. Nothing logged."

Carys appears puzzled for a moment. Does she realize Eric must have been paying his own flights, hotels, and meals while he took those trips? Whatever he was doing with Valeriya, he wasn't reigning her in.

"Until four or five months ago, Valeriya wasn't a problem?" I lean my elbows on the table, tired of bearing silent witness.

Ekaterina cocks her head while she contemplates the question. "Maybe the last year or so she hasn't been quite right—distracted, forgetful. But the last four or five months she was unbearable."

"And Eric?" I ask. "When did he start his visits?"

She takes her phone out of her purse and scrolls through it. "About six months ago. I had returned from a meeting in Moscow and found him at the warehouse with Valeriya. It was the first time I'd seen him in years."

She and Carys exchange a glance loaded with meaning.

"And the last time you saw him before that was…?" I relax into my chair and cross my arms. Carys might give me the backstory later if I ask, but I like to have the puzzle pieces.

"She flew to Chicago three months before I was supposed to get married, to tell me Eric paid for his mistress to have an abortion." Carys stares at the papers in front of her. Her voice is brisk and businesslike, but Jay gives me the side-eye. I've stepped in shit. "What was that? Maybe five years ago?" She looks to Ekaterina for confirmation.

As if she doesn't remember.

"Sounds about right." Ekaterina flips her phone face down on the table. "Anyway, you two remained close despite his obvious flaws. Frankly I had a hard time believing you didn't fire him, even if his actions had nothing to do with work."

Carys shrugs. She hated disappointing her dad. Much easier if she'd get over seeking his approval. Fire Eric. Let me kill him. I'm easy as long as he's gone. It's not as though her father has her best interests at heart.

"So," Ekaterina continues, "I didn't question his involvement in my branch. Apologies. I should have talked to you. I know better than anyone he's a master at deception."

Her final comment makes me wonder what else she's discovered. Is it only his cheating? Or is there more? One glance at Carys fixing an invisible flaw in her braid tells me not to push it. At least not here.

"Our information shows Valeriya was flying to Ireland to meet with the PLA. We also think she or someone associated with her might have been moving the product from the warehouse theft," Jay says as Carys passes papers to Ekaterina.

"Well, we put her in charge of finding the missing inventory. Makes it damn easy to cover it up if you're selling it, too." She scans the information in Carys's crafted charts. "Good thing European sales are strong overall or this theft would have completely fucked us."

"Still might." Carys's smile is tight. "Our fingerprints are all over those weapons now being used by an organization hoping to usurp their government."

"At least you don't have to worry about the FBI dickhead who was sniffing around trying to extort more money." Ekaterina mutters while she shuffles through the papers.

Carys, Jay, and I grow still, and the room hums with tension.

Ekaterina glances between us.

"What am I missing?" She focuses on Carys. "You warned me about him. He came nosing around while you were doing your bedside vigil." She tips her head at me. "I took care of it."

Carys tugs on her earring and sighs. I lean across the desk, on the cusp of losing my shit. Jay slides a piece of paper in my direction, and I glare at him. On the paper are the words *Calm the fuck down* in a hasty scrawl. Did he write that now or before he even came in the room?

My jaw clenches, but I focus on the message.

"The other half of his money never made it to him," Carys says. "His grievance was legitimate." She rolls her shoulders. "And you almost got me killed since I was there the morning you *took care of it*."

Ekaterina closes her eyes and presses her fingertips into her forehead. "The day before, I tried to call you on your mobile, but it was turned off. Then when I called Lilly in Chicago, she said you were on vacation and not taking any work-related calls." She sighs. "She said you were in Switzerland. You like initiative. I used mine. You warned me he might try to fuck you over. I thought I was helping."

Of their own volition, my hands flex into fists, and I force them to flatten on the table on top of Jay's note.

"If you ever need to talk to Carys, you can call me. I can always get in touch with her." Jay breaks the tension.

"Unless you fucking lose her in Ireland for hours on end." I pitch the words for his ears only. His Adam's apple bobs as he swallows. Gritting my teeth, I rise from my seat and ball up his note. "I've heard enough." I focus on Carys. "Come find me when you're done."

She turns to me with surprise and a hint of confusion. "Finn?"

I run my gaze over our guest one last time. "I'll double-check security at the front."

She scans my face before giving me a curt nod and then turns to Ekaterina. "I have a few more questions on a couple other accounts."

I close the door behind me. We've got what we need. Eric and Valeriya were fucking, and they're both mixed up in this PLA mess. The mystery of who shot Ricardo and whether the incident was a direct threat to Carys is also solved.

The biggest question is the same one I started the day with, and it'll be the one nagging me every day until something materializes. What is Eric planning?

Chapter Twenty-Six
Carys

Ekaterina answers my last few questions with ease and then says, "That was Finn Donaghey."

"It was." I gather my papers together into a neat pile.

"Rare for me to find a man intimidating."

I glance up and a smile plays on my lips. "Was he a little intense?"

"A little? Were we in the same room? The guy is all coiled rage and X-ray vision." She drops her phone into her purse and rises from her seat. "Are you—are you *safe* with him?"

Before I can answer, Jay chuckles on the other side of the large wooden table. "You were the only person in this room who wasn't safe today." He frowns as he picks up his pen. "And maybe me." With a shrug, he says, "Point is, he's not a threat to her."

"Why would he leave so abruptly?" Her expression is thoughtful. "He gave me that appraising once-over before he left, which meant something."

"Probably wondering how easy it would be to remove your head." Jay's voice is matter of fact, and if it wasn't for the horror on her face, I'd laugh.

"We do business differently," I assure her.

"Well, if you ever do business like him, I'm quitting."

Jay grins while he waves her out the door of the boardroom. "You know what Finn told me? Dying or going to jail were the only ways people got out of his organization in Boston. That's not Carys's policy." He takes a breath. "At least not yet."

Ekaterina walks along the hall beside him, their voices floating back to the boardroom. His words shouldn't be funny. Her face when Jay mentioned removing her heard was priceless, and her expression plays in my mind while I shred papers. When I'm sure I've hidden the paper trail, I head for the kitchen.

The sharp click of Lena's knife is audible before I reach her. As soon as I enter the wide-open space, I glimpse Finn wedged deep into a couch watching football.

Normally I'd chat with Lena to confirm dinner plans, but he exited the meeting so abruptly I want to check in with him first.

"You okay?" I sink into the spot beside him.

He grunts and doesn't look at me. "Just trying to figure out what we're missing. There's a clear timeline with Valeriya and Eric. It appears as though it's linked to the warehouse and the PLA. But it might not be. Then there's your father's involvement, which doesn't seem connected. But I heard them talking in the hotel, so I realize it is." He rubs his forehead. "I fucking hate sitting around waiting for shit to happen. I make things happen. People don't come at me—I hit them first."

"That's why you left the meeting?"

He chuckles, but the sound is without humor. "No. I excused myself because I wanted to drag Ekaterina behind the house and show her what her kind of initiative gets. Six fucking feet under."

Silence sits between us. My heart pounds as I picture him hauling her out of the meeting. His admission is appealing and horrifying.

Something isn't right with me. To love a man capable of that, who would enjoy that, seems wrong. It *is* wrong. But nothing about being with him is wrong to me. Not even a bit.

"We had a miscommunication." I rub his leg, and he links his fingers with mine.

"Almost got you killed." He squeezes my hand.

"But I'm still alive. And her intentions were good."

He turns to face me for the first time since I sat. His knuckles skim my cheek. "What she said means Eric and Valeriya were probably fucking."

"That crossed my mind."

"She called the Chicago office before leaving for Ireland. He admitted to your father he knew what happened to her."

"You don't have to dance around it. You think he had her killed."

Finn is silent for a moment, lost in thought. "Was she going to the PLA for protection? To blow the whistle on something Eric was doing? Does the PLA meeting have anything to do with this at all?"

I lean my head against his shoulder. "What do you think?"

"I don't know. But I will. I have three weeks to understand these connections before Eric makes his move."

~ * ~

The last two weeks have passed without incident. During the

day, I hole up in my office attempting to stay on top of everything at work. Sometimes I worry I neglected my company for months instead of a couple weeks. Maybe I did. God knows from the minute I saw him in Boston, half my brain zeroed in on him. I never quite got my mind back. Now I don't want to return to whoever I'd been before.

While I work, Finn and Jay track any lead they can find on Eric or my father. Finn is dogged, possessed, determined to find the truth before the clock ticks to zero. On the phone, on the internet, conferencing with people, calling in favors, and still nothing has turned up that satisfies him. He's even offered to fly to Chicago to shoot Eric and bury his body in my father's backyard. He was mostly kidding.

I laughed and told him I'd be too sad if he was arrested by the FBI to be happy about Eric's demise.

I should care more. Whatever they're planning should bother me the same way it does him. But I can't imagine he could ever say or do something great enough to sway me. Spending my days working in my office and my nights in Finn's arms, striving for the stars, is a new bliss.

Happiness is an addiction. Leaving him will be hard when I have to go back to Chicago for a while, but I'm not worried. We're solid—I've never been so sure of anything in my life as I am with him, with us.

In the kitchen, Lena peers at a security monitor on the wall. Finn has had cameras installed at the end of the long laneway, so we have lots of warning regarding visitors.

I stab at my salad and observe her staring at the screen.

"You recognize the car?" she asks.

I squint and shrug. "Generic. Rental? Or a limousine service?"

"You'd better call Finn." She waves a hand at the monitor as she goes back to prepping dinner.

"I'll text Jay." I pick up my phone from the island. Lena shoots me a disapproving look. "What? He's the head of my security, not Finn."

Lena scoffs. "I don't understand why you take such a perverse pleasure in pissing him off."

I take a bite of my salad while I text Jay with the other hand. There's a line with him I can tiptoe over. Finn on the cusp of real anger is my favorite. Texting Jay right now instead of alerting him will mean Finn will find me later, and he'll be angry with me. But not *too* angry. The kind of anger fueled by his love for me, his need to protect me.

Those needs lead to my needs being met in interesting ways. Me bent over a desk, pressed up against a wall, flat on my back with him murmuring how much he fucking loves me in my ear. *Delicious.*

So...I text Jay and give Lena an amused smile.

No time passes before Jay comes into the kitchen, his phone in his hand. "You got a beat on who is in the car?"

"Tinted windows." I put my plate in the dishwasher.

"Finn's on his way." His expression is all-knowing. "He's pissed you didn't text him."

I suppress my smile.

"One of these times this whole rile-him-up-and-have-him-work-out-his-anger-in-other-ways won't go the way you expect," he warns.

"Finn would never hurt me."

"Not you I'm worried about." He peers at the monitor.

My back is turned to the monitors, contemplating Jay's words, when he lets out a low whistle. "Carys, Mrs. Van de Berg has finally stepped foot in Switzerland."

"What?" I gasp.

In the years we've owned this place, my mother has never ventured here. She's aware of Lena, and my father's mistresses around the world, so she picks her vacations strategically. She's admitted none of her suspicions out loud. As a key member of the business, I have the locations of his long-term affairs memorized, and my mother has never gone to any of those houses.

Lena unties her apron, bundles it up, and shoves it into a drawer. "I'm going to my room."

I nod but can't tear myself from the screen. The woman is my mother, but her appearance is disorienting. Why would she come here?

A hand skims my spine and lips nibble at my earlobe. A shudder of desire rocks through me, and I press myself against him. He draws me tight to his body so I'm aware of every wonderful inch.

"You should have texted me," he growls into my ear.

"It's my mother," I whisper as the woman scans the house and fixes her blouse. I inherited her hourglass figure, light brown eyes, and blondish colored hair. When I was younger, people used to call us twins. Back then, the comparison felt like a compliment.

"Your mother?" Finn's tone goes from angry to surprised. "Opal is here?" He peers around me to take in the screen. "Well, I'll be damned. This can't be fucking good."

Jay's walkie-talkie blares out. "I've got a Mrs. Opal Van de Berg at the door requesting to meet with her daughter. Can you confirm?" The security guard's voice is professional, but he must wonder why my mother didn't make the list of safe contacts to enter the house.

Jay yanks his walkie-talkie out of his belt. "Roger that. Show her in." His gaze rotates between me and Finn. "I guess we'll see why Mommy dearest decided to come for a visit."

Has something happened to my father? I don't dare speak the words out loud. The thought of him dead or injured should be horrifying, but it's not.

Chapter Twenty-Seven
Finn

The tension between Carys and Opal is unmistakable. They're circling each other, current events, upcoming commitments, neither of them saying what they're thinking. Nothing has happened to Charles—it was the first question Carys asked—which is unfortunate.

With him gone, I could eliminate Eric or have someone do it. She would forgive me. Having her father wrapped up in whatever bullshit scheme they've cooked up makes it too complicated to get rid of one without the other. Especially since I can't yet uncover what they're planning.

I'm on the cusp of telling her to fire Eric just to see if that sets something in motion.

With our sleuthing, there are no hints of secret deals. No more sinister connections Carys doesn't already know. No paper trails. Unregistered or foreign bank accounts are noted somewhere. We haven't even come across more evidence of PLA involvement with Eric or her dad. What the fuck are they planning?

Opal's here perched on Carys's couch like a bird poised to take flight. Maybe I should ask her. Too fucking skittish for my liking.

"Well..." Her mother sips the cup of tea Jay made. "I'm not sure if your father mentioned we're having problems."

Carys narrows her eyes and brings her cup to her lips before glancing at Jay. "It may have come up."

Opal sighs, and her hand shakes as she sets her teacup on the coffee table in front of us. I've got my arm slung around Carys's seat. Her mother has barely acknowledged me since she arrived. She skims over me like I'm not here. That's fine. I'm not going anywhere. She hasn't asked about Lena, but I suspect she'll stay hidden, and we'll pretend she doesn't exist.

"Well—I—I wasn't going to tell you." Opal twists a lock of her blonde hair around her finger before tossing it behind her. "I've tried to ignore her. That strategy has worked for the last forty-seven years, so I thought the complication would blow over."

Carys lets out an exasperated sigh. "Who are you talking about? In the forty-seven years you and Dad have been married, has anything ever blown over?"

Her mother gives an unsteady laugh. "Quite a lot. If I ignore whatever is happening long enough and hard enough, everything is fine. It's always just fine."

Sounds unhinged to me. Or heavily medicated.

"What or I guess *who* did Dad do all those years ago? According to him, this problem is your fault." Carys slides her hand along my leg.

Whenever I was the go-between for Lorcan and my father, I never minded. I liked the power of knowing the minds on each side. Much easier to fuck with people when you're in their head. But Carys hates the tug-of-war. Has always hated that role with her parents. Once her younger brother died, her position only got worse.

Opal's teacup wobbles as she lifts it up off the table. With a huff, she pushes the cup onto the surface and fishes around in her purse. Her fingers latch onto something like a lifeline, relief descending. She pops the top on the pill bottle and takes two.

Medicated it is. Interesting. Whatever she's working up the guts to tell her daughter must be a doozy.

Opal presses the heel of her hand to her forehead, and there's a hint of panic on Carys's face. The medication must be a surprise. I squeeze her shoulder. Our eyes lock, and then I kiss the top of her head.

"What's going on, Opal? We can't help you if we don't know what's happening," I say.

"Help me?" She laughs. "Finn Donaghey is going to help me?" Another unsteady laugh tumbles out. "Though, I am strangely happy you're here." She meets my gaze. "I always wondered if you'd circle back. My daughter was so smitten with you. Didn't matter what you said or did."

"I'm sure you didn't come here to talk about him," Jay reasons from the armchair, cutting her off before she says something stupid to piss me off.

"No, no." She stares at Carys, and tears pool in her eyes. She sniffs and hesitates for another moment. "You have to understand this was forty-seven years ago. I didn't have the same options women have now. I—I was trapped, and your father saved me." She rests her face in her hands, and when she glances up, her mascara has smeared. "Or I thought he was saving me."

"Mom, what are you talking about?"

Opal sniffs and takes the tissue Jay passes her. "I was married before. I was married when I met your father. I married too young. He was an abusive man. He used to hit me all the time. I was hospitalized several times. But he was powerful, influential, unstoppable. No one messed with him."

"Oh," Carys breathes out the word and straightens on the couch. "I can't believe this has never come up."

"Your father saw me at a cocktail party with my husband. The attraction was instant. He wanted me. I wanted a way out. Charles had enough money and influence to help me escape. At first, he was so charming." Her face is full of naked pleading. "You know what he can be like. When the light in his eyes is on you, it doesn't feel like it could stray." She bunches up the tissue in her hand. "Then, later, I thought," her voice cracks, and she focuses on her lap before she continues, "well, at least he doesn't hit me." One shoulder raises in resignation.

"That's awful," Carys says while I make slow circles with my thumb on her arm.

Opal takes a shaky breath. "That's not the worst part."

Carys frowns. My family is pretty fucked up, so while this is interesting, it's not earthshattering. Not the commentary either of them wants to hear right now. Sometimes I can keep my inner asshole under control.

"I had a three-year-old daughter." Opal's voice hitches on the last word, and she almost doesn't get it out. "And I left her behind."

"Oh, Mom." Carys scurries away from me to hug her mother. "Your husband wouldn't let you take her or see her? You must have been devastated."

I sigh as she comforts Opal. She has such a good heart. If she considered the situation, she'd come to the conclusion I'm making. Her mother wouldn't be angry at Charles if her ex-husband kept the child from her. Would she feel guilty? Maybe. This guilty? Nope.

"I always wondered if that was why Lucas, your brother, died." She chokes on the words. "I abandoned one child—so God takes another to show me what I should have felt the first time." She frames Carys's face. "Nothing can happen to you. I can't lose you too."

"But if he wouldn't let you take her…"

Opal's expression is tortured. "I wish I could lie to you," she whispers. "But there's too much at stake."

There's a loaded silence, and I want Carys to put this together. Opal doesn't want to admit the truth. She won't get there without a nudge in the right direction. "It wasn't her ex-husband who stopped her from taking her daughter," I say. "It was Charles."

Carys turns to me and shakes her head. "Dad wouldn't do that.

He wouldn't. Why would he do that?"

Her mother's defeated gaze meets mine over her daughter. Even now, she wants to believe the best of her father. Or at least, can't come to terms with the worst.

My old man was a son of a bitch who killed his first wife to take a second. But he didn't abandon me. Lorcan's mother tried her hardest to parent me, but my father kept reminding her I was his son, not hers.

Whenever she tried to step in, coddle me, she was forced out. But she never stopped trying. Not even on her deathbed when she told me to leave the past buried.

Her death ruined me as much as my mother's. Looking back, I loved her, and she loved me. The problem was I didn't know what to do with those feelings once I had the truth. She asked my father to put her, his mistress, first, and he did. I raged against her love, seeking revenge and a warped justice. Fat fucking lot of good that reaction has done me.

"He did," Opal whispers. "I agreed. He wanted a fresh start. A clean slate." She takes a deep, wavering breath. "I wanted to be safe for the first time in years."

I've never been sure I wanted kids—maybe once, for a moment, the notion crossed my mind with Carys. She was so focused on those things, it was hard not to consider the future. But I understand the deep gash a mother leaves behind once she's gone. A gaping, jagged hole that never heals.

My life, so full of danger, never felt secure for a kid, even if I found someone who wanted to have them. While I might be sad Carys didn't get what she wanted, I'm not sad we'll be childless.

"Why are you telling her this now?" I lean forward.

She needs to be back on my lap so I can ease her hurt. This level of deception is like waking up from a vivid dream. Reality is altered, and it's hard to figure out what to believe, who to trust. The truth is fragile. I should know—that's how I felt when I found out my mother's death hadn't been an accident.

"My daughter—" Opal sniffs and takes another tissue from Jay's outstretched hand. "Pearl. She thought I was dead, until recently."

"So." Jay turns his attention from his phone, a pensive expression on his face. I hope he's already tracking this information. "She's not happy about being abandoned?"

Opal's eyes brim with tears. "It wasn't just his wife my ex-husband enjoyed beating."

Carys covers her mouth. "That's awful. I-I can't—I don't know what to say," she murmurs.

"She's furious I left her behind. Rightfully angry. I never thought he'd hurt her. I was selfish and stupid to agree to leave. But I was drowning in misery. I didn't think I could save us both." Opal stands and paces on unsteady legs across the front of the couches. "This last time she came to see me, she said the only way she could think to make things right was to remind me of what it's like to be afraid. She spent most of her life afraid."

Tears stream down Carys's face, and Opal is holding it together by a shoestring. They're focused on the emotion of Carys's sister, and I'm figuring out the angle.

"She needs to know your deepest fear," I say. "Then she has to have the time and money to go after it."

Opal stops pacing and examines me. "Which is why I'm glad you're here." She clenches her hands. "My ex-husband died two, almost three, years ago. Pearl found documents, and she realized I might still be alive. My ex was wealthy. Very wealthy. Pearl has never worked a day in her life."

"Sound cushy," I say. "Where do I sign up for that?"

"Finn." Carys reminds me of my personal vow not to be a dick during this conversation.

"She's out for blood?" I ask. Jay better be over there on his phone searching for information, a paper trail, a way to cut off the head before it becomes a hydra.

"I don't know," Opal says. "It might not be a real threat. But I couldn't let it go. I had to come tell Carys." She hesitates. "And you."

"We'll get to the bottom of it," Jay assures her.

Adding this on top of the stress with Eric and Charles isn't helpful, but I'd rather see what's coming than be surprised. "As long as there is breath in my body, I'll do everything to keep her safe."

Opal's brown eyes soften. "Somehow, I don't doubt that."

"Are you staying tonight?" Carys asks when she acknowledges her mother again.

With a shake of her head, Opal crosses to the couch and gathers up her purse. "I don't want to stay in case Pearl has people tailing me. I'm flying back tonight."

Carys rises, and I mirror her.

Silence sits between us for a moment as Opal searches her daughter's face. "I know how hard you tried to have a baby of your own, and abandoning a child must seem crass and unfeeling to you." She presses her purse to her shoulder. "It wasn't a choice."

"But it was," Carys whispers. "I could never abandon a child."

My hand is on the small of her back, and she sinks into the contact, turning to hug me around the middle.

"I'll show you out, Mrs. Van de Berg," Jay says from beside us.

She wipes away a few more tears that trickle down her face and follows him toward the door.

Chapter Twenty-Eight
Carys

When I slip into bed, Finn tugs me close but for the first time since we've been together, he doesn't run his hands along me in ways to make me think of sex. Instead, he wedges me in so tight my face is practically squished against his bare chest, and he smooths my hair before kissing the top of my head. Every bandage is gone, and sometimes I lie in bed tracing his scars, asking for their stories as my heart races at the danger and aches at the close calls. A world without him isn't a world at all.

"You okay?" he says. "You've been too fucking quiet since your mom left."

"I don't know," I whisper. Turning toward him, I'm comforted by the steady beat of his heart in my ear. "Anytime I hear someone gave up the chance to be a mom, it makes my heart hurt. I just—I would have done anything to have a baby, to be a mom."

He's silent as his hand strokes my back. "Sounds as though your sister had it rough after your mother left."

"Yeah. I can't process it. Being beaten by your father?" His arms tighten around me. "My mom has her faults, and so does my dad but they've been there for me. Even if I didn't always like what they did or what they said. They'd never set out to *hurt* me. And my mom is…well, she's my mom. I love her despite everything."

"Having a mom is important." His voice is gruff in my ear.

My heart skips a beat at the raw emotion in such a simple sentence. Through the sliver of light peeking through the curtains, I glimpse his face. "God, I'm so stupid. I'm sorry."

He chuckles and tugs me into a kiss. "It's all right. It was a long time ago." He runs his hand up my spine and fits me snug against him again. "Jay and I will find out more on Pearl tomorrow." His lips trail along my neck. "Is it wrong that when your mom said your sister's name, I was glad she lost her love of precious jewels when she named you? Not that I wouldn't have loved you if you were called Ruby or Amethyst."

I chuckle. "But? I sense a but."

"Not sure any of them would have the same ring to them."

"And that's important?" I kiss his chest, the heaviness from the day fading away.

"When you've yelled it out as you come as much as I have over the years, it's gotta feel right."

"Over the years?" I laugh. "Just how many Carys's do you know?"

"Nah." He smirks. "That's not it. Carys is the name of my right hand." He holds it up and wiggles it.

I giggle, and his lips find mine in the dark. "Sounds confusing," I murmur.

"Not as much as you'd think." He rolls me onto my back and braces one leg between mine as he peers down at me. For a moment, he searches my face, any trace of laughter gone. "Because I always knew it was you I was thinking about."

My heart dips to my toes. I'm not sure I'll ever get used to being this close, this connected to him. Before, I didn't believe these emotions existed with Finn—with anyone. I told myself it was impossible. Maybe I imagined them. Wanted something that wasn't there.

But he loves me, and I love him. And everything is perfect.

~ * ~

The next morning I've missed four calls from Eric and a text asking me to contact him right away. The urgency is confusing and takes a moment to sink in after just waking. I roll over to Finn, but he's gone.

Getting up, I throw on a robe to search for him. In the kitchen, he and Jay are speaking in low voices at the island, unaware of me outside the doorway eavesdropping.

"You going to tell Carys?" Jay asks.

"After yesterday? I don't know. That guy is fucking unbelievable."

"Who is?" I enter the open room as though I just arrived.

They turn to me in surprise. Finn's face flares with annoyance, probably that I snuck up on them. But it passes, and I'm not sure I like the emotion in its place any better. *Pity.*

Leaning against the island, he runs a hand along his cheek. "You don't want to fucking hear this."

"Try me." I bypass them and flip the switch on the coffee maker.

Jay and Finn exchange uneasy glances.

"Jay got a call from Demid this morning. Valeriya's body was released and is back to Russia." He splays his hands on the island and leans into them, focused on me across the granite expanse.

"That's great." The hiss of the water heating momentarily distracts me. "Who is fucking unbelievable? Surely not Demid."

Finn searches my face. Deciding something, he circles around the island and comes to where I'm standing, pressing his side into the counter and crossing his arms. He's close enough his body heat radiates toward me. "Valeriya was pregnant."

I grip my phone in my hand. Those calls from Eric. "Of course she was. Of course." Waves of shock and anger course through me. "Eric," I say in a monotone voice. "He was the father?" Frustrations spills out of me.

All these women. All these babies. None of them mine.

"Demid asked me if I knew who the father might be. I told him what I thought."

"You put a target on him."

"Maybe. Probably." Finn tries to catch my gaze. "I was going to ask you to fire him, even if it might drive a wedge between you and your father. Keeping him around is too risky."

"He'll be dead now—problem solved." The words slip out of my mouth as though I could not care less. Inside I'm morphing from angry to numb. I waggle my phone at Finn. "He's texted me once. Called me a bunch of times. An emergency, apparently."

"Have you listened to the messages?"

I shake my head. "I came to find you."

He accepts my phone and hits the voicemail icon. With the device to his ear, he paces into the living room as he listens to them.

The coffee drips into the pot beside me, and Jay catches my gaze. "You okay?" he asks.

Crossing my arms, I drop my gaze to the floor. A sigh escapes me, and I run my toe along the tiles in a back-and-forth motion. "Was Eric always a shit?"

When I glance up, a ghost of a smile flits across Jay's face. "Yes."

"Why didn't I see it? I mean, I saw it, but not like this."

His dark eyes are filled with sympathy. "You want me to play armchair psychologist?"

"Why not? I'm already paying you." I run my hands through my hair and then re-cross my arms. "You understand me better than most people. You've been working for me since you were twenty. What's that? Fifteen years now?"

Jay seems to weigh something; perhaps how truthful he wants to be. "Honestly, I always kinda figured your taste in men was related to your dad. You watched him treat your mom like shit for years. You expect them to be assholes." He tips his head toward Finn. "He's the biggest dick to pretty much everyone but you."

My gaze strays to Finn as he grabs a pen and paper from the desk in the living room and scribbles something down. "He's my big dick." A smile threatens.

"Hey now." Jay holds up his hands, but he's grinning. "Some things I don't need to be told." His smile fades as he stares across the island toward Finn. "He's an interesting guy—that one. But if you end up with him, if you stay with him, I'd never worry he wouldn't treat you well. He sees your value. He knows your worth. Even when you don't."

Tears prick at my eyes, and I have to look away from the kindness etched in his face.

Finn strides into the kitchen with the pad of paper clutched in one hand, my cell phone in the other. "Shit's hitting the fan. Eric's in Russia." His pale blue gaze lands on me.

"Demid?" I ask.

"No." He frowns. "Something else. He wants you to come, and he said you were welcome to bring me. Said he has information regarding the warehouse theft."

Jay laughs. "God, Eric is some kinda idiot."

Finn raises his eyebrows and uncertainty clouds his expression. "Jay, get us more security to take with us. We don't have a clue what we'll find. Looks as though we're headed to Russia."

"*Privet*, Russia." I raise my cup and sip from my scalding coffee.

Chapter Twenty-Nine
Finn

While Carys and I pack in our bedroom, I debate whether to let her come to Russia. There's so much we don't understand. I stuff more clothes into my duffle bag and glance at her as she wanders into the en suite to get her makeup.

Curiosity is a powerful thing, and I'm definitely curious about what Eric has been doing. He didn't sound scared in his voicemail messages, or even full of his usual asshole bravado. No, he was *excited*. Why? I stop packing and lean against the dresser while Carys continues to put things into her suitcase.

"Spit it out." She doesn't break her rhythm of sorting and discarding. "You're over there brooding about something."

"Don't come to Russia."

She laughs. "I'm going to Russia. He called me, not you, and he said you could come along for the show." She throws skincare products into her bag with a huff. "I don't care anymore about what he's doing. You're right. I'll fire him. I don't know why I haven't done it yet."

She knows why. I understand why.

"My father has disappointed me a lot in my life," she says. "So what if I disappoint him too?"

Except I realize she doesn't mean that. There are things people don't outgrow. "If he cares more for Eric than he does for you—"

She whirls on me. "Don't finish that. You think I can't get there on my own? I don't need you rubbing it in my face."

Her anger makes my frustration spike, and I spring away from the dresser. "That's not what I'm fucking doing. I'm saying you deserve better than both of them. Cut them loose." I throw up my hands. "Fuck it. Give the company to your father. I've got money now. We can start over—do something else—leave this bullshit behind."

"I—what?" Her expression is startled. "Where is this coming from?"

I sigh and resume my spot against the dresser. My anger

vanishes in an instant at the look on her face. "The longer it's taken me and Jay to figure out what Eric and your father were doing, the more I wondered why we were even bothering. You have the connections and the skills. I have the money. We walk away from their bullshit and start over. You and me."

"Doing what?" Her face morphs from confusion and surprise to consideration.

The fact she hasn't dismissed the idea outright gives me hope. "A smaller arms company, maybe? Work our way up. Security service." I meet her gaze. "Or, if you don't care, you can be my mafia doll." I wink. "I definitely understand how to build one of those empires."

She holds up a finger. "Nothing illegal. Not if we're starting over, okay? If I'm leaving everything behind for you, I don't want to worry you're going to be taken from me."

I walk over, smooth her hair, and peer into her amber eyes. "Sounds like a deal."

Her suitcase sits on her bed, open, partially packed. "So, are we going to Russia or not?"

"We make a clean break," I say.

"I own a house in Cape Verde. It's not huge, but it'll suit the two of us. We can restart there." She laughs and hugs me. "Are we really doing this?" She kisses my neck and squeezes me tight.

I'm glad she's so happy, but there's a part of me worried for later. Ever since I've known her, she's wanted her father's love and approval more than almost anything else. Leaving the company is guaranteed to piss him off.

The shrill ring of the house phone stops me from replying.

"Hold that thought." She grins.

The phone is on her bedside table, and she snatches it up. Her voice is full of happiness when she says hello. She smiles at me before wandering across the room, handset glued to her ear.

I perch on the side of the bed and riffle through her beauty products. Jesus, she has a lot.

"What are you talking about, Dad?"

That gets my attention. She's pacing, her expression confused. "I don't care what you're doing in Russia, Dad." There's a brief hesitation before she pushes on. "In fact, I'm—I'm giving the company back to you and starting something else."

Well, I guess we're doing this. I didn't realize she'd tell her father quite that quickly or over the phone. Best to fire the first shot. That's my policy, anyway.

She stops pacing and glances in my direction, but she's frowning, unfocused. "I don't understand."

Charles's voice is muffled, and I can't make out what he's saying.

"What the fuck?" I mouth to her, but she waves me off and keeps shaking her head.

"Yeah, fine." She turns to look at the wall, distracted, her face pensive. "I'll be there as soon as I can." When she hangs up, she stares at the phone. "I guess we're going to Russia."

"What's going on?"

"Dad says he needs me to meet someone in Russia. After that, if I want to quit, he won't stop me."

"So kind." I sway back on my heels. "Squeeze every bit out of you before he lets you go."

Carys crosses the room and stares at her suitcase in silence, her brow furrowed. "Such a weird conversation."

When we establish eye contact, I just raise my eyebrows.

"He was excited. The number of times my father has been excited for something could be counted on one hand."

This is the point where I should tell her Eric sounded the same way. Instead I keep that nugget to myself and mull it over. "I don't trust them."

Her shoulders slump as she re-arranges things in her suitcase. "Me either. But if I can get out of this company with his blessing, it'll make me feel better later on. You know, someday, when I look back."

With a sigh, I grab my bag and resume packing. "We've still got our plan?"

"It's just delayed." Carys fiddles with the lock on her suitcase. "That's all. A detour before we start out on our own."

Unease churns in my stomach. None of this is right. I take my phone off the dresser and text Jay to see how many more people we can bring to Russia for our team.

Even if Eric, Charles, and their acquaintance aren't a physical threat to her, I've steered Demid in Eric's direction. If something happens to her because I wanted him out of the way, I'll never forgive myself.

~ * ~

We spend the plane ride coming up with half-baked ideas and mapping out plans of action. She wants Jay and his family to come with us. Whatever she asks for, I'm agreeing. Anything to get her away from the two good-for-nothings luring her to Russia.

When the plane touches down, the sky is an inky black. On the tarmac, Jay briefs our extra security regarding the house, the known risks, and who is being posted to each position once we arrive. The only people who are going to enter the house are Jay and Tom, me, and Carys, in that order.

Although she's convinced Eric and her father won't hurt her, with the right motivation, they're capable of anything.

The property is outside Volgograd city limits which is why we didn't use it last time. She says her father purchased it almost a year ago, and as far as she knows, it's sat empty. My bullshit meter is reading off the charts. I keep trying to make the pieces fit together, but I never get there.

We're quiet in the main car as we approach the house. The two-story brick building might have been built at the turn of some century. Architecture isn't my specialty. Old houses harbor secrets—bodies, rooms, passageways.

Jay and his new partner Tom are going in first and then giving us the all clear. Once they exit the car, Carys and I sit in silence. I rotate a ring on her finger while we wait. Regardless of what her father said about letting her go, whatever or whoever is in that house is designed to draw her in.

It takes longer than I expect for them to inspect the property, and when Jay returns he avoids eye contact when I step out of the car.

"All okay?" I ask.

"No danger in there. But buckle the fuck up. Carys will need you."

"What?" I hiss at him as she climbs out behind me. "If there's something I need to know, you should have fucking taken me aside."

"You gotta see it, man. You won't believe me. *I* can't believe it."

"But she'll be safe going in there?" I tip my head at the front door.

"Physically, yeah. She'll be fine."

I place my palm on the small of Carys's back as we make our way to the entrance. My mind ticks through what could be in the house that would be emotionally or mentally damaging to her. As long as everyone is alive in there, I can't imagine what they've got or what they've done.

Jay and Tom slide through the door first. I follow, pulling her behind me, our fingers locked together. The gun holstered just under my jacket is a comfort. Without a doubt I'd kill anyone who physically hurt Carys, but with her heightened emotions, there's a good chance I'll shoot them for hurting her feelings, too. Ever since she talked to her mom, there's been something fragile in her.

When we enter the living room behind Jay and Tom, the high ceiling makes the place seem far grander than it should. The décor is a strange mix of modern and historic, as though someone came through and switched out pieces of furniture and wall coverings. Opal has clearly never been here either. Maybe Charles is announcing a divorce and re-marriage? But why would Eric be excited?

Her father rises from the couch at the far end of the room. "Ah, you're here." He grins and gestures for us to sit in one of the other couches. "I hope Jay didn't ruin the surprise."

I glare at Jay and don't answer Charles. She sighs and squeezes my hand tighter. Jay shakes his head but doesn't speak.

"Well, good." Charles's smile widens. "I've so been looking forward to seeing your face, Carys."

I frown and glance at her as she takes a deep breath.

"I flew all this way, Dad. Can we not dance around whatever it is you want from me? You promised if I came, you wouldn't be upset if I wanted to quit the business."

His eyes light up, and he peers at a small screen facing him on the table. "It'll just take a moment. I'm not delaying on purpose. You can't rush these things." He smiles at Carys. "You'll learn."

She huffs out a breath and glances at me. An uncomfortable silence sits between us. Then I catch the briefest of cries—like a puppy or a kitten. I rise to my feet, dropping Carys's hand.

"You got an animal in the house?" My hackles stand on end. What if it's dangerous? What if Jay didn't understand what the fuck he was talking about outside? Wouldn't be the first time.

Charles laughs, delighted. "Of a sort."

Jay won't meet my eyes.

The stairs creak from someone's heavy footsteps. They must be Eric, but even still, I reach into my jacket to rest my hand on my gun.

The stairs are at the rear of the house, near the kitchen. It only takes a moment for Eric to materialize in the doorway, cradling something in his arms.

Beside me, Carys digs her nails into my forearm.

What's in the blanket?

Eric ignores me, his gaze locked on her. He shifts the bundle ever so slightly when he reaches her. Her hand leaves my arm, and everything narrows, happens in slow motion. He places the squirming thing in her arms, and the tiniest sigh escapes her lips.

It's a baby. *It's a fucking baby.*

"Carys, I'd like you to meet Lucas. Our son," Eric says.

Charles claps and rushes forward to embrace her and the baby in a weird side-hug.

What the actual fuck is going on?

Chapter Thirty
Carys

I stare into my arms at the baby wrapped in a pale blue blanket. He has dark hair, and his eyes are closed in sleep. His fingers have the tiniest nails, and I want to touch everyone, count them, savor this moment. I'm so absorbed in the sight of a baby, it takes me a second to process Eric's words.

"What?" I glance up, a little dazed.

"Our son." Eric gives me an encouraging nod. "You weren't here for the birth, but I know you always wanted to name our boy Lucas after your brother."

I laugh self-consciously and shift the baby to hand him to Eric. "This isn't my baby." When I try to pass the bundle, he steps out of reach. "He can't be my baby. It's impossible."

"Not impossible," my father whispers. "You were searching for a surrogate when you two split."

"Exactly," I agree. "Eric and I broke up, and we destroyed the embryos. I signed paperwork to have them destroyed."

My father grimaces.

Eric shifts his feet. "This isn't the reaction I was expecting."

"I signed papers to have the embryos destroyed." I repeat the words, this time louder, hoping they'll stick in someone's brain. "This baby can't be mine!"

"You'll wake him, Carys. You don't need to shout." Eric's hand drifts to the baby's forehead, and it seems to soothe them both.

"You signed papers to have the embryos destroyed, that's true. But the leftover eggs were released to Eric." My father holds his hands up in a surrendering gesture.

"What?" When I start to shake, Finn's hand trails down my back to rest above my waist. "How? I would remember agreeing to that. I would. I wouldn't have done that. Why would I do that?"

Charles sighs. "It was after the last miscarriage." He searches my face for a moment. "You were in a pretty dark place."

My mind struggles to compute what he's saying. Yes, I didn't cope very well when I found out Eric was a serial cheater paying for abortions when I'd miscarried for the seventh time. A baby with Eric wasn't the solution to our problems. I knew it then, and I sure as hell know it now.

"I bounced back, Dad. I always bounced the fuck back." Then like a torrential downpour appearing out of nowhere, the truth drops. "*You* did this?" Disbelief rushes through me. "You had a hand in this?"

The baby wiggles, and I adjust my hold. But I can't acknowledge him. Each time I register that I have a baby in my arms and he *might* be mine, I no longer care quite enough how it happened, why it's happened, or whether the baby is even mine.

A baby.

"For years," Charles says, "you wanted a child. You went through so much to get pregnant, and then to never carry a baby to term? Destroying the eggs seemed foolish. They might have been your last chance to be a mother. I did what I needed to do to make sure you weren't throwing away an opportunity." He gestures to the baby in my arms. "Now you get to be a mom."

If it wasn't for Finn's hand on my back, I'd be unhinged. When I peer up at him, his face is impossible to read. It's granite. But inside, my heart is breaking. If this baby is mine, biologically mine, everything I've been planning with Finn can't happen. Or at least, it can't happen the way we envisioned. Does he realize that?

"We'll need a DNA test." Finn breaks his silence.

Eric smirks and shakes his head. "We can get as many DNA tests as you want. They'll tell you the same thing. That baby—Lucas—has two biological parents. Me and Carys." He beams at me. "We're gonna be a family. This time, I'm doing right by you."

The picture the coroner showed me of Valeriya not long ago pops into my head. He's making things right with me by doing wrong to a host of other people.

"Where is the woman who gave birth to this child?" Finn's voice is tight with suppressed anger.

I breathe a sigh of relief. He's asking the questions I should be asking. My brain is muddled, and half of it is already consumed with monitoring the minuscule movements of the baby in my arms.

"Upstairs." Eric gestures to the ceiling. "You're welcome to talk to her. She's agreed to stay on as our wet nurse. You were so keen to make sure our child was breastfed."

"Eric." My whole body goes cold. "That was five years ago. A lot has happened since then."

"You'd prefer he was bottle fed?"

173

A scream works its way up into my throat. I'm on the cusp of saying I'd rather he hadn't used my eggs to create a baby I no longer want, but saying the words are crass, not true. Assuming Lucas is mine, I'd never want him to hear that repeated later in anger by Eric. Kids can be weapons between parents. Any relationship with him will be a battlefield.

"You're being deliberately obtuse," I push out through clenched teeth. "Neither one of you even talked to me. You didn't ask me."

"Are you saying you don't want the baby?" Eric frowns.

"No—I—it's just—" I shake my head. Nothing sounds right. "I don't understand how you did this without me." My voice cracks, and Finn's arm tightens and shifts to my waist. He's the only thing holding me up.

Eric and my father exchange a look loaded with meaning. Was Valeriya part of this? The timeline Ekaterina mentioned sort of matches. Maybe her involvement with Eric, her involvement with this baby made her bold.

"Who helped you?" I ask.

"It's Russia." My father waves a hand. "The only help you need is money and a few connections. Lots of money. Once you've got that, you can make anything happen."

"First thing in the morning," Finn says, "we're getting a DNA test."

"Have at it." Eric chuckles.

Finn's fingers clench the material at my waist. I peek up at him, but his murderous gaze is focused on Eric.

The baby snuffles and wiggles in my arms. When I look down, his little face is contorting like he's about to cry. Eric checks the clock on the wall.

"Probably feeding time. I'll take him upstairs for Galina to feed him."

"That's her name?" I whisper as I pass him to Eric. As the baby leaves me, a heaviness settles in my chest. Part of me wants to snatch him right back, keep him tucked close. What if he's mine?

"It is." Eric grins. "Her English is impeccable. You'll be great friends, I think."

The tension radiating off Finn is unmistakable. It amazes me that Eric can ignore it, as though Finn isn't on the verge of releasing his gun and shooting him. If I turned to him and asked, I know he'd do it. Eric had better be telling the truth about the baby. Otherwise Finn will give him the shovel and watch as he digs his own grave.

But then, if he is telling the truth, what does that mean for us? I sink into the couch across from my father as the full weight of the realization settles. Does he want to be a father? My brain tries to extract the fragments of conversation from before, from now. He's never said how he would feel. A child was an impossibility. Even the miscarriage we sort of glossed over.

Would he be okay with parenting another man's child? How will Eric and I arrange custody? Where will the baby live?

I press my fingers into my forehead. Finn's hand strays to the top of my head in a soothing motion. *God, I love him.* His silence is adding another layer of fear. Will he leave me if the baby is Eric's? I didn't want this, but I can't say no to it either.

"I'm tired," I whisper to no one in particular.

Jay straightens as if coming awake. "We've got the hotel booked in the city." He comes around the couch from his position by the door.

"No need." Charles waves a dismissive hand. "This house is big enough. Seven bedrooms. Four upstairs. Baby Lucas. Galina. Eric. All have rooms up there. You can take the fourth, Carys. Finn, Jay, and I can sleep downstairs."

Finn tenses, and I jump in before he can say anything or even think it. "Finn will stay with me."

"Surely not now, given the situation with Eric," my father chides with a shake of his head.

"For fucks sakes," Finn bursts out. "She's a grown woman. Stop treating her like an errant child. She deserves so much better than this ambush."

My father sizes him up for a moment before muttering, "I'll never understand her attraction to you."

"You don't fucking have to, but you need to accept that it's her choice. Not yours. Not Eric's. Hers. Always."

Rising, I wrap my arms around Finn's tense bicep. He doesn't take his eyes off my father, but his seething rage comforts me. When he was so quiet, I couldn't read him. But this? I understand this. I'm supposed to feel the same. Hurt. Betrayed. Blindsided. Instead, I'm numb, clinging onto him like a lifeline.

"Take me upstairs." The words are a plea.

"Jay," Finn says.

"I'll get your bags." He heads for the front door. "And I'll bring them up in the minute."

As I'm led past my father, he says, "I thought you'd be happier."

"I can't talk to you right now, Dad. I need to wrap my head around... everything."

"Well," my father says, glancing at Finn. "Hopefully in the morning, you'll realize what a blessing this is. How fortunate you are to have this opportunity."

Bile rises in my throat. Finn wraps his arm around me tighter and guides me toward the stairs.

Chapter Thirty-One
Finn

The room Charles assigned to us belongs in a museum. Historical eras aren't my thing, but it's clear this place hasn't had any facelift since the house was built, which was probably a hundred years ago. From the doorway, everything seems clean enough, and nothing smells like mothballs or mildew. I sigh. These thoughts are just a distraction from the fucking fertility circus downstairs. A poor effort to calm the hell down, and it's not working.

As I close the bedroom door, I realize I should say something to Carys, but I don't have any idea where to start. My blood boils, rage coursing through me at Eric and her father creating this child without her consent. When she was at her lowest, they tricked her into signing away her rights to her future children. Their motives are inconceivable to me—and I've done a lot of shitty things in the name of profit or revenge. But this? Their plan is so misguided. How could either of them think a baby was the right solution?

My brain spent the whole conversation ticking through the complications. The situation is a fucking nightmare. Eric may be the only legal parent. There's no way I'm saying that to Carys because we don't know if the baby is biologically hers. Eric or her father could try to bluff through this or outright lie. Wherever we get the DNA tested in the morning, I'm following the kit like a bloodhound. They won't trick her again.

If they're lying? God won't be able to help them. Whether she wants them dead or alive, I'll be making them dig their own graves before I put a bullet between their eyes. To dangle motherhood in front of her and then snatch it away is unforgivable. Un-fucking-forgivable.

"You're very quiet." Carys's voice is hardly audible in the room.

There's a knock on the door, and I gather my thoughts while I go to open it. At the entrance, Jay passes me our bags. Worry is splashed across his face, and I shake my head. I don't have the slightest clue what to tell him. With a sigh, I close the door and set our luggage on the floor.

"Can you please talk to me?" she says.

Over my shoulder, I see her hand shake as she raises it to her hair. *Fuck.* What am I supposed to say? What do I do? I'm not this guy. Kill them? I can do that. No problem. Talk about feelings? Much harder.

"Why don't you tell me what you're thinking?" My voice is gruffer than I mean it to be.

"What if it isn't the same thing you're thinking?"

"That matters?" I shove my hands into my pockets. Maybe if I'd gone to therapy as a kid like Lorcan's mother wanted, I'd be better at this. Instead I'm fumbling around in the dark. And not the fun kind of fumbling.

She takes a shaky breath. "I was happy. I had you. If I have this baby, I'm afraid I won't have you. It just—" her voice cracks, "seems so unfair. I might finally have the two things I want, but I have to choose which one I want more."

There's no choice. I heard what she said to Opal the other day. She'd never abandon her child for a man, not like her mother did. Could I ask that of her? No, I couldn't. Even though not asking would kill me.

"As long as you want me, I'm here." I stand in front of her, out of reach.

She closes the gap and wraps her arms around my waist. "I want to be with you forever. That was my plan. Would you—could you raise that baby as your own?"

I clear my throat. "You're suggesting I could be a father to your child?"

She nods against my chest.

With a sigh, I draw her tight against me. "I'll be a shit dad, Carys. But if you want me, I'll do my damnedest."

"Really?"

I don't want to go in circles, and the complete truth about where my head is at isn't helpful. Did I want to be a dad? Not really. Will I walk away from her because she has a kid? Not a fucking chance.

Right now, I need to understand where her mind is at so I can figure out what I can do, what I should do to make that happen. "Logistics aside, what would you want from this situation if you could have it?"

Silence hangs in the room for a moment. "I'd have you. I'd get custody of this baby from Eric. We'd move to Cape Verde and set up a low-risk venture and raise him together. When I think of myself five years from now, that's what I want. You. Me. Lucas. On an island.

Unbelievably happy."

My heart squeezes in my chest. Her idea is so vivid I can almost close my eyes and put myself there, insert myself in her version of our life.

But in what world can that future happen? Eric was confident in her hotel room this maneuver would draw her back to him. She won't leave her child. He won't give up the child, his leverage, without a fight.

"That sounds perfect," I murmur into the top of her head. It does. Will the image of what might have been have to sustain me while I watch her live her life from afar? What might have been... What could have been... If only...

Because if they force her to make a choice. Well, for her, there's no choice at all.

~ * ~

Galina looks like a woman who gave birth two days ago. Darkness sits under her eyes from a lack of sleep, and her brown hair lies limp around her shoulders. Her middle is still expanded, as though there might be another baby in there.

Christ. I hope there's not another fucking baby in there.

"Breastfeeding is hard work," she says to Carys once we've introduced ourselves.

"I'm sure," Carys murmurs and focuses on her purse.

Last night, while lying in bed, I selected a DNA testing facility which guaranteed same-day results. We're waiting for the cars to be ready to get us there. Eric and Charles aren't getting near the scientific process. The facility agreed I can guard the DNA throughout the day. Only cost a few grand. Seems cheap for our peace of mind.

Carys threw up in the bathroom this morning. The sight of her makes my chest ache. The natural confidence radiating out of her is weighed down by today's outcome. Either result has grave consequences.

She told me she doesn't want to hold the baby again until she knows for sure he's hers.

As though reading my mind, Galina says, "Carys, I'm sorry. You must want to hold him."

Carys looks up, startled, and before she can say anything, I step in. "I'll take him," I say.

Galina frowns. "Eric said you weren't to hold Lucas."

Without meeting Galina's gaze, Carys says, "He's my baby, too. I say he can."

Aw. Shit. I don't want to hold him. The number of babies I've held in my life could be counted on two fingers. Galina shifts her grip and passes him to me. I hold out my hands and catch Carys watching me out of the corner of her eye. The smallest smile floats across her face. She's got to be laughing on the inside at how fucking awkward I am right now.

He's so tiny sitting in the crook of my arm, a swell of protectiveness runs through me. To think part of Carys might have become this tiny little man makes my heart pound. The baby yawns, and I glance at her. She's watching me and him with so much longing I regret saying I'd hold him. I was trying to make this morning easier, and now I'm worried I've made her day so much harder.

"I wish—" she says.

"I know." The pain in those two words is enough.

She nods and turns away.

Footsteps echo through the rear of the house, and I juggle the baby trying to give him to Galina before Eric can show up. Carys doesn't need a fight on top of everything else. My temper is lit, ready to explode. If he says the wrong thing to her, I'm likely to snap his neck. I still might get the pleasure if Eric has lied about this baby's parentage.

"All set?" Charles comes through the living room and into the entryway.

"You don't need to come," Carys says, half-turning toward him.

"Nonsense. Eric and I are coming to celebrate. My first and probably only grandchild."

She rubs her forehead, and I ease my hand across her shoulders. She shifts closer to me and seeks shelter in my arms. I keep focused on Charles as I kiss her temple. He frowns and turns away.

Jay pokes his head in the front door. "We're all set. Car seat installed. Everybody in. We gotta be there in an hour."

We're almost at the car when heavy footsteps sound behind us. I was hoping we'd be gone before Eric tagged along.

"Ah," Charles says with a grin. "Here you are. I was afraid we'd have to leave without you."

"Wouldn't miss it for the world." Eric smiles and tries to catch Carys's gaze.

She turns her face more into my chest. His gaze connects with mine instead, and his eyes narrow. "You're going to have that satisfied smirk wiped off today."

Carys stiffens in my arms.

I chuckle. "You know who else has a satisfied smirk these days?" When he doesn't answer, I continue, "Carys. Whatever happens today, that will always be true. I've satisfied her in ways you never could."

With that, Jay opens our car door with a flourish and Carys enters first. When I glance over my shoulder, Eric and Charles are deep in conversation. Eric's cheeks are red with anger, and Charles is trying to calm him down.

"Should you have done that?" Carys asks when I settle beside her.

I shrug. "Was I wrong?"

"No."

"Then he needs to realize he isn't winning you back. He's cheating. He's trapping you into something you don't want anymore. He's no hero. I'm not letting him walk around pretending he's some kinda savior."

She undoes her seatbelt and slips across the backseat bench. Her hand slides along my leg and she rests her ear against my chest. "I love this sound." Her other hand is against my heart. "I want to hear it forever."

I secure her close to me and kiss the top of her head. The selfishness I can't seem to shake rears its head. At the back of my mind is the mantra: *Please don't let Lucas be her child.*

Chapter Thirty-Two
Carys

Finn is somewhere in the building with the DNA samples. After a couple of hours, Eric gets up the nerve to speak to me. One plus of Finn insulting him—his confidence took a hit.

"We should discuss everything before he gets back." Eric sips the coffee he bought from the café across the street.

He's so tall standing in front of me that I'd have to crane my neck up to make eye contact or stand up. Neither appeals to me. I don't look at him and I stay seated in my chair.

"Or maybe we should wait for the results to make sure what we're discussing is appropriate." I flip through the Vogue magazine I found on a table.

"You realize Lucas is yours. Why would I lie about that?"

"Honestly, I don't understand why you thought any of this was a good idea. The inner workings of your mind are a bit of a mystery to me." I toss the magazine onto the nearest table and stand. "I'm with Finn. We're together. What you think you'll accomplish won't happen."

He raises his coffee and takes another drink. "I didn't want to head in this direction, but you're forcing my hand."

"Welcome to my world," I mumble.

"You gave up your rights with the paperwork your father had you sign."

"Which I did under duress. I was deeply depressed. That can be proven with a few inquiries to my doctor."

"Sure. Maybe. But your father will testify, if it comes to that, that you were of sound mind and body when you signed those papers."

A denial rises in me. But we're in this situation because my father believes he knows better than me. He doesn't like Finn. Those two reasons alone are enough to prompt his interference. Add in Eric as a surrogate son after my brother died, and my protest is a waste of my breath. Even if my doctor would counter my father's claim, the court battle might drag on forever. My father likes to win.

"Tell me what you want," I say. "Then I can tell you how much you won't be getting."

"You and me. Together. Marriage. Raise Lucas as a family unit."

"Not happening."

"Then I suppose you won't have much to do with your child. Shame. I guess I can always tell him you're dead." His eyes bore into me.

He knows about my mother. Doesn't surprise me. My father probably told him the whole sob story with his own slant on the details. "If that baby is biologically mine, you can bet your ass I'm not letting you raise him without me."

"If you're not part of our family—*fully* a part—then you'll have to take me to court to get access. That'll take years. Not to mention, we're in Russia. What are your Russian contacts like? 'Cause I've taken the last year to hone mine in the right circles. I've studied the chessboard, determined how to win no matter what move you made."

Oh, God. He's spent a year planning my downfall right into his arms. While I was buzzing around obsessing over Finn, overseeing his life from a distance, Eric was building a web so tight my escape appears impossible.

"We were good together," he says. "I screwed up. I realize that. This time, it'll be different. Wasn't so long ago I was the man warming your bed."

A shudder of revulsion goes through me at the memory of leaving Finn in the hallway to go to Eric. What the hell had I been doing?

"It wasn't long ago you were fucking Valeriya. In order for me to believe you've changed, well, you would have had to actually change. Convenient she died before a DNA test could be done on her baby."

"Oh, she was pregnant, was she? Such a shame."

"I'm sure the baby was yours. I'm sure you had a hand in her murder."

"Hmm." His brown eyes search my face and a smirk plays at the edges of his mouth. "Are you telling me you've got a problem with murder? 'Cause I'd have to call bullshit. You've been fucking a murderous psychopath for weeks."

Heat rises to my cheeks, but I'm not backing down. "There's a difference between killing someone because it's part of your business and killing someone because they're standing in your way."

"Oh." Eric raises his eyebrows. "You're going to try to defend him. Well, I suppose to that I'd say, do you honestly think Finn's never killed for no reason? 'Cause if you believe that, I've got swampland in Florida to sell you."

Jay, who is within earshot, tenses, probably at Eric's know-it-all asshole tone which is out in full effect.

"You're deluded if you consider him a better man than me."

I'm tempted to shove the coffee in his face and laugh as it burns him. An unexpected, almost uncontrollable rage surges through me.

Jay strides to me with a sense of purpose. "Carys, can I have a word?" He tilts his head.

Eric's gaze rakes over him before he focuses on me again. "You have a choice. You might not like the choice, but it exists. If you don't want to have a role in Lucas's life, I'll raise him on my own. I've always wanted a son I could mold into my likeness."

Bile rises into my throat at the realization my son could be anything like Eric. At one time, for whatever reason, his faults didn't seem written so large, so hard to ignore. But now, it's one character fault after another with no end in sight. Finn is a better man. Maybe not in the ways Eric counts, but he is better in every way that counts to me.

Jay's hand is on my elbow, and he's steered me away from Eric and down a hallway leading to the bathrooms before I have a chance to process Eric's words.

"What?" I snap. "What do you need?"

He releases my arm and takes a step back from me. "Nothing. I just thought you'd like to be outta that conversation."

I sink to the floor with my head in my hands. "What am I going to do?" When I glance up, his face is full of sympathy. "Did you hear everything? The things he said? How badly he's fucked me over?"

"I did." He deposits his phone into his pocket and leans his shoulder against the wall.

"You and Finn were searching for weeks. None of this was there?"

Jay shifts with obvious discomfort. "Maybe, looking back there were a few fertility-related things sprinkled in." He shrugs. "When I pointed them out to Finn, he said he didn't care who Eric was trying to get pregnant now."

I wince.

"Sorry." He rubs the side of his face. "I take it he doesn't realize the shit you went through and the things you and Eric did to get pregnant before?"

"No." I laugh, but it has no humor. "I didn't think it mattered."

We sit in silence. What's he thinking? My mind feels like a

bomb went off, and I keep searching the fragments of my life for what will make me happy. The pieces don't fit together anymore. Nothing makes sense.

"What are you going to tell Finn?"

"Fuck if I know." I throw up my hands.

He chuckles. "You sound like him."

"This is a nightmare. A baby shouldn't feel like a nightmare." My voice wavers. "If Lucas is my baby, I should be happy."

He crouches across the hall from me. A few tears trickle down my face, and I wipe them away. He touches my shoulder, and I glance up.

"Finn won't let you go without a fight."

"I know." My voice catches. "My greatest fear and my biggest hope."

My phone pings, and Jay's sounds at almost the same time. He removes his from his pocket before I can retrieve mine from my purse.

"Finn's in the lobby."

"Tell him to come here. I'd prefer not to do this in front of Eric—whatever way the results go."

Within moments, Finn is framed at the end of the hallway. His hands are stuffed into his pockets, but I can't read him. Is Lucas mine, or is he someone else's?

I rise from my spot against the wall, but I need to keep leaning on it. Hope and fear wash over me in alternating waves. Which way do I want it to go? I want both and neither. Nothing and everything.

Finn stops in front of me, and his pale blue eyes scan me. "He's yours."

A cry escapes me. Anger or relief? I grab Finn, hugging him, burying my face into his chest. His hands ease out of his pockets at a glacial pace and circle around me.

"Now what the fuck do we do?" Jay asks from behind me.

~ * ~

The whole day has been a blur, from Eric's pompous expression when I admitted Lucas was mine, to Galina taking me through the steps to care for him, to the distance Finn has put between us.

Or maybe I'm imagining his aloofness. Maybe I'm the person putting the space there. My world has tilted on its axis, and I can't shift reality back, make it level again.

The thing I do know? I'm exhausted. Emotionally and physically drained. When Lucas goes to bed for the night, or however many hours before he needs to feed again, I head to bed. Finn trails behind me, his hands in his pockets.

Eric tries to catch my attention, but I've been ignoring him all day. I don't give a shit if Lucas is biologically his baby too. Ever being with him in any way makes my stomach heave like I'm on a boat tossed around by the sea.

Finn closes the door to the bedroom and then leans back against it. "You look tired," he says before pushing off and ambling toward me. He tosses his wallet and other odds and ends on the nightstand.

"Did you want to talk?" I ask.

Finn's gaze searches mine. "About what? He probably wants me out of your life. I'm not fucking going." He hesitates and focuses on a spot above my head. "Unless that's what you need. Then I'll do it." His hand grazes my arm.

"Did Jay tell you?"

He chuckles and makes eye contact again. "He gave me the *Coles Notes* version of your conversation with Eric."

"So you know."

"He won't let you raise Lucas if you stay with me? Yeah."

"How do I get around his ultimatum? He's spent months locking me in without me even realizing it."

He presses his lips to my forehead. "I made calls today. He's not chasing me away. No one forces you into something you don't want."

"You won't leave me?" My voice hitches at the end as I hold back a sob.

"I'm not going anywhere unless you ask me to." His voice is gruff.

I kiss him. "Don't go," I murmur. "Don't ever go." But even as I say the words, anxiety eats at my stomach.

He deepens the kiss and jerks my shirt over my head in one swift action. There's a desperation in my movements as I tug on his jeans and remove his boxers. As though part of me needs the closeness to prove to myself that this, what's between us, is still real. We won't burn out or fade away because Eric is trying to extinguish us. But even as he slides into me, and I pull him tight against me, something has altered. I've got one foot out the door, and I don't know how to get myself back in.

He cups my face and stares at me. "Get outta your head, Carys. Be here with me, in the moment."

Tears spring to my eyes. "I'm just so afraid to lose you."

"Tell me what you need."

"Tell me you love me."

His lips brush against mine as he slides out and slips in again. I clutch onto him, keeping him as close as possible. "I love you," he whispers.

He keeps telling me over and over while we pleasure each other until I almost forget why he needs to say it at all.

~ * ~

When my eyes pop open, I'm not sure why I'm awake. I lay in bed for a moment with his arm draped across me and listen for a sound. Was the noise Lucas? Did I hear him? Galina's room is between ours. Could I have heard him? He'd have to be screaming.

What if he's hurt? Or sick?

Moving his arm, I sit on the edge of the bed, tense, listening.

"What's wrong?" he mumbles into his pillow.

"I'm going to go check on Lucas." I glance at him over my shoulder.

He runs his hand along my waist.

"Want me to come?"

I shake my head and then realize he still hasn't opened his eyes. A laugh escapes me, and he cracks open an eye. "No need for both of us to be tired in the morning," I whisper into the too-quiet room. "I just need to see him."

Finn's breathing evens out, and I can't help smiling. There's something so boyish about him in bed, asleep. The toughness vanishes, and in its place is a peacefulness he rarely shows when he's awake. My heart aches with love.

After throwing on a robe, I open our door and creep down the hall. The last thing I want is to wake Lucas if he's sleeping. His door is ajar, and I push it wide with my fingertips. The crib sits in the middle of an oversized room. There's a rocking chair, a recliner, a change table to the left, and a selection of books and toys in bins on the right. Earlier today, the details in the room made me wonder how long Eric intended to stay in Russia.

When I get to Lucas's bed, I stare at him, my swaddled bundle, and a surge of hope sweeps through my chest. *He's mine.* Someday this little person will call me Mommy, will tell me he loves me, will rush into my arms because he's delighted to see me. Every thought is amazing and terrifying. None of these dreams are new. Seven other times I had them when I learned I was pregnant. The joy, the hope, visualizing the future, making plans, buying things, in love with someone who barely existed. In each instance, my dream ended in tragedy. This time there's a baby. Not a ghost, not an idea yet to develop. *My baby.*

"He has your dad's nose."

I tense and half-turn toward the door where Eric is silhouetted in the entry. "I hadn't noticed."

He comes to stand beside me and gazes at him. "Your dad pointed it out, and I had to agree."

"Of course he did."

We remain in silence, and I wish more than anything he hadn't interrupted my moment with Lucas. It's the first time I've been alone with him today.

"Have you thought about what I said?"

I can't meet his gaze. "I don't want to be with you, Eric."

His hand trails along my side. "You'd get used to being with me again. We were good together once."

"That's not what I want anymore." I force myself to establish eye contact. Had I ever wanted him? Being with Finn makes everyone who came before or after him seem insignificant, unimportant.

He takes in my appearance, and his eyes darken. "You were always good for more than one round." He reaches for the tie on my robe. "And I don't mind Finn's sloppy seconds. Perhaps you need a reminder of how good we used to be."

I swat his hand away. "Eric. Don't."

"Relax, Carys," he mutters. "You've always been an easy lay. Don't start being a prudish bitch now." His hand catches a tie, and he yanks on it.

"Take your fucking hands off her," Finn growls from the doorway.

Eric whirls toward the sound of Finn's voice, and I breathe a sigh of relief seeing him standing there. I draw the two sides of my robe together and step around Eric.

"It's inevitable, Carys. If you want your baby, you'll say yes. We're a package deal."

In the entryway, Finn clenches and releases his fists. He lets me slip past, but I don't go too far. I'm afraid of what he'll do.

Before I can grab his arm, he storms Eric and wraps his hand around his neck, pressing him up against the wall. Eric lets out a startled noise.

"I'm thinking something might be inevitable. But it won't be Carys saying yes to you." Finn's voice, low and dangerous, sends a shiver down my spine.

Eric meets Finn's challenge with his customary ignorance. "We'll see."

His sense of self-preservation is lacking.

"I'll kill you before I let you lay another hand on her. You think you're the only person with Russian contacts? You think you can threaten her, and I'll just let it go? Inviting me here was a pompous, idiotic mistake."

"Finn." I ease my hand across his shoulders. The more Eric fights back, the angrier he'll get. He's used to eliciting fear. Eric should be pissing himself. At my touch, Finn's shoulders lower, his grip on Eric easing.

"Come on," I say. "Come on. Come with me to our room. Lucas is in here. Not in front of him, okay? I don't want him waking up to this."

Finn gives him a final shove, and Eric's head thuds against the wall. "You stay the fuck away from her, or you're dead."

When we get to the doorway, Eric says, "Inviting you wasn't a mistake. I wanted you to understand you can't win. The honorable thing would be to let her go. Let her embrace what she's always wanted. A real family."

Finn tenses and turns. His face is murderous. I wrench on his arm, dragging him back to our bedroom. Pushing him in first, I close the door behind us.

Chapter Thirty-Three
Finn

Before the door clicks closed, I'm striding over to the dresser where I stashed my gun. I check how many bullets I have. A full clip. *Perfect.* I only need one.

"Finn," Carys says from the doorway.

There are no words for the anger raging inside me right now. The warning in her voice is easy to ignore. He put his hands on her as though he was entitled to her body, as though she's an object he can take and use as he likes. There is no fucking way I let that smug asshole get away with that.

When I get to the door, she's pressed against it.

"Move."

"No."

"If I kill him, our problems go away."

"They don't. And if you think about it, you'll know why."

"I don't fucking care. He's not railroading you. He's not forcing himself on you. None of that is happening—ever."

"I love you, Finn." She molds herself to me.

I close my eyes and try to block out the smell of her. When her hands slide around my waist and her ear is on my chest, I can't hold onto my rage.

"I love you." Her voice is muffled by my shirt.

My arms stay at my sides, the gun still grasped in one of my hands. I want to kill him for putting her in this position.

"I love you." She lifts her head, but I keep my gaze focused above her. "Can I talk to you?"

"You won't change my mind."

"What would we tell Lucas? If I let you kill Eric, what would we tell him?"

"Nothing," I say. "He doesn't need to know. Dad's dead is enough."

"Is it? Was it enough for you with your mom?" Her voice is gentle, but her words cut like a knife.

"Not the same."

"You'd be his dad. Someday he might find out the truth—you killed his biological father. We lied."

"Fine. We'll tell him his bio dad was a dog who deserved to be put down." But she's got me. She knows me well enough to understand if she keeps at me, I'll concede her point. The situations may not be the same, but they're too similar to ignore. If I kill Eric, someday, in Lucas's eyes, I'll be no better than my father was. Instead of being someone he looks up to, I'll be the person who took someone from him. God knows if I end up loving this kid half as much as I love his mother, it'd kill me to know he thinks of me the way I think of my father.

"What has Eric done to deserve to *die*?"

With careful precision, I place my hands on her biceps and detach her from me. The anger still courses through me and touching her is dangerous. At the dresser, I take the gun apart as though I'm going to clean it. I'm not. The routine offers me a strange comfort to be away from her and doing something with my hands.

She sighs. "The truth is, I don't care all that much if you murder Eric. I don't care about him at all. The reason I don't want you to kill him is because of what it would do to us, to your relationship with Lucas, to my relationship with Lucas when he found out I not only went along with it but loved you more for doing it."

"Loved me more? Is that possible?"

I stay focused on the gun, but she's right. Killing Eric would be a short-term solution that would trap us into long-term problems. For years, I hated and feared my father. I don't want that kind of relationship with Lucas. It seems impossible to parent any other way, but I'm sure as hell gonna try.

"I love you more all the time Like right now? I love you more for listening to me, for being willing to do anything to protect me." She appears at my shoulder, but she doesn't touch me.

Her closeness is enough to wear me down.

"I hate this," I whisper.

I drop the gun and press my hands into the top of the dresser. Her hand rests on my back, tentative, light as a feather. Half of me wants to shrug her off, and the other half wants to gather her up, make her scream so loud with pleasure the whole fucking house knows she's mine.

She's saying the right things, but earlier she was slipping away, as though a crevice opened between us the moment Lucas became her child.

"I hate *how* I've become a mother. This situation would never have been my choice. I-I made peace with the fact I wouldn't have children. But now he's here and he's mine? I can't carry resentment into my relationship with him. I can't. Eric and my father did this, not him."

"I don't hate the baby." I turn to her.

She's been my foundation since I lost everything else. Until now, I haven't even missed my old life. Helplessness is the one emotion I can't stand. There's always an angle to be played, an avenue to take. There's one here, too. Murder. Simple. For once I have to think beyond the now, consider the future, a future with her and with Lucas. I won't become my father.

I clear my throat and stare at the dresser again. "He's so sure he's going to win, and I can't think of a way around what he's done." I push my hands harder into the polished wood. "He's given you the one thing I can't...I wasn't even sure I wanted you to have, even though I knew how badly you wanted it."

She's quiet beside me.

"I'm sorry I never offered," I say. "I didn't suggest—"

"Don't—please, don't. I would have said no. You didn't see me after the last miscarriage. There's no way I could have gone through the whole thing again. The hope, the disappointment, the crushing grief."

I circle my arm around her, tugging her into my side. Her expression would undo me, so I avoid meeting her gaze.

"Even if that wasn't true, I wouldn't have wanted you to become a father because I wanted you to. I still don't. If this isn't what you want—"

"I want you." I scoop her into my arms, securing her tight. "I'm not letting you go because the situation is hard, or not exactly what I thought our relationship would be. Fuck that. Maybe a better man than me would back off and let you figure this out with him. I'm not that guy."

"I don't want you to back off. You're what I want. We just have to make the circumstances work. In a few days, once things have calmed down, once he realizes I won't change my mind, maybe he'll be more reasonable."

I scoff. "There's no reasoning with him. He took your DNA and made a secret baby who he presented to you like a...prize or gift."

"What else can we do? Killing him is too risky. I doubt he's given me any legal rights to Lucas. And even if I should or can have those rights, we're in Russia trying to deal with Russian laws as outsiders."

My mind drifts to Hagen, but I don't want to call that fucker again in Boston for another international favor. Still, if he can pull strings in Russia and at least make sure Carys's name is on the birth certificate, we might have a hope in hell of securing some sort of custody agreement.

At the moment, we're flying blind. Hagen might refer me back to Demid, and I can't go to him with this problem. If the guy is like me, he'd murder Eric's child in retaliation for Valeriya's death. He wouldn't think twice about the baby being biologically Carys's kid too.

He didn't seem that ruthless, but the last time I underestimated someone, I was shot up in a warehouse and almost bled-out on the floor. That's not happening again.

"I'm tired," Carys says, against my chest.

I lift her up in my arms and carry her to the bed, then slide her under the covers. She reaches for me, and I shake my head.

"You're not coming back to bed?" she says.

"I'm going to grab a drink," I say. "Get some sleep. I'll come up in a while." I pick up my clothing strewn around the room and get dressed.

"Finn?" Her voice is heavy with sleep. "Leave the gun here."

The weapon is still in pieces on the dresser. "Get some sleep." I close the door tight behind me.

Downstairs, I search the kitchen for everything to make a pot of coffee. Carys will need caffeine when she gets up, and Jay drinks a cup, too. Those other fuckers in this house better not touch the pot.

I dig into my pocket and remove my phone. Scrolling through my contacts, I stare at Hagen's name. He is my worst option and also my most logical one. Nothing good will come from owing him. If Lorcan were here, he'd have a strategy, something I never considered, and times like these I miss the fucker, even if he chose Kim over me.

The coffee finishes, and I drop my phone onto the counter. I take a mug from the cupboard, pour the hot liquid into it, and then bring the caffeinated goodness to my lips. Carys likes to sweeten her coffee, but I enjoy it bare, undisguised.

"I smell coffee," Charles says as he enters the kitchen. "Oh, it's you."

I raise my drink to him. "It's me."

"When are you leaving?" He grabs a mug from the cupboard and takes the pot I made.

The temptation to snatch it away or punch him is pretty fucking strong.

"That would be never."

He finds the milk in the fridge and drowns his coffee. After heaping sugar into his cup, his spoon clangs on the porcelain as he stirs the liquid. "You'll stand in the way of her happiness?"

"Is *that* what I'm doing? Strange. That's not what she thinks."

"You've been an unwelcome and unexpected distraction for my daughter."

"Again." I press the cup to my lips. "Not what she thinks."

"My daughter has never been very good at sorting out her personal life."

"Oh?" I put down my coffee and cross my arms. "Please enlighten me. I'm fascinated to hear your take on her personal life since you seem so hell-bent on controlling it. Your life is such a shining example." I pin him with my gaze. "Remind me again. Where *is* your wife?"

He flushes, and liquid splashes over the edge. I hope it fucking burns him.

"Eric's a good man. He's the father of her child."

How did he become so deluded? Eric's behavior must be like staring in a mirror. They're both womanizing liars who believe control equals love. My father had a similar belief system. Being with Carys this last little while has changed my mind on how love and caring works. For years I treated Lorcan the way Charles and Eric are treating her. He only needed to understand what I wanted to tell him. Didn't exactly work out how I expected.

"I wonder if she'd let me kill you." I cock my head. The question doesn't need to be asked because I have the answer. I hope Charles doesn't.

The coffee slops over the edge again as he turns toward me, and he switches hands, shaking off the excess liquid. "What?"

"You heard me. You've been a shitty father. I'm not sure you'd be missed. What do you think?"

He gapes and sputters.

"When you chased me off seventeen odd years ago, I actually thought you were right. I wasn't any good for her. My temper almost got her killed. Her dad, I thought, he'll watch out for her. If he realizes I'm no good, he'll be able to recognize terrible men coming and protect her." I raise my eyebrows. "Instead you not only condoned but *supported* a womanizing, lying, piece of shit who murders pregnant women."

"Murders pregnant women?" Charles scoffs. "Sounds more like you than him." He gestures wide with the hand holding his mug and the coffee trickles down the side of the cup.

"The whole time he waited for your grandchild to be born, he was fucking Valeriya Kuznetsof who, it turns out, became pregnant with his child. Guy's got magic sperm and probably a host of venereal diseases."

Charles scowls. "I couldn't care less if Valeriya was pregnant. I'm not sorry she's dead—she betrayed us. He had nothing to do with her murder."

"Well, it must be true if you say so."

"She was selling company secrets to a third party. She was caught. Fled Russia and went to Ireland to meet up with whoever had been bankrolling her. We think it was the PLA. Eric and I flew to Ireland to head off the meeting, but we arrived too late. She was dead, but Carys was in trouble. We stayed to make sure she was okay."

"You knew this about Valeriya before you flew to Ireland?" He doesn't realize I was listening to his conversation with Eric. He didn't know shit about her or why she died until Eric told him.

"Yes." Charles gulps his drink.

Is there anything this man won't lie about? A waste of breath to talk to him. Eric probably fed him enough lies to cover up his own crimes.

Without saying another word, I grab my phone off the counter and drop it into my pocket. My coffee is only half full, so I refill it and turn to exit the kitchen. He's too deluded to deal with him rationally.

"If you don't leave, he'll take Lucas and run. Carys will never see him again."

I half-turn back and eye him over my cup before taking a drink. "Oh? Is that what a good man does? Forces a woman to abandon her child so she can be in a relationship with him?" I feign thoughtfulness as he flushes red. "Oh, no. Wait." I point at him. "You. You did that. What Eric's doing is so much better. You're right. He's such a good man. He doesn't force women to make impossible choices. That would be wrong."

Considering how red he is, Charles doesn't miss a beat. "I'm sure you've never forced a woman to make an impossible choice—human trafficking is such a decent way to make a living."

I clench my jaw. Guess he's been conducting his own research, but I'm not letting him rub my past in my fucking face. "I've never told a woman I loved her and then asked her to make a choice meant to break her. Say whatever the fuck you want about me. But that's the line I won't cross."

I start out the door and then turn back. "If I thought you and Eric engineered this baby to make her happy, your actions would a lot easier to swallow. But you didn't. This baby is about control, about figuring out a way to force her to bow to your wishes."

I leave the kitchen before Charles responds. Jay is getting a wakeup call, and he can get his own fucking coffee. We've got work to do.

Eric won't get a chance to run with Carys's baby. If anyone will run, it'll be me and her with Lucas. All I need to find are shackles for Eric, and right now, I'll take them literally or figuratively, whichever I can find first.

Chapter Thirty-Four
Carys

I wake up to find Finn gone. At first I panic and circle the bedroom, accounting for his things. Then I decide that maybe he didn't return after he got himself a drink. It's only eight in the morning. But that's late for me. Yesterday was exhausting.

After I've showered and dressed, but before I go downstairs, I creep down the hall to Lucas. In the rocking chair in the corner is Galina with Lucas, and she's attempting to burp him.

"Want to try?" she asks when she spots me hovering in the entryway.

"Oh, um, yes." I take the armchair next to the rocker. She passes him to me, and I mimic the movements I saw her doing. An awkward silence settles between us as I try to get a burp. After a deep breath, I say, "Is this your first time being a surrogate?"

Her face fills with surprise. "No, my third. Eric picked me because he wanted someone with a record of success." She hesitates and then says, "He said this was your last shot. None of the implantations in other surrogates took."

I absorb this information in silence. It's been so long, and I don't recall how many eggs I harvested when Eric and I started searching for a surrogate. A lot. I remember that much. More than we ever thought we'd need. I was worried about being too old. A laugh threatens. Now I have no choice. Too old or not, I'm a mom. *I'm a mom.* I focus on Lucas, letting the realization wash over me one more time.

My brain ticks to Galina's comment. He was trying to secure a baby from the moment we split. The deception is overwhelming. How many surrogates? How many attempts? Throughout, he was still sleeping with, and impregnating, other women. God, he's such a sleaze.

"I, um." Galina fiddles with the baby blanket in her lap. "He gave me the impression you and he were together. He said you didn't want to meet me because it was too hard to know someone else would be carrying your child. But it seems like you're with Finn? Did you and

Eric split up during the pregnancy? Is Lucas going into a good situation? There's so much tension in the house."

Lucas burps, and I take the blanket she offers to wipe his mouth and then cradle him in my arms. The weight of him is still surreal. A baby. *My* baby. I scan his tiny face and try to block out Galina's questions. Her worry is sweet, even if I don't understand how to ease it.

"He'll be fine," I say.

Eric's deception, how wrong this whole situation is for Lucas, for me, for everyone, shouldn't be her concern. I'll do everything in my power to do right by my baby. None of this is his fault.

Jay appears in the doorway. "Ah, here you are. First stop was your room. This was my second choice."

I smile and focus on the bundle in my arms again. "Where's Finn?"

Jay doesn't respond, so I glance up and raise my eyebrows. Once I realized Finn's things were in the house, I stopped worrying over where he might be. I should have known better.

"Gone out." His face is hard to read.

"Alone?"

"No, he took the greenest guys in the crew with him."

I narrow my eyes. He's telling me the truth, but he's being careful with his words. Out of the corner of my eye, I catch Galina watching us. Perhaps she's the reason. He doesn't want Finn's whereabouts to get to Eric. Since I haven't told Galina Eric lied to her, her loyalty will be with him. Telling her I hadn't been told about the baby doesn't make me more trustworthy if her primary concern is what will happen to Lucas.

I wander to Jay with Lucas secured to my chest. "Is everything okay?"

He gazes from me to my baby and back to me. "Not the best way to get here. But it looks good on you."

"Thank you." I smile and nuzzle Lucas as he releases a tiny yawn. "Parenthood is amazing…and kinda terrifying."

"Yeah, that's how everyone feels. You'll get used to it."

I turn in the doorway and say to Galina, "Do I need to bring anything with me if I'm just walking around the house with him?"

She shakes her head. "If you need me, I'm here."

With a head tip, I indicate for Jay to follow me down the hall. Once we're in my room, he closes the door behind us.

"Where is he?" I sway when Lucas squirms.

"He didn't want me to tell you." Jay shrugs. "So I'm not telling you."

I laugh, but I'm not amused. "You realize you work for me, right? I'm the one who pays your bills? Sends your kids cute outfits and expensive toys at Christmas and expensive toys. That's me."

"Yeah, well, when you threaten to cut off my balls, you'll be in his league."

I sigh. That's the kind of hardball I'm not willing to play. "When's he returning?" I frown, somewhat surprised he's gone anywhere. Last night he was determined Eric wasn't coming near me. Without him here, unease circles around my neck.

"Maybe tonight," Jay replies. "Maybe not till tomorrow. He told me to pretend I was glue and to stick to you." He grins. "Then he added," he squares up his shoulders in a good imitation of Finn's posture, "'but don't get too fucking close.'"

This time, my laugh is genuine. "I fucking love that guy." Lucas wiggles, and I peer at his petite features. "If his first word ends up being fuck, I'll be mortified."

"Yeah, we might have to dial it back. We've got a year to sort ourselves out. Maybe more if he's got his bio dad's intelligence." Jay winks at me.

His statement is funny and not. My child possessing any of Eric's traits or characteristics makes me angry. Some inheritance is inevitable, though. He is his biological dad. I'll have to get used to recognizing aspects of Eric, coming to love the parts of him in this little man.

"You're just going to follow me around all day?" I say.

"Exactly an arm's length away."

Amusement and unease war inside me. Finn can take care of himself. After our conversation last night and what Eric tried to do, I'm worried he's finding a way to eliminate Eric behind my back. He doesn't see himself as a protector, but I know better. When he loves, he loves hard. For years I watched as he tried to shield Lorcan from anything too damaging. Right now I'm the one he's trying to protect. How far will he go?

"Seriously, where did he go?" I say.

"Seriously, I can't tell you." Jay frowns. "He said he was going dark for the next twelve to twenty-four hours. Hence," he gestures to the space between us, "the glue."

"Please tell me he's not doing something rash or stupid."

"You think he ran his plan past me?" He tsks. "We're not bros. He only tells me what he wants me to know."

Lucas fusses in my arms, and I adjust my hold while I change from swaying to a light bounce.

"The only thing I care about, the only thing I want, is for Finn, Lucas, and me to end up together." My face is tight with suppressed emotion. "I'm close to having that. So close. But there's this knot in my stomach that won't ease."

"Eric thinks he's got you on the ropes."

Lucas quiets, and I sway again. "I used to watch Finn fight when we were younger. Want to guess my favorite part?"

Jay's lips quirk up. "No idea."

"How unpredictable he was. If you go to enough fights, you find patterns in fighters. They favor certain combinations or skills. Not Finn. And he always won. No one could figure him out." A piece of my hair comes loose from my ponytail and falls into my face. "That's what scares me. We're on the cusp of a knockout, and someone is going down. Who's going to hit the mat first?"

~ * ~

Every time the front door opened, or a car door slammed, I couldn't help peering out the window, staring at the entrance with raw longing. Eric only kept his distance until he realized Finn wasn't anywhere in the house. A few times, Jay redirected a conversation or stepped in the path of Eric's straying hands.

In a moment of weakness, I texted Finn. That was hours ago. While the message has been delivered, it hasn't been read. When I glance up from checking my phone again, my father is frowning. Eric is outside talking to a security guy about a video game they play in their free time. Occasionally, their voices drift through an open window. It's almost midnight.

When I stand up, tired from waiting, I tuck my phone into the back pocket of my jeans. "I'm going to bed."

My father rises and so does Jay.

"I'm flying out in the morning," Dad says. "It seems like Finn's come to his senses and gave you and Eric time to work on being a family. I can see how hard this transition has been for you today. But give—"

"He's coming back." I stare at him, wondering how he could get it so wrong. "Eric and I will *never* be a family. We'll raise Lucas as co-parents, but otherwise we won't have a relationship. I'm not leaving Finn. He's not leaving me."

"That's a mistake. Eric will never—"

"He doesn't control me. Neither do you." As I head toward the kitchen and the stairs at the rear of the house, Jay keeps pace beside me. "You can leave if you want. I couldn't care less," I call over my shoulder.

Not completely true. Even though he isn't exactly protective, he blocks Eric's snider comments. Eric can switch facets of his personality to suit his audience, and he never showed my father the sides of himself I saw. In some ways, I can't blame him for thinking Eric is better than he is—after all, Eric fooled me too for a while. Once the veil fell from my eyes, he could never get me to replace it the way he wanted.

When we get to my bedroom door, which is the first one at the top of the stairs, I turn to Jay and say, "You're off the hook. I'll see you in the morning."

He chuckles. "Off the hook? I'll be here outside your door until the sun rises or Finn comes home."

A protest mounts in my throat, but then I remember how Eric behaved last night, his lewd comments today before Jay could intervene. The smart choice is having a form of protection. He's always charmed me in the past, and now it isn't working. There is a chance he'll resort to force.

I swallow my words and nod. "Okay. I'll get you a pillow and a blanket in case you get tired."

"That's okay. I'm under strict orders to stay awake." Jay waves me off. "I'll be fine. Not the first all-nighter I've pulled."

"Thank you." I turn the handle to my bedroom door.

"That's why you pay me the big bucks." His grin is fleeting. "Lock the door." His gaze connects with mine before I close the door. "Make sure you've got your gun somewhere you can reach it."

I frown. "Is there something I should know?"

"Desperate, arrogant men don't make smart choices. If I go take a piss and come back to find Eric's knocked down the door, I want to be sure you can shoot him."

"Finn told you what happened last night?" I press my hand into the frame, remembering the spark of panic when he tried to push the issue.

"None of us wants a repeat." Jay adjusts the gun in the holster under his arm.

It makes me wonder if the gun was supposed to serve as a visual warning to Eric today. Normally he keeps his gun concealed.

"I don't think—"

"Has any of this been something you would have thought possible?" Jay's tone is kind even though his words slice through me.

"None of it." I shake my head. "If you'd told me six months ago I'd be with Finn, that Eric would deliver a secret baby to me, that my father would have a hand in the deception, I would have thought you were out of your mind." I sigh and prop open the door so I'm framed in the doorway. "Why do the best things and worst things seem to happen together?"

Jay mirrors my sigh. "Finn will return with answers or solutions, no matter what he has to do to get them."

"I know," I say. "That's what I'm afraid of." Longing has been my constant companion today. "If you hear from him, tell him I miss him."

Jay's lips purse together. "I'll be out here talking to my wife. This shit you two are going through right now makes me miss her more than normal."

"Tell Sofia I said hi." I shut the door and lean against it. My phone buzzes in my pocket, and my chest fills with hope. My mother's name appears on the display. With a sigh, I send it to voicemail. I can't deal with her drama on top of everything else. I flip the lock into place on the door as I hear the soft murmurs of Jay sweet-talking his wife. When we leave Russia, he should be with his family for a while or prioritize moving his family to wherever we're relocating.

My phone is almost dead, so I plug it into the charger over by the window and move around the room, getting ready for bed. It's impossible to keep my mind distracted enough to avoid thoughts of Finn. If we don't make it out of this together, I'm not sure how I'll survive. Having him gone today has been a slow form of torture, and I've realized Lucas won't be enough. I need them both.

Sliding under the sheets, I pull up the covers and stare at the ceiling. My meditation classes are going to come in handy tonight. I'm starting my breathing and visualization pattern when a chorus of loud, aggressive voices drift in the window.

"Carys," Jay shouts through the door. "I'm heading downstairs to see what's going on. Lock yourself in the bathroom until you hear from me."

Heart racing, I throw back the bedding. "Okay!" I yell in response. Grabbing my gun from the bedside table, I'm halfway to the en suite bathroom when I remember Lucas. He can't be left unprotected. I grab my robe off the bathroom door and shrug it on, pushing my gun into a pocket.

As I rush to the door, a few loud pops echo. Outside or inside?
Lucas.

Unsnapping the lock, I peek out the door and draw my gun from my pocket. Gunfire somewhere. Keeping my side against the hallway wall, I point the gun toward the stairway as I creep to Lucas's room.

An agonized scream streaks through the house, and my hand shakes. Whatever is happening, the noise sounded inhuman. More popping erupts.

The door to Lucas's room is ajar. My fingers squeeze my gun to keep it steady, and I use my free hand to open the door more. Heavy footsteps pound up the stairs behind me, and I whirl with the gun raised.

"Carys." Jay is out of breath, his white shirt stained with blood. "Don't shoot." He raises his hands, his gun high in the air. "We gotta get the fuck out of here. It's chaos down there. I don't understand what the hell is going on, but if I survive this and you don't, I might as well be dead."

"Are you hurt?" The gunfire and shouting drift up the stairs, through the windows, surrounding us, but distant enough my heart isn't booming out of my chest.

"No, no. Not me. We gotta move." He strides past me and my gun raised toward him. "We'll grab Lucas—"

"Wait." More pops sound below. Lowering my gun, I slip through the door behind him. "How are we going to—" My voice trails off when my gaze lands on the crib.

There, in the middle of the room, gun trained on us, is my father, Lucas cradled in his arms. "I need you to trust me," he says. "I can save us, but you have to trust me."

Chapter Thirty-Five
Finn

The kid who has been driving me around Russia for the last several hours is greener than a hill in Ireland after excessive rains. There were a few times when I worried he'd piss his pants at some of the hotshots I met. People don't mess around in Russian politics without consequences. Thanks to Hagen, I got face time with important senior officials. Even if Hagen was a total dick on the phone, he gave me decent leads. Two favors to him is bad business, but I'll deal with that when he tries to cash them.

"Hey, kid." I lean forward from the backseat to yell over the music he thinks keeps him calm.

We've spent the day together, and I haven't bothered to ask his name. There's no spark of promise in him. The desire for this life is the money, not the danger, not the violence. He's nothing like me.

He turns the dial on the stereo, and his gaze catches mine in the rearview mirror.

"We're headed to the house. You got no reason to shit your pants, so keep the music low, will ya?" I ease into my seat. "Your incoherent racket is giving me a headache."

"Sorry, boss." His English is heavily accented.

I thought we brought our security from Switzerland, but Jay must have picked up a couple of Russian kids at the airport when I demanded more muscle. He came in handy a few times when those Russian asshats tried to talk behind my back.

My lips quirk up with the hint of a smile. All day he's been calling me boss. Technically I'm not the one signing his checks, but it's so good to be in charge. To be *leading* the charge.

Out the window, the scenery around Volgograd races by us, eaten up by the car, by the darkness in the middle of the night. I hoped to return earlier, instead it's almost three in the morning. Jay better be camped out at Carys's door, or he'll experience my wrath whether or not Carys likes it.

"Uh, boss?" The kid says, as the car slows.

I meet his gaze in the mirror.

"The house is dark, sir."

"And that's weird because...?"

"The house has security lights. They aren't on."

Shaking myself out of my thoughts, I try to remember what the property was like a few days ago when we drove up. He's right. There were a few guards at the entrance, and the place was lit up around the perimeter. There's not a single light. If the kid hadn't told me we were nearing the house, I wouldn't have a clue.

"Park here. We'll enter on foot. Your gun loaded?"

His hand shakes when he picks up his weapon from the passenger seat.

Christ. He's going to be no fucking good to me. "Don't shut the car door when we get out. We'll leave them open, so the slam doesn't tip anyone off. Stay behind me. Avoid making any noise."

"When do I shoot, boss?" His voice wavers.

"Not until I do and not when you're behind my fucking head. You got me? You don't fire on anyone first."

Once I'm out of the car, I try to forget he's following. There's no way he's going to be worth anything to me in the next few minutes. It doesn't take long for us to come across our first body. One of the original security guys Eric and Charles had with them lies with his face in the grass. We keep moving forward, body after body.

The kid whimpers behind me.

When we get to the front door, thrown open, my heart is in my throat. No one is alive so far. If Carys is injured or worse, I'll hunt the people who did this, pound a stake into the ground, nail them to it, and light them on fire.

Back from the entrance, I turn to the kid. "Keep your gun in your hand. Search the perimeter. You find anyone alive, you come to the front door and wait for me. You don't shoot anyone unless I give you the order."

I will him to meet my gaze, but he doesn't. He's is in shock, but he's not getting an ounce of sympathy from me. This is the life we live, the sooner he knows this path is not for him, the more likely he is to remain alive.

"O—O—O—kay."

Carys would find his sudden stutter endearing, but it pisses me off. He's my only backup, and he's fucking useless.

Checking my gun one last time, I consider using my phone as a flashlight. Everything is pitch black. At least I'm dressed in dark colors, too. Harder to see. Harder to shoot. Instead of taking out my phone, I slip into the house.

There are two or three men dead in the main living room. None of them are guys I recognize. Doesn't mean much since I barely knew the security detail we hired. I left that up to Jay. Leaning down, I touch the neck of the nearest man. He's warm. Relief and fury surge through me in equal measures. If Carys is here somewhere, hurt, she could be saved. I'll give up the rest of my nine lives to save hers. My chest and throat are so tight I can hardly breathe. Wherever she is, I will find her.

My gun up, I sweep every hiding place on the main floor. I explore the kitchen at the rear. When I start up the stairs, a figure is sprawled on the landing. My heart kicks in my chest. A woman's outline. Taking them two at a time, careful to avoid the creaks I discovered earlier, my breath leaves me in a whoosh. *Galina.*

I don't stop to check for a pulse but continue toward Carys's room. Her door is ajar, and I keep my gun raised in front of me as I open it with my fingers. It's empty. I examine the whole room and en suite as quickly as I can. Her purse is on a chair, and her phone is charging by the window. Both are like bright, neon signs telling me wherever she is now, she was in danger earlier—might still be in danger. She wouldn't leave those items behind by choice.

Without giving myself time to consider where she might be, who might have taken her, I go through the rest of the rooms on the second floor. They're empty. No Lucas. No Jay. No Carys. No more bodies.

Just outside her room, I peer at Galina's dead body sprawled near the top of the stairs. Where are you, Carys?

Basement.

Whoever was on the property seems to have cleared out, so I don't bother to keep quiet as I take the stairs. I clutch my gun as I hurry to the middle of the house and the narrow stairway just off the living room that leads to the basement. In no time I've searched everywhere and come up empty-handed. At the bottom of the stairs, I examine the layout of the basement again. I'm missing something, but I can't put my finger on what's making my senses tingle. Pinning down the feeling is a waste of time.

What if they tried to run? What if they're outside somewhere? So many bodies.

My stomach has never been weak, but it rolls once at the thought of her scared, alone. From an early age, I learned to control my emotions, to quiet my natural sense of unease when I'm on the hunt. But right now, knowing she is most likely in danger, anxiousness is a vise around my heart, squeezing it so tight I'm not sure it'll recover.

Her name is a drumbeat against my soul. Finding her is my central focus.

When I get to the front door, I lead with my gun.

"Boss," the kid hisses when I step out.

At the sound of his voice, my shoulders relax. "What'd you find?"

"I got a guy, alive. Barely, but alive."

"Take me to him." I motion for him to lead the way. "Any female bodies?"

"Ms. Van de Berg isn't out here, boss."

Thank fuck for that.

"Jay?"

"Didn't come across him either."

Maybe they got away. But seeing the carnage here, their escape seems so unlikely. Did whoever came take them to hold as ransom or as a bargaining chip for a bigger game?

"The house is clear?" The kid asks as his head shifts around, his hand still trembling.

"Yeah." I follow him to a tall figure lying face up on the ground.

"He's coming in and out. Kept asking for Ms. Van de Berg when I could get him to look at me."

The body sends a wave of satisfaction over me. Eric's face is swollen so much he's almost unrecognizable. His clothes are torn, and in places blood is oozing out of him. Whoever was here, they spent time to work him over. I would have paid good money to watch that.

Demid? That's the only person who makes sense. But it also means Lucas was probably a target, and by extension, Carys. If she is hurt, there is nowhere in the world Demid will be able to hide from me. I'll hunt him and flay him open.

"Did he say who did this?"

"No." The kid shakes his head. "Just keeps saying, 'Carys' over and over."

"I need you to go search the bodies again for Tom or Jay. Check everyone. Even the bodies of the people you don't recognize. I want to know if anyone has orders on them—hints, clues, tips, anything. We need a lead."

"Got it." The kid hesitates for a minute. "Police?"

"No."

He nods and sets off toward the side of the house. I stare at Eric and then I crouch, shaking his shoulder, digging my thumb into a nasty wound.

He groans and turns glassy eyes in my direction. "Carys," he murmurs.

Anger spikes at him daring to say her name. This whole situation is his damn fault. "Who did this?" His head lolls to the side, and I slap his cheek to get him to focus on me again.

"Tell," he breathes out. "Carys."

"Who did this?" I grip his chin, forcing him to look at me.

His breathing is labored, and each breath appears almost painful. If he was anyone else, I might feel a tad sorry for the fucker. "Where is Carys? Do you know where she is?"

"Tell." He coughs and sputters. "Carys."

"Boss," the kid calls, from far away. "I think I got something, maybe."

"Meet me at the door." I gaze at Eric and grip his chin tighter, and I mutter, "I gotta put a dog down first." I cross to another man and snatch up his abandoned gun. After checking to make sure it'll still fire, I stand over Eric. I point my weapon. "In some ways this is too good for you."

"Carys," he mutters. "Tell her—"

Before he can finish, I fire two bullets into his chest and one to his forehead. Using the bottom of my shirt, I wipe my prints off the gun and let it fall to the ground beside him.

With a last appraisal of his still, mutilated body, I say, "I won't be telling her anything."

Chapter Thirty-Six
Carys

The room is pitch black and soundproof. Whoever is out there must have cut the power to the house and disabled the backup generator. None of us know the target of this massacre. It could be me, Eric, my father, even Finn.

Finn as the mark makes my stomach flip. Where'd he go, and what's he doing? Jay claims he doesn't have any details either. His phone died about an hour ago, but we weren't able to get a signal anyway. The panic room is built under the basement.

With my gaze pinned to the ceiling, I hope no one with a gun discovers the trap door and concealed staircase in Lucas's room. It's a steep, winding decent meant only for one person at a time. Jay was almost too broad to make it. Even now, having navigated it, I can't believe the passage exists. Who is up there? What do they want?

How will we know when they're gone?

Lucas makes a snuffling noise and snuggles into my chest, trying to find food. Soon we'll have to take a chance and leave. We can't let him starve, and I'm not sure when he last fed. He's been content to be cradled and rocked. Not for much longer.

"Do you think it's safe yet?" My father's voice echoes in the darkness.

"No." Jay's tone is bored. "We're waiting it out."

"For what?" My anxiety over Lucas eases as his breathing evens out again.

"Finn."

My father chuckles. "He left. We'll die of thirst or starvation."

"He'll be back. I'm locked in this panic room with the one person he actually gives a shit about. Come hell or high water, he'll find her."

"Do you think Eric's okay?" My father's voice is subdued, resigned.

"No." Exasperation enters Jay's voice. "He was the guy fucking screaming, Charles. Whoever came to the house, they came for him."

Demid.

I don't say his name out loud. Jay likely knows, and my father would never understand Demid was avenging his daughter's death.

"He only wanted to make you happy, Carys," my dad says.

I laugh. "He wanted to make himself happy."

Part of me wishes I could see my father's face, gauge his reaction. The other part is glad we're doing this in the dark. Maybe he'll be honest for once. "Lucas wasn't created to make me happy. This baby was a method of control, to get me under his thumb. Before the baby, I had the upper hand. I was his boss, and I had more money, prestige, connections." I bring Lucas to my chest, my voice hard in the darkness. "He might have given me a baby, but he wanted to take a lot more."

There's a heavy silence before my father speaks. "I wanted you to be happy. This was supposed to make you happy."

"Eric would never have made me happy."

"The plan wasn't about him—not for me. You wanted a baby so badly. Ever since you were little and you played with dolls, you wanted to be a mother. Watching you come so close and having the dream slip through your fingers…"

"You had no right." I wish I could see his face, his eyes, to determine whether he's sincere or trying to make the best of a shitty situation. We're his greatest chance out of this mess. At this point, Finn will be his savior. Must sting after how he's treated him.

"We haven't had an easy relationship, Carys. But I've always loved you more than I could express. Seeing you grieve over and over hurt me, too."

"You had no right." This time, my words don't have the same bite. "If we get out of this alive, I'm taking time with Finn and Lucas to sort through this mess. Then I'm quitting you and the company. I'm done. I'm out."

My father sighs. Jay's big hand lands on my shoulder, and he gives me a reassuring squeeze.

"You'll turn over the family company to someone else?" my father says.

"No," I say. "I'm giving it to you. What you do with it, that'll be up to you. But I want nothing to do with it…or with you."

"I haven't been a part of the company for years," Charles says. "I won't understand everything to step right back in."

"I'll come to the Chicago office for one week. One week. That's it. But not until we've got Lucas out of Russia and we're settled. You can hobble along until then. There are enough people there who know what they're doing. You'll be fine."

"All these years leading the company, all these years as your father, and I get one week?"

"You've been on borrowed time since you told Finn to stay away at the hospital seventeen years ago." Lucas squirms in my arms. "I understand why you did it. I do. But it doesn't change the fact you've been trying to make big life decisions for me for far too long."

"Ever since your brother died, I've tried to keep you alive. Anything to keep you alive." His voice is rough with emotion.

"We're in a panic room in Russia. I'd say your ability to decide who or what is dangerous stopped working." Truthfully, I'm not sure he ever had that capability. Of course, I don't believe he wanted to put me in danger, but he hasn't steered me down the straight and narrow either. "Finn loves me. And—and I have no doubt he'd do anything, anything in the world to keep me safe. I know it."

The latch above our heads creaks, and Jay tenses beside me.

"My kingdom for a light," he whispers.

His gun must be trained at the source of the noise, but it's so dark we can't see anything. A light shines, blinding us. Lucas stirs in my arms.

"Identify yourself!" Jay booms.

If whoever has found us wanted to shoot, we'd be dead. There's no cover in here, just a room, a ladder, and a few rickety chairs.

"Carys?"

Relief floods through me. "Finn," I breathe out his name, and I rise from my chair, wishing he'd shift the light so I could see his face.

The light doesn't ease, but there's the distinctive clatter of him descending the ladder, and I catch glimpses of his outline. Adjusting Lucas, I try to shield my eyes.

"Kid, get the fucking light out of her eyes. I don't want her blind, and I can see her." There's a slight pause, and Finn draws in another breath that sounds shaky. "I can see her."

My heart swells.

With that, the light moves to the side, and when the spots clear from my eyes, the relief on Finn's face before he scoops me and Lucas into his arms makes my chest tighten.

"You have no idea the things I'd have done if anything had happened to you." His voice is gruff in my ear. "For nothing can be ill if she is well."

My breath catches. A line from Shakespeare's Romeo and Juliet.

Once, when we were in Ireland, he said that line reminded him of me. Sometimes his almost-degree in literature reaped surprising benefits. I haven't heard those words in years, but those moments with him are my most vivid memories. Us at our happiest. Looking back, I don't understand how I didn't recognize his love. Blinded by youth and inexperience, I guess. His feelings are so clear now. Uncomplicated and perfect. My heart lodges in my throat.

He frames my face with his hands before his lips find mine and everything else fades away, becomes muted.

"I'm so glad you're here," I whisper when I pull back, my free hand cradling the side of his face. "How did you find us?"

"Tom had an old architectural drawing of the house in his front pocket. The kid," Finn indicates the person at the top of the ladder, "dropped out of architectural school to take this job. He saw what I would have never seen." A ghost of a smile flicks across his face. "Redeemed himself for being a piss-poor bodyguard."

He tugs me close, careful not to crush Lucas between us. His lips brush against my forehead, and I savor the smell of him, the warmth of him. Everything will be okay.

"Anyone alive up there?" Jay's voice breaks the silence.

"Me and the kid," Finn says.

"Eric?" my father asks.

"Dead."

My father's sharp intake barely registers. I can't stop staring at Finn. "Where were you?"

"We'll talk in the car on the way out of here. If the cops come along, I'd rather not be paying people off right and left. We'll go to the hotel Jay booked for us. Cover our tracks later with cash if we have to."

Lucas makes suckling noises. He needs to feed soon, which reminds me of another person who should have been on my mind. "Galina?"

Finn's lips graze my temple, and he mutters, "You're the only three alive." Surveying the light coming from the top of the stairs, Finn checks on the bundle in my arms. "Can you carry Lucas back up there?"

"I'll take him," Jay offers. "I carried my own kids all over the damn place when they were babies."

Arguing with him seems pointless, so I pass Lucas to him and he takes him with ease. "Sofia's lucky." I smile.

He chuckles. "She is. But so am I. That's why our marriage works."

We navigate the path back up to the surface in a single-file line. The house is dark, and the only lights we have are from Finn's phone and the kid's light in the lead. When we get to the front door, Jay grabs the diaper bag on our way out.

We trudge to the car, mostly in silence. The kid with Finn has my purse swinging from one of his hands, and our two overnight bags in the other.

"My phone," I whisper, realizing that leaving it behind tells anyone who comes that we were at the house.

Finn takes it out of his back pocket and waggles it. I lean into him and his arm circles me, securing me tight to his side. Once we're at the car, he opens the door and gestures for me to get in.

"We don't have a car seat." I stare at Finn and then at Jay with a hint of panic building in my chest. At every parenting hurdle, I'm stumbling.

"It's all right," Jay says. "The hotel isn't far. He'll be okay. It's the least of our worries right now."

When my father tries to slide in behind me, Finn puts his hand on my father's chest. "Nah," Finn says. "You can walk."

"You'll need my help to get Lucas out of the country."

Finn shakes his head. "What do you think I've been doing today?" His gaze sears my father. "I got a lawyer—a good fucking lawyer. And I greased some wheels. We fly out with Lucas and a Russian passport tomorrow."

My father frowns and crosses his arms. "You were going to run away with him?"

Finn chuckles. "I don't run. From anything. I would have taken Carys and Lucas and waltzed out the front door in the morning. There would have been nothing Eric could have done."

My father's gaze narrows in response, but he says nothing. I'm not sure it would have been as easy as Finn's making it seem, but we'll never know. We no longer have to worry about Eric. It surprises me I don't experience even an ounce of sadness over his death. At one time, I would have grieved his loss. Never in the same way, with the same intensity I did over Finn. But still, his absence would have left a mark. Now? I'm relieved the emotional manipulation is over. We're free.

With that, Finn climbs into the car behind me. Jay shuts the door and gets in beside the kid up front.

"He's walking? We're leaving him?" The kid's voice shakes.

"Yes." I gaze out the window, away from my father's dejected silhouette. "I should have done it a long time ago."

Silence fills the car as we drive. Every once in a while, Lucas stirs, and I remember we don't have a car seat. The situation is so precarious.

"Was it Demid?" I ask.

Finn grimaces and shrugs. "Seems like. It might be my fault he found you. I called Hagen to get leads on politicians and lawyers to approach with favors or bribes."

"Hagen sold you out?" I frown.

"If the price was right, he'd murder his own father."

I raise my eyebrows at Finn but say nothing. He allowed his father to be murdered for free. Not exactly a damning comment, given the source.

The baby wails, and Jay opens the diaper bag and starts doing something up front. A few minutes later, he passes back a bottle.

"What's this?" I turn the bottle to catch the passing lights out the window.

"Formula. Galina was using it to top him up at night."

"Oh." I stare at the bottle. "I think maybe you should be this baby's mother."

Jay laughs. "You'll be fine."

"We just left a shootout. We have no car seat. I would have forgotten to grab the diaper bag if you hadn't thought of it. I didn't realize Galina was using any formula." Tears spring to my eyes. "I don't know how to feed my baby."

He turns in his seat so we make eye contact in the dim light. Finn rubs my leg in soothing motions but doesn't speak. He probably understands less than me.

"Everyone figures out how to parent, how to care for their kid as they go." His expression is serious. Parenting is like this giant experiment that can screw up a kid for life." Jay shrugs. "You do the best you can and hope it's enough."

"Not very comforting," I say.

"The truth is rarely comforting. You got Finn, you got me, and when you decide where you're settling, I'm sure my wife will give you a hand, too."

"You'll come with us?" I ask.

"Yeah." He nods. "I talked to Sofia about relocating last night, before hell broke loose. She's on board for a move. The kids are still young enough they'll adjust okay."

"Approaching the hotel," the kid up front says.

"I want to go home as soon as possible." Looking over at Finn, I smile. "Jay?"

"On it." He whips out his phone. "I'll get the pilot and jet on standby for as soon as we get the passport. I'll call Lena and get her to pick up the baby essentials for the chalet."

"And book yourself a flight home," I say.

Finn protests, and I clamp my free hand over his mouth.

"Jay needs to be with his family. And we need to work on becoming a family, just the three of us."

Finn removes my hand and gives me the smallest smile. "Jay, hire us security for the chalet. Book yourself a ticket home to your wife."

I lean over and press my lips to his. "Thank you."

"Not sure how I feel about this whole compromise thing."

A laugh escapes me and then I sweep my gaze over his face. My chest floods with love and hope and so much joy I'm worried I might burst open. "I can't believe I'm getting everything I ever wanted." I stare at the entrance to the hotel for a moment. "It's almost too good to be true."

"You're getting what you deserve," Finn says beside me. "What you've always deserved."

I link the fingers of my free hand with his as we climb out of the car, a giddy grin on my face.

Chapter Thirty-Seven
Finn

Despite the twenty-four-hour security I've insisted on having here in Switzerland the last few weeks, I can't escape this nagging sensation in my stomach, louder than a whisper, not quite a roar. That sixth sense has never steered me wrong when I've listened to it, and it's going off like crazy.

The stupid part about this unease is that it's being overridden on a daily basis by an overwhelming satisfaction. Carys has agreed to give her father one week in Chicago to get the business in order for the transition, and then she's out—gone for good.

Things have been ticking along in Switzerland for the last few weeks between me, Carys, Lena, and Lucas. We've already paid for the renos to the property in Cape Verde, and Jay and his family are flying there this week to oversee the build. We greased some wheels and got approval to construct a hotel and casino on her waterfront property. It'll be fucking glorious.

Sometimes I wonder if that's my problem. There isn't something coming, not really. I'm uncomfortable with things falling into place so easily. My life has never been relaxing. Even as a child, my existence was fraught with danger. Death or jail was an almost certainty.

Now? I have Carys, a kid, and a legitimate business on the way. All my Christmases have come due at once.

"Finn?" Carys's voice drifts to me from upstairs, bringing me out of my thoughts.

I lower the volume on the TV and check my watch. "I'll be up with a bottle."

"Thank you."

Lena grins at me from the kitchen as I heat the water, pour in the formula, and shake it up.

"What?" I ask as I examine the consistency through the glass bottle.

"Just remembering that conversation we had months ago

before you went to Russia."

"Oh, yeah?" I raise an eyebrow. "Which one?"

"The one where you said you weren't the happily ever after guy." Her hand sweeps over me from head to toe. "Ta-da. Happily ever after."

"I'm trying," I admit as I give the bottle a few more shakes.

"I heard you down here with the baby last night. Seems like you're doing pretty well."

I chuckle and shrug. "I've always been a light sleeper. Getting up with him isn't a big deal."

Lena's smile is kind as she turns back to the dishes. "Maybe not. But those little things make a relationship stronger."

Silence fills the room for a beat as I shake the bottle. Relationship advice from her seems apt and odd at the same time. "Carys and I were talking about asking you to come with us to Cape Verde." I palm the bottle, letting the warmth of the formula seep into my fingers through the glass.

"Is that an invitation?"

"If you're willing to cut off her dickhead father, we promise you'll always have a home and a job with us." Hard to believe she shackled herself to that deadbeat.

She wipes the counter and doesn't meet my gaze. "Even if Carys had been my child, I can't imagine loving her more. If cutting off Charles is the only way I get to stay in her life and see Lucas grow up, then consider it done."

I point and narrow my eyes. "I knew I liked you."

She laughs. "You'd better get the bottle upstairs. Lucas has a strong internal clock."

I rotate the glass from one hand to the other and head for the stairs. I take them two at a time and go into the master suite. A bassinet sits in an alcove in our bedroom. Nothing fancy, but we're not sticking around here forever. This place is temporary, but what's between the three of us is permanent. Someday this kid will call me Dad. I intend to earn that name, unlike my father.

Carys is rocking him, and when I enter, she looks up. Her blonde hair is loose along her shoulders, and while she appears as tired as I feel, she's still the most gorgeous woman in the world. She takes the bottle and angles it into Lucas's mouth.

"Lena's coming to Cape Verde."

Carys's whole face brightens. "You asked her?" Her brow furrows. "She didn't buck at cutting off my dad?"

"Didn't even hesitate." I lean against the dresser closest to her.

"She loves you like a daughter."

When Carys glances up at me from watching the baby, her eyes are shining with tears. "Really? She said that?"

"Yeah, she did."

She turns her face to the ceiling and sniffs. "I'm so stupidly happy right now. I never thought I'd get these baby years—get to see a person change day by day, each day making him more mine." Her laugh is shaky. "It's coming together."

"It is." The gnawing in my stomach surfaces.

"Have you talked to Hagen? Did he have any idea if it was Demid's men who killed Eric in Russia?"

I shake my head. "I'm going to let it drop."

She frowns. "Someday Lucas will probably want to know what happened."

My gaze doesn't waver from hers. "Then we'll tell him the truth. Eric messed with the wrong people and paid the highest consequence. It's a good lesson not to fuck around with people more powerful than you."

"We're going to assume it was Demid?"

"We're in a good place right now. Do you want to take a chance we'll ruin it with too many questions?"

With a shake of her head, she says, "No, you're right. We're safe and we're happy. Part of me thought we might never get to be both."

If my conscience was louder, I might long to tell her the truth. Whether or not I shot the bullets in Eric, he was a dead man out there. Really, I did him a favor by putting him out of his misery. Perhaps the gnawing sense of dread that keeps reoccurring might be my conscience, worried she won't understand if she finds out. Unlike with my mother's murder, the only person who can reveal the truth to her is me. I suppose it'll stay a secret forever.

"You're caught up in your thoughts," she says with a smile. "Anything you want to tell me?"

"No," I say. "Just thinking about how good it'll be when you're back from Chicago and we can focus on what comes next."

She smiles as she tilts the bottle higher for Lucas. "Me too. One week, and then we're free."

He drains the bottle, and she puts it beside her to position him to be burped. "I thought I might be worried about leaving Lucas. He changes so much—something new every day. I'll miss that. I will. But you're so good with him." She stares at me, her features softened with love for me. "I can't believe how good you are with him."

With my index finger, I rub the top of the wooden dresser and don't meet her gaze. "With my old life, I wouldn't have been a good father—too much danger, too much violence, too much hate in me." I stare at the crisp whiteness of the dresser. "But we're building something I never knew I wanted, never considered possible." My voice becomes rough, and I clear my throat. "For the first time, my soul is at peace."

She adjusts Lucas and comes to me. She circles her free arm around my waist and settles herself under my arm. "Mine too." With a contented sigh, she rests her cheek against my chest, so close to my heart it's like they're one unit. "Mine too."

Chapter Thirty-Eight
Carys

Being in the office again is strange. Familiar and foreign at the same time. My father has been roaming around, but I've avoided speaking to him whenever possible. He doesn't have a place in my life anymore. Anytime he tried to make a personal comment about Finn or Lucas, I shut him out. We're not friends, and we're barely a family.

I thought my mother might stop in to see me since she and my father are living together again. Lilly gave me the gossip about them when I checked in with her at Reception this week.

My phone rings, and I glance at the call display. I break out in a grin as I prop it up and accept the FaceTime request. Finn and Lucas pop up on the screen. He has him supported with pillows, so it looks like they're sitting side by side.

"Happy Friday." He smirks and checks his watch. "What, maybe four more hours until you achieve freedom from that place?"

"Yes! We sign the papers at 4:30 today to turn everything back over to my father and whoever he's nominating as my replacement. I've been giving Daniel and Eliza the rundown on the accounts, procedures, and so forth so at least two people can keep this place running smoothly." I scan Finn's face, wishing I could be there in person. Only a few more hours. "My father has been putting his hands on every file, making comments about the changes I've made since he left."

"He can grumble all he likes. His opinion about anything doesn't fucking matter anymore."

I wince.

"I mean." Finn glances at Lucas. "Doesn't freaking matter anymore."

"One way or another, his first word will start with an F."

A knock sounds on my office door. "I'm on the red-eye back tonight. I gotta go. I can't wait until I'm close enough to touch you."

His gaze heats, searing me even through the phone. "You can touch me anywhere you want. I won't mind."

My thighs clench together at the thought, and another tap on my door draws my attention away from the two faces on my phone. "I love you! I'll see you tomorrow."

"We love you too." His voice is gruff when he says those words, as though they're rusty from ill use.

My heart stutters when I hear them from him. I'm the only person he's ever said them to, and he'd do anything to ensure my happiness.

With one last searching glance at the two of them, I end the call.

"Come in." I straighten in my desk chair and try to appear as though I've been focusing on file folders instead of staring at the faces I love the most in the world.

Lilly's long brown hair is the first thing I see before her round, brown face pops in the door. "I tried to call you from downstairs, but the internal phone lines seem to be down."

I frown and pick up the receiver next to me. Sure enough, there's no dial tone. "Did you contact someone to fix it?"

"Just before I came up, yeah."

"Do you need something?" I rest my forearms on the table.

"A time-sensitive package arrived for you downstairs. The courier was very insistent that you got it before four-thirty." She laughs as she hefts the box from between her feet. "I guess someone really wants to say goodbye to you or thank you or something before you leave here."

I've been receiving gifts all week from former clients, current associates, or just people I've met in passing over the years who heard I was leaving the company for good. Most of the people who knew my father had a variation of *what took you so long* in their message. That's the thing about family, though. It's hard to see their true colors sometimes. Or maybe we don't want to see them. The blinders are off where he's concerned. I have no regrets about leaving this behind.

"You can put it on the couch." I nod in the direction of the large cream sofa against the back wall. "Can you send Daniel and Eliza back in? I have a few other things to cover before we run out of time. I'm not sticking around any longer than four-thirty."

She struggles to get the box into her arms and then waddles over to set it on the couch.

"Return address?"

Lilly checks and frowns. "Nothing obvious. But they used a courier, so I'm sure I can track whoever sent it."

I shake my head. "No, if they used a courier it's probably Blake or Brooke Belamy. I haven't heard from them since I got back in the city. It would be like them to send something weighty and ridiculous at the last minute." A present for the baby, maybe? They had kids.

A smile floats across Lilly's face. "Yeah, they always liked you." She glances at me. "We all did. You've been a good boss."

I tip my head at her and return her smile. "Thank you. That means a lot. I'm sure the company will be fine without me, though."

"I always thought if you left, it would be Eric who took over." She crosses her arms and shifts on her feet. "I was sorry to hear he died. Though, he always made me a bit uncomfortable."

I run my fingers along my temple. "I'm sorry to hear that." What else can I say? I'm leaving, and he's dead. Had I known he was awful to everyone I might have done something. She's not the first one to tell me the truth now that he's gone. I'd like to believe I would have acted swiftly. I'll never know for sure. "I'm hoping my father picks Daniel or Eliza to take over. As of the end of business today, it'll no longer be up to me or any of my concern."

"The whole company will be someone else's problem."

"Exactly. Though, responsibility might be a better word." I smile. There have been a lot of good years for me here, in this building, with these people. I might not regret my choice, but I'll miss some of them.

"I'll send Daniel and Eliza in. If you need anything, I'll be at reception."

"I'll send my secretary if I have any urgent messages."

Lilly backs out the door and closes it behind her. I'm tempted to tell her to leave it open, but it might take her a couple of minutes to find our colleagues.

Rising from my chair, I circle the desk and go over to the box. Brook and Blake enjoy a bit of flair, so it's odd the box is standard cardboard. Still, I waited until I arrived in Chicago to announce my break from the company was actually a breakup. Might have taken a few days for the news to reach them. I finger the seal and consider opening it. A knock at the door draws my attention, and I step back. "Come in."

Eliza enters with Daniel on her heels.

"Oh," she says, spotting the box. "Another admirer?"

I laugh. "Not sure. I'll open it later. I have a few things to go over on these files I just pulled."

"Boardroom?" Daniel asks.

"That works," I agree. "We can spread it out a bit better so I can show you the account progressions and inconsistencies." Crossing back to my desk, I gather up the stack of paper files.

Daniel leads the three of us out of the office and along the hall to the boardroom. As I close the door, my gaze strays to the box one more time.

~ * ~

When I return to my office, it's almost four o'clock. As soon as I open my door, the package greets me on the couch where I left it. With a frown, I try to lift it, but it's heavy. Once my grip is adjusted, I get it into my arms and around to my desk. For a moment, I check over the box to see if I missed an address or a company name somewhere. Blank, apart from my office suite scrawled in black Sharpie.

In my drawers, I find a dull knife to slit open the packing tape. With a few quick movements, I slice through the points where the brown tape is keeping the contents secure. I yank up the four pieces of thick cardboard covering my surprise.

I furrow my brow, and then my eyes go wide. Inside is a large black device with a running clock that looks a hell of a lot like a bomb. My breath catches. The countdown is less than a minute and winding down too quickly. Too fucking quickly.

I can't watch it, and I can't seem to stop staring at the numbers running down. So fast. Too fast.

Shit. Shit. Shit.

There isn't enough time to evacuate the building. No time to call Finn. *Oh, God.*

Finn.

I shove my thoughts of him out of my head. A solution. Anything. Something. This can't be happening. This can't be happening.

Opening my desk drawers, I scan for a tool I can use to cut wires. The knife. The knife I used to open the box. Where did I put it? An agonized cry escapes me as I throw things around my desk.

My heart booms in my chest, overwhelming my ears so much I almost don't hear the beep from the box.

My chest tightens, and I peek over the thick cardboard edge, half-afraid, half-curious.

Time's Up. The words flash across the screen in place of the timer. There's a loud click, and I rear back but nothing happens. No explosion.

I run my hands along my body. Nothing happened. I'm okay. A joyous laugh escapes me. It's a dud. *It's a fucking dud.*

Then a second click sounds from the box and the whole thing explodes. I scream and clutch my chest, falling back into my chair as confetti falls like rain. The colorful tornado spins and swirls to the ground.

It was a joke. I'm okay. It wasn't a bomb. I'm okay.

My brain ticks through these realizations even as my desk chair rocks back and forth and confetti flutters around me, blanketing my office. Though the black machine wasn't a bomb, it exploded. Whoever did this wanted me to think it was a bomb. They wanted me to sweat.

"Carys?" My secretary calls from outside the door. "Are you okay?"

"Yes!" I call, staring at the chaos of my office. I cover my face with my hands and ease my fingertips over my brows. My heart rate is returning to normal.

There's a brisk knock.

Looking around, I take a deep breath and let it out. "Come in."

The door opens, and two men and a woman dressed in dark suits file in. Before they have time to say anything, Lilly appears in the open doorway, panting. The internal phone lines are still broken.

"Carys," she says. "The FBI are here."

"Carys Van de Berg, you're under arrest—" The lead suit continues to drone on about my rights as he flashes identification in my face. But I can't seem to snap into focus. Surreal. The scene is surreal, like a nightmare.

The second suit removes a piece of paper from his jacket pocket and places it on my desk. An excited buzz starts outside my door.

"What's this?" I ask, my brain sluggish.

"A search warrant for the premises. We already have agents on every floor."

"What is it—" I stare at him for a moment. "What is it I'm accused of doing?"

"In short? Conspiring with a terrorist organization. We'll get into the specifics in a secure location." The suit comes around my desk and puts his hand on my arm. "We'd like you to come with us."

"Do I have a choice?"

A hint of a smile flickers across his face. "Just about whether we use handcuffs."

I grab my purse and snatch my phone off my desk.

"Those things need to stay here. They're part of the warrant," he says.

I drop them on my desk. Hopefully, my lawyer can sort through this bullshit so I can get back to Finn and Lucas sooner rather than later.

"Looks like you were celebrating early." He indicates the papery mess while he escorts me out of my office.

My heels crunch across the confetti as I make my way to the door. It's 4:32. I should be signing papers, freeing myself from this place, from whatever will drag me under.

"I guess it'll have to wait a little while," I say when we get to the door.

The agent gestures for me to lead our exit out the door. "More like a few years," he mutters.

His comment gets my attention, narrows my focus. Whatever has led them here, they think they already know something, have evidence to get a conviction. Ice shoots through my veins, and my hand strays to my braid, tucking in a strand.

"I want my lawyer."

I don't say another word until Sook, my lawyer, is sitting across from me.

Chapter Thirty-Nine
Finn

When the phone beside my bed rings, I answer it before the noise wakes Lucas. He's not sleeping well without his mother here, but I sure as hell didn't tell her that. She would have been on the first plane back without freeing herself from her anchor of a father.

"Finn Donaghey?" the female voice on the other end of the phone asks while I rub my eyes and get my bearings. What time is it?

"Yeah. Who's asking?"

"Carys Van de Berg asked me to call you and relay information to you. My name is Sook Park, and I'm Ms. Van de Berg's lawyer."

My heart beats a staccato in my chest. "Is she all right?" I glance at the crib across the room outlined by the faint glow of a nightlight.

"She's been arrested by the FBI, Mr. Donaghey. They have accused her of conspiring with the PLA to commit an act of terrorism on American soil."

I frown and rub my forehead. "That's fucking ridiculous."

"The evidence the FBI has accumulated is," the line quiets, "significant."

"Get her out on bail or whatever you need to do, and let her come home."

"She's considered a flight risk. At this point, we're unable to arrange her release." Silence floats between us across the distance. "They know about you, Mr. Donaghey. Everyone knows about you."

Her words set my chest on fire.

I press the phone to my ear and crawl out of bed, heading for the door. Won't take long for me to lose my shit if this conversation keeps spiraling. There's no fucking way Carys isn't coming home. She sure as shit isn't going to jail. Once I'm in the kitchen, I take deep breaths while I pace. "Don't sugarcoat it. What the fuck are we looking at?"

"There's a lot of evidence. Sorting through it will take a while. We'll have to wait for a trial or try to secure a plea. She won't be back in Switzerland anytime soon." Sook takes a breath. "Carys asked me to let you know she's fine. The case against her will be fine, and she wants you to focus on Lucas."

I laugh, but there's nothing funny in what's happening. "That's what she wants me to know? What the fuck does 'anytime soon' mean?" The urge to throw my phone is almost uncontrollable.

Another pause and shuffling of papers. "We can never be certain how things will go in a case like this. Until we have a plea or a deal or a conviction, there's always a chance the case will be resolved favorably."

"You're fucking sugarcoating it. I told you not to do that. Based on your experience, what will happen?"

All I hear is her breathing before she says, "She'll go to prison. Unless we can counter their evidence, poke serious holes in their more damning arguments, Carys will go to jail." She hesitates again. "Either way, she'll be in the states for a while. Possibly for a very long time."

I stop pacing and stare up at the cathedral ceiling. Light streams in the large windows from the full moon. "How long?"

"Years."

My focus strays up to the spot outside our bedroom overlooking the living room. Lucas is up there, waiting for his mother to come home. "Years," I repeat the word, foreign, unknown on my tongue.

"We may be able to work out a deal. At this point, she wants to fight."

Fight—probably what I'd do. I've never gone into one where the odds were so stacked against me. With the law, guilt and innocence doesn't matter. The weight of the evidence is the only factor. From what Sook is saying and not saying, I don't like these odds.

"Carys can't speak to you, and for obvious reasons it would be ill-advised for you to try to visit her. She's asked me to keep you up-to-date on her case. We've got all hands on deck at the firm while we sort through the evidence."

"If a loophole exists—"

"We'll find it, yes." Her voice sounds confident for the first time since she called me. "Sometimes cases take an unexpected turn. Nothing is a guarantee in a case like this."

"Call me as soon as you have something. I don't give a shit about the time difference. Just call." I take a deep breath and pace around the room. "Tell her I'll do what she wants."

Sook breathes what sounds like a sigh of relief. "Great. Good. I'll let her know. That'll be a weight off her shoulders. Listen, I have to get going. There's a lot happening here, and I need to stay on top of it. Someone will call you when we understand more." She hangs up without waiting for my response.

I hold the phone, staring at it, letting the rage build, and then push it down.

"Was that Carys?" Lena's voice startles me. "I heard you talking. Is everything okay? You sounded upset."

"She's been arrested." My voice is dull, dead. "By the F-B-fucking-I."

"The FBI? Why would they want her?" Lena draws her robe tight.

"Conspiring with terrorists." My mind runs over the details Sook said and didn't say. "My guess is something to do with the stolen shipment we never traced or bothered to report. At least some of the product seems to have found its way to the PLA or someone similar."

"The PLA?"

"A bunch of fucking losers in Ireland who think anarchy is cool. Charles dealt with them in the past—left that shit for Carys." My focus keeps straying to our room upstairs and then back to my phone.

"When will they let her go?" She leans against the kitchen island.

I can't make the words leave my lips.

Her eyes go wide. "Oh, God."

A feeble cry sounds from upstairs, and in a minute or two, it'll become a full-on scream. Feeding time, and the kid loves to eat.

"I'll fix him a bottle." Lena gathers everything for his night feed in jerky movements.

I'm stuck to the middle of the floor, paralyzed by rage, indecision, and this intolerable frustration because we've come so far together to land here.

She gives me the bottle and puts her hands into the pockets of her robe. "What will you do?"

"I'm going to feed Lucas." I gesture to the bottle. "And I might contemplate joining a fucking religion or finding a god to pray to, or maybe I'll sacrifice something. Do any of those religious things actually work?"

She grimaces. "People believe what they believe because it makes them feel better."

"Well, the only thing I've ever believed in is myself. If Carys gets out of this mess and back here, I might have to become a born-again something." I step past her and head toward the stairs as Lucas ups the volume.

"That's the plan?" She calls after me. "We wait?"

"If you come up with a better one, you let me know. Until then, yeah, that's the fucking shitty-ass plan we're going with."

I take the stairs two at a time and then stand outside our bedroom door, calming myself. It's not good for me to go in there so wound up, even I understand that. When I've got the rage and frustration down, I turn the handle and start the shushing noise which signals someone is there.

When I lift him into my arms and stare at him, I'm glad he's not old enough to need an explanation for his mother's absence. 'Life is cruel' doesn't seem like a Carys-approved lesson, even if the sentiment is true.

Settling into the rocking chair, I tilt the bottle into his mouth and push off the floor with my feet. With each back-and-forth motion, a Plan B forms.

~ * ~

It only takes two weeks for me to decide Sook doesn't understand how the hell to get Carys out of this, and she's not coming home to us. The lawyer's last phone call tonight didn't go well. In a rage, I hung up on her, ripped the handset out of the wall, and threw it into the fire.

The situation is a setup—has to be. Maybe I just want it to be. Charles always took risks, and she picked up where he left off. Sook told me many of the dirty deals happened while she was recovering from her last miscarriage. Considering she ended up with an unexpected baby, it's easy to believe she might have made less than stellar decisions during that period.

That night, as I rock Lucas, I send two texts and book myself a flight out of Switzerland. When I put my phone beside me, he stretches his little arms and his eyes connect with mine.

"Don't worry, little buddy. I'll get your mom home."

The faint outline of the family photo Carys forced me to take when we returned from Russia is barely visible in the dim lighting. I've stared at the picture enough the last few weeks the image has become seared into my retinas. At some point, I'll close my eyes and the photo will haunt me—a comfort, a damnation, what might have been, what will never be.

Soon everyone will get what they deserve.

~ * ~

The next morning, I fill Lena in on my sudden trip abroad. While she holds Lucas, she searches my face, trying to figure out if there's any hidden meaning. One of my texts went through, but I don't have any idea if the second one did.

When I land in Cape Verde, Jay is at the airport to meet me. Carys insisted he stay here to keep everything on track with the casino, even after she got arrested. Sook told me that no matter what happens to Carys, she wants me and Lucas to have the life we planned to have together. Fuck that.

Fuck that.

Not being able to talk to her myself, to sort through this shit as a team, is driving me insane. "You heard anything?" I ask Jay as we drive to the island house.

"No. Did you think I would?"

"Nah." I sink deeper into the leather seat. I'd want the element of surprise. I'm sure he does too. Since our last conversation ended in a shootout, it's hard to be confident where we stand. Out the window, palm trees and rocky hills pass by in a blur.

"She'll never forgive you, man," Jay says.

"I don't care. I'm not leaving her to rot, to waste these years paying for something she didn't even fucking realize she was doing." I shake my head. "They're drilling her because of me. You can't deny that."

"Doesn't matter. I helped her haul your ass out of the warehouse, watched her bedside vigil until you were out of the woods. I've seen you two the last few months. You'll rip her heart out."

A lump surfaces in my throat, and I force it down. Her feelings, my feelings, can't be my focus. "If it was your wife," I say. "What would you do?"

Jay nods. "I get that too, man. I get that too." He squints before speaking again. "Probably seems dumb to you, but I've known Carys since I was little more than a kid. She's family." With a quick glance in the rearview mirror, he says, "I appreciate how you love her. I'm glad she's had that. She deserved it."

She deserved more than a few weeks of true happiness. Much more. I rub a hand along my face and then press the heel to my chest. The ache is back. Been gone for a while. Can't say I've missed the desperation. "I'm counting on your loyalty to her. Knowing you're around to pick her up, to keep her safe…" I roll my shoulders. "But no matter what happens to me—dead, alive, somewhere in between—I'll find a way to come for you if you don't do your job. You keep her safe."

He meets my gaze in the mirror. "You don't need to do that, man. I understand. I realize what she means to you."

We're driving up to the house, and he tenses at the wheel.

"What?" I pick up the weapon on the seat beside me.

"I don't recognize that vehicle." He throws the car into park and draws his gun.

Climbing out behind him, I keep my gun at the ready. He motions for me to circle the Mediterranean-style bungalow before coming in. I gesture to the left around the house while he opens the front door, gun drawn and calls his wife's name.

As I'm rounding the final corner, I check the window and glimpse a familiar sandy blond head. He fucking came. Quicker than I expected. Hustling around the last side of the house, I enter the front foyer cautiously. Could be an ambush.

Jay has his weapon aimed at Lorcan who is settled into the couch as though he owns the place.

"Brother," Lorcan says when he sees me. "You summoned me?"

"He's got Sofia and the kids somewhere," Jay says as I come into the living room.

"You in the business of taking women and children again, little brother?" I scan as much of the house as I can see from here, checking for anywhere obvious he might have stuck them. His partner in crime probably has them. "Or has Kimi finally joined the dark side?"

Lorcan glowers at my reference. "Last time we met didn't end well for any of us. I thought it best to come prepared to bargain." He glares at Jay. "Put your fucking weapon away. If I wanted a gun fight, I wouldn't be sitting on your settee."

I narrow my eyes. His accent always came and went, but it's thick now, the same as when he first returned from Ireland years ago.

"Where are my wife and kids?" Jay asks.

"Safe." Lorcan stares and raises his eyebrows. "For now." With a sigh, he relaxes into the couch. "What'd ya want, Finn?"

"Where are my wife and kids?" Jay's voice vibrates with rage.

There's fear under his anger. I recognize it. I've felt it.

"He's not like me," I say to him. "If my brother says they're safe, they are. We play nice, and they'll be fine."

Jay eases down his gun. "If you scared my kids—"

"You'll what?" Lorcan's gaze bores into him. "Take a fucking seat."

Jay shakes his head and doesn't sit. His gun is still clutched in his hand.

"This about Carys?" Lorcan swings his focus to me.

"Yes," I say.

"I can't help you." He rises and steps toward the door. "I would say I can't believe you think I'd help you after what you did to Kim, but that's always been you, hasn't it? Finn first."

I tuck my gun into the back of my pants and raise my hands. "You're risking nothing by helping me."

He barks out a laugh. "Risking nothing? We risked a fuck of a lot coming here in the first place."

Swallowing, my jaw tightens. This touchy-feely shit would be easier if Jay wasn't in the room, but he won't leave when his family is the collateral. "I should have handled the Kim situation differently."

Lorcan raises his brows, unimpressed with my admission.

"I probably should have handled a lot of things differently."

His hands on his hips, Lorcan's gaze narrows. "What are you on about?"

"I want to turn myself in to the FBI as long as Carys goes free—no chance of prison, no repercussions for any of the crimes she's accused of committing."

"You understand what that'll mean for you, don't ya?"

I grimace. "I plead guilty to whatever they want to throw my way. My freedom for hers."

Lorcan whistles long and low. He studies me for a moment. "This what you want?"

"If you can secure those conditions for me—Carys gets off free and clear of everything—then I'll turn myself in."

"Huh." He stares at the ceiling before giving me his attention again. "I always suspected you loved her with that intensity but never knew for sure."

"Will you help me?"

Lorcan's hand sweeps through his hair, and he sighs. "You shot Kim."

"I did."

"Right in front of me. Like what I wanted, how I felt meant nothing."

Instead of answering him, I purse my lips and then slide my gaze away. Can I justify or explain myself in a way that'll matter to him? "I'd forgotten."

"What's that?"

"What it's like to love someone beyond reason." I shrug. "I thought I was protecting us, and then when I realized you already had the truth—well, my impulse control has never been particularly strong."

"Kim," Lorcan calls out. "What do ya think? Sound close enough to an apology?"

Stepping out from the darkened kitchen, she makes eye contact with me. She's as striking as she was the first time I saw her. Long, dark hair, slender but fit, tan skin. The pull I once felt toward her as well as the anger is gone, evaporated.

"Not quite." Kim's gaze sweeps over me, assessing. "Is Finn Donaghey capable of a selfless act?" She crosses her arms.

"It appears so," Lorcan says.

"I'm in favor of you going to jail." She frowns. "Less in favor of how upset that'll make Carys. You understand what this will do to her?"

"She has a child," I say. "A baby boy. Lucas."

"I heard." Kim's voice softens as she says, "Named after her brother." She sighs and wanders over to stand next to Lorcan. "I'm familiar with the evidence they have on you. You'll never see the light of day. Turning yourself in will be a life sentence, several of them. You'll die in prison."

My brother tenses at her words, and my heart thumps. Her bluntness used to be refreshing. "It is what it is. We realized I was on borrowed time."

She studies me for another moment and then stares at Lorcan. Their prolonged eye contact is a silent communication. They must have known I might turn myself in, ask for a deal. I'm sure they discussed how they'd handle the negotiation.

Kim turns back. "A man named Zahir will call you."

"Sook can help with whatever paperwork I need to sign. She's with Carys right now." I hesitate before I make my only other request. Am I being selfish or fair? I left her one other time without an explanation. I can't do that again. "And I want to talk to Carys, alone, just once before they put me away."

"You're really doing this." Kim takes a deep breath.

"I don't know why everyone is so fucking surprised."

"Death or jail," she says. "Always thought you'd pick death if push came to shove."

"Not the dilemma here, is it?" I eye her. "She's is in trouble. I can save her. Nothin' I wouldn't do to keep her safe."

With a curt nod, Kim links her hand with Lorcan's. "We'll make the arrangements for the swap. We gotta go, or we'll be missed."

Before they've even taken one step toward the door, Jay raises his gun. "My family."

Her smile is sly. "We never had them. Watched them leave before picking the lock and disabling the alarm. You should tighten your security. They got a call from a new friend to go to a pool party. Completely legitimate. Sometimes," she says, "timing is everything."

Jay takes out his phone and dials his wife. Lorcan and Kim are out the door when Jay's relieved laughter sounds behind me. With a sigh, I wander to the huge windows in the living room facing the ocean. The ebb and flow of the waves lull me into a mindless state. Carys and Lucas will have a good life here.

Jay calls out that he's going to get his family. I wave over the top of my head but don't turn. It's easy enough to imagine Carys and Lucas here. When I close my eyes, the sun touches my face. The memory of her hand, starting at my shoulders and running along my back until she loops her arm around my waist is so vivid, so real. When I half-turn, I almost expect to see her there when I open my eyes. But she's not. We'll never get this moment.

From my back pocket, I remove the photo of me, Lucas, and Carys I stole from the frame in Lucas's bedroom before I left. That life already seems so long ago.

Happy. So fucking pleased with ourselves.

I trace Carys with a fingertip before I fold it, making sure the crease runs over my face, and slip it into my pocket again.

Chapter Forty
Carys

My heart pounds, and I drum my chipped nails on the metal desk. There are two windows to the right. Outside them is a hallway. People wander past, but they're faceless, nameless, and none of them distract me long enough to forget why I'm here, what's at stake.

Sook is supposed to be coming in with the paperwork for a deal. Anywhere in the five- to ten-year range and she thinks we should take it. Part of me wants to snatch the deal out of her hands and sign it immediately, anything to guarantee I return to Finn and Lucas someday. The other part wants to tear it up and tell them if they listed things *I* actually did, I'd be a lot happier.

Happier. What a stupid, stupid word.

We were so close. So, so close. I press my fingers into my forehead and try to block out those thoughts. That path is gone. Now I have to focus on what I can get, what I can have.

The evidence and charges they've piled on me are unreal. Most of it, I either don't remember doing or didn't do.

Even from the grave, Eric is fucking me over. I've been trying to pinpoint when I lost my focus, but between the miscarriages and my renewed interest in Finn, I can't recall the last time I *was* focused on the business. I should have quit years ago or stepped away, done something else so this steaming pile of shit didn't land on me.

People walk past the room in a steady stream. What is taking Sook so freaking long? There's no clock, but I've been waiting for hours, haven't I? Out of the corner of my eye, there's a familiar movement in the hallway. The man is surrounded by bigger, broader FBI agents. This glimpse of something recognizable vanishes when I look close enough.

This time, I want the scene to be a mirage, a trick of the light. His head is turned toward Sook, but I'd know those shoulders anywhere. Pinpricks dart along my spine, and I stand, my chair scraping against the floor.

"No," I whisper.

Where's his gun? He shouldn't be walking around with escorts like this. Shooting people, pulling me out of this room, the two of us fleeing together, those are things he does. Not this. He can't be here if he isn't fighting his way through.

When his shoulders rotate, the handcuffs become visible, and panic wells in my chest. "No." I go toward the window.

As if he senses me, Finn turns. His gaze is shuttered, but when we make eye contact, I realize what he's done. My stomach rolls.

"No." I shake my head and shove my hair behind my ears.

Sook leads him away from the window, and I bang on it, trying to follow them down the hall. "Get him out of here," I scream, my voice echoing around the room, mocking me. I rest my forehead against the cool glass, my fist banging against the window, and a sob releases.

When the door opens on the other side of the table, I'm crying so hard I can't look at whoever has entered. My chest is caving in, and it hurts to breathe. I can't breathe.

"Hey." Finn tugs on me, drawing me away from the window. "Hey."

The handcuffs clink, and I throw my arms around him, burying my face into his neck. I can't stop crying, deep wracking sobs as I cling to him.

"It's gonna be okay."

"Please tell me you didn't," I choke into his ear. "Please tell me you didn't." I say the words over and over, but he doesn't respond, just nestles as close to me as he can.

"I love you so fucking much." His gruff voice in my neck restarts the flood of tears.

"We were happy. We were gonna be happy." The last word catches on another sob. "I don't want us to end like this. We weren't meant to end like this."

"You go home today to Lucas. You grab the life we planned."

My chin wobbles. "I'm not leaving you here. I won't leave you here. Please don't do this. Don't do this, okay? Don't do this."

He backs away from me, and his cuffed hands cup my cheeks, his pale blue gaze scanning me. "It's done. It's already done. If you'd taken their deal, he wouldn't have known you. A boy," his voice cracks, "needs his mother." He brushes my tears with his thumbs and kisses my forehead. "Boys need their mother."

I hold in a sob, my chin trembling as I try to keep myself together. Tears stream down my face. "I would have gotten out, eventually." A voice niggles the back of my brain. He's right about my relationship with Lucas. He understands from his own childhood. Still this price is too high.

"But you—" I suck in a deep, shaky breath. "The evidence they have on you." I stare into his eyes. "You'll never…we'll never…" My lips won't form the end of those sentences.

"You'll be safe. Lucas will be safe."

"What about you?" I cry, clinging on to him. "I can't—I can't—"

There's a knock on the door, and over Finn's shoulder, Sook comes into focus. A man in a suit enters behind her. "Time's up," he says.

"No." I hang onto Finn. "There has to be something. We can't. No. We need more time. We need more time." The words come out broken and garbled, desperate.

His lips find my ear. "Be safe. Be happy. Raise him up to be a good man. I love you." His voice is raw, as though even he might be on the verge of a breakdown. Then he steps back from me and tears run in rivers against my cheeks. He stares at me, and agony coats his face. With a tortured expression, he slides his hands along my jaw as he pulls me into one last kiss.

I clutch onto him, trying to memorize the warmth of him, his scent, the way his tongue glides against mine, his palms warm on my cheeks. Banking each thing, hoping I've deposited enough detail for all the days to come. When he draws back, his forehead grazes mine.

"It would have never been enough," his rough voice whispers.

This time when he steps away from me, there's no hesitation, and when he slips out the door forever, I slide to the floor sobbing.

Chapter Forty-One
Finn

Attachments have never come easy for me. One way or another, people let you down. My father, Lorcan's mom, Lorcan—all of them fucked me over. Saving Carys is the only time in my life when I've let someone down by doing the *right* thing. This decision feels like shit, so it's no wonder I've never bothered before. Who would choose to have their heart ripped out?

When I'm called for my first visiting hour at the federal prison, I debate having them tell Carys to go home to her kid. But the only remedy to this terrible ache is likely her, even if the relief happens through a glass partition. I'm weak, so fucking weak when it comes to her. I travel to the cubicles like a man walking the gangplank.

Yeah, I'll feel better gazing into those whiskey eyes. Then when she leaves, my chest will burn a hell of a lot worse. She can't stay; I can't go.

I take the seat across from her, and we scan each other in silence. A frown mars her face, and she picks up the phone. After a second, I do the same. Already a crushing tightness threatens to make talking about anything important impossible. To be sure this is as close as I will ever get to her again is like being repeatedly punched in the nuts.

"You have a bruise on your cheekbone." Her hand clenches the receiver so hard her fingers are white.

I smirk, trying to gloss over her concern. She doesn't need the details. "You're not sleeping." I graze my knuckles across the ugly darkness blooming on my cheek. "Lucas keeping you up?" Her makeup can only hide so much when I know her so well.

"I'm getting you transferred to a different prison. I have Bradley working on it."

"What happened to Sook?"

"I fired her."

I stare at her, tempted to ask why but not sure I want to get into it. The things we can't bring ourselves to say float around us.

I shrug. "This place is as good as any. Don't trouble yourself."

"No, it's not. I've been doing research, and I can have you moved somewhere better."

With a shake of my head, I shift the phone to my other ear. "I told you to go and be happy. Live the life we planned."

"I can't do that. I won't as long as you're in here because of me."

"*I'm* the reason I'm in here. You have no clue the shit I did before you came back into my life."

"Sook gave me a copy of the things you pled guilty to. I realize exactly what you were up to, and I'm all out of fucks to give. You think I haven't understood who you were this whole time? Please. Give me some fucking credit."

A chuckle escapes me against my will. "I figured I'd be the reason his first word was fuck."

The fire goes out of her, and a ghost of a smile crosses her lips before she whispers, "Me too."

We stare at each other in silence. I take in every peak and valley of her face, store it away, but I can't hold on to her image too tightly. My memory never does her justice. "You can't keep coming here," I say.

"How will you stop me?" Defiance flashes across her face.

"I'll refuse to see you."

"Are you going to do that?"

Am I? I should. I really fucking should. "How's Lucas?"

"He's good. On target with his developmental milestones. He's at the hotel with Lena."

"And Jay?"

Another brief smile. "And Jay."

"You're in Cape Verde now?"

"We are."

"Long flight to be here for an hour."

She sucks in a deep breath. Is she surprised I know the length of the flight? "Worth it."

"It's really not." I lean forward and give her a taste of the thoughts raging inside me. "Every month that passes, our lives get further apart. Soon we'll have nothing to talk about. You'll come here so we can sit and stare at each other and remember what might have been, what we used to have." I sit back, annoyance spilling out. "No thanks. I'll pass."

"That's not true." Her voice lacks conviction. Those whiskey eyes connect with mine, and she straightens in her chair. "I didn't want this. I would *never* have agreed to this."

"Come on, Carys. Did you think I'd let you spend years in prison while your son was out there growing up? The only thing you ever wanted was to be a mother."

"Our son, and raising him wasn't the only thing I wanted."

"I understand what it means to miss a mother."

"And that's why I'm not incredibly fucking angry with you."

"You're still angry with me. But I did the right thing."

She scoffs. "Oh yeah? This choice doesn't seem rash and impulsive to you? Ill thought out? You're telling me you lie awake at night thinking about how *right* this is? Fuck off." Her voice breaks. "Don't pretend like this situation is easy for you."

The silence between us is charged as I glare at her, considering every response I could give her. None of them change a damn thing, though. I'm still in here; she's still out there. Offering her even a grain of hope is wrong. She can cling to her anger. Easier for her to move on.

"Don't come again." I stand and put the receiver on the holder.

She rises with me and bangs on the glass, but I don't turn. I can't. I'll cave, sit back down, continue in this circle leading nowhere. Doesn't end, doesn't get better.

The guard peers over my shoulder toward Carys, but since the glass is soundproof, whether she's saying something or has left doesn't affect me. So tempting to check, one last glance.

Down the hall and through the checkpoints, my chest grows tighter and tighter the further away from her I get. When we're at my cell, the guard closes the door, and I lie on my bunk, listening for the lock to click.

I can't keep looking back, and I can't let her either. The future we might have had is gone. The lock on the door tumbles into place. Given enough time, we'll figure out how to exist without each other. We already did it once.

Chapter Forty-Two
Carys

The waves roll into the shore and a breeze kicks up tendrils of my hair. I tuck them behind my ears and run my hand along Lucas's back. He's against my chest, snug in the baby carrier, fast asleep. There's nothing like his skin, his breath wafting across the space under my chin built just for him. It's a huge comfort to focus on him, to keep his happiness and wellbeing in sight instead of falling apart. The swishing of footsteps in the sand are familiar. The tread of those feet, the ambling confidence, could only be Jay.

"You all right?" He appears at my shoulder, a comfortable distance away.

"Just thinking." A lot of thinking since I got back from seeing Finn. My mind is in a tailspin—has been since he left me sobbing in a heap at the FBI office. Every time I remember he's in prison forever, I want to burst into tears or throw up. I'm on a rollercoaster, and I can't figure out how to get off. This tiny little guy pressed to my chest is my stabilizing force.

"Yeah, I got that part. We've been here a few days now. You have a beat on what you'll do? Are we going back next month? I gotta book the flights early to get the best deal."

I shake my head. "No."

Finn leaving me in the visitation cubicle stung, and I've taken time to process the rejection. Whether or not he likes it, I understand him.

Jay draws in a deep breath. "I don't know exactly what he said to you—"

I give him a wry smile. "Nothing I wanted to hear."

I half-turn toward him, and the wind catches my hair again. It flies around me, but I don't bother trying to tame the strands. "He thinks he doesn't want to see me. Fine. He won't see me. He can stew over my absence next time his visiting block comes up, and I don't appear."

Jay digs his big toe into the sand and squints, gazing over the vast expanse of ocean. His light brown skin has grown darker these last few months here. "That'll set him straight?"

A hint of a smile threatens at the thought of Finn going straight. "Probably not. But he needs me. He doesn't want to need me, but he does. I know it. When we're sitting across from each other, even in stupid prison, I feel it. He can have his month to cool off, to remember having me in his life is better than being cut off." I cup my hands under the carrier to ease my back for a moment. "Just as long as doing this doesn't kill me, too."

A squeal flies out the open sliding doors from inside. I glance over my shoulder toward the house. "Sofia is okay with the kids?"

"She does it all the time." Jay shrugs.

My lips tip into an almost smile. "She amazes me."

He chuckles. "Sofia. She's my steel magnolia. Nothing that woman can't do. Lena is there, too. She just returned from grocery shopping." He puts his hands in the pockets of his dress pants and lets the silence envelope us for a beat. "I gotta pop over to the casino build soon. You tagging along or staying here?"

"I'll come." I rub another hand against Lucas's back, and he makes a snuffling noise as he turns his head to the other side and snuggles in.

"Did you ever get confirmation about who killed Eric?" I say.

Jay shuffles his feet. "I can call Demid directly. Might stir things best left to rest. Evidence points to him."

Do I need a confirmation? Maybe not. Eric is gone, and he paid for what he did to Demid and his family. He might not have admitted he had Valeriya killed, but I'm confident her baby was his. If he stood any chance of getting me back, he couldn't let me see what he'd been doing. Doesn't seem to matter. The truth always worms its way free.

"No. It's okay." I shake my head. "Finn was probably right about leaving that situation alone."

Running a hand through my hair, my feet sink deeper, going from the warm dry sand to the cool dampness underneath. "Sometimes I think Demid was the one who sent me the final box."

"The confetti bomb?"

"Yeah."

"Why would he?" Jay arches an eyebrow.

I grimace. "I brought Eric to his doorstep."

"The choices Eric made were his. You aren't responsible for any of them."

Another breeze kicks up the sand at our feet, swirling it around us. "No luck tracking the courier used to deliver our little joke?"

He shakes his head. "Dummy company. The courier Lilly listed on the sign-in sheet doesn't exist. Surveillance cameras were useless because of how the person carried in the box and exited the building. Whoever it was understood what they were doing."

"I wish I'd let you tell Finn about the confetti bomb. Seemed so pointless then. A stupid joke we could trace later once the FBI was finished with me."

There's a lengthy moment of silence while we both watch the waves roll into shore. Jay doesn't bother telling me things would have worked out differently. What would he have done? Would he still be in jail? He wouldn't have left the threat unanswered. If I'd given him another focus, he might be free.

A few boats zip across the water in the distance, the buzz of their engines audible until the wind shifts. We'll have a good life here. If only I could figure out how to mend this massive hole in my heart.

My hair drifts in front of my face, and I weave the ends together. An idea has been brewing I haven't dared to voice. The proposal is desperate, but maybe that's where we're at. Finn's bruised cheek appears every time I close my eyes. He's not getting any younger. Neither am I. Life is slipping away from us.

Turning to Jay, I say, "There has to be a way to get Finn out."

"You saw the shit he pled guilty to. Life sentence on top of life sentence on top of life sentence." He gives me a side eye. "Please tell me you're not considering a jail break."

"I wouldn't have any idea where to start." I give him a sly smile. "Who could I possibly ask to help me acquire that information and those skills?"

Jay rubs his face. "Is this you asking me?"

I shrug. "Is this you telling me you can help?"

"I might have made inquiries a few months ago when this went down. At the time, I was wondering about getting *you* out. Thought for sure that'd be Finn's solution if you pled guilty to even something so minor as jay-walking." He chuckles.

"What'd you find out?"

"It'll be hella hard."

"But."

"Not impossible. You got enough money and connections—"

"And nothing is impossible." I smooth my hand over Lucas's head, loving the softness of his fuzzy hair against my palm.

Lucas is living proof. Even if the route to motherhood wasn't what I wanted, I'd never trade him or this experience. Finn turning himself in enrages me because I'm convinced we could have found a better path. But I understand why he did it. In some ways, I love him more.

Death or jail. He'd rather die than end up in prison.

Turns out he'd rather go to prison than see me or Lucas suffer. We are suffering, though, just in a different way. At least we have each other.

For nothing can be ill if she be well.

I close my eyes, and the sun kisses my face while I remember what it felt like to have him murmuring those words in my ear as he held me tight. I'd do anything to have him again—to be safe, protected, loved.

As I take a deep breath, the wind kicks up, stirring my partially braided hair. "Find me the best person to break him out. This isn't the end," I say to Jay, my face turned to the sun. "It's just the beginning."

Resurrection is the second installment in the Donaghey Brothers series. Carys and Finn's story concludes in *Redemption* coming early 2021.

Acknowledgements

To my agents and friends, Amy Brewer and Patty Carothers—thank you for your continued support and guidance.

A special thanks to Champagne Book Group for taking a chance on my novels. Kelli Keith and Cassie Knight—your keen eyes helped shape this book and the previous one into something we can all be proud of.

Thank you to my husband, Jay, and my daughters, Hannah and Autumn. I would not be able to do this without your love and support.

Thank you to everyone who contacted me after they read *Retribution* to discuss the characters, my writing process, or to muse about where this second book would go. There's nothing better than sharing this world with you. Your excitement is a gift.

A special thank you to Nicole Bontaine who has read so many of my drafts with enthusiasm and discussed my characters and plots with me at length. It's so nice to have a friend to talk books with.

Thank you to all my first readers: Rositza Bratovanova, Wairimu Kibathi, Carmen Insfran, Jennifer Thompson, Juliann Semon, Ashley Haltom, Maya Hamed, Sirone Booysen, Celeste Williams, Karen Sampson-Venzon, Stephanie Kazowz, Sherylin Barrientos, 2user38, Camilla Gunzel, Sadaf Batool, Meagan Tate, and Purnima Kar.

Each one of you has given me such an incredible gift by offering encouragement, criticism, and passion for my stories when I've needed it most. I'm here because you stuck with me and made me feel like my work had value.

Thank you, Cole Lepley, my writing bestie. Without you, who always seems to root for the "bad" guy, I'm not sure this book would have happened.

About the Author

Wendy Million is a high school English teacher who has spent the last sixteen years teaching in England, Bermuda, and Canada. She loves conveying her passion for storytelling to her students.
Currently, she lives in Ontario, Canada with her two daughters, two dogs, and one husband.

Rarely without a book in her hand, she enjoys reading and writing stories with fierce women and high stakes. *Resurrection* is the second novel in the Donaghey Brothers Series.

Wendy loves to hear from her readers. You can find and connect with her at the links below.

Blog/Website: http://www.wendymillion.com
Facebook: https://www.facebook.com/authorwendymillion/
Instagram: https://www.instagram.com/million.wendy/
Linkkle: https://linkkle.com/authorwendymillion
Pinterest: https://www.pinterest.ca/million3505/
Twitter: https://twitter.com/Wendy_Million

Thank you for taking the time to read *Resurrection*. If you enjoyed the story, please tell your friends and leave a review. Reviews support authors and ensure they continue to bring readers books to love and enjoy.

~~~

Missed *Retribution*, book 1 in the Donaghey Brothers series? Turn the page!

AN UNDERCOVER FBI AGENT
TWO DANGEROUS BROTHERS
A DEADLY CHOICE

TURN THE PAGE
FOR A LOOK INSIDE!

Chapter One

The phone in my front pocket vibrates. Checking it is the only thing I want to do right now. I shift in the metal chair and keep my hands clasped on top of the aluminum conference table that has seen better days.

The warehouse is deserted except for the six of us. It's a weird setup, but I learned a long time ago the right questions to ask and the ones to avoid. At least there's a table. This is a negotiation, not a confrontation. The table is important.

My heart thumps a violent rhythm in my chest, but I've gotten used to that too. The erratic heartbeat is my tell, and I'm thankful the people I work with can't hear it, even when it pounds in my ears. I've been well-trained for this double life, at least on the outside.

"Look," I let impatience seep into my voice. "Carys is going to be pissed when she finds out you guys are screwing her over." My first indication this meeting wouldn't be lucrative should have been the lack of heat in the building. It's so cold that each time I speak, I wonder if I'll see my breath. Teddy is too cheap to pay the prices we need to make this deal worthwhile.

"Next time, she comes to the meeting herself or we'll be taking care of business in a different way." The metal of Teddy's gun twinkles at me as he flips his suit jacket with false casualness.

I give him a mild glance and suppress my eye roll. Guys who have this burning desire to whip out their gun as a substitute for their dick piss me off. *You got a gun. Good for you. I have four.* The one up the sleeve of my leather jacket would nail him between the eyes before he even unholstered his archaic piece of crap. It's no wonder he's searching for an arms deal.

"I have a feeling she's not going to want to do any business with you after this stunt." I keep my features neutral. This is a wasted opportunity, and frustration eats at me. "Call me when you're serious about working with us. Maybe she'll still be interested." I nod to the two men who came with me, and they mirror my movements, ready to follow my lead.

"What's she paying you, Kim? I'll double it." Teddy readjusts himself under the table.

As I amble toward the exit, my throat fills with unease. My brain should be engaged in this conversation, but I can't stop thinking about the message on my phone. I call over my shoulder, "You couldn't afford me, Teddy. I'm above your pay grade."

"You got balls of steel." He chuckles when I keep walking. The warehouse is large and has too many of his steel products lying around which doesn't absorb his voice. His voice echoes, drawing my attention even when I'd prefer to ignore him. I'm not sure what he wants with Carys, but I doubt it has anything to do with guns.

Pausing before the exit, I shake my head, half turning back to him, flanked by Carys's two burly men. "I'd take a pussy made of diamonds over balls of steel any day."

Teddy's grin fades, and his chair screeches across the concrete when he stands. The two men with him are like shadows. "You want diamonds? I can arrange that."

"Forget you know my number." I push the emergency exit door, and it pops open. "Unless you have money for the deal."

The door slams behind my last man as we head to our black SUV waiting in the deserted gravel parking lot. The sky is blue-black, and the snow on the ground is melting, creating puddles in the potholes. Spring is on the way, but it isn't here yet. At some point, we'll get another blast of winter.

"What a waste of time." I pull out the phone in my pocket as it vibrates again.

"That Carys?" Jay raises his dark eyebrows as he opens the rear passenger door for me. His close-cropped brown hair is ruffed by a sudden breeze.

"Could be." I duck down, folding my almost six-foot frame into the car, but I don't take the phone out. Why am I being contacted? The FBI programmed the phone with a unique vibration for agency texts. When it went off in the meeting, I worried someone would notice my reaction. Creating suspicion in any of the people I work with could get me killed—shot dead without hesitation.

Dead.

The car jerks forward, and Jay mumbles an apology as I focus on my hands, turning them over.

Dead.

My pocket vibrates again, and this time when I look down at my hands, they're covered in blood.

"Kim?" He tries to catch my gaze in the mirror. "Carys is going to be ticked."

My head snaps up, and I tuck my hands under my thighs,

sliding along the black leather, and release a dark chuckle. "I told Carys I didn't think there was any way Teddy was buying from us. He hasn't got enough money, and no use for guns." Carys making me the point person for the deal was a step in the right direction. So, I didn't argue too much.

"He's got lots of use for you." Jay meets my gaze.

"He wouldn't be able to handle me." I ease back into the seat and stare out the window as Chicago zooms by. The skyline is one of the things I love about this city, and dusk brings it to life, the lights dancing across the lake's surface.

"You ever work for a man before?" Jay checks his mirrors.

The new guy beside him, whose name I can't remember, pipes up, "She's too much of a ballbuster to work for a man."

Jay gives him an annoyed look. "Carys will shoot you herself for chirping Kim like that."

"I'm perfectly capable of shooting him," I say, my tone mild. The cityscape outside the window rushes by. I can't stop thinking about my phone, but it's too risky to take it out right now. "Yeah, I've worked for some men. I try to avoid it. They're too preoccupied with their balls."

The new guy laughs, and Jay gives him another sideways glance.

"I can see why." He isn't getting Jay's silent message. Over the seat, he's scanning my dark ponytail secured near the top of my head down to my Lululemon pants. "What are you, anyway? You're like, exotic or something. I can't put my finger on it."

Giving him a cold stare, I say, "Your fingers don't belong anywhere near me." Compared to me and Jay, this kid is as pale as a ghost.

"You're getting fired, man." Jay shakes his head and adjusts his hands on the steering wheel as we merge into heavier traffic. "If you keep talking, you're going to end up in concrete shoes at the bottom of Lake Michigan."

The only bit of color in his face disappears. At least the new guy has the good sense to take Jay's comment seriously. He's probably in his early twenties, a kid looking to make a quick buck. Everything about him reminds me of someone I don't want to remember but can never forget.

"That's not a real thing." His voice quivers.

"They're all real things," Jay says. "You don't mess around with these people, Paul. The stereotypes, the rumors, the shit you see on TV—most of it is taken from someone's real life."

250

Ah, a name. Not that I'll need to remember it after the conversation we're having.

The car glides to a stop in front of my four-story brown brick apartment building. The trees lining the street are mature, hanging over the sidewalk and road. The streetlights work, and the front door has a security guard. Not that I need one of those. I chose this neighborhood on purpose. It's not too run-down, but it's not new and shiny either. Carys has offered to let me live with her outside the city. I can't, though. While it might make aspects of the job easier, it would make others infinitely harder.

"I didn't mean anything by my comments." Paul's voice is uncertain.

He isn't as big as Jay and, standing up, he and I are about the same height. I'm maybe ten years older than him, but that gap is massive right now. I've been on this job with Carys for almost a year, but in some ways, it's my whole life.

"You're not cut out for this, Paul. Quit before someone kills you." I'm half out the door when I turn to Jay and say, "Tell Carys I have some personal business. I'll be back in a few days."

"Your brother?" His brown eyes are full of sympathy.

"Yeah." I give a curt nod. "Anniversary of his death."

"I'll let her know."

I slam the door behind me and enter the building, waving to the security guard at the desk. In the elevator, I put my hand over the phone in my pocket. How much time will I have?

At my door, I slide the key in the lock. My steady hands belie my racing heart as I slip inside. I flip all the locks in place and tug the phone from my pocket.

It's been almost six months.

Airport. Two hours.

Glancing at the current time and when the text was sent, I'm pretty sure I can make it. It's going to be tight. Opening the entryway closet, I grab the prepacked bag and then undo the locks on the door.

I disappear into the night.

Chapter Two

Malik likes meeting at the same hotel, same room, every time. It's a mid-level chain in a mid-sized city. Everything about the meeting is constructed so I don't have the run-in we dread. Being undercover and seeing someone from either version of our lives is one of the few things that makes people like me wake up in the middle of the night, covered in sweat, making sure there isn't a bullet lodged in our brain.

When I slip into the hotel room, the scent of stale cigarettes hits my nose. The rooms need to be renovated, but I never question Malik's desire to meet here. This is his area of expertise, not mine. He stops pacing when the door clicks shut behind me. His dark face and eyes soothe my unease.

He scans me from head to toe, assessing. "I wasn't sure you'd be able to make it."

"Your message didn't come at the best time. Carys let me take another meeting today. It was a waste of time though."

"Like the last one," he says, finishing my thought.

I shrug. "It'll come. She's giving me more and more authority."

"So that explains why you're dressed like a ninja supermodel." His smile is half-hearted. "What have you got for me?"

Twisting, I swing my black bag forward until I can dig into the pocket for the latest USB drive. It's full of whatever documents I've managed to get off devices in the office, screenshots of texts and emails, anything that might have a shred of evidence to build a case against Carys. I hold the device between my fingers, flipping it over and over.

With a sigh, I drop it into Malik's open palm. He doesn't say anything. I'm sure he knows. Carys is the kind of woman I like, and gathering information on her doesn't sit well with me. She's not a bad person, but sometimes she does bad things.

"I have some...news," Malik hesitates.

I glance up, trying to catch his attention, but he's not looking at me anymore. "Something I won't like."

"Maybe you will."

"Malik, seriously, you've been my handler for a few years." I let out a huff. "The way you started this conversation tells me I'm not going to be happy. Are they pulling me?"

"Yes." Malik sighs, his shoulders dropping. "Probably."

"I'm getting somewhere. It takes time." I've never been pulled off an assignment before, and it stings more than I expect. Time, that's what I need. She trusts me.

"It's not what you're assuming." He sits on the edge of the double bed. The white duvet cover is too pristine, too pure compared to the rest of the dingy room.

I sit next to him, and he takes my dusty brown hand in his two darker ones. My body relaxes as though it's releasing a giant breath. I've been holding myself in for weeks. Being on high alert is exhausting. Here, with him, I can be me, Kimi. Out there, I'm Kim and keeping my lies straight is like walking a tightrope. One wrong move, and I'm falling to my death.

With a side glance, I appreciate the familiarity of him, his broad shoulders, muscular biceps, and angular, open face. From the first time I arrived at a hotel room to find he replaced my previous handler, we've had an easy, steady relationship.

"For what it's worth, I asked them to keep you on this assignment. You might stay. It depends on whether you're picked or whether we can slot you in easily."

"Picked? Malik, you know I hate riddles. Out with it."

"Are you familiar with the Donaghey family?"

I frown, ticking through the operations I've been part of the last few years. "No," I admit. Something about the name is just out of my grasp. The name spins around my consciousness searching for the last time I heard it.

"Hmm. That's probably good. We couldn't find any direct employment connections even though you grew up outside Boston. You consistently use Kim which makes it easier compared to other undercover agents."

A name close to my own keeps me grounded. Some people need to divorce their normal selves. For me, weaving details is easier than inventing them, then remembering my inventions.

"What about the Donaghey family?" I remove my hand from Malik's to rub his thigh in slow circles.

"Brothers. Mafia in Boston. The head of the organization, Eamon Donaghey, their father, was murdered."

Now my brain latches onto what I saw on TV a while ago in Carys's office. She knew the brothers and liked them. Or she liked one of them. My eyes narrow, trying to remember what she said. Her wording was precise, as though there was more to the story. At the time, I wondered if I should pry, but it hadn't been information I needed for either job.

"The organization is fracturing. Lorcan and Finn are on the cusp of an all-out war."

"And?" How well would Carys know these men? Sometimes connections between people are stronger than they appear.

"The younger brother, Lorcan, has been low-key looking for a female bodyguard to add to his staff."

I freeze and remove my hand from Malik's leg. "They want to undo months of work on my part to make me a *bodyguard*? Are you kidding me? I'm practically the second in command with Carys. This is ridiculous. Off the top of my head, there are at least ten FBI women who could do this."

"Any of those women read, write, and speak Irish Gaelic?" He cocks an eyebrow.

I frown. "They only communicate in Irish?"

Malik's shrug is almost imperceptible while his dark eyes search my face. "Our mole says most top-secret communication happens in Irish Gaelic—emails, verbal conversations, text messages."

Shit. I can see why they'd want to move me. My father, after my older half-brother was killed, developed an obsession with Irish Gaelic. It was all he spoke until his death. I had to learn it.

"So, I guess that answers the *why me* part." I sigh and stand up, crossing to the mini-bar and plucking out a couple of bottles. I pour Malik a whiskey in a coffee cup and pass it to him and then pour one for myself. "Am I getting an introduction? Is there a plan?"

"You're not mad? You're okay with being close to home?" Malik eyes me while he takes a sip of his whiskey.

"I'm not thrilled." I put my own glass to my lips and breathe in the sharp aroma.

"You might be able to slip away and see your mom."

Tension radiates through me at the mention of my mother. On the wall is a painting of a lone boat in the middle of stormy seas. Each time we're in this room, it catches my eye. Something about it reminds me of my mother, or maybe it's me. She's all I have left.

"A plan?" I prompt again.

"We think Carys knows them."

I laugh, the tension easing out of me. The whiskey burns my throat when I take a sip. "Carys knows everyone. But she's not going to broker an introduction. Why would she hand me over or even consider giving me up?"

Malik grins and takes a long drink. "*How* do they know each other?"

"An arms deal makes sense." The conversation with Carys about the brothers refuses to resurface from the caverns of my memory.

"And yet, that's not it. Or at least we don't think so. What's near and dear to the heart of your beloved Carys?"

His tone is teasing, but it still pisses me off. I hate when he pokes my weaknesses like it's a game.

"Kids with cancer," I mumble. Carys funnels a lot of her money into charities which aim to treat or support childhood cancers. Her brother died from a brain tumor when they were in high school. A few months ago, we got drunk and traded dead brother stories. Well, she got drunk. I pretended to be drunk.

"Lorcan also has a soft spot for cancer patients." Malik tips back the rest of his drink and stares into the coffee cup. "There's a cancer fundraiser coming up in Boston, on the cusp of being big, not there yet. We've asked them to highlight children's cancers and breast cancer—that's how his mother died. Lorcan has confirmed he'll attend."

"So, I only have to convince Carys? Fly from Chicago to Boston on a whim?" That's a tall order without raising suspicion.

"Not quite. We've arranged for her to get an invitation. You need to give her a gentle nudge. If Lorcan and Finn do escalate into a full-on war, it'll be ripe for arms deals."

"If she doesn't take the bait?"

"I have no doubt you can be persuasive." He puts his empty glass on the TV stand. "We'll figure out a way to broker a meeting another way if you can't make it work. We have a substantial file on the father but not on the two sons." He nods to the duffle bag in the corner of the room. "I brought some information so you're not going in blind."

"The assignment goal? An arrest? War?" I stare into what's left of my drink, swirling it around.

"No, no war. We want to avoid that. Civilian causalities would be out of control. Both brothers are prone to escalation. An arrest is best if you can get the right information but otherwise, try to keep the situation stable. We'll tackle whatever information you acquire."

"You'll stay my contact?" I glance up at him, worry eating at me. He knows and understands me better than anyone else at the bureau. His replacement would never be good enough.

"I will." Malik smiles.

I move to him, sliding my glass onto the table beside his. "Did you want another?" My voice dips low.

We're almost the same height, and the way I've lingered with my fingertips on the table means we're inches apart. His gaze flicks from my eyes to my lips and back again.

"I'll never say no to you." His tone matches mine.

I shift closer, my chest grazing his. "In case I die tomorrow, I'm going to live for today."

His lips lift into a half smile. "Have I ever told you how much I love your motto?"

"A few times." I take in his dark features under my lashes, enjoying the hunger I see. "What are you waiting for?" I murmur. "Make me feel alive."

It's the only invitation he needs before his lips dip to capture mine. His hand tugs the elastic out of my hair, releasing my long, dark strands. I sigh, pressing my body tight to his, the parts of him that have come to life brushing against mine. We may only do this dance every few months, but I know each step by heart.

Familiar. Easy. Safe.

All the things I usually hate.

Chapter Three

Hot pink. It's not a color I would choose, but it goes well with the darker coloring I inherited from my father. Carys insisted on buying my dress for this function. Convincing her to come was the least of my worries. I had more trouble talking her out of the ridiculous wardrobe choices for me.

"So, Native Barbie, are you enjoying the spectacle?" Carys clutches her champagne flute in her manicured hands.

I give her a sideways glance as I sip from my own glass. "Only *you* could get away with that."

There's a lot of lily-white in me, too, courtesy of my mother. People who need to classify me think I look odd, difficult to pinpoint. My focus skims around the high-ceiling ballroom and catches on the crystal chandelier that lends the majority of the light to where we're standing. I let the fingers of my free hand graze the gun attached to my thigh. For an event that was supposed to be small, it seems to have grown much bigger in the weeks since I met with Malik. Women and men in expensive dresses and tuxes mill around us, chatting in loud voices before wandering off.

"You go write your soul cleansing check yet?"

Carys laughs. "And only *you* could get away with that." Her amber eyes soften when she gazes at me. "How's your dad?"

Still dead.

"Same as always." I give a slight shrug. "The anniversary of Chad's death is hard." Not a lie. At least the emotions aren't, but the details of his death are different for every job. The date, the place, the method of murder are fabrications.

"Well, I hope you and your dad can work out your issues someday. Family is important."

Family. The word echoes around my brain, bumping into memories I keep buried.

Carys flags a waiter to deposit her empty glass and takes another. She signals to me, but I shake my head. "First you insisted on a dress you could move in, and now you won't drink with me. I swear you think someone's lurking around every corner waiting to kill you."

I laugh with her, even though it's not outside the realm of possibility. "You like that I'm prepared."

Carys sighs. "It's true." Her hand nudges a piece of her blonde hair back into its intricate braid. "I'm starting to think Lorcan's not coming. I should have called him and scheduled a meeting. You're right about the territory being ripe for deals if the two of them explode."

"Is it wise to pick a side?"

"Hmm. My side is probably obvious. At least this way it might appear like a genuine coincidence. The charities we support are here, and we happened to run into each other."

I'm about to ask Carys why her side would be clear when I catch sight of a blondish-brown head coming through the open doors of the ballroom. He's dressed in a dark blue suit and a pink tie, not a tux like many of the men. Two men flank him, as tall and broad as the man in the middle, but their suits don't scream money. I tip my head in his direction. "Who's that?"

Carys glances over her shoulder, and her lips curve into a smile. "Speak of the devil."

"Lorcan?" It's him. Malik had photos. They didn't do Lorcan justice. In the flesh, the man is the kind of dangerous, rugged handsome which makes others glance in his direction without realizing they've done it.

"In the flesh," she says as though she can read my mind.

"Have you ever?" I force my focus to Carys. She's fifteen years older than me, which makes her ten years older than Lorcan. Time has been good to her. Well, that and she has a dermatologist and cosmetic surgeon on call.

Carys shakes her head, but her attention lingers on Lorcan. "Being a woman in this business, you have to be careful who you get into bed with—remember that, Kim. A man will get you killed."

"Not all men." My mind strays to Malik.

Carys stares at me before nodding at the bar. "It seems Lorcan's been waylaid by one of the organizers before he got to the bar. I know what he drinks."

She orders three whiskeys and then sashays to where he is talking to a petite blonde who is giddy with nerves or attraction. Either is possible. He is bigger and more intimidating in person. Above his head there might as well be a flashing neon sign that reads *danger*. Tension circulates in the air, surrounding him, enveloping us.

"Lorcan," Carys drawls, allowing her southern accent to pop out. Her hips sway in a manner she reserves for those she trusts. No one takes a woman seriously in this business if they seem too womanly.

His head whips up at the sound of her voice, and a grin splits his face. He sidesteps the over-eager woman to embrace Carys. "I didn't realize you'd be here. It's been an age."

"A delightful coincidence." She flicks her attention to the other woman before focusing on Lorcan. With a slight bow of deference to Carys, the event organizer wanders off, hands clasped.

While he and Carys chat, I take in his features: the goatee, the slight dimple in his right cheek when he almost smiles, and his hazel eyes which are alight with surprised amusement.

"Who is this bright spot of loveliness behind you?" He nods at me. He searches my face, appraising, but his gaze never travels my body in an assessing way.

"This is Kim." Carys gestures with her hand flung wide. "She's the best at what she does."

As an introduction, I couldn't have hoped for better. The grin on my face is genuine while she slings an arm around my waist in a motherly fashion.

"What's that?" His voice carries a hint of an accent that isn't Bostonian. Of course, I know from the file his parents sent him and his brother to boarding school in Ireland.

"Everything." Carys beams at me.

"That's quite a compliment." Lorcan takes a drink and tilts it in my direction. "What do you think of that?"

"It's not much of an exaggeration."

He chuckles and again his gaze roves over my face as though he's trying to piece me together. My hot pink dress is garnering little attention from him. Should I be pleased or offended?

"You got any mates? I'm looking for someone like you."

Carys tightens her grip on me and sips her whiskey. "She's taken. Keep your mitts off her."

He raises his glass, eyeing me over the top. "People who can be bought aren't for me, Carys. You know that."

She scoffs. "Not true, Lorcan. I *do* know you. I've played this all wrong. I should have told you she was thinking about leaving my organization."

"I *am* terribly unhappy." My gaze connects with Lorcan's, and I offer a mischievous smile.

An answering smile spreads across his face. "That so? Now, Carys, you need to treat *your everything* woman a touch better before someone swoops in and sweeps her away."

"As long as you aren't *the someone*, Lorcan." She glances at me. "I appreciate the effort, but I'm afraid once he's on the hunt, he can't be deterred."

"You make me sound terrible." Amusement pours out of him.

"I used to like you," Carys says. "Finn, on the other hand…"

"…is an acquired taste." Lorcan's grin fades. "One I've gone off recently."

She glances at me and then back to Lorcan. I've seen that look on her face before. She's trying to figure out the best approach.

"Sorry to hear that," I murmur, surprised by the sudden chill in the air.

His lips quirk up. "You wouldn't be sorry if you knew him." He empties his whiskey. "It's been a pleasure, ladies. Thank you for the drink. You know me well, Carys." With a nod to his men, Lorcan drifts into the crowd, leaving me and Carys to finish our drinks on our own.

"Shit." She sighs and taps her glass with a fingernail. "I should have left Finn out of it."

"Can't ask him if he wants a deal without letting him know there's a deal to be done."

"Their organization buys arms, just not from me." Carys purses her lips. "It should be me. It'd be a good time to slip in there. Maybe we can still salvage it later."

"Are you doing that or…"

"If you get a chance to ask, fine by me. Plant a seed, see if it grows."

Lorcan breezes through the crowd with his two burly security guards trailing behind him. He's a small fish in an arms world. Carys does much bigger, more ethically comprised deals than this. She hasn't let me near those yet. If I get out of here tonight with what I want, I'll never see them. I'm going to need to work fast to recapture his attention. His late arrival means there are two hours until this event finishes, and he's cut our conversation short.

"I'll see what I can do."

"You're not one to be charmed," Carys draws out the words, and I think she must be watching Lorcan like me.

I smirk and raise my eyebrows. "Is there a but?"

A smile plays on her lips. "No, I suppose there isn't."

"You've got nothing to worry about," I say. "If I can get him to consider a deal, I will. And, if not, it's been a pleasant evening. We haven't been to an event like this in a while." I knock back the rest of my whiskey and wiggle my glass at her. "Another?"

"No, I have people I want to connect with. Tonight is bigger than I expected."

"I'll be at the bar."

Carys and I move in opposite directions as she heads off to make or solidify her contacts. I sidle up to the bar and place my empty glass to the side. This end of the bar is for standing, but farther down, there are a number of stools with people perched on them, chatting away to each other. The ballroom is vast and airy, though the perfume and cologne circulating are enough to cause an asthma attack. Above the bar, pendulum lights are set low to match the rest of the mood lighting. Most of the charitable events I've attended with Carys have been dimly lit. It must seem too intrusive to ask for money with the brightness turned to full.

I'm waiting for the bartender, wondering how I can slip myself into conversation with Lorcan when a shoulder brushes mine.

"Be a shame for someone as talented as you to be unhappy with your employer," a deep voice says in my ear. His lilting accent is a sound I could get used to. It calls me back to the hours my father spent devouring anything Irish.

He's so close, Lorcan's hazel eyes are piercing in their intensity. The musky scent of his cologne floods my senses, and I'm glad for my training. Cool. Unaffected. "How do you know I'm talented?"

"Carys isn't one for bigging people up who don't deserve it." He turns away to signal the bartender with a finger. "Two whiskeys."

In this business, men are everywhere. But there's something in the curve of his shoulders, the slant of his jaw under the goatee, which makes him familiar. Part of his appeal has nothing to do with appearance and everything to do with the way he carries himself. Confidence seeps out of him, oozing over everything he touches.

The bartender passes the two glasses to us, and I pick mine up with my fingertips, swishing it around, letting the ice clink against the sides.

His back is against the bar railing, and his elbows are on the wood, so he can stare out across the wide expanse of the room. When he shifts toward me, his gaze connects with mine over the rim of his glass. "When are you heading home?"

"Tomorrow afternoon. Carys offered to show me some sites around Boston."

One side of his mouth twitches as though he's holding in his amusement. "Sounds grand."

"Does it?" I avoid looking at him directly, keeping my back to the room.

"Not quite as grand as coming round to mine for a meeting."

"What would we be meeting about?" I peer into my glass, hope rising in me.

"See if one of us can make the other an offer they can't refuse."

"I get offers all the time. I refuse them all." Our little game of cat and mouse amuses me, but I keep my features smooth.

"You never had one from me."

Somehow, I've managed to finish another drink. "I guess we'll see what you've got then. I'm a tough nut to crack."

He places his finished drink onto the bar. "I'm counting on it. Tell Carys to call me."

When I turn around, he and his men are gone.

Out Now!

What's next on your reading list?

Champagne Book Group promises to bring to readers fiction at its finest.

Discover your next
fine read!
http://www.champagnebooks.com/

We are delighted to invite you to receive exclusive rewards. Join our Facebook group for VIP savings, bonus content, early access to new ideas we've cooked up, learn about special events for our readers, and sneak peeks at our fabulous titles.

Join now.
https://www.facebook.com/groups/ChampagneBookClub/

Manufactured by Amazon.ca
Bolton, ON